By Lauren Nicolle Taylor

Clean Teen Publishing, Inc.

This is a work of fiction. The characters, incidents, and dialogues are products of the author's imagination and are not to be construed as real. Any resemblance to actual events or persons, living or dead, is entirely coincidental.

The Wall
Copyright © 2013 by: Lauren Nicolle Taylor

All rights reserved. No part of this book may be used or reproduced in any manner whatsoever without written permission except in the case of brief quotations embodied in critical articles or reviews. For information address:

Clean Teen Publishing
PO Box 561326
The Colony, TX 75056

www.cleanteenpublishing.com

For more information about our content disclosure,
please utilize the QR code above with your smart phone or visit us at
www.cleanteenpublishing.com.

For my sister Kristen,
your strength and courage were the inspiration.

You tell yourself, *I won't survive this. If one more bad thing happens, I will shrivel up and die.* But there's always something more you can take. Because what's the alternative? Death? Death would be easy. Death would be boring too. I have too much to do, too many things to complete. Death clips my wings, leaving me stunted. An unfinished person with her legs half-buried in the ground. Yes, death would be easier. But living is what I have to do.

1

Waiting

I was waiting for something to happen. Anything at all. Bad or good. But time continued on, soundless and dull. After everything we had been through, all the walking, and then the running. Dying. I was stuck in the mud—the more I wriggled, the deeper it pulled me in. I didn't want to be this person, this pathetic wretch, so I fought it, my feet making sucking noises as I managed to pry one foot out, only to have the other foot sink deeper.

We sat like rounded pebbles at the bottom of the stream, uncomprehending. Not hearing because of the rabbling water overhead and only seeing a distorted, blurry version of the world above. We didn't know where we were and why we were here.

People came in and people went out, and Joseph stayed the same like an epitaph to what could have been.

After a two-week break, Deshi returned on most days to lecture me. We argued. A lot. It didn't take much to set me off. I was throttling for a fight. I needed somewhere for my frustration to go. Otherwise, I may have leaned over Joseph, lying in the bed next to me, and shaken him senseless.

Deshi brought Hessa to me, swinging him in the crook of one arm.

He was a real child now. Aware. Sitting up with the aid of a pillow, blinking and grasping at things. And he smiled, a smile that broke my heart and rejuvenated it at the same time, because it was his mother's.

As I watched them, so comfortable, so natural, I wondered what Clara would think of me now. I wanted to believe if things were different, if she were here, somehow, I would be different too. I could be the mother my baby deserved. But I was never like her and I never wanted this. I was drowning. I struggled with everything. Without her slender hand to hold onto, I was lost.

"How's it all going?" Deshi observed me over the tip of his nose, disapprovingly. His dark face was perfect and thin, self-righteousness emitting from his dark eyes. He knew exactly how it was going.

"It's hard," I complained.

"You're making it much harder than it needs to be." He shook his head in disappointment. I peered into Deshi's face. Joseph already had a light beard. Deshi's face was smooth. *He was a boy*, I thought, unkindly.

"Being a mother doesn't come as easily to me as it did to you," I snapped, trying to upset him.

He raised his eyebrows and pushed his lips together in a fake pout. "If you're trying to insinuate that I'm a woman, then I think you need to come up with something a bit more clever than that."

I poked my tongue out at him. The corner of his mouth twisted up, just a little.

This was our relationship now. We bickered like an unhappy, married couple. But no matter how rude I was, he kept coming back. His love for Joseph, and his dissatisfaction in me, was motivation enough. He had the wrong idea. Forcing me was the wrong tactic. Making me feel guilty was superfluous. I already felt awful about it, all the time.

I leaned my cheek towards him, "Why don't you just do it?"

Deshi raised his eyebrows in surprise, "Do what? I'm not going to be your surrogate Joseph!"

I blushed. He thought I was asking him to kiss me, which would fit with the married part of our scenario. "No. Slap me. I know you've wanted to since the day you met me." I lowered my eyes. "Maybe even before that."

Seriousness created pinched ridges along the top of his thin nose. Slowly, he brought back his arm, sweeping it through the air. I squeezed shut the eye closest to him, imagining it would feel like being slapped with a wet towel. It would sting, but wouldn't have much force behind it. I felt a breeze, but when I looked up, his hand was hovering millimeters from my face, and then he dropped it into his lap.

"Don't be stupid. I don't want to slap you. I just want you to realize you can do this. With or without Joe, you will be able to do this. You don't really have a choice." He patted my arm awkwardly and stared longingly at the beautiful, sleeping man behind me. He missed him almost as much as I did.

I looked down at the new life in my arms. This rounded blob with simple but unending needs. I sighed. I knew the baby was part of me and, in some ways, I was more sorry about that than comforted. I knew I was supposed to be his mother. Things would be so much easier if it had just clicked, but it didn't. I felt disconnected. I said I would try harder but the more I did, the worse I felt.

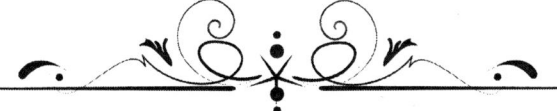

At night, when no one was around, I would climb into Joseph's bed.

His face was scruffier now. A light beard touched his face. He was alive, his hair grew, his nails grew. He had a pink flush to his face. Blood was pumping, but not enough. I whispered into his ear, "Wake up, wake up, wake up," over and over. But he never did. Sometimes I envisioned punching him, straddling his chest and hitting him over and over until I had startled him out of his sleeping state. That was when I truly wondered if there was something seriously wrong with me, something more than *defective*.

One night, I turned the light on above his bed and crept over, the glow of his life-support machines illuminating my face and hands in reds and blues. I bit my lip and let out a breath through my nose. I just wanted to see them. I needed to see that green, with flecks of gold in it. I gently peeled back one of his eyelids, but his eyes retreated. I tried the other one, so frustrated, so ashamed of the way I was behaving. I didn't hear the footsteps coming towards me until a hand was on my back. Matthew.

"Ahem," he coughed, but I could sense there was a laugh in the back of his throat. "You won't be able to wake him up like that."

I scrambled back off the bed and stood, looking up at him, my hands behind my back like a naughty child. "I... I know... I just wanted to see him, see his eyes, just for a second."

He nodded. Of everyone here, he had been the most patient with me. He wasn't judgmental; he didn't force the baby on me like Deshi. He understood I needed time.

My eyes flitted to the door. I had requested they move the baby into the room opposite mine so I could go in there at night, to feed him or attempt to comfort him. It was difficult. Every now and then, a feeling would start to rise inside me. I jumped on it, trying to trap it like a mouse that had run across the floor. But every time I thought I had it, it wriggled out of my hands and disappeared down a crack in the floorboards.

Matthew interrupted my thoughts saying, "Actually, Rosa, I'm glad you're up. I was hoping you might join us tonight. We need to discuss something with you."

His face was casual but his tone was serious. I nodded my head and followed him, not bothering with shoes—the cold floor kept me alert. The baby cried out just as we passed his doorway.

"You can bring him with you," Matthew said.

"Ok. Umm, Matthew?" I said, blood rushing to my face. I wanted

The Wall

to say something, but it was difficult. My instant reaction to things was always suspicion, defensiveness. But these people took us in and I was grateful for that. I didn't understand it but I was grateful.

"Yes."

"Can I say thank you?"

"Yes," he said, amusement tickling his tone.

"I mean, thank you. You could have left us to die. But you rescued us. We would all be dead if it wasn't for you and the others."

Matthew stared down at me with an unnerving, determined expression.

"It is our responsibility. Our duty." Shaded memories of Class rules echoed in my head, and then he said, patting my pointy shoulder gently, "Rosa, this is what people should do for each other."

I supposed he was right, but selflessness was not big in the Woodlands. It was microscopic.

He resumed his casual demeanor and leaned against the doorframe, waiting. I fumbled around in the dark, trying to find the blanket I usually wrapped the baby in. Giving up, I just pulled the crying child out of the cot and put him on my shoulder. He started to calm. Despite my ill treatment of him, he always wanted my presence. Soon, I could hear his breath slipping into a dozy rhythm.

I followed Matthew down the corridor, still not used to the quiet. There were no trees rustling, no animals disturbing twigs as they padded along the earth. Sound was swallowed here. Like the place was designed to absorb it.

Matthew told me the Russians built it. A contingency plan in case the Woodlands didn't succeed. They hid people here during the time when the Superiors were 'cleansing' the earth of the remaining occupants. Cleansing. What a word. Like scrubbing dirty laundry, like the earth was refreshed and sparkling clean from all that death. It made my stomach twist in dark nausea.

The dwelling had provisions, cleverly hidden solar power, and enough space to survive for at least one generation.

But as the Woodlands became a success, the Russians on the outside, the ones originally settled in Birchton and Radiata, abandoned the people inside. They locked them in and left them to die. Powerful cowards. They couldn't even kill them; they shut the door and walked away like somehow, they could pretend it was never there. Squeezing my eyes shut, I pictured the people drumming on the doors, trying to get out, their screams bouncing back on themselves like a loop of never-ending pain.

I shook my head in disbelief. "I don't understand—why didn't they try to get out when they realized they were locked in?"

Matthew frowned. "They didn't know. Not at first. The orders, as far as they knew, were to stay underground for one generation. They fulfilled their mission but by then, it was too late. They were locked in, they had run out of supplies, and foolishly they sat and waited for the Russians to come back. Even when some decided they'd waited long enough, they were locked up and punished. By the time they had accepted that they had been abandoned, most were too weak from starvation and dehydration, so that only a handful of people were strong enough to tunnel out. Even then, there were several failed attempts and collapses before they succeeded."

"Jeez, they shouldn't have waited so long," I said, tucking a strand of wild hair behind my ear.

"You, of all people, should understand the power of orders and rules. People follow; they don't think they have a choice. Sometimes the threat of certain death is the only thing stronger than the fear of your superior," he said tiredly.

He was right. I did understand. I looked at the floor. "Sorry. I do. Understand, I mean."

He shrugged. "It's all right, Rosa. Luckily for us, after two-hundred and fifty years of Superior rule, records of this place appear to have been lost. And lucky for me, some of them did get out, or I wouldn't be here," he said, smiling sadly.

I cast my eyes around the hollowed-out hill. Now it was like a tomb. A reminder of where we started and how far we had come, which was not very far.

Matthew turned to me as we walked. "Have you been outside lately?"

I shook my head. I barely left Joseph's bedside. He knew that.

"The snow is starting to get heavier now."

"Hmm," I murmured absently.

I pictured our little cabin with a thick blanket of snow on its roof and smoke coming out of the chimney. My heart squeezed and then a little sliver slid off. We were such idiots, coming from where we had, to think we could make a life out here. Our knowledge was so limited. I should have known better. I clenched my fist, feeling like I could punch something. But there was a baby on my shoulder so I settled for digging my nails into my palms.

I wondered where this was leading. I knew that this was not the Survivors' home. When I had asked about it, Matthew had been a bit closed off. He dodged my questions, smiled, and said, 'Oh, you'll see soon enough'. We had been here for six weeks. Maybe it was time to move? I half-hoped so. I hated being underground. It felt like we had gone backwards. It hurt me in an unexplainable way that my child had been born down here, unlike Hessa, whose first experiences had been stars, firelight, and swaying trees. My baby was born under fluorescent lights. It angered me that part of what was planned for him by the Superiors had come true, in a way. I resolved to take him outside and show him the trees.

After several unnaturally shallow footsteps, we arrived at our destination. A strong shaft of light streamed out of the doorway, along with smells of food, coffee, and the whisper of hushed conversations.

We walked in and everyone looked up at me from their cups and meals. I knew what they were thinking. *There's that poor girl who lost her love and rejected her baby like a broken animal. How damaged she must be.* I tried to stop myself from glaring. I then registered the shame on their faces as I glared at each and every one of them anyway. Apella was there, as well as Alexei, Deshi, and five other people I didn't recognize. Careen was absent. They offered me coffee, which I declined. It kept me and the baby up. Apella also declined. She looked green, covering her mouth while waving away imaginary smells from her nose. She was suffering from nausea with her pregnancy. I took a sick kind of satisfaction in it. It shouldn't be easy for her.

Matthew sat down and I sat next to him, feeling eyes on me the whole time. A man spoke first. He was older, maybe fifty, with grey hair and a full beard. He was thin and wiry, like everyone here. He seemed to be the leader. I scanned the others at the table. They all looked like survivors, quite literally, like they had come out of the forest swinging axes, with dead rabbits hanging over their shoulders. It clashed so humorously with the way they were sitting, hands clasped with serious expressions in a carved-out, metal-clad room, small, shiny readers in their hands, the screens illuminating their faces. Like technological cavemen. It was a world away from Pau, the Classes, everything.

"We need to talk about the move," he said, his voice deep and scratchy, full of authority. "We've already stayed longer than we should have. The diversions we have set up are running out. They will turn around soon. The boy has not woken. One has already left with the first group." So that's where Careen was—nice of her to say goodbye. "I think we have to make a decision sooner rather than later, before we get trapped here, under meters of snow."

I leaned into the table, squishing my poor child against the metal rim. He squeaked, and I eased off. Anger was bubbling up. The boy? He had a name. Matthew put his hand on my shoulder and pulled me back, gently. Across the table, Deshi had the same offended look in his eyes.

"I hear you, Gus. But we can't move him like this. The life support is not portable. Can you give me a few more days? There is one thing I haven't tried," Matthew said evenly.

Everyone shifted in their chairs. The metal legs screeching on the stone floor made my teeth ache. They were waiting for the bearded man to speak. One woman looked bored, rolling her eyes and looking longingly at the door. *Get out*, I thought. *If this doesn't interest you—why are you here?* Gus stared at his nails; they were caked with forest floor. I inhaled deeply, trying to calm myself. I could almost smell the layered leaves, the decomposing matter that held such richness and life. Gus picked at his nails and flicked a bit of scum onto the stone. Mulling.

"Matt, we need to be practical. You can't bring these wounded birds into our house and expect us to change our plans so you can save them. Some of them can't be saved." Several of the survivors shot him an appalled look I didn't quite understand.

My fingernails from one hand were digging into the underside of the table. What could I do? I had no influence over these people. I knew what I wanted to do. Launch at him. Scream Joseph's name. He was a human being. He was a good person. He deserved a chance.

Someone else spoke up. A young man. Not much older than myself. He had dark brown, curly hair, curly like Joseph's, but longer. He had it tucked behind his ears, which stuck out like sawed-in-half saucers. They were dressed so differently from anything I had seen before. No uniforms. Everyone seemed to have their own style. There were different colors, materials, and cuts. My mother would have been fascinated. As soon as I thought it, I pushed the idea out my head. Mother was gone.

This boy was wearing a t shirt, something they called 'jeans', and a soft sweatshirt that had a hood sewn into it. He pulled a strange face as he spoke, like it was hard to get the words out, as he toyed with the toggle attached to his hood.

"Dad, imagine it was me, or Saz. You would want Matt to do everything he could to save us. Wouldn't you?" the boy stuttered, each word louder than the one before as he gained confidence.

The man, Gus, wiped his forehead, leaving a dirty streak across his weathered skin. He rubbed his temples like he had a headache. He looked to the boy and smiled, a warm, familiar smile, full of affection. "All right, I'll give you a few days, Matt. The rest of you need to start packing up your groups and preparing." He took a sip from his coffee, swallowing it with a sour expression. Adults—always drinking stuff that tasted bad for the after-effects.

The rest of them shuffled out of the room, talking to each other and ignoring us. This left our original group sitting around the table, along with Matthew. We all wanted to hear his plan. I jolted up once the others had cleared the room, pumping my legs, jiggling the baby to keep him sleeping.

My heart sank and then jumped up in my chest repeatedly. Hope. It's a strange feeling, and one I've had very little experience with. It made you feel buoyant, like you were pulling the clouds down to meet you.

"What are you planning?" Apella asked, her voice vibrating, face still green. Alexei was patting her back too hard, in a distracted way like he was trying to dislodge something she was choking on.

"A broken heart operation," he said, like we should all know what he was talking about. "But we'll need blood."

She nodded, somehow she knew, or could guess. "Blood type?"

"O," Mathew replied

Apella frowned. "What have you got?" Hope was bleeding out. Something was wrong.

"None. We need to ask people to get tested and donate."

I stuck my arm under his nose. "Take as much as you need," I said enthusiastically, pointing to a nice, big vein that wanted to volunteer.

Matthew smiled and pushed my hand aside. "Sorry, Rosa. You're not compatible."

I frowned. Of course. Our differences included our blood.

They started to make plans. There were only twenty people left. The rest had already moved back to wherever they came from. We would divide those people between us, send them to the clinic to be tested, and hopefully have their blood collected.

I made my excuses and ran back to my room. The corridors looked brighter, glossier than before, like a light was shining behind them, like the building was swelling with hope for Joseph. I skipped down the halls, imagining those beautiful eyes. Totally distracted. I thudded into a soft but solid mass. I looked up to see the boy who had helped buy us some time staring down at me awkwardly.

"Sorry," I muttered, attempting to walk past him. The baby would be hungry soon. I wanted to get back.

He put his hand to my shoulder. "Your shoelace is untied," he said, smiling kindly. Warm hazel eyes looked from my shoes to my face.

"Oh. Here, hold this," I handed him the baby and knelt down to tie them, ignoring his surprised expression at my use of the word 'this'. The boy gazed at my child, rocking him back and forth as he held him.

"He's cute. What's his name?"

I fought back my suspiciousness. "He doesn't have one yet."

"Oh." Was he looking at me with pity? No, it was something else, sympathy and camaraderie, like he got it.

"What blood type are you?" I blurted out. Standing before him, all I could see was blood. He was a walking bag of blood.

"O," he answered warily.

Our eyes connected and I smiled at him. A real, full smile, my teeth catching on my lips, not used to the ascension. He returned my grin, his eyes sweeping over me. I stiffened. That made me a little uncomfortable. I thanked him hastily and snatched the baby back, brushing his hands lightly as I did so. I ran back to our room. I had to tell him.

"My name's Cal!" he called after me.

O. O. O. O.

I could see him again. It could work out. *Please, please, please, let this work.*

2.

Hope

I barreled into our room and the baby cried. He didn't seem to share my elation. I sat down on the bed and fed him. He looked dreamy and satisfied after. Lit by the fluorescence and reflective black rock ceiling, his little face was so pale compared to my own. His defective eyes twinkled as he watched the changes in the light. I wrapped him up tightly in a blanket and held him. *Hurry up,* I thought. *Sleep.* He closed his eyes and then opened them again, peering at me, making sure I was still there. I smirked, thinking my suspicious nature had been passed to this tiny bundle. "You trust me about as much as I trust myself, don't you?" I whispered, rolling my eyes.

Finally, he stopped checking for my presence and I took him to his room. Creeping across the hall like I had stolen the child, I laid him down in his crib. I leaned down and kissed his tiny head. He stirred and his forehead crinkled for a moment before it relaxed again. My lips had never touched something that soft. It was the first time I had ever done that. Smoothing his tiny, blond curls from his face, I smiled again, the sensation less and less foreign.

I left our son and returned to Joseph. My heart still hurt. It was wrapped up in a dark shadow that would squeeze inside my chest at the sight of him. His body was suspended in gold, waiting. I climbed into his bed, lightly touching his resting face, almost scared it would cave in if I pressed too hard. I whispered, "I love you." Another first. My tears stung and fell on his unresponsive face. Yes, hope is a dangerous thing.

Matthew knocked on the doorframe, interrupting me. I wasn't embarrassed. After he caught me poking Joseph's eyes, this was nothing. I sat up, wiping my away my tears.

"I want to talk to you about the operation," he said seriously. He walked to my bed and sat on the edge, crossing his legs like he was a preschooler sitting on the mat in front of a teacher.

I wasn't sure I wanted to know. I just nodded.

"It's a very complicated procedure. If it works, though, Joseph will be as good as new. Maybe better."

"So why didn't you do it before?" If it would fix him so completely, why wait until now?

"It's very risky, the success rate is…"

"Stop!" I turned away from him, closing my ears, closing myself off to the prospect of complications and slim chances. That cloud of hope was trying to return to the sky. I didn't want to let it, not yet. I held onto it tightly, clutching it to my chest like a pillow.

Matthew put his hands up in surrender. "All right. I just want you to understand that this is his last chance. If it doesn't work…"

"It will work. It has to." I knew I was being stubborn, but I couldn't leave room for the possibility the operation wouldn't work. That was not an option. Joseph wouldn't leave me here on my own.

Matthew smiled. He understood. For some reason, he cared about us. I trusted that he would try his best.

"Do you have any questions?" His kind eyes assessed my restless state. I was all over the place. He was much older than me but his casualness made him seem young, like he was a surgeon that still climbed trees and played. Maybe he was.

"What can I do?" I asked anxiously.

He chuckled. "Find people with O blood and get them to report to the clinic."

"That boy... Cal. He had O; I'll go get him." I jumped up, about to fly out the door.

"Not now. Tomorrow." I scowled. I didn't want to wait. "Get some sleep, Rosa. Tomorrow will be a very difficult day for everyone."

No. Not difficult. *Wonderful*. He could be fixed.

I relaxed back into the bed, sharing a pillow with Joseph. I wondered if they had any technology that could fix me. I know what I would ask them to do. Before the baby, I would have said my eyes. That would have been the first thing. Now, I would ask them to install a few doors or blocks between my brain, my mouth, and my body. I would probably break through them all but at least it would slow me down. Stop the continuous flow of stupid or dangerous that seemed to pour out without warning.

I pulled Joseph's limp arm around me and fell asleep, dreaming of the squeeze I would feel when he woke up and pulled me to him.

3

Blood

We were to meet at midday with our results. I had asked everyone I came across what their blood type was, probably more than once. I wasn't registering their faces; they sloshed down the halls, walking IV bags, in my eyes. I found myself winding up tighter and tighter like a rubber band about to twang and take out someone's eye. Each person I asked seemed genuinely frightened when they told me *no*, like I was going to squeeze blood out of them like juicing an orange. And I couldn't find Cal. I hoped someone else had.

I made my way through the maze of corridors to the clinic with the baby in my arms. It was up a level. I followed a series of metal-rung ladders and platforms. My footsteps sent muffled sounds up into the ceiling, with no rebounding echo. Dull, like we were living inside a damp sponge. It was dark and cold, much colder than when I first arrived.

Hope. It's a foolish feeling, one that lifts you up only to cut your wings and send you crashing back to the ground.

I entered the clinic, blinking. It was a shiny, white room, too bright. The smell of disinfectant and out-of-place mustiness swirled up my nose. As I scanned the room, I felt like a giant had stepped on me, squashing my body, twisting his foot to push me deeper into the dirt. There was only one person sitting in a chair. Only one. He looked pale. Bags of blood were piled next to him, a needle protruding from his arm. Cal.

Apella was talking to Alexei in sharp whispers. I'd never seen him so angry. His bottom lip was quivering and his pale face was twisted into a very dissatisfied expression. She shook her wrist free of him, looking into his eyes, her own teary but determined. She slipped passed me without looking up and went into the hall. Deshi was hanging back, squeamish from all the blood.

"Is this it?" I asked no one in particular as I spread out a blanket on the floor and put the baby down. I felt a little crazed, the morning's disappointments weighing on me. *How could this be it?*

Matthew walked over to Cal and patted his shoulder. "That's it for you; you've given more than enough." Cal tried to speak but he could barely whisper. His face was white as a sheet. He tried to grab a glass of water from the table next to him, his hand shaking. He quickly gave up when he realized he was too weak. Letting out a small laugh, he said, "I think I keep grabbing for the imaginary one. I can see two glasses dancing in front of me right now."

I walked over to him and held the glass to his lips. "Thank you," I whispered, my own body trembling. This couldn't be it. It wasn't enough. Cal managed a tiny nod and looked up at me with his kind, hazel eyes.

"Is this it?" I repeated, this time aiming my question at Matthew, who had collapsed in a vinyl chair. His face showed stress for the first time. He pinched his eyebrows and stared at the tabletop like it was talking to him.

"There's one other, but it's complicated." He pushed the words out. They had a bitter edge to them.

"What... what's complicated about it?" I ignored their faces, even though I could tell there was something deeper going on. I was trying to boil my blood. Change it to O. I wished I could give Joseph my heart. I would have given him anything.

Alexei stormed out of the room, slamming the door weakly behind him.

"Is it Alexei? Let me talk to him. I'll change his mind. I'll make him see...." Desperation was clear in my voice.

Matthew still wouldn't look at me. He shook his head. "No, it's not Alexei. It's Apella."

I felt myself shrinking, my body condensing into a scrunched-up ball. "Well, she owes me at least this," I whispered sharply.

Matthew stood up and looked at me or almost through me. His eyes changed from kindness to judgment. I leaned away from him, scared. I knew I could take things too far but I didn't think it was unreasonable to ask for this. She could give me some blood.

"Does she owe you her baby?"

"What does her baby have to do with it?" I snapped, not quite grasping the link between the two.

Matthew's words pierced right through me as he said, "Apella is forty-three. She's underweight from the journey and she's high risk as it is. The amount she needs to donate would put her body under a great deal of stress. It's not a certainty but giving this much blood will put her baby in danger."

Oh no.

No.

Not even I could ask that. Pain swelled in the room. Everyone could feel it. It was hopeless. Apella would not give her baby up. I would never ask her to. It was over. I started to sink.

Deshi spoke, "Ease up, Matt. She's not that kind of person. Even Rosa has her limits."

I crouched down on the ground, feeling a physical pain like being stabbed in the stomach. The knife was twisting back and forth but stayed in my gut, all jagged and rusty.

The hopelessness of it threatened to crush me. I was going to lose him. "Oh God..." I whimpered. "I'm going to be sick." Matthew ran to me with a bowl and I threw up. He looked surprised. I think he expected me to run after Apella and demand she do it. "I could never ask her to do that," I said, sliding myself towards a wall so I could lean against it. *Let*

The Wall

me turn to stone here, I thought. *I'll become part of the mountain. I'll never leave. I'll never grow. I'll just stop, with him.*

"You don't need to," he said softly. "She's already decided."

My back straightened. "What? No!" This was a debt I could never repay. "Where is she?" I was searching the room like she would jump from behind a curtain. I had to find her and talk her out of it. "Will you look after the baby for me? I'll be back soon," I said to Deshi. He nodded, adding an eye roll. He was getting sick of watching the baby for me. I didn't have time to placate him. "Last time, I swear," I threw over my shoulder.

I stood up and walked briskly out of the room. I had an idea of where she might go. I climbed down the ladder and made my way to the big, metal door, composing my speech as I went, changing it several times.

I stood at the big, metal door. The one they had hauled my screaming, pregnant body through six weeks ago as I watched them drag Joseph's lifeless body past me. A lifetime ago. Something needed to change. For too long, we had been stuck in a nowhere land. I took a deep breath and unwound the cog, pushing hard.

4

Gifts

I could feel her hand linked in mine, pulling me backwards. A warm breath on my neck made me pause and a deep rumbling voice whispered, "Don't do this." I shook them both free.

The moment I breathed in the cold air, everything hit me at once. This was where I was supposed to be. I had lost myself to my grief, to my struggles with the baby, and to Joseph. This was not who I was. This was not the girl he fell in love with. My heart ached at the thought, a splinter of grief for my own losses splitting me open. My eyes found the landscape unrecognizable. I had craved winter, so long ago. Back in the Classes, I'd wanted the peace and quiet to wander the garden without kids staring at me. This was more beautiful than an arboretum. This was real. It was breathtaking but harsh and cold, bitingly so. Nature never waits; it layers the world, changes it, circles it, and brings it back again.

The woods were heavily laden with white snow. Glimpses of evergreens sparkled with crystal icicles. It filled me. I crunched onto the snow, my feet instantly frozen. I quickly jumped towards the cabin, snow up to my knees. I could see a faint path, the thin slip cut into the snow only someone as small as Apella could have made. She must have been inside.

I poked my head in the door. Everything was exactly as we'd left it. A circle of beds, backpacks stacked neatly in the corner. A pile of firewood. I fought back tears as I looked at the pile of stones on the floor. An unfinished puzzle dropped the second we saw Joseph walking towards us. Apella was huddled in the corner, shivering. I sighed. The wood was *right* there. If I hadn't come, she would have frozen to death. She looked up at me with an expression I couldn't read—sad, expectant, angry? Maybe all of those things.

I retrieved a backpack and pulled out a lighter, building a fire. Memories of orange and yellow warmth flooded through me. But it was an unpleasant memory. That jagged knife was turning around and around, sending veins of pain creeping through my whole body. This place was no good. It felt like it held all our dashed hopes, all our fears. The fire warmed the corner but with no door, it was still horribly cold.

I took one of the blankets, draped it around her slight shoulders, and sat close. I wanted to speak but I wasn't sure what to say.

"Don't do this," I stammered. My teeth were chattering, from the cold and from the fact my body was trying to stop my mouth from moving. It didn't even make sense to me but I desperately didn't want her to do this. I knew what it meant if she didn't, but I couldn't put the two outcomes together. I couldn't owe her this. The debt would crush me. I wondered in the blackest corners of my mind whether she would regret it and resent us. Of course she would.

She looked at me, her big, blue eyes unblinking, and her hand on her stomach. "Rosa, do you know how many girls I watched them hurt?"

I didn't answer. I didn't need to. I remembered the sickening rosy cheeks. That glow of pregnancy that sat so wrongly over the unaware girls. Their skin stretched thin over their stomachs and their faces, like it was all they could do to hold themselves in. Those girls were probably still walking around the roped-off yards, still fighting the oppressive fog of drugs, stuck in their own contained nightmare. They were so young. I was so young.

"I did nothing. I let them treat those precious, young lives like animals, worse than animals, and I did nothing. I was selfish," she continued.

I put my hand on hers. It was cold as ice and still as stone. I watched her face—watched it change.

"I understand now. I don't get to have a baby. I don't deserve one. I have to let it go." She had no tears. Her face was accepting.

"But I can't…" I started to say, feeling hysteria pulling me down, the weight of too many lives sitting on my tiny shoulders. "I don't know how… it's too much." I burst into tears. She put her thin arms around me and held me close, wrapping me in a paper-thin cocoon, making shushing noises and stroking my hair.

"It's all right. I'll be all right," she said calmly.

"You'll hate me. If you do this for me, you will end up hating me." I wasn't even sure why I cared so much. I had hated her. I blamed her for so much.

Apella laughed a soft, sad, gasp of a laugh. "I'm not doing this for you. I'm doing it for Joseph and for our strange, little family."

I nodded, still unable to control my tears, sniffing and shaking. We couldn't lose anyone else. But this sacrifice was more than anyone could ask. And I guess that's why no one would. This was her choice. I had to abide by it.

"How did this happen?" I asked

"How did what happen?" Her voice was serene.

"All of it."

"It's like you said, Rosa. We always have a choice," she replied, dipping her chin and staring into the fire.

Damn it! My own words were coming back to bite me. I smiled, genuinely. Tears froze on my cheeks. We picked up a few things and left, our arms around each other. Apella would give her blood and might lose her baby in the process. We just had to hope it would be enough and that Alexei would forgive her.

5

Gone

Apella insisted on having it done straight away. I urged her to stop and think it over but she wouldn't listen. We looked for Alexei but he was still hiding. Apella wasn't upset, but I was. She needed him. He should have been there.

They sat her in the beige, vinyl chair, its oversized arms and back dwarfing her tiny body. Cal was lying in a bed next to her, still looking quite white but his color was returning with every passing minute.

Matthew put the needle in, pressing the cold metal hard against her skin and puncturing her willowy arm. I observed the tattoo she had stolen from the dead girl at the Classes and truly wondered if she could ever make up for all the horrible things she had done. But I sat with her. If she was letting go, then so should I. I held her hand, watching her dark red blood track up a tube and into the bag. There was a bond growing between us I had never expected. That was what bonded us, blood. Clara's blood, her child, Apella's gift of blood to Joseph. We were becoming a family.

Everything was fine for a while. They took two bags without anything seeming to happen. Then she started to sway. Matthew walked over and said, "Ok, I think that's enough." He went to disconnect the tube but her hand shot out and grabbed him.

"No, you need at least this last bag if you want to have any chance of saving him. Let me finish," she said through her teeth. She looked so frail and yet so much stronger than I thought her capable of.

Where was Alexei? I had unfair visions of him crying in a corner somewhere, cowering like a child.

The door swung open and he appeared. He stumbled over to her chair and sat on her other side. His eyes connected with mine. I wanted to say, *I tried to stop her*, but my mouth was dry and wouldn't open to the words.

He looked down at Apella and smiled. "I'm sorry, darling. What you are doing... I'm proud of you."

She looked up at him, her face paler than I thought possible. I could almost see through her. They looked at each other forever. I finally understood what they had. This was an old love but a strong love. It was unconditional. They couldn't hurt each other because it would be hurting themselves.

Apella let out a small cry, tiny. It shot out of the room on a breath of wind. I know she didn't hate me but I hated myself. It shouldn't have happened. Matthew ushered me out of the room, telling a much brighter looking Cal to leave also.

"When I'm ready, I will come down and collect Joseph. Wait for me in your room," he said as he turned his back to us, closing in on Apella. She was braver than I'd ever thought possible. Somehow, she had become a mother without a baby. She was protecting her family. Maybe she would come out of this stronger, shake the old life off like shedding a skin, papery remnants of a horrible existence floating to the ground. It was something to aspire to.

I was staring through the small, rectangular window, intruding on their personal pain, when I felt a hand on my shoulder. "C'mon, we need to give them some privacy," Cal said. He guided my rigid body towards the ladder.

I shrugged his hand off and tried to steady myself but the floor was heaving under my feet. An imaginary gust of wind churned around me

The Wall

and tried to knock me over. If only things would slow down for a second, if the world would stop spinning, I could catch my breath. His face stretched and blurred before my eyes. "Whoa!" Strong arms caught me and then... darkness.

6

Cal

I awoke propped up against a wall in a dark hallway. Hard, jagged rock poked into my back, wet with condensation. A shaft of light sliced through the blackness about a hundred meters away. I stood quickly, bumping my head on a low-hanging pipe, a comical 'boing' sound shimmying away from me.

"Rosa, isn't it?" a vaguely familiar voice asked. I pulled my legs up quickly, hands in front of my face in defense. "Don't panic. You fainted."

"Oh. Um. Sorry. I'm just not used to all the blood," I lied. If only that were true.

"It's all right. Lucky I was there or you would have fallen down the ladder," Cal said a little too proudly. I could barely see him in the dark, just his ears poking out, giving him a recognizable silhouette.

I started to stand. "I better get back. Matthew said to wait in my room."

A hand clamped on my shoulder, holding me in place. "Hey, there's no rush," Cal said in an odd, syrupy tone. "They'll be a while."

I stood up, swaying a little, and walked towards the light. It felt uncomfortable being in the dark with this boy. I picked up the pace, ducking my head when I got to the door so they didn't see me, and swinging myself down the ladder.

"Wait! Can I come with you? Keep you company while you wait?" In the light, he still looked pale. He was only a couple of inches taller than

The Wall

me and he was leaning up on his toes. Eyes earnest, he stared at me expectantly, one hand in his pocket, the other tucking a stray curl behind his ear. He seemed harmless.

I weighed it up. This boy had just donated all the blood he could to Joseph. He must have understood our relationship. Besides, what I was thinking was preposterous. I was not desirable in any way. I was a teenage mother, a mess. Whatever had made me uncomfortable, I ignored it. My instincts weren't to be trusted anymore, look where they'd got us so far.

"Ok," I shrugged. He followed me to my room, silently. I kept a good few feet between us, not entirely trusting him. The only sound was the standard-issue canvas sneakers squeaking on the linoleum floor.

I entered to find Deshi sitting, rocking an inconsolable, screaming baby. He looked stressed. Hessa was rolling around on the floor. I smiled down at the darling child.

"What happened?" Deshi asked, his eyes showing concern for both of our family members, as he walked to me and handed me the baby.

"She went through with it. Matthew is coming down to get Joseph soon." My face felt thin, stretched over my bones too tightly. My heart felt similar.

"Do you want me to stay?" he asked, his eyes moving from me to Cal and back again. I wanted to say yes. But I was being silly. I would be fine.

"No, it's ok. Joseph's here," I said with a weak smile.

Deshi rolled his eyes. "Well, I'm going to put Hessa down for a nap." He tapped his hand on Joseph's shoulders lightly. "Good luck, Joe." He kissed his fingers and placed them on Joseph's forehead. Then he was gone.

The baby screamed. I climbed onto the bed and put the child to my breast. Not even thinking about Cal. This had become second nature to me now. The boy shyly looked away as I fed my child, his curls forming a curtain over his bowed head. When I was done, he pulled up a chair and sat facing me eagerly. Maybe he was just being friendly.

"So, have you thought of a name yet?" he asked, trying to be kind or interested.

I stiffened. "No, not yet. I mean, I can't."

His eyebrows rose in confusion. "Oh, why's that?"

"Not that it's any of your business but I always thought his father would name him," I snapped.

The boy was offended. His eyebrows turned down, his eyes wide, but he quickly swallowed it. He seemed overly sensitive.

"I'll help you," he said, half-standing out of his chair, his hurt flipping to inappropriate enthusiasm.

Now I was confused. "What do you mean?"

"I'll help you come up with a name. He's going to be pretty tired and confused when he wakes up." Cal gestured to Joseph's resting form. "The last thing he's going to want to do is name a baby."

He was irritating, but he had a point. And I wanted to show Joseph I wasn't completely incompetent.

Cal devised a plan. He started asking me questions, personal questions. The first being—how did you feel when you first found out you were pregnant? I eyed him suspiciously, replying that I was really, really angry. Violated. Seeing that was not a great line of questioning, he continued to ask me about the baby. How I felt, when did it change, what made me think I could be a mother?

"Stop. None of this will help me," I said crankily. My patience was not thin, but non-existent.

"Ok, ok. I know," he said. Rubbing his chin, he pointed at Joseph. "How does *he* make you feel?"

I closed my eyes, dreaming, thinking of Joseph's warm arms around me, his soft lips parting mine. The way he pressed me up against a tree and buried his face in my hair, kissing my neck, sliding his hand down my arms to my waist.

"Like gold," I whispered, forgetting I was answering a question, forgetting there was someone staring at me. I opened my eyes and my cheeks flushed hot at Cal's intense gaze.

"Hmm. Like gold," Cal grinned with a faraway expression. He paused and I waited for him to snap out of it. When he didn't, I rattled the arm of his chair. "And you are of Spanish origin right?" he said chirpily, coming back to reality.

"I suppose. I mean, in old terms, I guess I'm half-Indian, half-Spanish." It felt strange to say it. These terms were rarely used in Pau, banned outside of the classroom. They were considered inflammatory.

Cal stared at me a long time, picking over my features, his eyes pausing over my nose, my ears, my neck, and to my chest. I wanted to kick him. He returned to my eyes and kept peering, until I coughed and turned away, giving my attention to the baby as I wrapped him and tried to rock him to sleep. The way Cal looked at me was completely foreign. I didn't know whether to be scared or flattered.

"Interesting," he said, peculiarly fascinated. "Those eyes…" He stopped talking mid-sentence and pulled out a small reader from his pocket. At least that's what I thought it was, until he started typing things in and reading. I was curious but something told me not to get too close, so I hovered above him from my bed.

"What about Hema?" I screwed up my nose; it sounded too much like Hessa. He laughed, a low sound that didn't quite touch his eyes. It sounded like Joseph and I didn't want to put the two together in my mind. "Ok, maybe not." He returned to the screen. "Oriole, Orville, Hemen, Kunal, Orlando, Kin, Jin, Paz."

"Wait. Go back a few."

"Kin?"

"No."

"Orlando?"

I paused. Orlando. I turned it over in my head, pulling it out and laying it across the child like a blanket. Orlando. He opened his eyes and looked at me. One blue and one brown eye framed with long, blond eyelashes. My eyes, Joseph's frame. I wondered if there was a nice-sounding name for defective. Probably not. I let out a giggle. No, Orlando fit, a beautiful name for a beautiful child, a one-of-a-kind child. Something materialized in me, or maybe was there all along, and now it was making its presence strongly felt. When I looked at this baby, I saw beauty. I saw love. The connection was there. I took his tiny hand in mine and put it to my face. Soft and sharp.

I nodded. "Orlando is good."

Cal was looking at me with a quizzical expression. He opened his mouth to speak but Matthew entered the room, flanked by two women I didn't recognize.

He just stared at me with tired, worried eyes and I knew what he was going to say. I watched his lips moving slowly, noticing the dryness in the corners. The words came out like they were underwater. A dull thrumming noise that I understood to mean 'Apella will probably lose her baby' and the words not spoken, 'It's your fault'. I felt the pain of his words, each one smarting like the lash of a cane. Leaving a message slapped into my skin, a debt I could not repay.

"Can I see her?"

He shook his head. "Give her some time," he said, his usually bright face looking worn, tired. I felt so very sorry for him. He seemed to have invested so much in our well-being and I could tell this was weighing on him heavily. If the operation wasn't successful, Apella's sacrifice would be for nothing.

I wanted to say something comforting but all that I could think was: *You have to make this work* and *you better make this work*. So I kept my mouth shut. I didn't want to add to the pile of rocks and bodies Matthew already had teetering atop his shoulders.

He managed a weak smile, thin-lipped, no teeth. "We'll take him now. If you want to say something, now would be the time."

I nodded. "I just need to put the baby, I mean, Orlando, to bed." Matthew raised his eyebrows at the name but didn't comment. I padded off quickly. I laid the child down in his cot across from my room. My eyes washed softly over the tiny bundle. If Joseph didn't survive—at the thought of this I felt my insides turning to stone, like a snap frost it crept up my spine and spread like poison—would I be able to make this work? Unfortunately, I knew the answer, so I didn't finish my thought.

I walked back to my room slowly, inching my feet forward. I felt like I was moving through high grass and there were animal eyes on me, waiting to pounce. Matthew was watching me too, hands on his hips, tapping his feet. He was anxious to get moving. Drawing it out was not going to help. Invisible arms shoved me forward. I tripped over myself and into the room.

Cal was still sitting in a chair, looking at his feet. I moved to Joseph.

His face was a memory. I filled in the spaces, inserted pink to his yellow skin, added weight to his thinner body. I leaned down and kissed him. The smallest glint of gold sparked through me. He was still there. I leaned down to his ear and whispered, "I named our son. But I'm not going to tell you his name until you ask me." An ache shot through me as I remembered one of our first conversations back in Pau. Joseph had said he wouldn't bring up the subject of my father until I asked him. We still had so much to talk about, so many things to learn about each other. It wouldn't end here. It couldn't.

The nurses disconnected him from the machines. One put a suction cup over his mouth attached to a balloon and squeezed it at even intervals. I let my hand trail the edge of the bed until it connected with nothing. They disappeared.

"This will take all night, Rosa. I suggest you try and sleep," Matthew said, rubbing his tired, creased forehead.

I rolled my eyes. "Yeah, sure thing." As if I could sleep.

Now it was just Cal and me.

"Do you know what they are going to do to him?" I asked, blinking away stray tears.

He looked up from his feet, his eyes hopeful. "No, but Matt's very good, the best."

Something was stirring in me. Old feelings of curiosity long suppressed. "How did he get that way? I mean, do you have Classes like we do?"

Cal laughed at me, and I hardened. I glared at him and he swallowed the laugh like a bitter pill. "No. No Classes. Matt wanted to be a doctor so he studied to become one."

This was an amazing and confusing revelation for me. People could choose their path in life? The idea of that amount of freedom was, surprisingly, a little terrifying. And like that, the seductive distraction of finding out more about the Survivors took over. I leaned into Cal intensely. "What else can you tell me?" His cheeks were pink, surprised by my sudden closeness.

"Not much, I'm afraid. I'm not supposed to say much until you take the pledge. Besides, you really need to see it for yourself."

"The what?"

Cal explained that all survivors had to take a pledge. It was a way of securing your allegiance, to the secrecy of their home and also to each other. Everyone had to take care of each other and help any other survivors who came along, which was not many, apparently. We were the first in many, many years and the only known escapees of the Woodlands. So that's what Matt meant when he said it was his duty. It sounded nice but a tiny warning light was flashing, a faint, red glow. Was I swapping one cult for another?

"So you can't tell me anything?" I sighed.

The Wall

He responded to my obvious disappointment, eager to impress. "I can show you some things," he said, extending his hand. I eyed it apprehensively. I wasn't sure, and I really should have stayed right where I was. I talked myself into it; waiting was not going to achieve anything anyway. I took his hand. It was warm and dry. A shiver ran through me, a reminder, and I let go abruptly. I walked to the cot to check on the baby. Hopefully, he would sleep for at least an hour. "Ok, lead the way."

Cal grinned at me and started walking down the hall away from where the people were. Then as it got quieter and darker, he broke into a jog. I jogged behind him, wondering why I was mindlessly following this strange boy but feeling a sense of freedom. My footsteps sent a new energy through my body as I ran. A sense of my old self, impulsive, mischievous, was surging forward. He told me to hurry up. We were nearly there.

He pulled up suddenly and turned to face me. In the dark, I could barely make him out and I slammed right into his stationary body with a thud. We were both panting, breathless. I laughed. So did he.

Once I couldn't hear footfalls anymore, another sound was pushing up out of the darkness. Barking.

The air was heavy down here. Cal found my hand and I didn't pull away because I couldn't see where I was going anymore. It made me feel intensely uncomfortable and I was starting to regret my decision. He placed my hand on a metal rail, patting it once, and told me to climb down. I gripped the rails and clumsily tried to find the rungs of the metal ladder with my feet. Cal was right behind me and stepped on my hands.

"Ouch! Watch it," I snapped

Cal scoffed, "Whoops, sorry."

Hitting the ground, I adjusted my eyes. I could see light again. I followed it; hearing the sounds of dogs barking, the unpleasant smell of animal closeness creeping up my nose. I came to a door. Cal opened it for me, putting his hands in the small of my back and pushing me through gently. I jerked away from his touch and stumbled into a room full of wolves.

I turned to run, my blood thumping in my ears. But Cal was just smiling casually at me, like the room was full of bunny rabbits. There was a man in the corner fiddling with what looked to be a carriage. He looked up and waved a hand at Cal. "Hey, Bataar," Cal said. The man just grunted. His dark brows pulled together in concentration as he tried to untangle meters of rope.

The wolves were jumping up excitedly, their claws click-clacking against the stone floor. Cal approached them. I squeaked out a "No," but they knew him. They were licking his hands and he was patting their heads, pulling on their ears and talking to them.

I didn't notice I was pinned against the wall until he brought one over to me, holding it by the collar. I gulped drily; I had nowhere to run. I peeled myself off and leaned down towards it. "This is Bold." It wasn't a wolf, at least not like what I had encountered. Its eyes were a golden yellow and its coat was thick and fluffy. It looked at me, teeth bared in an almost human grin, tongue hanging out. "It's ok. He won't hurt you." I reached my hand out and patted it stiffly on the head. It leaned into my palm, taking the pat as a sign that it could jump on me.

I surprised both men when I firmly said, "No!" The dog tilted its head and planted its bum on the ground. I laughed. "Good."

"You're a natural," Cal said admiringly. The man in the corner sniggered and spat on the ground.

"What is this? I mean, why have you got animals down here?" I had the sudden and ridiculous fear that maybe they ate them. I chided myself.

"This is our transportation," Cal shrugged, like it was obvious.

My eyes grazed over harnesses, carriages, stacks of containers piled

The Wall

against the walls of the big, dark cavern. I grinned. This could be fun. But I instantly felt a stab of guilt at enjoying myself when Joseph was under the knife and Apella was grieving her baby. I sat down against the wall and sighed deeply. Would I ever be able to enjoy life without something pulling it away from me?

Joseph, please wake up.

One of the dogs sidled up to me and laid its head in my lap. I ran my hands through its fur, rough and prickly on the outer layer, but when I pushed my fingers deeper, it changed to a soft down. My happiness was attached to these feelings. A mixture of fear and love had pushed me into a tree and created the most amazing night of my life. I held my chest, afraid of my ribs parting, my heart falling out and dropping to the dirty floor to be covered in dog hair. I laughed halfheartedly as I imagined someone picking it up, dusting it off, and handing it back to me saying, 'Here, you dropped this.' I felt like I was going crazy. I *was*.

Cal played with the dogs and I watched him create mini-tornados of dog fluff and dust. Yawning. Distraction didn't last very long. He walked over and sat next to me, our legs touching. It was too close. I edged sideways, putting a gap between us. The dog snored in my lap. I wished I were him.

"Why are you being so nice to me?" I blurted out, harshly.

He was taken aback but he answered me kindly. "Because I know what you're going through."

I snorted. How could he possibly?

"I lost my sister six months ago. She got sick. Matt tried to save her but he couldn't." He looked sad. Tired. Grief does that. It wears you down. So all you feel is bluntness and loneliness.

"I'm sorry," I said, shoulders slumped, suddenly feeling so weary I could barely keep my eyes open.

"Close your eyes and rest," he said. "I'll wake you in half an hour."

I didn't reply, the heaviness of the day was pressing down on me, one life slipping away while another fought to hang on. Half an hour. I could rest and then I would go back to the room and wait. A heavy, furred head on my lap lulled me to sleep with its warmth and rough snoring.

Wrong One

I was running through the forest, the light streaming through peppered trunks. It was warm; the autumn colors shone Technicolor bright, as if painted on. The trees leaned into me, whispering secrets as they swung their arms back and forth in a slow dance. Someone caught up to me. A big, warm hand clasped my own. It started to rain, but I didn't feel wet. It showered down on me but only sent pinpricks of pleasure through my free body. Joseph chuckled and stopped running. I gazed into those beautiful eyes, the green of the forest living in them. The gold of my heart scattered around the irises. He started climbing a tree and I followed, vaguely aware of dogs barking in the background. We sat together on a branch and he pulled me into his lap. It was light, brighter than light, everywhere. It folded over us like a warm blanket. He held my face in his hands and pulled me closer. I parted my lips just slightly, breathing in his warm breath. I closed my eyes and opened them again.

Cal's face was about an inch from my own. Before I could stop him, he leaned in and tried to kiss me. Shocked, I froze. My lips set hard, my whole body stiffening like a plank of wood. I leaned back, trying to put my hands on his chest and push him away but he had a hold of them, grasping my arms at the elbow. He pushed towards me. I pulled my legs up quickly and kicked. He flew back, knocking over water bottles that made lonely, metallic, rolling sounds against the rock floor.

"What the hell do you think you're doing?" I yelled. Dogs joined in chorus.

His eyes were unapologetic. "You just looked so beautiful lying there I couldn't help myself," he said with a shrug.

"Help yourself?" I should have followed my instincts in the first place. My instincts were now telling me to get out of here as soon as I could.

His face fell. "Sorry. It just gets lonely here. I thought we could be friends."

Friends? I was furious. What was I going to tell Joseph? "Friends don't kiss!" I said damningly.

He nodded.

I stormed out of the cave, embarrassed, angry, and ashamed. People were horrible. I thought about going back in there and punching him in the face, but thought better of it. There was a sense of violence to that kiss, a forcefulness I didn't want to revisit. Stumbling around in the dark cursing, I found the ladder and made my way back to my room.

8

My Heart

I popped my head into the baby's room. He was still sleeping soundly. The clock read almost midnight. That idiot let me sleep for hours. I crawled into bed, my eyes falling upon the empty one beside me. Doubt slunk its way into my head like a burglar. If he died... No I wouldn't think it.

I pulled the sheets up over my knees. Sitting. I was too scared to sleep. I shuddered as the memory of Cal's slobbering lips on mine. It sent sharp shakes of disgust right through me. I didn't feel guilty. I was just plain angry. Why would anyone do such a thing? Maybe there was something wrong with me that made him believe I was an easy target. I wanted to scrub the memory off my face and take a layer of skin with it. No one was allowed to touch me like that, not without my permission.

A nurse came in and gave me an update. My angry face gave her pause. I tried to relax it, forcing it into a calmer set, but it felt like trying to push air from a barely blown-up balloon, squishing things to the sides awkwardly. She looked tired, her light brown hair pinned back messily, and her eyes squinting as she talked. The operation was going well, very well. Then she said a whole pile of medical stuff I didn't understand. I just nodded. I didn't need to hear anything other than 'going well'. She said they were halfway through and then she hurried off. I sighed. It would be a long wait.

I wandered across the hall. Orlando's eyes were half open but he was asleep, his little chest moving up and down faster than an adult's. I grimaced at the thought that Cal had helped me name him. But it was his name now. Hopefully, I would forget the rest. I picked him up and brought him to my room. Lying on my side, I placed him in the crook of my arm and watched him sleep. He had been a good baby so far. Better than I deserved. He had more personality than I remember Hessa having at this age, but maybe that's what a mother sees in her own child. A mother. The word made me feel deathly frightened and comforted at the same time. The responsibility of it was heavy in my chest.

I whispered to him, "You'll look after me, won't you? We defectives have to stick together." He sucked in a breath and shivered. I pulled him closer.

I recalled my conversation with Alexei, when he told me that if my baby had my eyes, we both would have been 'disposed' of. A small fire started inside me that grew to a blue-and-white flame. A rage I couldn't name. I smiled, a solid sternness to it. If this is what it felt like to be a mother, maybe I was more suited to it than I thought.

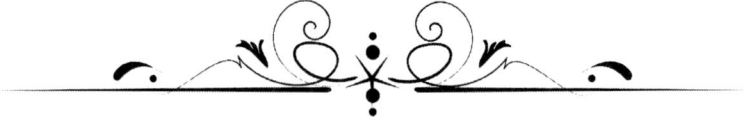

There was never any easy way to tell whether it was morning or night in here. The lights always glowed, footsteps travelling softly past the door. Someone was always busy doing something, but what? I didn't know.

I had been watching Orlando sleep, breathing in and out, rolling his little eyes, the pink of his cheeks strange compared to my dark ones. He was so warm and comfortable. I was quite the opposite, wound up like a tight coil ready to spring headfirst into the rocks above me. My mind wandered in different directions. I worried about what Joseph would be like when he woke up—would he be weak? Would he be upset? Would he still want me? The last question, I didn't dwell on too much. I had in

The Wall

my mind that I would remind him he did, somehow. When my thoughts went to Cal, my hands turned to fists—a hard feeling wrapped around a soft one. I wondered what he was after. If I hadn't stopped him, what would he have done? Strangled by the idea of telling Joseph, I became angrier still.

And Apella. How was she feeling right now? It felt odd to worry about her. I had spent so much time hating her, despising every single thing she did, and taking pleasure in her discomfort. All these new feelings assaulted me like a spray of cold water. Things I never thought I would feel, waking me up, making me want to defend my old self, hold onto it, even as I watched it wash away. It was impossible. I used to say nothing changes, but I was so wrong. Everything changes so fast you feel like you're grabbing the edge of the train as it takes off, your feet scrabbling to lift up onto the platform, your hair swirling about your face. I wondered whether I would ever catch up.

I abandoned it all in favor of counting the points on the rock wall above our heads. Watching the light bounce off the shiny black, the way it looked like a dark sea of oil almost moving and swelling in a nonexistent storm, mesmerizing. I pulled Orlando in tighter. He wheezed. My eyelids were heavy. I didn't want to sleep but my body had other ideas. After the last time I slept with a child, I decided to put him down in his cot. Memories of the burning heat in my hands as I held Hessa out over the flames woke me up enough to drag myself reluctantly out of the room. I laid the baby down and backed out quietly. I retreated to my bed, and into a dream.

"Should we wake her?"

"Let her sleep."

"Anything we need to do before we go?"

"No, thankfully, for better or worse, it's over."

Something familiar was missing. My brain was still under a cloud of exhaustion. I was listening for it, although I wasn't sure what my ears were searching for. Monotony had trained them. Thinking about absence, no beeps, no blips. I exhaled slowly.

I felt a hand brush my face, collecting strands of hair and pulling them away from my forehead. Warm hands. Fear jolted through me. I snapped my eyes open and slapped at the hands. "No!"

Blinking, it took a while to focus. And then I was staring at those eyes. Those beautiful green eyes with flecks of gold in them. I was melting and on fire at the same time. Tears filled my eyes and I sprung at him from my bed, embracing him, squeezing him hard until he let out a small squeak of pain as he struggled to keep his feet. I relaxed my grip a little and he chuckled.

"You had me worried for a second," he said as he stepped back to look at me. He ran his hands down my arms and then brought the backs of his fingers across my now-flat stomach. I shivered. I smiled. I could have burst through the ceiling! This was the closest we had ever been and yet it wasn't close enough. I looked up at him and gave him a toothy smile. I touched his beard, tracing his jaw. He looked better than I'd expected, his strength was not immediately apparent but his color had returned. Whatever they did to him was remarkable. He was standing in a hospital gown and cotton pajama pants that were too short. He swayed a little and steadied himself against the bedrail. I moved to him. "You should sit down before you fall down," I said.

"It feels so good to hear your voice," he said as he obliged me and sat with a thump on the edge of the bed, his knees wide apart. I sort of shudder-shivered at the sound of his.

I felt brave. He did that to me. I fit myself between his legs and stood on my tiptoes. Pulling his head down towards my face, I laced my fingers in his hair. He smelled like antiseptic, but also of Joseph. Of all the things I had craved for weeks, even if was I imagining them: wood fire, pine, fresh air.

He moved slowly, at first, and as painful as it was, I matched his pace, savoring it. This was not our last kiss. He brushed his lips over mine unhurriedly. It was torture—good torture. When he added pressure to it, I sank, waves of molten gold crashing over my head. *Was this real?* It felt like a dream. He moved back onto to the bed and pulled me on top of him. Kissing me like he never had before. I willed myself to stop but it was not going to happen.

Until pain crossed his face.

I sat up and shuffled back. Reluctantly, I stepped off him and sat back on my heels on his mattress. He was grinning.

"What?"

"Oh nothing," he said, looking at the ceiling. I stared at him until he answered. "It's just—I should fall into a coma more often."

I sighed and stared up at the ceiling. At least this hadn't changed.

"So do you know what happened to you?" I asked, realizing that he may not know where we were or who these people were.

He nodded. "That man, Matt, filled me in, briefly." Then his eyes squinted at me and he pulled his mouth to the side. "Is it true you tried to poke my eyes out?"

I was a little embarrassed. I grinned at him. "Well, you wouldn't open them. I had to try something! Is that your only question?" He laughed. I had missed that sound like breathing.

His expression went somewhat serious but he couldn't control his happiness any more than I could. "I do have more questions I'd like to ask. How's Apella and Alexei, Hessa and...?" A baby crying interrupted. He stilled, looking from me to the half-open door and back again.

I'd been dreading this. "Just a minute," I said as I jumped from his bed to the floor, feeling his eyes on me as I walked.

I took my time, feeling flushed and nervous. I had to remind myself that he knew me. He knew how I'd felt about the baby. I couldn't change my behavior or act a certain way. Anyway, it wouldn't fool him. I changed the baby's nappy mindlessly, probably putting it on backwards for all I knew. When I was done, I slung him over my shoulder. He liked to be up and looking around when he was awake. I waded slowly back to our room, pushing through my insecurities like I was moving through jelly.

The door was slightly ajar and I slipped inside.

Joseph's eyes were wide and soft. I knew he was trying not to assess the situation and I tried hard not to get my back up about it. As soon as I stopped, Orlando started crying again, throwing his head about on my shoulder, looking for something to eat. I sat on my bed and swung him around, lifting up my shirt. Joseph was watching, quietly, intently, his chin resting on the heel of his hand.

This felt wrong. I couldn't help but feel that sense of backwardness. He'd never seen me naked. It seemed unfair to me that this was the first time he would see my breasts. I paused.

"Can you, um, not look?" I whispered, self-consciously.

He blushed. "Oh, sorry," he muttered and stared at his hands. So patient. It was so quiet. All I could hear was his deep breathing.

"You can talk to me, though," I said, my voice sounding a bit shrill.

I heard him grunt or laugh, I wasn't sure. "How has it been for you and the baby?" The words seemed hard to get out. Was he afraid of what I might say? I thought I should be honest, but maybe not too honest.

"It was hard at first," unbearably so, "but we're doing ok now." I looked down at the beautiful boy and smiled. Yes, we were doing ok.

"I'm so sorry I wasn't there to help you." He sounded so regretful. He always jumped to blaming himself for things, things that were out of his control.

"Don't do that," I snapped "This is not your fault. If anyone's to blame, it's me. I should have listened to Apella, not made us stop and build that damn cabin." It hurt just thinking about it, bits of me fretting around the edges. Apella. I needed to find her, thank her… forgive her.

"Don't be ridiculous, Rosa. This was no one's fault," he said, waving his hand dismissively.

The Wall

I scowled, though he couldn't see me, he was still staring at his hands. I finished with the feeding and swung my legs over the edge of the bed. "Look up."

Joseph's head rose tentatively. I took the two steps to his bed and handed him our son. He inhaled deeply and I could see his hands were shaking, "He's beautiful," he whispered as he lightly touched the baby's forehead, swirling his fingers through his light curls.

"You would say that—he looks just like you!" I scoffed.

Joseph rolled his eyes, tracing his son's brow with his large finger. Orlando opened his eyes and Joseph smiled broadly. "Ha! Hardly. Oh, you poor boy. You have your mother's eyes." He shook with laughter, his gown slipping down to reveal a zipper-like wound in the middle of his chest. He touched two fingers to the wound and winced. "Oh, ouch, it hurts to laugh."

"Good," I said with a smirk.

He slowed his breathing and stared at me while I stared at the wound on his chest. It moved as he spoke, "Rosa, he's perfect. Well done."

I thought, *don't thank me. Thank the scientists—who concocted him in a lab*. But I bit my tongue. "What's his name?"

I flinched a little, and then tried to cover it up by smiling, but my mouth felt strained. The memory of Cal pushing himself on me was too fresh and unpleasant. It didn't mix well with how I was feeling right now. "Orlando."

Joseph screwed up his face. "Orlando? I guess it's better than Leech. What does it mean?"

I closed my eyes, the light shining through them making my vision pink. "Gold…"

There was silence. Maybe he understood, maybe he didn't. How I felt was probably different for him. But when I opened my eyes, he just gazed at me for as long as I could bear before I turned away. I think he understood. He held out his spare hand and clasped my own. He was here. We stayed like that for the longest time. Neither of us willing to move or disconnect from each other.

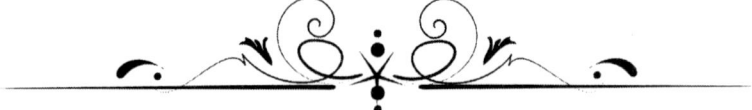

Eventually, I left Joseph with the baby and excused myself to shower. The truth was I needed some time to myself to decompress, sort through my feelings. I needed to work out where I fit in this instant family. It was very hard to shake the wrong feeling. The backwards feeling.

I was also suddenly aware of my appearance. I undid my untidy half-up and ran my fingers through my very knotty, rat-nest hair. I'd barely looked in a mirror since we arrived here and I suspected I looked like a wild girl that had just stepped out of the forest, dirt, leaves, and all.

But I was happy—thrilled even. The rest was going to take time to sort through, bit by bit. I was a crumbling wall. People kept taking bricks from the bottom and stacking them on the top, leaving the whole structure wobbling and unsound. It stretched to the sky but was unlikely to ever reach it. I just had to hold onto to the fact that Joseph was awake. That fact alone filled me to the brim.

9

Insights

I took a towel from a stack by the door and entered the women's bathroom. It was empty but I locked the stall and undressed in there. Hot water was such a luxury. I could have stood under the stream forever. I stared at my feet and let the water drum a steady beat over my back.

Two women came in, talking seriously.

"You know, he used all of it. If anyone else gets hurt, there won't be anything we can do until we get home," a high-pitched, whiny voice complained.

"Don't start. He did what he had to do. He was just following the Pledge. That's what we all have to do."

"I suppose. But the girl—I don't think she'll go along with it. She seems, well, young. Young and stubborn."

Stalls closed and they stopped talking. I let the shower continue to run until I heard toilets flush, sending sporadic spurts of hot and cold water over me, making me hop up and down, trying not to scream. The bathroom door closed. It didn't sound too good. I had been so caught up in my own tragedies I had lost sight of all the questions I should have been asking.

I held my trust in a locked box, deep inside myself, obstacles and booby traps safeguarding it. I'd never given it to these people but I'd forgotten to remind them of that. The woman was right; I was unlikely to 'go along' with anything.

I finished up and dressed. There was always an abundance of clean clothes to choose from, but I found the process difficult. I was used to grey-green and green-grey. Here there was every color and every cut. I chose a red, button-up shirt and a pair of jeans. My white sneakers were high cut and fit nicely around the cuff of my pants. My reflection showed a girl of bizarre proportions, my hair was ridiculous. Untended, it had morphed into a giant, dark mane that fell nearly to my waist. I needed to ask for some scissors.

Funny where dark memories can surface from. The most mundane things can trigger things long buried. An ache appeared in my chest. If Clara were here, she would help me with this stuff. She could also advise me about what to do about what I just heard. Although she would probably say to trust them and then I would go ahead and ignore everything she said. I plaited my hair as best I could and walked back to our room. I would play dumb, try to observe. Talk to Joseph—see what he thought about it all.

10

Recovery

My head felt heavy as I made my way back. Someone was lying to me but I wasn't sure why and whether it was something to worry about. Somehow these halls had become a soggy mess of me dragging my feet, through jelly, through grass, and now wet cement. I'd had enough. I needed to get out of here.

Matthew was arguing with Gus just outside our door. Lights flickered above. When they saw me, they stopped talking, their behavior seeming even more suspicious. Either they were talking about me or having a lover's quarrel. Ick! Gus was a bit old for Matthew. Matthew approached me and said Joseph would need at least a few days to recover before they moved him. And by the look on Gus's face, that must have been the issue. He had wanted to leave a while ago. Delaying the trip by even more time would definitely upset him.

"I'm going to restrict visitors to just you and the baby for now," he said softly. His eyes trailed a disgruntled Gus as the man stomped quietly down the hall. I sympathized. When you wanted to stomp around this place, it was very unsatisfying, the noise absorbed before it could escape from under your boot.

I was surprised by Matthew's orders. "Why?"

"I have scheduled an ultrasound for Apella later and if it shows what I think it will, she is going to need some time. This way, it's out of everyone's hands. Think about it as a forced recovery, for everyone."

"Can I help? Can I see her?" I said in clipped excitement. I knew he would say no. I knew Apella well enough to know she was a private person and would want to handle this on her own, but I had to ask.

He shook his head, his faced creased and grainy from tiredness. I touched his hand and thanked him. He said he would keep Deshi, Apella, and Alexei updated. I had questions I wanted to ask but he seemed so stressed. I had the feeling he needed some time also.

I was upset at first, but when I thought about it, a bit of time could be nice. Could we just pretend we were somewhere else and forget what was going on around us? I decided to take this recovery time at its word. Recover some of the time we had lost and enjoy being alone with Joseph. I postponed talking to him about the women from the bathroom, about Cal. It could wait. The world could wait for a while. It was doctor's orders anyway.

We spent our days talking. Joseph was supposed to lie down so we faced each other, hands clasped together, Orlando sometimes lying between us. I was buzzing from his touch, not one single shred of that charge had waned.

He wanted to learn everything he could about Orlando and I tried really hard not to look like the inadequate mother I knew I was.

"So how often does he feed? Do you bathe him? Can I change his nappy?" he said in one hurried breath.

"Um, I don't know, quite a lot, yes and definitely yes. Please!" I answered. He was hilarious, so enthusiastic, as I knew he would be. He was already a great father, but then, he'd always wanted to be one. I felt a little tug at the idea that soon, he would overtake me.

He raised his eyebrows and sighed, "Does it hurt?"

"Does what hurt?" I asked, confused.

"Feeding him."

"Oh no, not really. Maybe a little at first but now it just feels normal," I said, flustered by the turn in conversation.

"Now don't get angry," he said, pumping his hands infuriatingly, like he was fanning flames.

"If you don't want me to be angry, maybe you shouldn't say what you're thinking of saying." I eyed him suspiciously, trying not to give away my amusement.

He took a deep breath and I wondered what the hell he was going to say. "It's just… I'm really proud of you. I shouldn't say 'you've come so far'," his eyes were glinting with mischief. "But you have certainly done a great job with Orry." He looked at the boy with adoration. He had already shortened the baby's name, but I liked it. It made it more Joseph's doing and separated it from Cal.

I thought back to that day in the forest. How enormous I was, my belly getting in the way of everything. I was huge and on a hormone-induced anger rampage. Everything had blown up from one small comment. *You've come so far.* I remember feeling deficient, like he was saying, *Look how far you've come from the unfeeling, incompetent mess you were before.* Looking back, I could see how silly I had been. But then, it's always easier to look back and say things like that. Given the time again, I'm not sure I would have done anything differently. I decided to make him regret saying it again, just a little.

I snorted. "You're hopeless. I can't believe you brought that up!" I made a show of turning my back to him and crossing my arms. I felt him approaching me, his arms sliding under my arms and around my stomach.

"Rosa, I'm sorry, I didn't mean to…"

"Humph!"

"Rosa…?"

That was enough torture for the day. I grabbed his hands and brought them to my lips, laughing. "You really are an idiot."

He smirked and turned my body to face him. Kissing my neck and saying in between his lips touching my skin, "You... really... shouldn't... tease... me... like... that."

I leaned away from him, finding his eyes. "You love it!"

"No. I love you," he said earnestly.

I held his gaze for a moment before I dropped my eyes and jumped at him, saying loudly, "So cheesy!" I swept my arms around his neck and pulled him towards me for another kiss. Brimful of warmth and gold, I was nearly overflowing.

Even though Joseph was getting stronger every day, Matthew embarrassingly told us to be 'gentle' with each other. He didn't exactly give us a sex talk but he may as well have. Joseph thought this was the funniest thing he'd ever heard, even more so when my face flushed pink and I nearly choked on my lunch. I didn't care too much. His laugh echoed through my body, sweeping the dark corners, pulling out the bad parts and leaving some spaces empty and ready to be filled.

We pushed our beds together and, although it was difficult, we did respect the doctor's orders. Every single touch was sufficient for me anyway. It was more than I thought I would ever have again so I reveled in the tiniest contact. But it did start to pull at the threads I had agonizingly stranded myself back together with. I was always just a little scared that he would find the loose end, start pulling, and reveal me for the pile of dirty rags I was.

All the same, I could have stayed like this forever—in denial and suspended in time.

I wish I'd known the time was not ours to keep, that there was a huge trade-off for taking it. It wasn't mine; I stole it from the others. And,

The Wall

unfortunately, I could never give it back.

On the day Matthew confirmed that Apella had lost her baby, I proved my terrible acting skills. The sadness I felt, the guilt, was eating away at me. Little bits of me started falling away at the edges. Picking them up was exhausting. They were fast forming a bundle that was getting heavier and heavier to carry.

I walked into our room and Joseph was trying to one handedly put his trousers on while holding the baby. The image would usually inspire a sarcastic remark. But all I could think was, *Just another thing I have taken away from someone.* Apella will have no baby—these funny events, these moments will never happen to her. The finiteness of that realization slapped me in the face. *Never.*

How could this possibly be fair? Apella had a lot to answer for, but how did it work out that her baby died and I had a healthy baby I never wanted?

My foot was dangling in the air as I thought this, like one more step would send me careening off a cliff. Joseph stared at me cautiously. He knew something was wrong. And I was desperate to tell him. I wanted to melt into his arms and tell him everything, confide and let someone else bear some of the burden. But I couldn't do it. Instead, I made a choking, gulping sound, held my chest, and backed out. I stumbled towards the bathroom, hoping I wasn't coming undone, that I hadn't left a part of me, some guilty secret, lying in the hallway.

Telling myself to breathe just made it harder. I slammed into the door with my shoulder and pulled myself towards a stall. Crouching down inside, I placed my palm against the door and focused on the pressure I had to apply to keep the door shut. Knees to my chest, I rested my head on them and sobbed. Things were easier when I didn't care about anyone, when I flitted from bad idea to even worse idea, not caring about the consequences. Now the result of every decision hung over me like a fat cloud, dripping like a sponge that couldn't hold any more water.

I pulled the door ajar and lifted my blurry, puffed-up eyes. Someone had left a toiletries bag on the counter. I dragged my soaking-wet body off the floor, rifled through it, and found what I was looking for. The gold-edged blades shone hopefully under the dangling light bulbs.

I hacked through my thick plait, feeling some physical weight dropping to the floor. It lay there like a dead animal. Scared it might raise its head or scuttle across the floor, I threw it the bin, holding it like you would a poisoned rat.

I could see her reflection in the mirror, taking in my red, puffy eyes and my brutalized head of hair. She left as quickly as she had entered, returning a few minutes later with a chair. She guided me by the shoulders and sat me down. I let her. She took the scissors and painstakingly started to undo the damage I had done. It was calming—therapeutic in a way. My hair fell around me in a circle like pine needles from a tree. If only I could grow and heal so easily.

When she was done, she smoothed down my now shoulder-length hair with her hands.

"There, that's better," she said, smiling, nodding her head in satisfaction, like she had just pulled a cake from the oven and it met her approval. She put the scissors in the bag, collected up the hair, and threw it in the bin, taking the toiletries bag with her. She never asked me what was wrong. I think she had the sense not to.

These people were kind. I didn't deserve it but they were kind to me.

11

Reunion

I gazed at myself in the mirror, my blue and brown eyes blinking back at me. I looked… ok. My hair swished about my shoulders like a beaded curtain as I turned my head. I sighed, my shoulders pulling down. I felt so tense. I had to go back. He would be wondering where I was. I tied my hair back into a ponytail but then all you could see were my red cheeks and puffy eyes. I shook it out. At least this way I could hide behind it. I walked towards my room, feeling a mixture of apprehension and self-consciousness about what would come next and stupidly wondering if he would like my haircut.

When I rounded the corner, I was faced with a flurry of activity centered around our doorway. People were stacking small backpacks against the wall, all white. Others were walking into our room as some were leaving. Had it been a week already? Deshi stood at the door with Hessa. He looked like he was trying to build himself up, convince himself to go in there. He eyed my new haircut critically, a slight curl in his upper lip.

"You know, he's doing really well. You don't need to be nervous," I said, shaking my hair around to annoy him.

He wiped his hand across his mouth. "Yeah, I know. It's just… oh, I don't know."

"It's ok. I won't be upset if you hug the life out of him, I kind of expected you to."

Deshi just nodded and gazed down at Hessa, who was busy trying to jam his finger up his nose.

"After you," I said as I pushed the doors open for him.

Deshi took a deep breath and seemed to straighten up, set his shoulders, and strode into the room like he owned it. I guess everyone's an actor at different times. "Look at you!" he exclaimed loudly, but I could hear the quiver in his voice and it made me wince. It was easier for me. I could jump on Joseph, cover him in kisses, and no one would blink an eye. Joseph had chosen me. For Deshi, every single event, touch, and smile must have been tainted with heartbreak. He was always on a tightrope, gripping his bar and trying to maintain the balance between love and friendship.

Joseph was standing with Orlando casually in one arm. I hated that he made it look so natural, like he'd been a father forever, and not just one week. He was out of his pajamas and was busy trying to button his shirt with one hand as he talked in low tones to Matthew and Gus. I inwardly chastised myself for thinking how desirable he looked right then, with his shirt unbuttoned and that serious look on his face. When he heard Deshi, he looked up and grinned at both of us. He pointed at the back of his head and put his hands up, mouthing "Your hair?" I shrugged, hoping my face didn't reveal how much I'd been crying. His eyes lifted, asking me if I was ok. I waved him off and nodded. This seemed to suffice.

Deshi slapped him on the back and gave him a massive hug with his spare arm. Joseph wheezed from the pressure. "Whoops, sorry," Deshi said, easing off. I held out my arms for Hessa, the beautiful boy slapping at my hair like he was batting a rug.

"Bring Hessa over here," Joseph beckoned. We brought the babies together, darkness and light. "Orry," he said, "this is your brother, Hessa." Deshi looked uncomfortable. He smiled but it was tight, his eyes dark and thoughtful, as he stared down at his feet.

The Wall

I heard the whisper of a cough and turned to see the pale, blond couple. Apella sitting in a chair, looking like death. She reminded me of the bolts of delicate fabric my mother used to lay across a chair as she worked, translucent and feather light. Alexei was rubbing her shoulders, while trying to participate in the conversation. He spindled his way through everything, looking out of practice at whatever he was attempting. But he was trying. I pushed my way into the middle of the talking to catch up with the conversation.

"So how much time do we have?" said Joseph, his face serious, his hair curling around his ears and falling in his eyes. People stopped and turned their attention to him. That assured tone of voice made everyone want to listen.

"The diversions we set up have all been discovered and discounted. I think they will be coming back around for another sweep soon," Gus muttered, the words tinged with accusation.

I felt a warm hand on my shoulder and I jumped. Cal.

"The dogs are ready to go, Dad," Cal said. I stepped towards Joseph and let Cal's slimy palm slip from my shoulder. Joseph folded me into his spare arm. I turned to his chest and helped him with the remaining buttons on his shirt, looking up and fake-smiling thinly. I was never good at acting different to how I felt. I swear I could almost feel Cal's eyes boring into the back of my head. Maybe kissing an unconscious girl meant something different to him than it did to me.

Everyone was talking at once, giving orders or asking questions, the room crowded with bodies and opinions. I felt like a child trying to get attention, having to stand on my toes just to put my head in the cloud of clashing voices and ideas.

I was done being quiet.

"Excuse me," I shouted, but no one was listening. I put my fingers in my mouth and whistled shrilly. Everyone stopped for a second, which was long enough. Wiping my hands on the back of my jeans, I said,

"What's going on?"

Cal spoke, I wish he hadn't, even his voice gave me the creeps now. He directed his speech towards me, sending it on a dark, grey sloth of a cloud, his words hitting my face like wet mud. "The Woodland soldiers are doubling back. Surveillance shows they will be here in approximately two hours. We need to evacuate. Now." He sounded all soldiery. He reached his hand out to me like he expected me to take it so he could pull me out the door. I glared at him, willing him to spontaneously burst in flames. Poof! Into dust! I imagined a swirl of Cal ash being sucked up into the air-conditioning vents. Sadly, no luck. He just stood there blinking, clueless.

Joseph's arm gripped me a little tighter. I happily dissolved into his chest.

Everyone stared at me now, but I didn't have the effect Joseph did. They looked at me like I was an annoying interruption. It was times like this I wished I was taller. "What do we need to do?" I asked, already feeling the adrenaline of flight taking over. This is what we do. We run.

Gus spoke this time. He was all business, which suited me fine. "Pack your possessions and meet us at the dog room. We'll fit you out and show you what to do."

Throughout the commotion, Apella looked shell-shocked frightened, her big blue eyes wide, her tiny body shaking. I walked to her and took her hand. Her eyes were glassy, vacant. She wasn't doing so well. "Apella, look at me." She stared right through me. "It's all right. Look at me. I need your help." I considered slapping her, my hand kind of aching to slap someone. Instead, I took Orry from Joseph and placed him gently in her lap. If I gave her something to do, maybe she would snap out of it or at least be distracted. "Can you look after him for me?" She tipped her chin ever so slightly. "You packed up?" I asked Alexei. He nodded. "Ok. I'll meet you down there. I need to get something."

People filed out of the room quietly. Now that we knew what we

The Wall

were doing, the arguing was over. Then it was just Joseph and me. Cal turned back and gave me a lingering, wounded look as the door closed. I wished it had hit him in the face.

Joseph swayed a little and sat down on the bed. I rushed to him. He was still a little weak. He pulled his hair from his face and searched my eyes. I gulped. Holding out his hand, he pulled me towards him. He laced his fingers in mine, heat running through them. If I closed my eyes, it would be so easy to forget everything that had just happened and fall into a pond of golden warmth. "What's going on?" he said.

"You heard them—we need to get moving," I said, avoiding eye contact as I started throwing things in the pack we were given. I was vibrating. My heart not settling to a rhythm, fast, slow, beat one, beat one, two, three…

He held me still and put his hands to my face, turning it slowly against my resistance to meet his eyes. "I have two questions. One…" he leaned down and kissed my top lip, sparks dancing in our eyes, "why are you and Apella so chummy all of a sudden? And two…" he moved in again, his mouth pulling at my bottom lip, those sparks igniting into flame, "why were you staring at that boy like you were trying to saw him in half with your eyes?"

Lie, I thought. I bit my lip, blinking, stalling. I was trying to come up with a decent lie, anything. Putting my hands in my pockets, all I could fish out was lint and a ball of paper that had been through the wash so many times, it had become a solid ball. I didn't want to answer either of those questions.

"For your information, I was trying to make him spontaneously combust!" I said.

He let his hands fall but didn't break eye contact. He rested his forehead against mine.

We didn't have time for this. "He kissed me," I blurted. His eyes dropped down, hurt, angry—I don't know. I put my finger under his chin, trying to lift it but it was like he was made of stone. Even in a weaker state, he was too strong for me.

"And what did you do?" he muttered softly, still staring at the floor.

I was indignant. What did he think I did? Jumped on him and had my way with him in front of the sled dogs? "I kicked him," I said, standing back with my hands on my hips.

I could see his brows rise beneath the curtain of blond curls. He pounded his hand in his fist. "Where is he? I'll kill him." I felt panicked. The last thing we needed was a fight. I looked at him, bewildered.

He lifted his head, his eyes gleaming. He chuckled.

"It's not funny!" But I was smiling. It was ridiculous. Only I could manage to get myself in this much trouble already. I threw a coat over his shoulders and started dressing myself. Everything they gave us was pure white.

Pulling on the thick, padded boots, I paused, something occurring to me. "Why aren't you angry, or at least surprised?"

He shook his head, laughing a little. "Rosa, I'm not an idiot. You're a beautiful girl. You don't think men might try and take advantage of you?" I snorted. He was an idiot. Was he serious? "But I also know you can take care of yourself." His confidence in me was startling and probably unwarranted. I blushed, covering it by throwing him the boots and a hat, which he caught easily. He put the boots on and stood. I walked up to him and pulled the hat down over his ears, giggling. He looked hilarious. His hair was poking out at all angles under the white, wool cap. But his eyes, his eyes looked amazing, the white providing the crispest backdrop for the green. I tried not to get sucked into them and show how easily I could lose myself.

I cocked my head to the side like I was listening for something. "Is that why you like me, because you think I'm beautiful?" I hated that my heart was tripping over itself. That it mattered at all. It was a stupid question. No answer he gave me would be a good one.

The Wall

He looked down at me and put his hands on my shoulders, like he was going to give me a stern talking to.

"No," he said, finitely. I shouldn't have been hurt. I had asked for it. I stared at the floor. My white outfit made me look like a giant marshmallow. "I love you because you're beautiful and you don't seem to realize it."

At this I laughed, waving my hand in the air as I took a step back from him. "You know, you should write this stuff down. You could make a pamphlet and hand it out to inept boys who have trouble talking to girls."

He smirked, irresistibly. "Well, honestly, you already think you're right all the time. You're pushy. I can't imagine what you would be like if you were vain too."

"Nice," I said sarcastically.

He pulled my hat down over my ears, as I had done to him, and kissed me softly. "We need to go," he whispered.

"I'll meet you there."

"You can't go," he said, his voice laced with worry. "I'll come with you." He determinedly stepped towards the door.

"No. Go get ready. I won't be long. Didn't you just say I could take care of myself?"

"Not fair, Rosa. I don't like you using my words against me," he said with a wary smile.

"Too bad," I said as I walked to the door. He grabbed my hand and we walked together, our hands straining as we went through the door and moved in opposite directions. Our fingers parted and he gave me one last, checking look. "Don't be long," he said in low growl that made me shiver.

He fell into line with the others. I waited until he was out of sight and hurried towards the big metal door by our cabin.

I sprinted, my lungs burning. I imagined someone was chasing me, that something was biting at my heels, and it made me run faster. I passed dark opening after dark opening. The rooms that had been filled with the noise of people talking, the smells of food cooking or coffee brewing, were now hollow, empty caverns, the doors swinging on their hinges from rushed exits. This place was even more tomblike than it had been before.

I got to the door and started turning the cogs, but it was extremely hard to open. I touched the metal; it was ice cold and stuck to my hand. It was frozen shut. I hoped Apella was already down there with Orlando. I shouldn't have left him alone.

As I was considering abandoning the door and turning around, the ground shook violently.

12.

Collapse

Not just a small shake. It rumbled, groaned, and threw me off my feet so I was hanging off the door handle, wondering which way was up and which way was down. I heard a woman scream and a man shouting words I couldn't quite make out. It all churned up together and came out a chorus of terror. But there was no damage that I could see. No rocks falling, no vast cracks in the ceiling. I stupidly decided to continue. I gave the door the biggest shove I could, only managing to open it a crack, but it was enough to squeeze my small frame through. The snow was up to my waist and I pushed through it as quickly as I could, my white suit keeping me camouflaged and very warm.

The cabin was right there. I could see it. Just the gaping eyes of the windows showed in the snow.

Four more steps.

I heard a mechanical whirring sound, metal clashing with rock, flinty chinking. The kind of sound that makes your hair stand on end and your teeth ache, like fingernails on a blackboard.

I couldn't see where it was coming from at first. My eyes scanned the nearby hills, searching for the origin. It didn't take me long to see the cloud of dirt and blackened smoke on the hill opposite. Three metal blades attached to a cylinder were glinting against the snow. It was burrowing its way into the hill, like a metallic flower retreating to the earth.

I entered the cabin and grabbed Hessa's old capsule, feeling a swell of affection for the rough-made pack. I slung it on my back and ran towards the door in the hill, pulling myself through the snow as best I could. Desperately trying to find the edge of the door, I patted the dripping ice with my bare hands. I didn't shut it but the light, falling snow had hidden the crack. I kept looking behind me. There were no choppers. All I could hear was the clattering and clanking of metal on rock. Then it stopped abruptly. The forest breathed a sigh of relief—way too soon.

It wasn't slow; there was no build up. It was quiet and then there was so much noise… I couldn't find myself in it. My body shook, my brain squished and vibrated. I covered my ears but it invaded my head, a ringing, resounding, booming racket. The ground shifted and, thankfully, so did the door. I turned to the hill opposite, but it wasn't there. It had collapsed in on itself like a sucked-out eggshell. It was nothing but rubble. The carcass showed the intricate steel frame that had held it together all these years. The twisted, broken metal looked frail and delicate, like it had been cut out of balsa. I searched the rest of the view—several other hills had been blown apart all in a line. Two more to go and we would be next.

They'd found us.

I had no time to stare. I wasn't even sure if I should go back in, but that's where everyone else was. That's where Joseph and Orry were. I had no choice.

I squeezed through the door and ran, darting in and around fallen pieces of ceiling and shattered light globes. As I approached our room, I looked up and saw three stories clear above me from a giant hole in the ceiling. The shift in the earth was causing our mound to collapse. Looking left and right, I clambered over a fallen rock, only to hear a moan coming from under the debris. I pulled the mangled metal and coils of wire away, my hand getting shredded by broken glass, and found half a person. The woman's torso was all I could see. Her legs gone, squashed under the giant, black rock. Her face was covered in dirt. I swallowed hard and swept it away from her face. She pursed her lips and let out a small sigh. Her airways clogged with dirt and rubble, she coughed. I found her hand. It was cold, the life leaving it. I was breathing so fast, my eyes darting around, trying to find something that would help. I couldn't leave her here. I searched frantically for the rest of her. I put my shoulder to the rock and tried to push it over but it wouldn't move. I let out a sharp cry in frustration. Her hand gripped me tightly, perfect fingernails digging into my wrist.

"Tell them I did my duty," she said, her eyes rolling around like she was selecting the words from the air. "Tell them," she insisted, gripping me even tighter.

I nodded, tears making my vision blurry. She coughed again. Her body lurched and convulsed once and then she was still, shock making my own body still.

But I needed to run.

I wiped my face with the back of my arm, sweeping dust into my eyes. I looked back and watched her body disappear into the wreckage as more of the ceiling rained down on her. Just the small bump of her tightly pinned hair protruded from the chaos. *Is that what happens in death? Your body returns to the earth, or molds into whatever you die with?*

The ground shook again, the remaining ceiling collapsed, and she was buried. No time. They would be here soon.

I ran down the hallway. The ground lurched and jolted under my feet. I pushed through the dark halls, occasionally seeing flashes of light behind me that lit up the hall for seconds at a time like a camera flash. I swung myself down the ladder, skipping most of the rungs and landing on my feet unevenly, pain shooting through my heels. There was a single stream of light coming from the door. I could hear them yelling as I approached. Joseph's voice was the loudest. "I'm not leaving without her," he shouted. Dogs barked excitedly.

I burst through the doors and was confronted with panicked pairs of eyes. Joseph ran to me, tripping over ropes and nearly knocking me over. "Damn it, Rosa." His hands were shaking but he pulled me to him so tightly that I could barely breathe. I leaned back and looked at him. "I'm ok, but there was a woman… she's gone. I mean, squashed. Oh God." I covered my face with my hands to hide my embarrassment at that terrible announcement.

"Mila," Matthew uttered quietly, holding a charm that hung around his neck to his lips and closing his eyes.

"Mila," they all said in unison, each holding something similar up and copying Matthew's actions. They didn't seem that upset. It was like they had expected it or maybe they had accepted it already. I didn't have time to contemplate their weird behavior just then.

I threw the capsule on the floor, trying to shake the dead woman's face from my mind.

Apella was already settled in a sled, her arms folded neatly in her lap like she was about to go on a scenic tour. Alexei handed me Orry and slid in behind her. One of the survivors stood behind them. All the sleds were pointed directly at the wall, the dogs hooked up, jumping and straining at their harnesses. I didn't understand what was happening. How could we ride out of here? We were underground. I laughed loudly at the idea of us all speeding directly into the wall at full pace. Splat! Everyone stared at me for a second. I was deaf from the blast. My 'loudly' was booming.

I popped Orry in the capsule, padded it with scraps of fabric, and slung him on my back. He was secure. Gus stood in front of us and yelled out some basic instructions, left, right, stop. Joseph nodded. I wanted to scream. We couldn't do this.

I insisted Joseph sit in the front. We were having a ridiculous tug of war about who wanted to put themselves in danger more. But while my back was turned, he climbed out and stood in the driver's seat. A woman slid into the front of our sled and I squatted behind her, an idiotic pang of jealously hitting me. I wanted to drive.

The ground shook again and the door to the dog room twisted on its hinges. It screamed in metallic twangs as half the ceiling around it fell down a few feet, intact but looking like a burgeoning dam about to burst.

This could have been the worst time possible. But I felt like the words would choke me if I didn't spit them out now. I turned to Joseph and shouted, "I love you!"

I wish I could say the world melted away in that moment, that time stopped and it was terribly romantic. What actually happened was he snorted, his eyes glowing. I wanted to smack him and throw my arms around him at the same time. I knew exactly what he was thinking. *Now? Now is the time you choose to tell me you love me?* I tried to wink at him but I think all I did was blink both eyes. At that point, he threw his head up in the air and, although I couldn't hear him, I could feel his whole-hearted laugh deep in my own chest, spreading warmth through me like no one else could. I rolled my eyes. I was so good at making a fool of myself.

I was speedily ejected from my happy state as the ground become unsteady under the sled and the nauseating sense of movement that was out of my control took over as the floor started rising.

We were on some sort of ascending platform, like an open elevator. Everyone's faces were tense. Their mouths were set hard, looking up. I didn't blame them. As we rose, we could see the destruction around us. The cavernous hideout was being scooped out like an old pumpkin, patches of sunlight streamed through vast holes. Big blobs of snow dripped and spilled over the edges like melting ice cream. The dogs were barking and everyone was clinging to their sleds for dear life.

We rose, wobbling, teetering. It felt like we were a plate balancing on a broom handle. It was dark and then suddenly we were pushed out into the frozen air like early spring saplings.

People sighed collectively in relief, but voices were quiet. We had come out on the other side of the hill and were hidden only by the mound that was fast collapsing. We didn't know where the Woodland soldiers were. We were about a mile from the tree line. The survivors shouted at their dogs, urging them forward, and the dogs obliged.

The shouting morphed into a shattering bellow as the supports for the platform we were on started to give way. Metal creaked and strained as it swung one way and then fell to the side with a clang. The lip of the circular plate was barely touching the edge of the bank surrounding the hole. It looked so precarious it could have been clinging to a single snowflake. We were at the edge closest to the trees. Joseph shouted and the dogs started to run, our sled bouncing off and over a growing gap between the plate and the ground as it started to recede unevenly into the ground.

But there were still groups behind us.

I turned to see their sleds swing sideways and one, two, three of them slip over the edge and fall into the cavern below. Dogs yelped as they tried to find a hold on the metal plate that was now tipped at a 65-degree angle with their claws. They were running in the air as they fell. I wanted to jump up and help them but there was nothing we could do. The people didn't even scream. I caught the stony face of the bored woman from that first meeting. Air whipped around her face, her sled spun, colliding with the dogs attached to it, making a hollow thud as it slammed into their ribcages. Then they disappeared into the ground in a tangled ball of human and animal.

Who was left? I could see Gus and Cal at the front. Matthew was with them. Apella and Alexei were there. They were disappearing into the snow as the camouflaged sleds and outfits shrank into the whiteness. But where were Hessa and Deshi? My ribs strangled my heart as I searched ahead and behind me, but I couldn't see them.

I thought I must have been screaming—my voice as loud as the destruction, but my mouth wasn't even open. My head was rattling, the ringing from the explosion and the pounding panic confusing me. *If Hessa dies, I will die*, I thought. I won't survive it. I won't. I won't. I could feel Orry's warmth on my back, realizing I had to. I had to survive anything and everything. It would keep coming, pelting me with new torment, and I would have to keep going, for him.

I kept searching for them and we kept getting further away from the hill, or what was left of it. Joseph expertly controlled the sled. I tried to see his face, to make eye contact, but he was firmly focused on the horizon. We reached the trees and snow-covered branches slapped me in the face. It was so cold it burned. The sharpest pain, a thousand tiny needles burying into my skin. I imagined I could remove my whole face in one frozen mask. My body was warm but the wind on any part of my exposed skin was like a punch.

The woman in front of me was leaning every time we turned and I copied her actions. It made the sled move more smoothly. She was quiet and calm. These people were crazy—or so far removed from crazy, they didn't seem human.

As opposed to me, who was frantic. Hessa. Where was Hessa? My eyes skittered in my head as I snapped back and forth, combing the frozen tundra for some sign of them. There were none.

I wondered how far we would travel. It was so cold out here. My bones felt brittle and liable to snap. We wouldn't survive for very long without shelter. A small sense of relief reached up when I realized the dogs couldn't go on indefinitely. We would have to stop. Then I could make them turn around. I could go back and look for my baby nephew.

But we didn't stop. Not for a long time. The explosions had either ceased or we were too far away to hear them. The other sleds disappeared into white and I found myself disappearing too, bowed inwards like the answers lay in my belly button. I imagined the soldiers would be searching through the rubble now, stepping over the bodies and doing headcounts. My own head was going over all the possible scenarios. If Deshi and Hessa had survived the fall, they would be back in the Superiors' custody. That thought pierced through me harder than the cold. They would be better off dead. Then the guilt that accompanied that thought was unbearable. I wished I could talk to Joseph but it was too hard to even turn my head, let alone open my mouth. I tried but my neck was stiff, my voice carried away by the wind and the chorus of panting dogs and paw pads.

We just went on and on, moving through the trees. The sled cut a light track in the snow, gliding over it, almost flying. Everywhere, things that were once familiar were almost unrecognizable. The trees were bare. The light too bright, too shiny, like the sun itself had turned into a giant, cold, fluorescent light, giving off no heat but burning everything with its stark brightness.

We turned a corner and the woods stopped abruptly. A cold, dark line of trees gave way to a perfect 45-degree slope. The other sleds were pooled at the base. The dogs strained to pull their masters up the hill. Some people disembarked and pulled the exhausted dogs up by their collars. We got to the hill and Joseph did the same. His knees reached up as he waded through the snow, looking like he was doing high kicks. I jumped out too, or more like pried my frozen butt off the seat, and battled my way up the incline with Orry on my back.

"Wh-wh-wh-ere do you think we're going?" I said through chattering teeth.

"Beats me," Joseph said between his boots crunching through the snow.

The woman who had seemed like a statue up until now spoke. "We're going home." She smiled and turned her eyes frontward again, still sitting comfortably in the sled.

Joseph put his arm around me and pulled me close, our hips colliding softly. Heavily padded suits provided an unwanted barrier. "Oh, and by the way, I love you too," he said as he winked at me and then imitated my attempt at winking, blinking both eyes hard.

I blushed, thinking the snow must be melting around my feet. Must he show me up at everything?

I bumped him with my hip and he fell forward into the snow. We both started laughing, a kind of hysterical laughter that drew away some of the stress we were feeling. He pulled himself up, gave me his irresistible smirk, and we dragged the sled dogs to the top of the hill. The dogs were panting, their long tongues hanging out the side of their mouths. They were spent.

We got to the top and my body cracked, the laughter throttling out of my lungs like a vacuum was sucking the air out. My frozen limbs pulled up and away from me as I remembered.

Run.

The need to flee was so strong, I wanted to jump off the incline and roll down the hill. Keep running and never, ever look back.

13

Tunnel

Joseph stopped still, his beautiful eyes unblinking. Disbelief stung right through us both. The woman in our sled grunted impatiently and finally climbed out. My eyes flitted to her, irritated at why she had waited until now to help us. She pulled the dogs. It was a battle, though. Now that we had stopped running, the dogs seemed to think they had done their part. Their legs were still. Breathless, they leaned down to lick the snow, little puffs of steam floating from where their warm tongues had touched the ice.

I put my hands to one of their heads and rubbed between its ears, burying my fingers into the soft fur and holding on like it was an anchor. It whined before the woman yanked the harness violently and urged them forward.

Neither of us could move.

I pulled Orry from my back and Joseph carefully shook him free of the capsule. His cheeks were pink and his nose was cold but he was ok. With his other arm, Joseph pulled me close to him. I moved stiffly, my legs buried in snow, my heart somewhere in my stomach. Never in a million years did I ever think we would be back here.

"It's ok. It's not the same one," he said close to my ear, his warm mouth tickling my skin. I nodded weakly. If it was ok, how come he hadn't budged either?

The rails were mostly buried with snow. But the shape of their path was still evident. Small sections of rusted steel poked out from the white here and there like vague zebra stripes. This twisting path led directly into my nightmares.

The black hole laughed at me. Its stone border grinned with chipped and stained teeth. I could almost see it screaming and howling, with ghosts flying out of its ghastly mouth and flames licking the walls. I felt her arm link in mine but she didn't push me. She was waiting. She would move when I moved. "Cla—" The name caught in my throat and stayed there, gravelly and uncomfortable.

Joseph started towards the entrance, following the others, assuming I would follow. The tunnel whispered, 'Hessa,' for my ears only. I squatted down in the snow, removed my gloves, and plunged my hand into the ice. I let out a squeak as it both scalded and froze my fingers. It hurt but I wanted to feel something else, just for a second. The ice around me turned pink from my cut-up hands.

I shrank back. Blood. Always more blood.

Joseph stopped when he noticed I was still stuck in the snow and beckoned me with his spare hand. *Get up and go*, I thought.

I was the kind of person that needed time. And I seemed to be someone who was always running out of it. Always having to kick myself, force myself to get over it and move. I wondered if this would ever change or if I would always be fighting and wading against the current.

I trudged on, feeling a strong sense of *deja vu*. But as we got closer, I could see what Joseph was talking about. It was not the same. Not at all. I hesitated anyway... until the horribly familiar sound of blades slicing through the air started me running to the entrance. I burst through and crouched in the shadows, waiting for it to pass. It got louder and then the sound dissipated into the atmosphere as the chopper swung around and headed back in the direction of the mounds.

Turning my gaze inwards, everyone was unpacking their stuff and stacking it against soot-smattered walls. The dogs were being watered and fed. The weird thing was they were all pinned against the wall like the tracks might rip up and bite them. I stormed in, ready to demand they take me back to look for Deshi and Hessa, when I heard a voice yell, "Rosa, wait!" before I slammed into something solid, hitting my nose quite hard, splinters of pain shooting into the backs of my eyes. The solid thing clanged and then it flickered before me.

"What the...?" I reached out to touch it. It was cold, metallic feeling, but felt thin as paper, like I could push it in with my finger and make a dent.

Deshi laughed loudly. "Ha! That was great—can you do it again?"

My heart danced at the sight of him. I pinched the bridge of my nose and said in a nasally voice, "You're not very nice to me, you know."

Deshi frowned theatrically. "Oh coz, you're *always* sweetness and light..."

I used my hands to guide myself to him, around whatever it was, and slammed into his chest. Wrapping my arms around his neck, I kissed his cheek and squeezed his thin body.

Deshi went rigid, his arms tensing for a second, before he started shaking with laughter. "Are you confused or something? Joseph's over there," he pointed.

I stepped back, embarrassed. "Sorry. I'm just glad to see you. I thought you... um... I thought we had left you and Hessa behind."

His eyes softened, something occurring to him. "Oh... Nah, we're fine. We left before the rest of you. I think Hessa's a little daredevil; he loved the sled."

"Where is he?" I asked eagerly.

"Hessa?"

I just glared at him. Who else would I be talking about?

"He's in there." He pointed to the air above the cleared railways tracks. I sighed, tired of everything being a riddle. I wished someone would just sit me down and tell me what the hell was going on.

The Wall

I put my hands on my hips. "Where?"

Deshi sighed too, impatiently. Then he took my hand, guided it over the smooth surface, and pressed. Something pulled back with a whoosh and again I saw it flicker. It was like a rip in space. I stared at the dull blue floor and purple upholstered seats, facing each other over a plastic table. And there was Hessa, strapped into a seat, slapping his hands on the table. He gave me a toothless grin when he saw me.

I rushed to him, covering him in kisses and stroking his beautiful, black hair, cursing myself for not being more present in his life. Joseph poked his head in the door, beaming. Like this was all normal—like it didn't surprise him at all that Hessa was sitting in an invisible bubble hiding tacky upholstery. I wished I were more like that, able to roll with things. "Orry, do you want to sit with your brother?" Joseph asked the baby in his arms. Deshi's face darkened a little, a twisted expression, almost like it was a painful thing to hear. I was offended. Did he think Hessa was too good for Orry?

"Orry can't sit yet," I said. "Besides, we are not sitting anywhere until I find out what's going on." I set my mouth in a hard line. Joseph looked at me and nodded. Agreeing? Wow!

I stepped out of the room and the door closed behind me. Peering at it closer, I could see it was not invisible. Its surface flickered and wobbled as I moved around it. When I stood in front of it for too long, it started taking on the colors of my white suit, my dark face, and, amusingly, my brown and blue eyes. The brown and white swirled together, polka dotted with blue. Very clever. Then I pressed my nose to it, observing all the little mirrored panels that made up its exterior. All of a sudden, I was confronted with a gigantic pair of defective eyes staring back at me. I jumped.

"Can you stop staring at yourself and come over here?" Deshi yelled.

I used my hands to guide myself to the end of it, feeling reverse blindness—a seeing person in an invisible world. I found the group of

Survivors talking close to the other entrance of the tunnel. Although, I guess they were the survivors of the Survivors now. Alexei and Apella were positioned against the wall behind them. He was trying to coax Apella out of the sled, to no avail.

There were seven of them left. Only seven. I expected them to be grieving or angry but they were busy discussing the next move.

Gus spoke first. "We should wait until nightfall and take the spinners." Cal was standing right next to him. When I peeked around the corner, his eyes lit up like I was on fire or something. Standing next to his father, it was surprising how alike they were. Same height, same hair, even their faces were almost identical in shape. I wondered if Gus went around kissing people without their permission. I grimaced at the thought of that thick, scratchy-looking beard anywhere near my face.

Joseph was listening, stroking his chin and swaying from side to side with Orry in his other arm. I tried not to gaze at the golden facial hair he had grown in his coma, adorable little brushstrokes of pure, spun gold, catching the light. His expression was stern. "I need to know your names and what your intentions are before any decisions are made," he said flatly. Apart from Matthew, everyone was looking up at him. The way he spoke, no one was going to argue.

Gus walked over to him and shook his hand, introducing himself as the coordinator of the group. We already knew Matthew. Gus introduced Cal as his son and a contributor. Coordinator, contributor, these were words we didn't understand the meanings of. Joseph shook his hand also. I saw Cal smirk as he approached and then wince when they shook, Joseph squeezing his hand too hard. I didn't think that was necessary. Cal was still pumping his sore hand behind his back when Matthew introduced two other men and two women. "This is Gwen, Elisha, Bataar, and Hally," He motioned to a tall, young woman, the woman who had ridden with us, and two dark men, similar in age to Gus, their skin leathery and wrinkled like raisins, muscular and gruff. We nodded

The Wall

in greeting.

"As for our intentions… we could ask you the same thing," Gus stated, his dark brows knotted in conversation with each other.

I scoffed. "We don't have any intentions; we're just trying to survive."

He shot me a disapproving stare at the same time as a cold wind shot through the tunnel. It swirled around us, shrieking, drowning out my irritation. Memories knocked me back like the wind was trying to dig icy fingers into my arms and drag me backwards through time. Back there, Clara would die all over again. I felt an arm on my shoulder, light and shaky. Alexei.

"I think what Rosa is trying to say is… we appreciate everything you have done for us but we need to know that we can trust you," Alexei stuttered, dragging Apella by the arm into the circle. "Everything has happened so fast."

"You've been through a lot, I know, and it is hard to trust people, people different from you. But you can, trust us, I mean," Matthew said clumsily. He seemed somewhat unsure of himself, which was unlike him.

The woman, Gwen, interrupted. "We don't have time for this!"

She was right.

The two groups stood opposite each other, like warring tribes. Lines drawn and redrawn. It dawned on me that we were no longer part of any tribe or group. We were only part of each other and those bonds were loose and fraying at best.

Joseph stood up tall. "Look, I am just trying to protect my family."

My shoulders pulled together at the words. I had the urge to make an excuse and creep away, slide along the wall like a thief and run into the woods. Instead, I took a few steps into the middle of the group. "If we need to go, then let's just go. But we need answers. Whoever is willing to give them can ride with me." I scanned the group. Cal went to step forward but I shook my head. He was a worm I wanted to crush under my foot. Anyone but him. I wanted it to be Matthew but he was avoiding my eyes.

Gwen stepped forward. "I don't know why we're making such a fuss. We have nothing to hide. I'll answer any questions you like," she said, her voice like a whip, tight and lashing. I didn't recognize it from the conversation in the bathroom and was a little disappointed I couldn't use what I had heard to catch them out. Gus looked like he was going to object but she glared at him and he turned away. Right then, I liked her.

Everyone pushed their things into the remarkable carriages. Piles of crisp white sharper still against the blaring purple and dusty blue. Tracing the shape when the door was open, they were like giant marbles with a second sphere floating inside them. I heard Alexei exclaiming that they must be electromagnetic, whatever that meant. I squinted at the edge of the door, trying to decipher how they worked, but dogs barking distracted me and we were told to get in. Dogs and sleds went in the rear carriages with Bataar, and the rest settled in to wait for cover of dark.

We took off our suits and piled in. Our entire original group squished into one carriage with Gwen, who sat cross-legged on the floor, staring up at us. She was athletic looking, her limbs svelte under the thin leggings and a cotton top she had on underneath her suit. She was much taller than me, and tanned. She was like a cricket, with strong upper thighs and spindly thin calves. I imagined she could jump very high. Her hair was long, black, and plaited down her back. She played with her fingers as we tried to get comfortable, chewing on her nails and spitting them on the floor. My guess was she was not much older than us, maybe mid-twenties.

She scrunched up her face, creating dimples high up on her cheeks. "What do you want to know?"

"What, er, how did you build this amazing train?" Alexei asked. I wanted to slap him. That wasn't important right now.

Gwen looked amused. "Borrowed technology. Next." She flicked a nail upwards and it landed on the table in front of Apella. Disgusted, but

The Wall

at least showing a tiny sign of life, Apella used her pinky finger to flick it off.

"Yes but the reflections or absorptions…" Alexei stuttered.

Rage was boiling up—could he ever focus on what was important? Joseph took my hand, lacing his fingers with mine, Orry sleeping comfortably in the crook of his arm. I rolled my eyes; he would have to put that baby down eventually.

"Alexei, can you save those questions for later, please?" I said, trying not to sound too annoyed. I was trying to simmer it down to the one most pertinent question. All the questions mixed together in a whirlpool as the temperature rose and some floated away with the steam. *Why had they rescued us? Why did they help us? Where were they taking us? What was expected of us when we got there?* No. *What was it?*

Simple.

"Who are you?" I asked plainly, realizing I should have asked this about six weeks ago. Staring into her dark eyes, they looked like fiery black coals. I identified with that kind of attitude.

She raised her eyebrows and gave me a quick smile. Then her face turned serious. "I am a survivor. I live beyond the wall. I give shelter to those that need it. I am not chosen but I choose to live."

A shiver ran through me, icier than the frozen land surrounding us.

14

QUESTIONS

Everyone went quiet for a few minutes. The words pulled at us. They were stern and accusatory. Full of heavy meaning we could not weigh. Apella stared at her wispy fingers. Alexei was deep in contemplation. Deshi was trying to stop Hessa from climbing onto the table. Gwen resumed her attack on her nails as we absorbed what she had just said. The last words echoed in my mind, a mirror image of what we had always been taught. *I am not chosen but I choose to live.* We were chosen—we were told that we were the lucky ones. Maybe we were. But I doubted it.

Everyone was staring at their hands or at the walls. But I didn't feel this guilt. I didn't ask to be chosen. Neither did they. Besides, now all we were chosen for was recapture and probably death.

"Is that the Pledge?" I asked, surprised faces all around.

Gwen nodded. "That's part of it."

"Do we have to take the Pledge?" I know Cal said we had to but I needed someone saner to confirm it.

"It's preferred."

"Or what?"

"Or nothing—we're not going to force you to do anything."

I didn't believe her.

Joseph looked up. Gwen seemed startled by his intense gaze and blushed. He smiled, trying to make her more at ease I suppose, or using his good looks for evil. I shifted uncomfortably on the vinyl seat. A shred of jealously peeked out from behind my eyes. Watching him, it occurred to me that if you knew how, you could brandish your looks like a weapon, but I doubted it would work for me.

"Where are we going?" he asked, fluttering his eyelashes slowly, sweeping his hair back and handing me Orry without breaking eye contact with Gwen. He was giving her a look that said, *You're the most important person in the world right now.*

"To our settlement; it's about a day's ride from here," she answered, her voice stripped of its earlier attitude, lower and softer than it had been minutes ago.

Joseph then launched into an absolute tirade of questions, but, as with everything, he handled it so well. His words poured from his mouth in a hard-to-keep up kind of way, sweetened like honey. She was like a fly caught in a trap. She answered everything as best she could, eager to please him. I wished I could be suave like that. Not just bust in and threaten people to answer me with my fists up and my eyes ablaze. Sometimes, well, most of the time, I didn't really understand what he saw in me.

"Are you the only ones?" Joseph asked.

Gwen shook her head, not as an answer but in dismay. "Pretty much. We are the biggest group, at least. There used to be tiny pockets of people all over but your Superiors took care of most them. If there are any leftovers, we certainly haven't heard from them in years."

"How have you managed to stay hidden for so long?" Joseph said in a complimentary way.

Gwen smiled. "Your Superiors have become lazy of late. All they seem to worry about is their new projects and experiments," she said, holding her fingers in mock air quotes. I cringed. I was one of those experiments. "We hid for a long time, never staying in one place for too long, but when we realized no one was coming for us, we built a settlement."

I hated that she kept referring to them as 'your Superiors.' I didn't want to be linked to them. I had enough blame hanging over my head without adding the Superiors atrocities to them.

"But I guess that's changed now," Gwen muttered sourly.

Joseph leaned down and touched her arm gently. Steam rose slowly from the top of my head and I tried to wave it away. "We're sorry," he said.

She looked up at all of us. "Don't be," she said plainly.

When asked what the settlement was like, she wouldn't go into any detail, just grinning and saying, "You have to see it for yourself." Like it was some kind of inside joke we had to see to understand. I prayed it wasn't underground.

Deshi, who had been listening intently but not volunteering any questions of his own, suddenly spoke up, his voice tight. "What are you going to do with us?" Hessa, as if reacting, slammed his fist on the table like an angry father, like my angry stepfather.

She flipped her head up to look at him. "You? We want help deciphering some of these borrowed technologies we can't work out."

She pointed to Apella, whose pale face had barely shown a flicker of interest since Gwen started talking. "You? We need help with our infertility issues." Apella looked away, her expression that familiar mask. She and my mother could compete for who could be the least outwardly emotional. I knew they would have a hard time convincing Apella to go down that road again, if at all.

She continued to point at each of us. Joseph, they thought would be useful in their surveillance group or maybe helping out in their hospital. Alexei was a wealth of information about the Superiors.

"And you?" Her finger hovered as it pointed at my face. "I don't know what they want to ask of you."

"Ask?" I said, confused.

"Yeah. Well, I mean, they'll ask you to help with those things but if

The Wall

you don't want to, that's fine. But you have to contribute in some way," she said, waggling her finger at us as if we were children.

In some ways, I suppose we were. We were fledgling Survivors who had been previously raised by an uncaring and ruthless society. Everything she said was so foreign it was hard not to be overwhelmed. But it sounded fair. And impossible. So different to what we were used to that it just didn't seem plausible. Everyone looked nervous, playing with fingers, eyes darting around, looking for a way out. Choice was not something we were overly familiar with.

I leaned into Joseph's shoulder, yawning. Hessa was playing with my fingers, looking under my flattened palm like he might find some hidden treasure there. Joseph laughed. "People will never believe you're brothers," he said, looking from one to the other.

Deshi stood and yanked Hessa away from me. He made Apella and Alexei shuffle out of their seats and quickly exited the carriage.

"What's wrong with him?" Joseph asked, confused.

I thought I knew. "I'll go check on him," I said.

Joseph shrugged but there was a tautness to it. The muscles around his shoulders and neck were straining, like he was holding in something nasty he wanted to say. He was all edges and sharp bits. "I don't get it. You and Deshi are close now? Apella looks like she's been hit by a train and you're not enjoying it? What's going on?"

Gwen took this as an excuse to slip out. I didn't blame her. That was enough questions for now.

I swept his hair back out of his face gently. He shook me off furiously. "Rosa, just tell me." He held my free hand, warmth and fluttering closing out the bizarre surroundings for a second.

I wanted to cry, in truth, blubber and confess all the dark secrets. But this was not my story to tell. If Apella wanted to tell him, it was up to her. I looked at her and she shook her head. My body slumped as I exhaled. Think of a good lie. He put his hand to my face, begging me to look at him. I felt his lips brush the top of my head.

"Some things are just not worth hanging on to anymore," I whispered. I looked at Apella, a big 'thank you' reflected in her face. It would kill him to know the sacrifice she had made for him. I slipped out of Joseph's grasp like I was shimmying out of a dress, handed Orry to Apella, and went to find Deshi.

There weren't many places for him to go. The tunnel was short, light shining through both ends. I remembered the other tunnel, the way it curved around for a mile. I couldn't bear to leave it and leave her behind. And when I got to the end, I was blinded by the loss and the white light of morning tried to pull me from the ground.

Deshi was pressed up against the wall with one foot up, holding Hessa, frowning deeply.

"What's going on with you?" I asked.

"What do you care?" he snapped.

"You know, you sound like a child." I came out here to be nice. So much for that.

His dark face looked older. Older and grumpier. I stared at him for a long time, trying to stir a reaction. He glared at me for a while and then did something so unexpected that I nearly erupted into laughter. His face screwed up tight and I thought he was going to say something rude like he always did but instead he burst into tears.

My eyes widened and I took a step back. I wondered if I should hug him or pat his arm but something told me this would not be received well. This was not our dynamic. I knew less how to comfort him then I knew how to tame a bear.

"What's the matter with you, you big girl?" I said, apprehensively. My lips curled up only because I was forcing them to.

The Wall

He snorted, wetly, and wiped his face with his sleeve. Hessa reached up and touched his tear-stained face, which only made him go another round of bawling.

"Don't take him away from me, please," Deshi begged, shaking a little.

Confusion messed up my thoughts. The unfair, but very strong, urge to smack him and tell him to pull himself together was making my hands shake like they were straining at the bit like the sled dogs. My total lack of sympathy reinforced to me what a terrible mother I was.

"Why would we do that?" I asked. I thought he was upset about Joseph and me and of course, I was wrong.

Deshi took a deep breath and narrowed his eyes, considering his speech. "Well, now that you and Joe are all happy families, and Joe keeps calling Hessa and Orry brothers… I guess I thought maybe you were going to make that official."

I laughed. Deshi looked offended. "You have been more of a parent to Hessa than I will ever be. I wish I were better, but I'm not. I would never take him away from you," I said, realizing that may not be how Joseph felt, but I would make him see. I hoped.

He stopped sniffing and ran his hands down his shirt. He straightened up, clearly embarrassed by his behavior. "All right then. Good. Thank you." Hessa nuzzled into Deshi's chest. I knew it and hopefully Joseph would see it too. They belonged together. He started walking back to the carriage. I stayed where I was. What I had said was right. Deshi was a much better parent than me. How long would it take before Joseph realized that and his disappointment started to affect our already strange relationship? As if hearing my thoughts, Deshi turned around, his demeanor much calmer now.

"You know, you're not a bad mother," he said. "I don't think anyone expected you to be the kind that fussed over her child, or clapped every time they did something uninteresting like blinking." I just stared at him. He was saying I was cold. "You don't realize that this mother thing, well, you've been doing it this whole time. You care for your son; you feed him, change him, and respond to him when he cries. I've seen you rocking him for hours. I guess, what I am saying is, you *are* a mother. You love your son. Stop being so hard on yourself."

I sighed and nodded. He tipped his chin just slightly and walked back to the group. Maybe he was right. But I still felt lacking, like I had made promises I hadn't kept. Sometimes, it was so easy to get lost. I had lost myself to my grief for Joseph. I needed to start keeping my promises. Beginning now.

Just one thing I needed to do before we left.

15

FAREWELL

Matthew was sitting at the front of the carriages. Everything about the way he sat oozed sadness. It rolled off him in waves. His shoulders were hunched and he was squatting down, observing rocks in a distracted way that made me think his mind was elsewhere. I leaned down and touched his back gently. His muscles tightened. He startled but quickly composed himself, giving me a thin smile.

Matthew was different from the others. He seemed less able to let the fallen go, more likely to cling to life. I could see the rest of them kissing their necklaces and following each other off a cliff if that's what they were told to do. Matthew was a fighter. Not like me, though. I just closed my eyes and started flailing my arms around, hoping to connect with something. Matthew was a quiet, contemplative fighter with a plan and actual technique.

"What's the matter, Rosa?" he said wearily.

"I was going to ask you the same thing," I said

He waved me off. "Oh, I'm fine. It's just been a long day. A lot of lives lost, which happens, I mean, it happens all the time, people die but…" He seemed unsure of himself again, stuttering. The survivor philosophy was shackled to him but it didn't quite sit right on his shoulders.

"It's ok to be sad about it," I said, trying to sound comforting.

"I know, dear, but it's not useful," he replied, standing and dusting off his pants. He was handsome for an older man. I wondered if he had a wife or kids at home.

I screwed up my face at that. "Who cares?" I wasn't even sure what he said was true. If death was a part of life, so was grief. It was important. It made me think that everything needs a proper goodbye.

He laughed weakly. "I like you, Rosa, but there is a lot you don't understand."

I tried not to snap at him. My mouth was bursting to give him a smart-mouth retort. I put my hand to my lips, physically trying to keep it in. I shrugged my shoulders. "I came to ask you something. Can we go out to the woods for a bit?" It was getting dark.

"I suppose," he said. "Just keep your ears open for choppers." Then he returned to staring at the ground. I remembered when I sat staring at the rails, thinking they were the only thing keeping me from being swallowed by the ground, half-wishing I had the courage to just let go and let myself be swallowed. I frowned at the memory but then smiled at the fact that, somehow, I got through it. With help, I got through it.

"Ok."

I took a lighter and a knife from one of the men's bags and made my way back to the carriage where our snow suits were stacked inside the door. After putting the outfit on, I tramped out into the woods. The cold was a shock but I pressed on, looking for a nice circle of trees with low, protective branches.

The trees were kind to me, bending down. The snow pulled the branches towards me in an embrace and hid me from the menace in the skies. There was barely any greenery, just different shades of brown, iced with fluffy white. The sounds of my feet crunching over the ice were not that different to the crunching my boots once made over the gravel of the railway line. Thoughts were dangerous but I let them take me back, laughing at the fact that all that time, the rails were in use. It explained why they were so intact. If we had stayed on them, perhaps we would have been run over by one of their invisible trains. It wasn't really very

The Wall

funny but you could either laugh or cry. It was much easier to laugh.

It took me about half an hour but I managed to get a fire going after digging a hole in the snow, right down to the frozen dirt. I made sure it would last and then walked back to the tunnel, still finding it hard to make that initial step into the darkness. Like the moment my feet touched the shadows, I would be pulled into a nightmare again.

I convinced them to come with me, reluctant to explain until we got there. They dressed up in their snowsuits and followed me out into the cold. Confused faces looked bluish against the white. I was starting to feel a bit unsure myself. It seemed like a good idea before. Now I wasn't really sure what I would say, and whether it would do any good.

As we walked, I kicked the snow off some low-lying shrubs and pulled off the leaves. I snapped off some of the branches and showed them to Orry. "This is a rhododendron." I held the straggly, wooden branch in front of his face. His eyes blinked as drips of cold water splashed on his face. Joseph looked amused but he held his tongue. Ignoring him, I continued. "I know it doesn't look like much but in late summer to autumn it will have a beautiful, delicate, papery flower. It could be pink or red or even purple..." Joseph took the twig out of my hand, his eyes twinkling.

"Eat or don't eat?" he said. The words filled me with equal parts joy and sadness. I felt tears come to my eyes.

"Don't eat," I said quietly, blushing in the cold.

We walked towards the orange glow of the fire and everyone stood around it, not wanting to sit in the wet snow. We gathered up some more firewood and threw it on until we could feel decent heat radiating from it.

Apella's face was sorrowful, but at least it had some color to it, although that could have been from the fire. Now everyone was looking to me expectantly, asking me with their eyes what the hell we were doing here.

Softly and very unsure of myself, I said, "I wanted us to say goodbye." They looked puzzled. "Um, not to each other, but to this, to what we have been through, sort of like a memorial for our journey along the Great Siberian Railway," I finished with a flourish. I could feel tears coming quite fast. I hadn't realized until now how much I had missed being out here, how even though we were running, even though we'd suffered a great deal, parts of our journey were some of the best times of my life.

I moved to the fire and threw on a branch. "For everything I have learned about myself…"

It was a weird thing to do and I was embarrassed but I felt we had to give weight to it. I didn't subscribe to the Survivors' philosophy. It was ok to feel sad, to feel loss, and to acknowledge those experiences.

Alexei stepped forward and threw some snow on the fire. It sizzled and left a blackened spot that was quickly engulfed with flame. "To the sacrifices and to the friends we've made… Um, also to the knowledge we have gained."

I rolled my eyes.

I took the knife and moved towards Deshi. He looked wary at first. I held up a curl of Hessa's hair. Deshi nodded. I cut the little, springy curl from the boy's head as gently as I could. I gripped it tightly in my fist before throwing it into the fire. "Clara. I miss you so much, I…" Overcome with sadness, I couldn't finish.

Joseph stepped in. "Clara, you were wiser and stronger than the rest of us put together. We will never forget you. You wouldn't let us."

Deshi rolled his eyes. I knew he thought this was a bit stupid but he surprised us all with what he said, "To love. Love lost and love found. I don't think any of us thought we were as strong as this. And I think, now, together, we can do anything."

Apella was a bit shaky but looked at each and every one of us. "To our family. I never thought it would turn out like this but I'm so very glad it did." She looked at her feet and muttered, "I love you all." I took her hand and squeezed.

Joseph broke the reverie. I'm glad he did before we all took hands and started singing or something.

"To those damn hinges! You know, it took me ages to find them and work them out of that window," he said.

I jerked my head up to stare at him, disbelieving. "Window? Are you serious?" I asked.

He took a step back, hands up in the air. "I couldn't get them out of the door. Why does it matter?"

"How big were they?" I asked.

He held up his hands awkwardly, while cradling Orry, leaving a tiny space between them. He looked totally confused. "Why?"

The ridiculousness of it could have sent me spiraling into depression. Instead, I smacked his hand and let out the biggest, heartiest laugh. Bending over, I could barely catch my breath. I heard Deshi mutter over my own hysterics, "That's it. She's lost it."

Joseph bent down to find my face. He swept my hair back to reveal my eyes, and when they connected with that beautiful green, the gold looked like it was sparking in the firelight. I calmed myself.

"What's so funny?" Joseph asked, concerned.

"Oh God… They would have been way too small. They never would have held up the door."

This news could have destroyed us.

I heard Apella cough and then a noise came out of her I had never heard before—a laugh. It tinkled and whispered, almost musical. When I looked at her, she covered her mouth and I could see her whole body shaking with laughter, tears in her eyes. Then they all started. We laughed and laughed. Alexei fell backwards and landed in the snow, which made us laugh even harder.

Maybe we would be ok. Just maybe.

The fire was dying and we watched the life drain away from it. The orange coals dulled to red and then black. The babies were sleeping and we were jumping up and down to keep warm. It was time to go back, to put our faith in the next part of our journey and see where it led us.

16

SPINNING

When we got back to the tunnel, everything was covered in black shadow. We must have looked strange with big smiles on our faces, eyes red and puffy like we had been crying for hours. Confident that our bond was now as strong as ever, we separated into different carriages for the long ride. Gus said we should be able to sleep provided we didn't get chased, which wasn't very reassuring. Joseph, Orry, and I were alone. Deshi, Hessa, Apella, and Alexei were in the carriage next to us. We could see them if we pulled up the blind of a small window behind our heads. I fed Orry and laid him in the capsule. It fit, just, across the seat. I yawned. I was tired, but also hungry, not having eaten since the morning that seemed a million years and as many miles away.

We were offered some food. Sandwiches, which were pretty ordinary, just dried meat and cheese. No fresh stuff. And some drinks in pretty red cans. These were something very different; I had never seen anything like them. Turning mine around in my hand, I observed it curiously.

Gwen grinned at me as she passed our carriage door. "Don't shake it up."

I traced my finger over the letters. It sounded like some nonsense language, 'Coca Cola'. Joseph shrugged and we both opened our cans, which made an odd "pfft" noise. Inside the can, the liquid looked dark, like coffee, and it was sizzling. I was wary but Joseph took a swig without thinking, holding his chest and wiggling his nose. *Oh God, they've poisoned him*, I thought. He let out a huge burp and grinned. "It's good, try it," he said, taking another sip, this time more slowly.

"You're disgusting!" I said in mock disdain.

I held the can under my nose. It didn't smell bad—all it really smelled like was sugar. I took a small sip. The bubbles fizzed down my throat and some tingled in my nose. It wasn't unpleasant but I'm not sure I enjoyed it either.

Joseph put his arm around me and I put my legs up on the bench seat. He looked down and chuckled.

"What?" I asked, narrowing my eyes.

"Nothing, it's just you're funny. So suspicious," he said, copying my narrowed eyes and then opening them wide, letting them shine in all their beauty and drawing me in with that look. The only girl in the world look. "Funny, suspicious, and beautiful."

"You're an idiot," I said, knocking him with my shoulder. I took another swig, the taste improving on the second intake. A small fire was starting to smolder, and every time he looked at me like that, he was fanning the flames.

The carriage jolted and we were pulling out of the tunnel, heading towards what could be our new home. We slid silently away and I then understood why they called them spinners. We were encased in a bubble. Two bubbles actually. One that spun around, pushing us forward, and another that floated silently inside it. And that wasn't even the most amazing part of this train.

It was hard not to feel cold even though the temperature was comfortable enough to wear just a t-shirt and jeans. The side walls of the spinner were transparent. The ends facing the other carriages were solid blue, but the ones revealing the view were so clear. Like we were floating, like we could reach through and touch the trees that leaned in so close some branches slapped the sides. It was dark, but you could still

The Wall

see light bouncing off the snow. I couldn't help but gasp. And then shiver from the imagined cold.

I snuggled in closer, breathing in Joseph's scent, feeling his chest rise and fall under my head. Slowly sipping my drink, and feeling it pull sleep out from under me.

I flipped my head up and looked at him so his features were upside down. "Do you think we're safe?" I asked, knowing full well what he would say, but needing the reassurance anyway.

"Yes, I really do," he said confidently. The words vibrating through his chest were so comforting, I almost believed him.

"I hope you're right." Maybe this was what he saw in me. I provided the counter weight to his over-trustfulness.

I tried to close my eyes but they wouldn't comply. The brown liquid was swimming in my stomach and fizzing in my brain, but I didn't feel like talking anymore.

I turned around to face him. His eyelids were fluttering. The drink seemed to have little effect on him. On both sides the world was buzzing and falling away. The spinner was moving so fast it made me feel dizzy. Heavily wooded areas gave way to sparse expanses of pure white. I dreamed of what was under them, remembering the fields of flowers, the swaying high grass, dormant, not dead, just waiting for its opportunity to press down and spring forth.

My nose was millimeters away from his. I leaned in a fraction and they touched. He opened his eyes drowsily at first but they quickly brightened. He put his hands on my waist and pulled me closer. It was uncomfortable because the table hung over the bench, the harsh plastic pressing into my side, but I didn't really care. I closed my eyes and found his lips. We needed to make up for the time we'd lost and we could do that now. My hands and feet were jittery. My mind darted all over the place. Questions I shouldn't ask popped into my head like—did you dream when you were in the coma? What were you thinking when you were running towards the cabin? Why didn't you tell me about the bite on your arm?

His hands were running up under my shirt and I was thinking about the coma? I needed to breathe. I pulled back.

"Sorry," he said, eyes downcast. "Was that not ok?"

"It was fine. I'm just jittery from that brown stuff." No one told me reunions would be this hard, but then no one told me much of anything. I was searching for some middle ground. We had already skipped several important steps. Now it seemed he couldn't wait to skip some more.

He seemed hurt. "Are you ok?" I asked.

"Yeah. It's just… this is hard. Now that you're not pregnant and the baby isn't standing between us, literally. And Matt said I'm pretty much healed…" He looked down at the table, tracing patterns with his fingers. "It's really hard to keep my hands off you."

If it's possible, my dark face went a shade of deep red. Well, that's what it felt like anyway. What he said was thrilling, intoxicating, kind of scary, but in a good way. I put my hand over his and tried to still it.

I smiled at him. "Close your eyes," I said. He pursed his lips but did so.

"Now what? Are you going to disappear?" he asked, clicking his fingers.

I moved towards him slowly, climbing towards his chest until our faces were level. He started moving his hands towards my hips. But I put them at his side. I could tell he was frustrated by the consternated look on his face but he kept them there. I started at his neck and made my way to his face slowly. When I got to his mouth, I parted his lips with my own and let my tongue run along the underside of the upper one. He exhaled slowly through his nose, like it hurt. Then we kissed properly, softly at first, but passion and want getting the better of us. To have this almost felt like too much. Like I didn't deserve it.

Orry's rustling interrupted us. Joseph sat up straight and went to

The Wall

attend to him immediately. I put my hands on his chest, holding him where he was. He looked at me, concerned. I put my finger to my lips. "Sh!"

Orry let out a small cry, turned his head, then his fingers found his mouth and he settled himself. We both relaxed, but Joseph looked upset. His hands clasped in front of him and his hair covered his eyes.

"What's wrong?" I asked, bumping him with my shoulder.

Joseph shook his head. "It's just that I've missed so much. I wish I'd been around to learn these things about him with you."

I thought about it. If Joseph had been awake, if he had been with Orry from day one, I wonder how different things would have been. I knew the answer. It was a bizarre alternate universe we had ended up in but, in a way, I was glad it had happened like this. I needed time on my own with Orry or I may have never bonded with him. When everyone stepped out of the line, I was left with no choice. It was hard but somehow I got there. Well, was still getting there.

All I said was, "You didn't miss much. You'll catch up soon enough."

We talked about everything he had missed with Orry. How he liked being wrapped tight. How if he was awake, he wanted to sit up. How he never seemed to have a pattern for feeding. Joseph listened and nodded with this awestruck look on his face. I realized maybe Deshi was right; I knew everything about my child. I had paid attention.

Barely thinking at all but needing to get at least one thing out the way, I blurted, "Hessa and Orry aren't brothers."

Joseph looked at me semi-surprised but mostly curious.

"Is this about Deshi's little tantrum before?" he said unkindly.

I never thought I would be defending Deshi but I responded with, "It wasn't a tantrum. I think he has a right to be upset. He needs to know that we support him looking after Hessa on his own, that we aren't going to take him away."

"I don't know. I always thought we would all be together," Joseph said.

I started to panic a little. I couldn't look after both of them. Joseph seemed to notice and he stroked my head gently.

I took a deep breath. "Look. I know it's hard for you, but while you were sleeping, life kept on going. Deshi cared for Hessa exclusively. I don't think we could separate them even if we wanted to. They are each other's family now." He looked down and I could tell he was considering it carefully.

"All right. For now anyway, Hessa stays with Deshi." That would have to be good enough. I suspected he could see the sense in it but didn't want to give in all the way as a matter of principle.

After a few hours, I was still buzzing from the drink but I could see Joseph was getting sleepy. It had been a ridiculously long day. He had just begun to feel better, was allowed to have visitors, and then all hell broke loose. Now we were on our way to the Survivors' settlement. The place and people Apella and Alexei had been searching for. The place neither of us thought existed. I was excited and nervous. There was so much we still didn't understand about these people, but like it or not, we were survivors now too.

I still hadn't answered his question about Apella and, thankfully, he didn't bring it up again. Hopefully, we would have time to talk about it later.

After a while, I could hear him snoring. He had fallen asleep sitting up. I tried to move him but he was much too heavy. Asleep, it felt like he weighed two-hundred kilos. I shoved a jacket behind his head and snuggled into his chest, still shivering every time I looked out the window.

The world was racing by. I didn't like it. I wanted to walk out into the snow, touch it, smell the pines, and let the cold air burn my lungs. Being

The Wall

behind a wall, even if it was clear, was too much like being enclosed, captured. Now that I had experienced real freedom, I'm not sure I would ever get used to walls again. Walls loomed, leaned in, and whispered nasty things in your ears. They imposed and imprisoned. I hated them.

I closed my eyes and inhaled. I would get back there soon. I had to. I was like a bendy, juvenile tree. Without the air and sunlight, I wouldn't thrive. I would slowly kneel to the ground, my trunk cracked and splitting, and wither.

I took Joseph's warm hand in my own; he murmured something but didn't wake. I told myself, *one thing at a time. Don't want everything at once—don't demand things from these people. They have helped you. Be kind and try to listen.* But I knew I wouldn't listen, not even to myself. I had to wait. Wait and see what this place was like before I made any decisions.

I hated waiting.

17

MUSIC

Too soon light was shining through my slitted eyes. Like a whitebone needle it was working its way between my lids and forcing them apart. It hurt. I was groggy and I'd barely slept at all. My teeth were furry. I cursed that brown stuff but then the memory of it made me crave more. That convinced me it was bad.

The sun rose over the icy plains, painting the horizon with drips of color that hit the snow and splashed across it, seeping in like the ice could hold it. The stunning beauty of it was enough to stop me from feeling so tired, for a moment. In front of us were low hills shimmering under the sleepy sun's rays. I hoped we weren't going under them but then going over them would be nauseating. I imagined spinning over the edges, teetering, with no hold on the tracks and my stomach rolled.

I pulled up the blind between the carriages. Everyone was awake and Deshi waved at me. He looked happier, more secure.

The train glided smoothly to a stop and the carriage door opened soundlessly. The blast of cold air was like a smack in the face. Joseph woke up very suddenly, sitting bolt upright, like someone had given him an electric shock. Looking at him crumpled from sleep, he looked boyish, his hair sticking up at all angles, his eyes squinting and not wanting to open. It made me want to grab his hair and pull his face down to mine. He made me feel like I was sitting at the edge of a pool, that feeling of warmth touching my toes and begging me to dive in. He smiled down at

The Wall

me, leaned in, and pressed his lips to my forehead.

Matthew poked his head in the door and smiled. His light brown hair showed strands of gold in the light. "Hungry?"

We both nodded. He threw some sandwiches at us.

He was wearing his stethoscope around his neck and was carrying a small bag. "I thought I would ride with you for a bit. I need to give Joseph a check-up," he said in a too-cheery voice. His mood from last night was shoved somewhere. Maybe being closer to home helped him. I didn't know what that was like. There was no place I felt a pull towards except maybe the woods and they were dangerous. We were like trees with nowhere to sink our roots, Joseph and I. Instead of finding the ground we wound them around each other.

Matthew put Orry's capsule on the floor and slid into the seat opposite us. Orry seemed so tired from the stress of yesterday, he didn't even notice the movement. We opened our food and talked while eating.

Matthew cleared his throat and tapped the end of his stethoscope. "How are you feeling?"

Joseph breathed in and out slowly as Matthew listened to his lungs and tapped his chest lightly. "Stitches are itchy but apart from that I feel really good," he answered, grinning at me. He did look really good. The hollows of his cheeks were already starting to fill out, his color was great, and if anything, he looked stronger and healthier than he did before he got sick. Which wasn't right.

I tightened my eyes at Matthew. He leaned back a bit and raised his eyebrows. I was so used to people reacting that way to me it didn't give me pause anymore. "What exactly did you do to him?" I asked.

"Rosa..." Joseph started to say.

"It's all right." Matthew put his hands up. "She has a right to ask, so do you."

"Yeah, but she doesn't have to glare at you like that."

I turned my eyes on Joseph. "Don't talk about me like I'm not here,"

I snapped.

He chuckled and ran his hand through his hair. He was so annoying and annoyingly adorable.

Matthew explained that the operation they'd performed, the 'broken heart' procedure, was one of the borrowed technologies discovered when they started building the settlement. It involved removing the heart and placing it in a glass box. At this point, I snorted. It sounded stupid. I felt sure it was a lie. Matthew assured us it was true. They didn't know how it worked but, coupled with a complicated machine, it could completely regenerate the damaged tissue. It could replicate any organ or body part. So if you were badly burned, it could generate new skin. It was like Joseph had been given a new heart. Joseph was fascinated. I was looking out the window. As long they hadn't hurt him or changed him in some fundamental way, that was explanation enough.

When they had finished their doctor talk, Matthew asked Joseph to unbutton his shirt so he could look at his stitches.

"Would you turn around please?" Joseph said to me, making a circle with his finger, a wicked grin on his face.

I poked my tongue out at him. "If you hadn't just had surgery, I would punch you."

The train started moving. Matthew slammed into Joseph's chest with his stethoscope and he winced. "Ha!" I laughed.

I could tell Matthew didn't quite understand our dynamic. But he ignored us, focusing on pressing around the edges of the scar as Joseph gritted his teeth.

"All looks good," he said. "How do you feel?"

"Good. Really good. Thanks, Matt."

"How's Apella?" I blurted out before I could stop myself.

"She's fine," Matthew said looking at me with his kind, blue eyes.

"What? What's wrong with Apella?" Joseph asked.

"Umm…" I was never good at coming up with a lie on the spot.

The Wall

Matthew took over. "Apella had a miscarriage while you were in the coma. She's very sad, but physically she's doing well."

Joseph shook his head sorrowfully, "Oh no. That's awful." He went quiet, taking on her grief. It made me love him more, that he would be so affected by her loss. He wouldn't make the connection between his miraculous recovery and her miscarriage unless we pointed him that way. I made eye contact with Matthew and he seemed to understand nothing more should be said.

The spinners were climbing now. A labored electrical noise hummed in the background as they pushed upwards. We were like a strand of beads being pulled along and now we were heading uphill, I could hear a slight strain.

Matthew said we would be there soon. He tapped his fingers on the table and glanced out the window absentmindedly. Trees sprouted out of the snow and I felt more at home with the green pressing into the tracks. With the sun so strong, the snow was melting, pulling the white back from the leaves, revealing the life underneath. It was there, just waiting, ready to grow and change the scene. I wanted to run out there, to shake and whip the branches and tell winter to hurry up and finish.

As we climbed further, an alien noise punctured the silence. Matthew uttered, "Gwen." He rolled his eyes and stared out the window more intently, like that could block out the noise. Tiny speakers in the four corners of our carriage emitted static and I thought they were going to make an announcement. It threw me back to the announcements in Pau. They were never good. I found myself unwittingly gripping the sides of the chair and grimacing. Then the sound came.

Joseph and I both jumped in our seats. Orry followed the noise around the room like he could see the sounds floating around on the air. I could almost see them too.

It fit into the scene like it was made for that exact purpose, an accompaniment. It slipped in and around the trees, hopping up and down on the leaves, sending sprays of melting snow running from their shiny fronds. It leapt into the clouds and burst through like rays of light. I found myself tapping my feet and swaying my head.

Then the singing started. A man's voice ebbed in between the springing, echoing noises of strings being plucked and wood being hit. His voice was sweet and soft; the painful bemoaning edge to it brought tears to my eyes. I thought of Clara. She understood music. In Pau, the only tuneful sound came from absent humming or whistling and that was usually swallowed pretty quickly for fear of being reported. This was the first time Joseph and I had ever heard anything like this, an organized, yet almost organic, melding of voice and instrument. It filled my ears, my head, with pleasure and aching and I wondered if that was the intention behind it. I couldn't even hear the words. The sound was overwhelming enough. When it stopped, I wanted to reach out and tug it back through the speakers. But another song started and brought us through another journey of the singers making.

I was lost to it.

Matthew watched our reactions in a gentle but clinical manner. I wouldn't have been the least bit surprised if he had pulled out a notepad and started jotting things down. I guess it would be fascinating to see a person's first reaction to real, recorded music.

When the collection of songs ended, I leaned into Matthew, my eyes wide. "Is there more?"

He laughed. "More than you can possibly imagine."

I crossed my arms and collapsed back into my chair, hugging my ribs. More. Any place that had more of that couldn't be half bad. I glanced at Joseph's face, which was somewhere between a smirk and a laugh that didn't quite get out. I could tell it affected him, but not as intensely as me, because he took new things on so much more easily than I did. It didn't send him into a spiral of wonderment and sadness; he could accept it into his head like it had always been a part of him.

The Wall

"Do you have your own music, too? Like a favorite song?" I asked.

Matthew's eyes creased and a flash of pain crossed his face. I had upset him.

"Sorry, I didn't mean to…"

"No, it's fine, Rosa. Like you've just experienced, music can evoke strong emotions. My favorite song is hard for me to hear; it brings up memories of the people I have lost."

"I'm sorry," I said, wishing I could say something more meaningful but there was nothing.

Matthew told us that he had a wife. At the very beginning of the building of the settlement, people emerged from China. They had been hiding in the hills around the edges of a bombsite. He told me, his eyes going soft and distant, that she was beautiful, smart, and fierce. She was very protective of her people and it took him a long time to convince her that he could be trusted.

Joseph silently chuckled. "What?" I asked.

"Oh, just sounds like someone I know," he whispered.

When Matthew finally won her over, it didn't take long before they were married, or what Survivors' called being married. It basically meant living together.

His favorite was the song they played at their union party. It was *their* favorite song, and that's why he couldn't listen to it anymore. He didn't need to continue—I understood. This is what life was like, not just here but everywhere. There were no happy endings, just endings. Things rarely seemed to work out the way they should.

"I knew she was sick when we got together. Perhaps I should have kept my distance but then…" he smiled sadly, "I think it was better to have had those short months with her than nothing at all."

I tipped my head gently, agreeing. Even though it was more painful than I could possibly have imagined, I would never want to give up knowing Clara. Her loss stung me a thousand times a day in a thousand different ways. Even though I was barbed and ridden with holes from her, I couldn't regret our friendship.

Deep in thought, I didn't notice we were slowing down until we started rolling backwards, clanging gently against the other carriages like marbles on a slide.

"We're here," Matthew said, satisfied, full. He was happy to be home.

18

WALLS

It was about lunchtime when we stepped out of our carriages onto a concrete platform in timid shuffles, like we were stepping onto thin ice that might crack at any second. Our group of newcomers was quiet and anxious.

The Survivors looked relaxed. They were home.

All I could see as I scanned the vicinity was the curve of a metal shelter reaching up like a wave. It was similar to what we had seen when we'd approached the ruins of the city, but more sophisticated.

The cold still bit into us with gnawing teeth. We were told to put our jackets on and follow them.

Gwen was half-skipping, half-walking. "Why are you so excited?" I asked distrustfully, listening to her hum a repetitive tune.

She turned to me and smirked. "It's my bros birthday. I thought I'd miss it. I'm gonna sneak up on him and surprise him." I tried to return her smile but it came off looking forced and confused. Siblings were allowed, of course. So much was new. It filled me up to the point where I felt like one more piece of new information would make me burst like a bubble or that I would float away like one.

I saw Bataar unloading the dogs and wondered what he was going to do with them. At this point, I wouldn't have been surprised if he'd miniaturized them and put them in his pocket with his pipe.

Our little group looked like a herd of startled deer. Survivors pushed us this way and that, our legs skittering across the concrete, our eyes wide as we searched for clues, skimming over everything, looking for one shred of similarity we could hold onto. Where was this settlement?

As we were steered past the shelter, something close to a convulsion went through me. We found that shred of similarity we were looking for... though I wish we hadn't. It hit us like a sledgehammer, so much so that we all stopped still and the Survivors in the back bumped into us. Apella shot forward and her thin hand gripped my arm like a bird claw. I heard Alexei whimper. Joseph wrapped his spare arm around my shoulder protectively. I tried hard to breathe but the air felt thin, laced with fear. Not again.

The wall was as high as the Woodland walls but made of a different material, crumbly-looking stone that seemed like it was before the time of the Woodlands. I wondered if this was where the Superiors got the idea. Theorizing didn't help; it was a wall and it was terrifying, and if we couldn't see the settlement on this side of it, it must have been within the ominous structure. My expression hardened and my stomach twisted awkwardly, like it couldn't digest the sight.

It stretched both ways as far as the eye could see. A dirty brown color, the wall was constructed of cut stone. Our standstill had created a traffic jam but the Survivors didn't push us, they just parted their people sea and went around. It didn't intimidate them. They didn't break stride as they made their way towards it.

As they passed, Gus grunted and pushed Cal towards Joseph and me forcefully. Cal stumbled, pulled himself up, but stared at his feet as he talked. "I... I wanted to apologize for my behavior. It was," he looked to Gus meekly, who nodded, "inappropriate." He annunciated every word carefully and I knew Gus had written Cal's apology for him. I stared at

Cal, embarrassed and angry that he had even told Gus, mortified to be having this conversation in front of Joseph. I nodded. "Ok, well as long as it never, ever happens again…"

Cal looked only at me, ignoring Joseph looming possessively over me, whilst I felt like I was shrinking to the size of an ant. "It won't. I promise. Friends?"

"Um, friends," I lied. I truly hoped this would be the last time I would ever see him.

He walked away with the rest of them, looking over his shoulder like a wounded animal, like he expected me to follow him.

We were left staring silently at the wall that encapsulated our worst fears. The fear that we had not come to a better place and this was exactly the same as where we had come from. The thought hurt a great deal, pushing old memories I had barely buried back up to the surface.

Matthew stood with us for a while, and then broke the quietness. "It's not what you think."

"You don't know what we think," I snapped without thinking. It felt like this was all a trick. The very small amount of trust I had afforded Matthew sprung back to me like it was attached to elastic. The need to protect my family, my new family, whose bonds were tenuous as it was, was overwhelming. I took a deep breath.

"I'll go with Matthew. I'll check it out. Then I'll come back for you. If I'm not back in thirty minutes, leave," I said, trying to sound sure of myself, but I was shaking as I talked.

"No," Joseph said. His eyes were panicked, wide and pricked. I felt the same way at the idea of us being separated but this seemed like a decent compromise and I didn't trust anyone to do it other than myself.

"It's not up to you," I said. "We'll vote. Out of everyone here, who is the most suspicious, the least trusting?" All eyes were on me. Not proud, but satisfied, I continued, "Then it should be me."

I kissed Joseph gently, his lips were still, set so hard it was like kissing his elbow. "Take care of Orry. I won't be long," I said. He didn't respond.

I turned away from the group and put my hand on Matthew's shoulder. "Let's go."

As we peeled away from them and made our way up the incline to the great wall, I wasn't afraid. Apprehensive maybe, but not afraid. I was half hoping I was going to hate it and we could leave. Return to the woods. Matthew's mouth was turned up at the corners. Clearly he was amused by our behavior, which was infuriating. He didn't understand where we came from. He didn't understand the kind of dread that a walled-in town would fill us with. A little ball of hate that had been seething in the pit of my stomach grew a little. The Superiors had damaged us all.

We were both quiet, just the crunch of our boots in the snow. I felt hot under the sun. Hot in anticipation. Slipping and falling as we struggled to find a foothold near the base, Matthew gripped the bricks of the wall and swung himself into a small hollow. Holding out his hand, I took it and he pulled me in. There was an iron gate, which was already propped open with a rock, and dark, unlit stairs wound upwards. Matthew flicked on a torch and I followed him up the narrow staircase. Everything was wonky, like there was little thought put into how the stones might fit together but somehow they just did. It was dusty and smelled stale.

We came out of a hole and stood on top of the wall. I looked down at my hands and traced the letters carved into the rock, 'LH was here 1983'. There were hundreds of similar carvings. Ancient scrawl, the only thing left of a civilization now gone. Another one caught my eye: EV loves RJ. These people were long dead but their little dedication of love survived. It was kind of sweet. I remember someone got caught scratching words into the wall of Ring Four. They had their fingers crushed with a stone while everyone watched.

I expected to see other people up there but the survivors were nowhere.

The wall was very different to the Rings, which was a relief. It was

The Wall

as wide as a road, a low barrier on either side. And when I stood and surveyed the greater area, the sight baffled my eyes.

It looked like the spine of some gigantic creature that had laid itself gently across the hills and breathed its last breath. The world grew up around its remains. The tail of the monster was endless. Curving and following the hills until it disappeared to a line and then a point. Sandy grey stone perforated the forest but seemed a part of it.

Matthew was grinning, hands on hips, so pleased with himself that I wanted to slap him.

"Where's the settlement?" I asked. Looking over the edge of the wall, all I could see were trees—the place was thick with them. I couldn't for the life of me see any signs of people, no houses, no light, just woods. It was like Gwen and the others had stepped into the clouds.

This was all a big joke to him but I didn't get it. Then he walked over to the edge of the wall and pointed to a small, metal disc that was stuck to the parapet. When I observed the sides more closely, I could see they lined the whole side of the wall that faced away from the train station. I walked back over to the opposite side and waved at Joseph and the others but they didn't respond. Then I yelled. Heads moved in my direction but they still couldn't see me. Confused, I walked back to Matthew.

He took my hand and placed it in front of one the metal discs. The sky flashed and a shaft of a view appeared before me. Roofs of houses nestled in amongst the trees. Little cabins with light-colored, wooden shingles covered in snow, narrow roads with people walking along them. I gasped and then I smiled, big and full, the grin splitting my face. I removed my hand and the view was replaced with the woods again. Then I covered another one, revealing a slightly different view that was connected to the one before like a sliding puzzle. Further out, past the wooden shacks, I could see a city in the distance. The most important thing I couldn't see was another wall. The land was divided by the great structure but not surrounded by it.

Matthew explained. "This was once called the Great Wall. It spans most of the border between Mongolia and China. We didn't build it, but it was perfect for our needs. I think it's at least a few thousand years old."

I wasn't really listening. I was thinking of those little cabins surrounded by trees. Each looked different, each one was handmade, not handed over, with a character of its own.

"How do we get down there?" I asked, jumping a little, curiosity sending shivers of excitement through my whole body.

"There are some stairs a bit further along. We just walk down."

"Then what?" I felt confused, but only wanted to know more, the instinctual runner in me didn't kick in this time.

"You'll have to go through quarantine and then you can choose a place to live."

"Ok," I said excitedly. "Show me the stairs."

Matthew showed me the entry point, a neat set of metal stairs held up by scaffolding, which led to ground level on the other side of the wall, and then we went back to the others.

They had taken some convincing, aside from Joseph, who still wanted to walk head first into danger without a second thought. Watching him dipping his shoulders and trying to squish his hulking form up the narrow stairs was amusement enough. Now we were all standing up there—they looked so confused. Apella stared this way and that, as I had, looking for evidence of people. Alexei blinked like a mole staring at the sun. Deshi distractedly squeezed Hessa's chubby little arm too tight and he started crying.

It was mean, but I couldn't help myself. They followed me and we walked along the wall a way. I'd asked Matthew to be quiet and let me

The Wall

explain it to them but I hadn't told him what I was planning to do.

Without warning, I stood on a parapet, talking as I walked. "It's pretty fascinating really, this wall was here way before the war, before the Woodlands, all of it." Jumping from parapet to parapet and back again, I pretended to lose my balance, teetering and flailing my arms. I stepped off the wall, concealing myself behind the projection that kept the town camouflaged. Crouching on the first step, I snickered as I heard them scream and gasp. Then I popped my head back up, my body cut in half by the projection, like half of my body was missing and I was a floating torso in the sky.

Joseph growled at me, his brow furrowed in a worried anger I had seen many times before, "That wasn't funny Rosa."

I shrugged and walked back to them. I thought it was hilarious.

"Ingenious," Alexei muttered, flapping his hands back and forth over the discs.

"Apparently, they were used for festivals and such, projecting giant images in to the sky for an audience to watch," Matthew said. "This used to be a tourist destination."

I rolled that word around in my head, tourist. We had learned about them in class, about the wastefulness of our predecessors. We were told people used to fly around the world on 'holidays'. Poisoning the earth and wasting time they could have otherwise spent working. The idea of a holiday didn't sound that sinister to me but then I was never a true believer in the Superiors' propaganda.

They all took turns sticking their heads over the edge to see what we were getting ourselves into. We all agreed we would try it.

"There is one stipulation," Matthew said seriously. "You will all have to go through quarantine before you can become part of the community. It means two weeks in hospital. If you are ok with that, then I'll take you now."

I wish I had thought about it longer. Not just said 'yeah yeah' and ignored half of what he was saying. I was too anxious to get down to the trees. They called to me and the rest was just dull humming.

We agreed to the conditions, not thinking to ask why they needed us to do this and what exactly it would involve. We all stepped off the edge of the wall and hit the metal steps with a clang, like we were diving off a board into silky, black water. There was no turning back now.

It was beautiful.

No. More than that. If I had concocted an idea of the perfect home for my child and me, this would be it. I stomped down the steps, enjoying the metallic vibrations, and held out my hands, sweeping the frozen leaves as I went. I wanted to climb. I wanted to run.

There were people watching us, people of different ages mixing together. Maybe I did invent this. I was the one in the coma and this was my dream. I shook it out with a light laugh.

Joseph took my hand and I wound my fingers in his. Breathing in deeply, the smells of wet leaves, dirt, and wood smoke was unmistakable and wonderful. It brought me home. It swam around my heart like a warm drink and made me whole.

Stones made up the road. There was a track cut down the middle and spinners moved soundlessly through the streets. It was a bizarre mix of old and new. Cottages were dotted against the backdrop of the ancient wall, each with a generous plot of land begging for vegetables to be grown when the sun actually warmed the earth, not just threw its light sparingly across it with distaste.

The modest, wooden cottages stood on stacked-stone foundations, simply shingled, with thick, glass windows and smoke coming out of the stone chimneys. They must have been built individually, not by some Class team, as each one had its own personality. They were new too,

The Wall

maybe about five to ten years old. And the plants... My chest swelled at the possibility of it. They had the freedom to plant their own gardens. Any tree, any flower. It was too much to take in. Too much but not enough—I craved more.

This was what my eyes, my heart, took in in the five minutes we had before we were ambushed by people in white coats. Before we were barreled into a spinner and rushed towards the grey, ramshackle town down the hill. I let out a strangled sigh as we got further away from the cottages, my hand pressed to the wall of the carriage, willing it to shatter. I put my head in my hands and swore I would get back there, somehow. Joseph's hand made a fist in the small of my back.

Matthew explained that it was necessary, that although it seemed like they had it all together, most of their technology was borrowed and pieced together. Survivors were scroungers; they had eked out an existence here after much trial and error and a new disease would devastate the community. He explained this as we were manhandled up the stairs of a dark, dingy building. He pleaded for our patience as we were stripped of our clothing and forced to stand before scrutinizing doctors, thrown white pajamas, and pushed down halls into a room where we would be separated by glass. Then they made him leave and I was glad. I was having trouble restraining myself. He had not been clear and I knew why. Because he knew we would say no. And they wanted us here. I wasn't sure why, but they wanted something from us.

Now we sit.

Each room has a bed, a bathroom with a privacy curtain, and a chair. In the corner, to keep us occupied, are stacks of books and a device for playing music with headphones. My first modification to our accommodation was to throw everything at the humming air-conditioning vent and let it land in a pile by the door, which was always locked. Books flew like shot-gunned birds, flapping their wings once before tumbling inelegantly to the ground, bent and splayed open, spines twisted. The next morning when I woke up, they were neatly stacked back where they were originally.

I was so unhappy, contained.

But they did one thing, a thing that made their behavior unforgivable in my mind. They took Orry.

19

CONTAINED

The books they gave us were all nonsense to me. Made-up stories. No history books, no how-to guides. They didn't understand we knew nothing of this past world. Although it was interesting, coming from where we did, the 'fiction', as they called it, seemed frivolous and self-indulgent. Flicking through a book called 'Alice in Wonderland', I dragged my chair over to Orry's cot. They had pressed it up against the wall so I could see him and he could see me. It was of little comfort. He turned his head at the sound of my muffled voice.

I read a little bit of the story to him out loud, but when I got to the part where the Queen of Hearts started ordering beheadings for stealing pies, I slammed it shut. It sounded too much like Pau.

My mood shifted between periods of shaking wordlessly, to screaming at no one, to trying to breathe and stay calm. I didn't want to remember these things but being here in this sterile, scraped-down environment brought back memories I didn't even know I had. Scenes that, up until now, had been pinned under a cloud of fog, started pushing their way up to the front of my already-crowded brain.

"Rosa," Joseph said, his voice throttling for attention. But I was gone; I stood in the center of the room, my body rigid. My face stinging from a memory that hit me like a broad board of plywood. "Rosa…?"

I was lying on a metal table. My wrists and ankles tethered. My feet pushed up into stirrups. My head lolled around and someone dabbed at my mouth with a tissue.

"Is she worth keeping?" someone asked.

"For now she is—we'll just have to wait on those eyes." A pause and a sigh. "She's ready for implantation. Transport her as soon as possible. Oh, and keep her heavily sedated; she keeps waking and fighting."

The memory pulled away like a blanket and I was standing back in the white room, shivering from imagined cold, with Joseph watching me. I ran my hands over my wrists, reliving the way the restraints rubbed away at my skin. They hurt still. I shook my head and made my way over to him, my eyes watery, my body feeling pinched and weak.

"Get me out of here," I said. "I don't want a baby."

"What?"

Where did the old world end and the current one begin? I felt half-in, half-out.

"Oh, sorry, I don't know what I'm saying." I put my hand to my forehead, confused, like I'd been drugged.

Joseph's voice was calming, but had an edge of a grumble to it. "It's ok. You'll be ok. Just hang on."

They said two weeks. Joseph argued with them, especially on my behalf. Being trapped held a special sense of horror for me that it didn't for the others. But I heard them all at different times, pleading and yelling. Deshi was beside himself too. They had placed Hessa on the other side of a glass wall as they had Orry.

The doctors were kind. They were patient with my attitude. They assured us we were safe. They encouraged us to ask questions, but my trust was not so easily won. Joseph tried to be more forgiving but even he found it frustrating.

Watching another woman feed my baby was agonizing. They gave

The Wall

me a pump so I could express milk for him, which I did. When I initially refused, thinking I could blackmail them into bringing him to me, they shrugged and said they would give him artificial baby milk. I was desperate to maintain any connection to him so I relented.

They took blood and did physical tests. *It all looked good*, they said. *We should be cleared in no time*, they said. *Now?* I would ask. *No, not yet. Soon.*

If Joseph wasn't there, I think I may have hung myself from the shower rail. He talked me down from my panic. We pushed our beds together and talked through the glass, our breath fogging around our faces. Joseph found music he thought I would like and noted the tracks, telling me to find them on my music device. I stared into his green eyes and counted the gold flecks. I put my hand to the glass and imagined I was touching his hand—that I was lying next to him.

He chewed through the books. I watched him read and wished I had the strength to sit still and try, but I didn't. My skin was crawling; the bugs and itches of the past ran through my body and surfed alongside me. I felt and knew I was one meltdown away from completely snapping.

When they took Orry's blood, the snap echoed like a tree falling, a dry crack and splinters creaked and cried out. He screamed and screamed as they pricked his little heel and squeezed drops of blood onto a piece of paper. All I could think was, *They took my baby*. And no matter how many times they told me he was safe, no matter how many times they pressed his little body up against the glass, I didn't care. He should have been with me. I couldn't take it anymore. It had been a week. The glass was smudged with my desperate, pattering hands. Layers of tears and terror clouded my view.

Before I knew what was happening, my body acted. I picked up a chair and banged it against the glass as hard as I could. It rebounded. The glass wobbled but it didn't break. I smashed it again and again. The rubber stoppers on the legs squeaked down the pane. Joseph watched me, exasperated and helpless.

I hit and hit until my arms were bowed and shaking from the exertion of holding the chair over my head.

I walked to the center of the room, my hands in my hair, and screamed.

"He should be with me! Bring Orry to me," I yelled, and then I whispered to myself, to my body that felt fragile and broken, "I can't do this anymore."

Joseph's muffled voice called to me. "Rosa, come here." He had his hand on the glass, bumping it gently with his fist. I didn't want to look. I shook my head, listening to the rhythmic clunk of his hand on the glass. He wanted to calm me down and I didn't want to be calm. I wanted to build angry flames around me, set the sprinklers off, and let the doors open. Let the whole place burn down for all I cared.

"Rosa, come here!" His voice was more frustrated now, the word, "please," choking on the way out.

He was kneeling on the floor, banging on the glass, trying so hard to get me to turn around. Reluctantly, I shuffled over to him. This was unbearable. After six weeks apart, we only had a week together before they separated us again.

He breathed in deeply. I watched his chest rise and fall. The scar from his operation moved as he talked. "Just breathe. It will be over soon."

"But, how can you trust them? How can you be sure...?"

"It will be ok. You know this is killing me too." He pulled his hair back with both hands, his muscles tensing, and whispered through gritted teeth, "Don't you know how much I want to punch through the glass and touch you?" A shudder of agonizing pleasure ran through me. His eyes were so intensely focused on me, all of me. I couldn't stand it. "But we have to wait," he continued. "We agreed to this and now we have to wait."

The Wall

I banged my head on the glass, a little too hard, the thud reverberating and rippling up to the ceiling. "I hate it," I sobbed.

"I know," he said.

We touched hands, and I swear I could feel the heat burning through, like if we concentrated hard enough on reaching each other, we could melt the glass. How was I ever going to survive another week of this hell?

That night I slept in fits and bursts, my body knotting and unknotting around the cool, white sheets. I continuously woke screaming but there was no one to hold and comfort me. Most of the dreams I couldn't remember. But I knew my mind was taking me back to the facility, to the four months I lost. And I wished they'd stayed lost.

I awoke with my hands around my throat. Not screaming but gurgling and gasping for air. Joseph was kneeling on his bed, trying to get my attention. His eyes panicked, his muscles tensing at the fact they couldn't reach me. When I shook myself free from the dream, I slumped down on my pillow and shoved my face against the cold, cotton pillow, letting out one pathetic whimper.

The dull thud on the glass continued until I turned to face him.

"Tell me what you dream?" he asked, his eyes flicking back and forth, searching my own.

"I don't want to," I said with a scowl. *How could I?*

"Why?" He looked down at his knees, the bed bowing and squeaking under his weight.

"It will hurt you."

He sighed, frustrated. "I can handle it. You need to stop protecting me." He used his eyes against me, staring deep into mine, until I felt incapable of resistance.

"Ok, but I warned you." I kept it as brief as I could. "I'm in the underground facility. I wake up, suddenly aware of what they're doing. I start to fight, to scream, and try to pull myself out of bed but they're always there in a second. People in white coats hold me down, tie my ankles and wrists to the bed with leather straps, then they put a mask on my face. A man holds me by the neck and presses his hand down on my forehead because I'm thrashing my head around so much. Then I feel like I'm dying. Or I'm dead. Like I've floated away, out of my body. But it's not peaceful; it's terrifying and I'm always fighting, scratching, grappling to get back to myself."

His mouth twisted and I could see his neck and shoulder muscles tightening. I knew it hurt him. I knew he found it hard to hear but all he said was, "Thank you for sharing that with me, Rosa. I appreciate it," in an oddly formal tone.

"S'ok," I shrugged, a little confused.

"Can you sleep?"

"Probably not, but you should." I could feel the dark, craggy fingers of sleep trying to wrestle me under but I was fighting it.

"No, I'll stay with you until you fall asleep. Close your eyes." He lay facing me, propping his head up with his hand. His body caused the rollaway bed to sag in the middle, his big feet hanging off the edge.

I lay on my side facing him and closed my eyes, opening them a couple of times to see if he was still awake. He was. He just watched me softly, his eyes muted in the safety lights, his warmth radiating through the glass and wrapping around me.

Eventually, my eyes became heavy and I slept without a single nightmare. But I knew as long as I was in here it would only be a temporary reprieve.

20

SAVED

After my meltdown, Matthew came to visit. He casually walked up to the glass like this was a normal experience, knocking like it was my front door. And if it were, he would have got no answer. He explained that he and the others we were with had been quarantined too. But they were allowed out earlier because the doctors already had most of the data on them. I tried to avoid his eyes.

"You lied to us," I muttered sulkily.

"No, I didn't, Rosa. I said you had to go into quarantine," he said unconvincingly.

"Don't pretend like you didn't keep details from us so we would go more easily. Just don't. I am so tired of being lied to or half-lied to or whatever."

He sighed, pulling his shoulders back proudly like he was shaking me off, moving on to the others who were happier to talk to him. I was disappointed and resigned. Maybe he was done with me. After a while, everyone was.

"How much longer do we have to stay here?" Joseph asked.

"One more week," Matthew said.

"She won't make it," I heard him whisper. "You have to understand—this is much harder for her than the rest of us. It brings back too many bad memories. I think she's traumatized or something." I stiffened at this. The number of times I'd heard someone say that about me was starting to add up.

Matthew's tone was terse when he replied, "Look, this is just the way it has to be. You have no choice."

No choice. *Back to the Woodlands we go*, I thought.

Most of the time, Matthew seemed ever-patient and willing to help but sometimes something else slipped through—a shred of impatience, a tight knot of rope that constricted around his throat when he spoke, like the burden of being our caregiver was wearing thin.

After that, Matthew stopped talking to me. He would wave, but took his steaming mug of coffee and pulled up a chair at one of the other pens. I didn't acknowledge him. But a parade of guests started arriving. I don't know whether he sent them or if they came of their own volition but they were all unwelcome.

I was an animal on display. A static exhibition—an example of a Woodland citizen. *See how she snarls at passersby. It's because of the way they treat people over there. They have lost their humanity*, the tour guide would say.

First was Cal. I was so rude to him but he didn't seem to get the hint. Pushing my headphones on my head, I turned my back and ignored him. But he just sat there, tapping along to imaginary music, and smiling gawkily at me.

Joseph tapped on the glass and beckoned him over to the far corner of his room, as far away as he could get from me. I watched them curiously while trying to seem uninterested. He whispered something and then I saw Cal's eyes widen as he nodded. He waved to me and left, walking jauntily off like he had just heard fantastic news.

I walked over to the glass separating us and glared at Joseph, who had a ridiculous grin on his face, distracting me with his white teeth. I picked out my favorite one, the broken one, and focused on that instead of his eyes.

"What did you say to him?" I was sure it was something unkind.

The Wall

"Nothing," he said mischievously, his hands behind his back, looking up at the ceiling.

"What?" I threatened. Most of the time, I wanted to break the glass so I could hold him. Right then, I wanted to get through so I could shove him over.

He wouldn't answer me but was obviously very amused with himself.

"Well, at least you think yourself funny," I snapped. I flopped down on the bed and put my finger to my mouth. I'd started biting my fingernails. Nervousness and fear had manifested itself and my nails were disappearing. I flashed back to when I had first seen Clara ahead of me in the line of dopey, pregnant girls. Her hands were raw and painful looking like someone had tried to strip the skin from her fingers with a vegetable peeler. Would she have been able to make this easier for me or would she have found it just as hard because she was also 'traumatized'?

Careen finally came to see us. I think they asked her to. She repeated some lines I was sure they'd fed her about how she'd been through it too. I knew it wasn't her own words because she talked slowly for once, her mouth chewing over every word carefully before she spewed them out. She told us it really wasn't so bad and once she was out, she was free to do whatever she wanted.

"Which is what?" I asked.

"Um. I'm in the hunting party," she said, twisting uncomfortably under my gaze for a second and then jumping up and down like a toddler again, lifting her butt off the chair with her arms and legs swinging. "Yeah, I get to use all sorts of weapons. We hunt for food and share it with the rest of the people. It's fun. When you're out, I can show you how, if you like?" Her words mashed together.

Take a breath, I thought. I wanted to pinch her lips together with my thumb and forefinger. I'm pretty sure that would be the only way to stop her from talking. But I was glad she had found something she enjoyed, even if it was slightly disturbing.

"How fun for you," I said sarcastically. I was being unkind, but I was jealous of her freedom, and jealous of her ability to assimilate into this new society so easily.

She sat cross-legged on the floor and her face went smooth and serious. Her tied-back hair revealed a scar seamed across her left temple I hadn't seen before. It was jagged, like the skin had been split apart or burst. "I never told you this before but my father was a butcher," she said. "He taught me everything about the trade. I know it sounds terribly simple. I mean, to want to be a butcher, but I had a dream that I would set up my own shop once I left the Classes. But then I got pulled into Guardian training and that was the end of my dream."

This threw me. My assumptions about Careen flew off her body and landed in a pile at my feet. Another person I was wrong about. Her dream was not dissimilar to my own. There was a question I wanted to ask her, but it meant bringing up my own downfall at the Classes. I hadn't told Joseph yet... I'm not sure I ever would.

I said it anyway. "What did you do to end up underground, with me?"

She shrugged and held her stomach, holding a baby long gone. "I said 'no'."

Her eyes meandered around the room, avoiding mine, and I knew she wasn't going to say anymore.

I put my hand to the glass, remembering the hammer breaking my face, breaking my dream apart in an instant. "Me too."

There was a moment's silence, then she shook her perfect hair free of the tie and started jabbering again. She talked about the surrounding woods, which were overflowing with life. There was good game in there. The words just made me ache and I started to feel like the walls were closing in on me, or that I was getting smaller. The glass cube would fold

The Wall

over on itself and I would disappear.

Eventually, when I found a break in her prattling, I asked her to stop. She skipped off to say hello to the others and then left the area. One more week left of hell.

The next morning, I awoke to gentle tapping on the glass. I peeled one eye back and then the other, pulling myself slowly to sitting. What time was it? It felt like I'd barely closed my eyes and now someone was waking me up. I was about to snap at them when my blurry eyes focused and I was rendered speechless.

Matthew stood behind a tiny woman, his hand affectionately on her shoulder. I dragged myself up and walked towards her timidly, fascinated.

She cocked her head and smiled, missing teeth on the bottom row, her crinkly lips curling around her gums like they were searching for moisture. "So this is the one who's giving you all the trouble?" she said, eyeing me carefully. Her voice sounded like gravel rattling in a paper bag. "She doesn't look like much." I would have been offended but she said it with a twinkle in her eye, like she was challenging me to prove her wrong. "You can stop staring, dear, and shut your mouth. You're liable to catch flies."

I clamped my lips together with some effort. I'd never seen anyone like her before. I stumbled over my words, selecting probably the most offensive ones my brain could come up with. "I'm sorry. It's just, you're so old."

Joseph chuckled in the corner. He had seen older people before. I'd never seen anyone past the age of sixty. The Superiors' attitude was everyone had to get around on their own steam, so if you were too old to walk that far, you never made it to the center circle.

She patted down her clothes like she was looking for something and then replied, "Am I? I'm only twenty. This is what living on the outside does to you."

My eyes were bulged out of my head in disbelief. Matthew covered his mouth with his hand and laughed. The woman turned to him, cupping her hand over his ear, and whispered dramatically, "I thought you said she was clever?"

At this point, Joseph fell backwards on his mattress and started laughing uncontrollably. I walked to the glass and glared at him.

"Ooh, ouch," he said. "If looks could kill."

"If only!" I said.

Matthew tapping on the glass brought me back. "This is my grandmother, Adleta."

Grandmother? I know I looked confused. My face scrunched up like if I refocused my eyes, she would look young again and things would make more sense. Suspecting my confusion, Matthew explained, "She is my father's mother."

"But how is she still alive? How did you find her?" I said, feeling more stupid every time I spoke. But this crumpled-up bag of skin didn't look like a person to me. Her words sounded real enough, she seemed to have a lot of life in her, but I couldn't quite grasp the idea of this being allowed, or even possible.

I nodded slowly, taking her whole form in. "Adleta," I repeated. She was tiny, shorter than me. She looked like it was just her clothing holding her together. Her skin was sagging over her eyebrows, her cheeks slipping off her face like melting wax, but she wasn't frightening. Just foreign. I could see Matthew in her bright eyes. That kindness and kinship was there.

"Call me Addy, please. I'm alive because I want to be. And he didn't find me; I've always been here. I'm like the furniture, dear, old but sturdy," she said, smiling crookedly; it looked like an effort to move her cheeks that far up her face.

The Wall

Orry cried. He let out one long, howling note and then took several sharp intakes of breath like he was panicking. It was a noise that pierced right through me. He missed me. I knew it. I could feel it.

"May I?" she asked me.

"I guess," I said shyly.

She approached the door without putting on the gloves and mask.

"I thought you were all worried we would make you sick or something," I challenged.

"Like you said—I'm *so* old. I shouldn't even be alive. I'm not scared of your Woodland germs," she said dismissively, waving a wrinkled, bark-like hand at me.

Matthew stopped her. "Addy, you need to put on the suit. Otherwise, we will have to quarantine you as well."

The old woman made a clucking sound with her tongue. "Very well, doctor man. You're the boss." She held her hand to her head in mock salute. He smiled back at her with such affection I felt embarrassed to be party to it.

Matthew helped her into the big, plastic coveralls, booties, and facemask while I watched her old limbs struggling to lift and maneuver their way into pant legs and armholes. She made an inordinate amount of noise for someone so small. Each movement of her bony body crackled and sighed like she was made of brittle sticks. It was almost too painful to watch.

Finally, she bustled through Orry's door, large bag in hand, her oversized, plastic suit swishing with static. Placing the bag on the floor, she pulled out a knitted rabbit and placed it at the end of the cot. Matthew sighed and rolled his eyes. "You'll have to leave that bag there now," he said, trying to sound aggravated but coming off more amused. She rolled her eyes back and made a 'pfft' noise.

She scooped Orry up, who screamed at first, wriggling and fighting. *Just like his mother*, I thought. But she wrapped him up tightly and rocked him back and forth. She was strong. When she picked up Orry, I imagined she would crumple like a paper figure but she had him. He stopped crying. He felt secure.

She started singing.

"Are you trying to torture my child?" I asked.

Why would you sing about a baby falling out of a tree? It would give them nightmares. She paused, smiled, and changed the song.

Her voice was soft and dusty at first, but once she brushed it off, it was beautiful. The words were lilting and comforting. Rhythmic. And Orry responded to it immediately. The rise and fall of the melody brought tears to my eyes. How I ever lived in a world without music, I'll never know. She sang about trying to get home. *Once there was a way to get back home.* The words flew over me and transcribed our experiences perfectly. *Sleep, pretty darling, don't you cry*. I thought she was finished but then the last part gave me goose bumps all over my skin. How did she know?

Golden slumbers fill your eyes.

Smiles await you when you rise.

Sleep, pretty darling

Do not cry.

And I will sing a lullaby.

Orry calmed down and the old woman placed him gently in his cot. She stretched her back after he was down and planted herself in a chair in front of my cage.

"What was that?" I said, desperation pitching my voice higher. I was clinging to it.

She clucked her tongue. "You've never heard The Beatles before?" She shook her head like she was so very sorry for me.

"Can you teach me?"

She nodded. "Sure, but first you have to do something for me."

"Ok," I said, suspiciously. Matthew had walked away, talking to one of the other doctors.

"It's give and take here," she said in a matter-of-fact voice. "What can you do, apart from be a smart mouth?"

I paused. It had been so long since I'd done anything useful. I noticed the chair she was sitting on was wobbling, creaking every time she shifted her weight.

"If you bring me some tools, I can fix that," I said, pointing to the chair.

"Deal. As long as it doesn't end up a pile of splinters or slammed against the wall," she said sternly but with a hint of humor to her voice.

So my education with Addy began.

Every day she brought me things to fix and in return, she helped me with Orry. She taught me songs, gave him toys, and answered my questions.

When I asked her about the Survivors, she tried her best to answer everything in detail. I wore her out, though. Quite often, she would fall asleep in the chair mid-conversation and I would have to wait until she had rested before continuing. Her age, and the way she behaved because of it, was intriguing to me. She was smart and aware like an adult, but she needed as much sleep as a baby.

I managed to find out the Survivors had been nomadic for the most part, moving from town to town until they settled here about twenty years ago. It seemed close to the Woodlands but it was far enough away that the helicopters, which were battery powered, always ran out of juice and had to return to the solar-charging stations before they could reach the settlement. The people were mostly of Russian, Mongolian, and Chinese descent. There were only a few Chinese—the Superiors hadn't lied about that—as they were almost completely wiped out. Clothes were scavenged from abandoned factories, as were canned and processed foods, like the fizzy drink. They liked to grow their own when they could.

Beyond the city was nothing, a vast blackness of dust and destruction.

People who had dragged themselves from those ruins were diseased, or almost dead. Hardly anyone survived the first few years.

The population was small—maybe three thousand.

She had the same small charm around her neck, which she played with while she talked. It hung between her collarbones, her wrinkly skin and neck trying to envelope it with their sagginess. "What is it?" I asked.

She removed it and looked both ways before passing it through the door. She dropped it and it landed on the ground with a metallic chink. Examining it closely, it was just a simple circle of metal with a square hole in it.

"During a routine scavenge, we found a big metal box, as big as a house, standing out against all the rubble. Inside, we found millions of these, as well as stacks upon stacks of small slips of paper. We took some and thought it would be a useful way of identifying members of the community. Everyone has one. You'll get one too."

I tried to imagine a young Addy, agilely climbing over rubble and searching out treasures in abandoned buildings. I couldn't quite do it. In my mind, she looked the same but bounded across the rocks like she had springs in her shoes.

"What if I don't want one?" I said.

"You will."

I smirked. "You're a bit of a know-it-all, old lady."

She crimped her lips together in a fake frown. Then she grinned, showing all her teeth and several holes where teeth used to be.

"Get back to work!" she said, flapping her hands at me.

Joseph watched our interactions quietly. He peered over his book every now and then, the pages shaking like rustling leaves when he laughed to himself.

Addy saved me.

I needed something to do. And she gave me a sense of purpose. Or maybe it was just distraction. Whatever it was, it stopped me from going

The Wall

crazy. The nightmares still came but I felt like I could handle them. The week went by more smoothly because of her.

Her presence also gave me hope. If she were allowed to exist, if she had a relationship with her grandchild, maybe things were different here. In the Woodlands, old people were just shoved to the edges and I don't even know what happened to them if they didn't have the common decency to die quietly. Addy was loud, opinionated, and people listened to her. It was strange, but a welcome strange.

On a day when there was more silence between us than talking, I tapped on the glass lightly to get Addy's attention. There was something I wanted to ask her but I wasn't sure how to phrase it. It bothered me that I didn't know enough about the elderly. I wanted to know what it felt like to live on the edge of death.

Addy's head was hooked under and she was snoozing in her chair again. "Addy, Addy," I said, between tapping. She snorted awake, sounding like an ailing lawnmower. "Goodness! What, dear?"

"Can I ask you something, er, personal?"

She narrowed her eyes a little but she had a smile on her face. "Depends on what it is."

"Right." I looked at the floor and breathed in. "Um... are you afraid to die? I mean, since you're so old?" Joseph had his back to us against the glass wall; it shook from his sniggering shoulders.

Addy's eyebrows rose but she looked at me kindly. "I don't want to die, dear, but I accept that I will. What about you, are you afraid to die?"

I thought about it. I hadn't really considered the reality of death. But when I was in Pau, I always felt that my life would be a short one. Like the fireworks they released over the Great Wall at New Years, my life would be a brilliant flash of sparks and color but would flame out all too quickly. Now I didn't know. Orry and Joseph had changed the way I thought about my life.

"Hello in there... I'm dying of boredom over here," Addy said, waving her hands in front of my eyes.

"Sorry," I replied, snapping out of my thoughts. "I think, no. I'm not afraid to die. What's the point of being afraid of something inevitable? But I really want to live for as long as I can."

Her eyes reached me, grey but warm. So compassionate. "That's good. Very good."

21

RELEASE

I woke up to something shaking me. Rough hands that felt like they were made of spun, dried grass, light with no substance to them. I batted them away, unwilling to give up sleep. "Rosa, wake up," a raspy voice urged.

Addy.

I opened my eyes and her face was two inches from my own. I jumped.

"Your face is way too scary for this time of the morning," I yawned.

She was sitting on the edge of the bed, scowling. She smacked my leg but it was like she'd tapped me with a straw broom. I barely felt it.

"Didn't your mother teach you how to speak to your elders?"

I cringed. "Is that a trick question? Or is that just one of your silly sayings?" I hated it when she brought up family. And she always did. She was like a dog with a bone. She couldn't let it go... unless she was just forgetful. It was hard to tell sometimes.

She patted my leg again and smiled. I tried to shake off my morning crankiness. I needed to remember I actually liked this woman and I shouldn't be so rude.

"Is she always like this in the mornings?" Addy directed at Joseph.

"What?" he smirked. "Beautiful, captivating, beguiling?"

I blushed and then snapped, "I'm pretty sure those are all words for the same thing. You've been reading too many romantic novels."

Addy clucked her tongue and grabbed my face with her crinkled hands. "Today you get out."

"Really?" I pulled myself up straight. I couldn't believe it. The last week had flown by.

She nodded, her light grey eyes sparkling. Even if she was ancient, I felt like we were so similar. *Cut from the same cloth*, is what she would say. I pulled her to me in a tight embrace. Unidentifiable sweet smells emanated from her clothing and it was like squeezing a bird, her thin bones, her body, was so delicate I was afraid I would crush her.

I released her and she clapped her hands impatiently. "You all need to get dressed and get ready to face them. Today you get to meet the rest of us."

Matthew and a few other doctors came up to the doorway, which was now propped open. I was torn, wanting to run to Joseph but also wanting to grab Orry. Joseph made the decision for me, slamming through his door and coming towards me in what looked like painfully restrained steps. Addy shuffled out of the room so fast it was like she'd grown wheels in her feet.

After two weeks of staring at each other through glass, it was all I could do not to jump on him and knock him over. But I tried to stand still, aware of other people watching us. Joseph didn't seem to care. He grabbed me around the waist and lifted me to his chest. I threw my arms around his neck and breathed in him in. Golden cymbals clashed around my ears, blocking out any other noise, any other distraction. I wrapped my legs around his waist and lifted my face up to meet his. It was too easy for him to hold me up. Like it was no effort at all.

It's funny how every kiss seems to have a slightly different meaning, a different intention behind it. This kiss was more desire than any others before it. Lips were hungry. Tastes magnified. Not just warmth, heat. If we were alone in that moment, it would have led to something much more. But someone coughed loudly. Deshi.

The Wall

Joseph whispered into my ear, his warm breath sending tiny shivers through my body. "Do I have to let you go?"

I only managed, "Mhmm," and a nod.

He let me down but kept a hold of my waist.

"All right, you two, that was disgusting," Deshi laughed. "Can we get ready to go now?"

Reluctantly, I let Joseph go but it was like he took half my beating heart with him. The feeling scared me a little. The want to be so close to him, as close as I could possibly be, was powerful. Overwhelming.

Addy agreed with Deshi, muttering something about 'a time and a place'. She brought Orry in to see me while Joseph got dressed. It felt so good to hold my son again. He felt heavier, his eyes brighter. How did he change so fast?

Once everyone was dressed, we lined up and Matthew gave us a talk. Addy busied herself packing up her bag, giving me a wink every now and then. I sidled up to Apella and gave her a gentle squeeze. She managed a weak smile. We were all nervous, none of us knowing what to expect.

"Ok, everyone. From here, we will go to the meeting hall. It's nothing special, but everyone wants to meet you," Matthew said.

This filled me with dread. I pictured an angry mob armed with Coca Cola cans ready to aim at our heads. We were responsible for the deaths of several of their community members. I didn't know how the others were feeling, except for Joseph. I sensed he was thinking of nothing else other than being alone with me; it was the dominant feeling in my mind. He kept his hand around my waist, slipping it under my shirt so he could touch my skin as we walked. It was driving me crazy and I wanted to swat him off but at the same time couldn't bear the idea of losing that connection. As we neared the glass doors of the ward, Matthew grabbed the back of my shirt and gently pulled me backwards towards the hallway. I turned towards him, irritation radiating from my eyes.

"Can I speak with you?" The others were walking on ahead, only

Joseph hung in the doorway waiting for me.

"What do you want?" I said tersely.

Matthew grabbed my wrist and opened my fingers, pressing something into my palm. My fingers closed around four small, plastic wheels, pills radiated around the outer edges, the days of the week in tiny writing below them. I looked at Matthew confused.

"Am I sick? Did the tests show something?" I whispered. Joseph caught the concern in my face and started towards me.

Matthew laughed quietly, "No, no. It's just… I don't know what your plans are in terms of adding to your family but if you take these every day on the day specified, well, you can control when you want to have another baby."

My face bloomed crimson. Who knew such a thing existed? "You mean I won't get pregnant?"

Matthew nodded. I closed my hand around the discs and slipped them into my pocket. This really was a strange new world. Joseph and I weren't even close to having to worry about another baby, but a choice would be nice.

"Thank you," I managed.

I caught up with Joseph and we were ushered down a hall and then… sunlight. It was cold but the air had the promise of spring in it. I stood and breathed it in. My lungs danced, reaching out to grab more, more air. My eyes instantly skimmed back towards the Great Wall, back to the simple, wooden shacks. They were there. I hadn't imagined them.

When I returned my eyes to what was in front of us, I could see the city was just as Matthew had described the Survivors' whole lifestyle—pieced together.

The roads were narrow and grey asphalt. It was cracked and you could see the well-worn paths people used to avoid the bigger potholes. There were spinner tracks running down the main street. The buildings looked old, ancient, and if they were designed for a specific purpose,

The Wall

they had definitely been repurposed. It was a cheery, hopeful kind of construction. If something was broken, it had been fixed or propped up with new timber or bits of shiny-colored tin, giving everything a half-finished, half-old, half-new look. No space was wasted. It was neat, tidy, and absolutely ramshackle. A patchwork city.

"Since the sun is out, we'll walk," Matthew announced. We followed him and he pointed out different things as we went. "This town used to be a huge tourist destination. People came from all over the world to see the Wall." Why would anyone want to visit a wall? "They had masses of restaurants, shopping centers, movie theaters..." I couldn't keep up with him... every second word was foreign and had little or no meaning to me.

The whole town sloped downwards like it was tilted towards something. Up ahead, people were walking downhill, dressed in all manner of clothing. They were coming from every direction, heading toward a big, stone-fronted building with red and gold paint peeling off its ornate, carved-stone frames. It had a large verandah that was sagging at one end. Wooden and steel scaffolding held up the worst side. Blackened plastic casings that once held light bulbs lined every straight edge of the structure.

As we walked, we could see most of the buildings in this area were once shop fronts. Some were still used as such but most had been turned into homes. Colorful, painted flowerboxes filled with dirt hung out of windows ready for warmer weather. I imagined flowers spilling over the edges, dripping with vibrant petals. Brightly sewn curtains hung in the windows. I peered through the panes and saw a small display of miniature models of the Great Wall behind us, some carved from wood, some set in plaster, all with little, metal placards glinting in the sunlight that read: The Great Wall of China.

This place was a standing contradiction. Amazing technology set amongst a self-made mishmash. It boggled the mind. I was in awe of what they had managed to do.

"We'll sneak in the back. This used to be an old movie theater. It seats about four hundred. The rest will probably be standing."

The rest? I stifled an eek.

We stared at him like he was speaking a foreign language. None of us knew what the words 'movie' or 'theater' meant. I was aching to find out though.

We ducked into a side street before the theater and Matthew guided us through a door, into a dark space. I walked straight into heavy material, hanging from a very high ceiling. It was shedding bits of red fluff and smelled like dust. Velvet. Very extravagant for curtains, my mother would have said. All the while, Joseph kept his hand on me, leaning in to smell my hair. When we stopped, he placed his chin on my head, making it hard to think of anything other than unbuttoning his shirt and laying my head on his muscled chest. I sighed but it came out more like a grunt as I pushed the air out and forced myself to concentrate.

We could all hear the voices. They melded together into one collective hum. Odd smells of rancid butter and heat from too many bodies wafted through the air. Exchanging glances nervously, we shifted from foot to foot uncomfortably, like we were stretching for a race. The unfamiliarity of it, the noise, and the oppressive heat hovered over us like a starter gun poised to fire. We were used to running. It was our first instinct.

Matthew looked at us sympathetically. "It's all right. They just want to meet you."

Oh God. I really didn't want to go first.

Joseph took a deep breath and spoke, his voice deep and calming, "Let's all go out together." Then he grinned and said, "And if they turn on us, we'll throw Deshi to them and run like hell!"

Deshi punched him lightly. "Nice."

"No one's going to turn on you. They're just curious," Matthew said. He strolled through the curtains and out onto a dark, wooden stage. I

The Wall

peered after him. My heart pounded in my chest as I saw at least a few hundred pairs of eyes following him as he walked to the center. The voices settled down and they waited for him to speak. "Ok, they're here. Be nice…" He beckoned with his arm. The crowd started making noise again. Maybe they weren't that interested in us anyway. Joseph walked out and Matthew introduced him, then Deshi, and Alexei. Apella was standing next to me holding Hessa, her feet stuck in the same glue as mine. Then those dried-up old hands started shoving me ineffectually. "Just get on with it, dear." The crowd still hummed. Not really paying attention. Someone yelled out, confused, "I thought there were more?"

All right, I thought, *one, two, three*. I stepped out with Orry in my arms and dragged Apella with me.

I don't know what I was expecting. Not this.

They looked impressed. People clapped and cheered. I recognized some faces. Gwen, Gus, Cal, all smiling, with admiring expressions everywhere.

I felt ridiculous standing there on show. I waved at the ones I knew and sat down on the stage, my legs dangling over the edge. I looked up at Matthew as if to say, *What is this all about?* He leaned down and whispered, "You're the first escapees from the Woodlands. They're impressed."

People started approaching us, offering clothing, food, someone mentioned a vacant house they would help us fix up if we were interested. They also asked for help. Asked us what skills we had. A lot of people just wanted to touch Orry and Hessa, leaning over them cooing and fussing like they'd never seen a baby before. It was too much and I found my eyes tearing up. Kindness. Was this how people were supposed to behave?

Joseph was smiling but he looked tired. This was overwhelming, even for him. He held out his hand and I took it. Cal was staring at me again, looking back and forth between my face and our joined hands. I hoped it was a friendly stare but it made me feel uneasy.

The way they were all fussing over Orry and Hessa made me think. I scanned the crowd and could not pick out one child. Sometimes, I wished I had a notebook I could get out and jot down all the suspicious questions I had accumulated in my head. Where were all the children?

There was no time to ask. We found ourselves sucked into the crowd and carried outside on a wave of people. I looked back and could see Addy waving at me from the stage with a big grin on her face, her ruddy features becoming smaller and blurrier as the rush of people pulled us out on their tide.

My chest seized. *No.* We were letting ourselves be carried out on this current of strangers. I turned and battled my way back through the crowd. I wasn't going to leave anyone else behind. Joseph was inadvertently pushing me forward with the heel of his hand so when I turned around, he pushed me in the chest. Face to face, I frowned at him.

"I'm going back to get Addy," I said.

"Why?"

I ignored his question. It was too hard to explain. The others had stopped at a shop front that had been converted to a home. Red and white poles decorated either side of the door and a picture of a man's head floated over the entrance. These glimpses into the past had a bitter taste to them. The floating man with initials KFC, was probably dead, his dark-rimmed glasses and bowtie buried with him. They were inspecting it, I suppose, as a possible home.

I twisted my head to look at the sky, watching a black scribble of a bird lazily wind its way around in circles. I had longed to be free of them for so long but now the idea of us living apart frightened me. We had become each other's safety and comfort, an annoyance but an anchor in a too-fast changing future. I kept pushing past the flow of foot traffic, making my way to the theater. Joseph sighed his Rosa sigh and came thumping after me. Addy, I could trust. I wanted her advice on what we should do.

The Wall

When I got to the door, Addy was climbing carefully off the stage. I looked up at the red-velvet curtains. From here, they looked grander. I wondered about the people who had time to sit in these seats and watch a performance. It seemed lazy to me.

"What are you doing back here, girl?" Addy asked, raising her eyebrows.

"I... I want you to come with us. I didn't want to leave you behind," I said, not really sure why I came, just that I couldn't turn my back and walk away from one more person.

"Oh, I'm fine, silly girl. I would have caught up to you eventually," she replied, waving me away.

"I doubt it, the way you move," I laughed.

She took my arm and we walked outside, very slowly. The others were still standing at the shop front. I approached them and asked what was happening. A small group of Survivors was still around us, including Cal.

The Survivors had been busy while we were in quarantine. They'd found us all possible places to live—two here, and one up the hill. It made me very uncomfortable that we were being helped so much. I got the sense we would be asked for something in return soon enough. It was their way.

A woman, who introduced herself as Odval, swept her long, brown hair behind her ears as she talked in dips and mumbles. She pointed out all the main rooms, the patchwork pieces of furniture salvaged from various places. Her eyes were warm, dark pools framed with short, dark lashes and her skin was wrinkled, though only around her eyes and mouth. She looked down at the babies and sighed, sweeping Hessa's hair back gently with her finger. She emanated loss. I could tell, because it was same grief that sometimes steamed off my body in plumes. Where was her child? Did she lose one or just wished she had one? My mouth pursed as I thought. How did you even go about asking such a question?

Addy spoke, "How's your husband, Odval? I'll have those scarves and hats ready for you early next week."

Odval's sweet voice responded as though startled from deep thought, "Scarves? Oh yes, thanks Addy. I'll bring those casseroles over this afternoon."

Odval continued with her tour and then we were back at the front door. It was meant for one of us but we had to choose who would stay here.

After talking amongst ourselves, it was decided that Deshi and Hessa would stay. He wanted to be close to the hospital and science labs. We left them, promising to meet up later.

Apella and Alexei, who had been surprisingly quiet, were now whispering to each other. I wondered if this is what they had hoped to find. It was more than I had expected, but whether it met their expectations, the dream they had come up with when we left the Woodlands, I wasn't sure.

All I knew, as we walked to the next dwelling with Cal hovering too close, was, for now, we needed to rely on these people's kindness. But as soon as I could, I wanted to start repaying our debt.

22.

THE BLACK

Apella and Alexei chose the dwelling nearest to Deshi. It was on a second floor of a dilapidated apartment building and afforded them a view of what lay beyond the city. Like the wilderness around the Woodlands, the trees pressed up against the ruins. I decided to climb to the roof of the building. The survivors followed: Cal, Odval, and three other men.

We tripped up concrete stairs. Addy stayed behind, complaining of sore legs. The air was cold and had that barely breathed taste to it. Most of the rooms in this place were empty and the windows were blasted out. I shuddered to think of this town full of people. I felt that ball of hate for the Superiors rolling around, gathering weight and fire as it churned my insides. How could they live with so much death on their hands? They stood atop a giant pile of bodies. Innocent people.

We came to a heavy door and Cal tried to open it, pushing with his shoulder, but it wouldn't budge. Joseph tried to kick it in, but it just sent a shock through his leg and he limped back and sat on the stairs. I sensed a bit of male ego jousting going on in front of me.

"Why are we here anyway?" Joseph asked. He looked weary, but still managed to slide his hand up my calf. I smiled down at him. I didn't really know.

"I just want to see," I said simply, placing my hand on his neck and winding it around to his ear, raising goose bumps as I went.

One of the older men sighed, rolled his eyes, and pulled a pocketknife from his jacket. He jimmied the lock until we heard it click.

The big, metal door creaked open and we walked out onto a flat, concrete roof. It was windy and hard to hear what people were saying. I handed Orry to Odval and made my way to the edge. I wanted to see what lay beyond the city, beyond the woods.

It was like strips of color had been laid down across the earth. The lines unnaturally defined. There was the grey of the city pressed up against a line of trees. Then, beyond the woods, far enough away that it looked like the horizon ended close to it, was black. A curved line of grey retreated away from the tree line and disappeared into a menacingly dark abyss where no color touched or reflected. A bombsite.

I sensed a body behind me and thinking it was Joseph, I leaned into it.

"That's why they won't come here. We're too close to it," Cal said, his lips tickling my ear. I jolted forward and Cal grabbed my shoulders as I over balanced and nearly went over the edge.

He pulled me close against him so that I could feel his uneven breathing and gripped me tightly for a second before releasing me. I glanced wide-eyed over his shoulder to Joseph. His eyes showed strain but he seemed to be forcing his body not to react. I almost wished he would let himself go and punch Cal, but I didn't know how the others would react. Besides, if someone was going to punch him, it should be me.

"Is it safe? I mean to be this close?" I asked. Although I'm not sure what difference it would make. They were stuck here for now.

"On the whole. But we do have our problems," one of the men replied.

"No babies?" I guessed.

"No babies," he confirmed.

Odval stepped forward, cradling Orry like he was the sun. Beams of

The Wall

light touched her face and made her seem younger.

"Most of us came from places where the bombsites were much closer, so sadly the damage was already done before we even arrived here."

"I'm sorry," I said, touching her hand.

She just tipped her chin and gazed at Orry.

Joseph slid his arms around my waist and pressed his lips to my neck. The cold air burned away and my heart cartwheeled like it was trying to escape my chest.

"Where to now?" he whispered

"I want to go home," I said, angling my chin towards the Wall.

23

HOME

We collected Addy on our way down and were directed onto a spinner. When I said goodbye to Apella, I was surprised how it made me feel. I was leaving security. My replacement mother. If I left, I was admitting myself to adulthood. I wasn't sure I was ready.

I took her hands and squeezed, trying hard not to cry. "I'll see you soon," I said in a voice that was not my own, girlish and unsure of itself.

She put her hand up like she was going to touch my face but then put it back down and took a handful of her shirt instead. "You'll be fine, Rosa. And yes, you will see us soon. We are not far away."

I pressed my hands together and nodded. "I know."

I reassured myself that we would see them again. Soon.

The spinner hummed and did its miraculous twirling, revolving and revealing the view. I couldn't take it in. Exhaustion was getting the better of me. Joseph's hands and eyes were getting the better of me too. He gave me the look, like I was the only girl in the world, like he could close out everything else going on around us and just see me. He surety, his unwavering belief in us, was unnerving. Because, for me, everything felt tenuous, like at any second it would be snatched away. I believed in our love, but I knew it couldn't stay this way.

We arrived back at the Wall. The mid-afternoon shadow pressed down on the houses that lined the stone structure. Addy was talking,

The Wall

her striated lips moving, but I wasn't really listening. We piled out of the spinner and one of the men, who had only talked in grunts and sighs up until now, spoke. His voice clear and higher pitched than I would have expected. He spoke in short, clipped sentences. "Follow me. It's not much. It will need some work."

We followed them past several shingled shacks until the man turned suddenly and headed up a path. I clasped Joseph's hand tighter.

On either side were dormant plants sleeping under a layer of ice, which was starting to melt and pool in places. We climbed up three wooden steps and onto a narrow verandah. It was small. It was wonky. It was *perfect*.

The man swung open the door and showed us the simple lounge room, a couple of rickety chairs, a simple plumbed bathroom, and woodstove and kitchen in the corner. It had one bedroom with a wooden bed.

"Sorry there's no bedroom fer yer baby," he apologized gruffly, swiping his large hand across the back of his neck.

I laughed. It seemed ridiculous to apologize for such a thing. On the end of the bed were piles of folded clothes, blankets, and sheets. It was too much.

Set against the wall was the capsule I'd made for Hessa. It felt out of place in this homely picture.

In the corner metal glinted. I let go of Joseph's hand and walked over, the floorboards creaking under my weight. Kneeling down, I could see it was a pile of woodworking tools. My heart swelled and stayed large in my chest, taking in all this kindness and being at a loss as to what to do about it. My eyes connected with Joseph's. He was grinning, his hands clasped in front of him like he wasn't sure what to do with them.

The man introduced himself as Viktor. He shook both our hands roughly and explained that he lived two houses down the road. "Call in if you have any trouble. And err… I have a chipped countertop. I need it repaired. Keep catching my clothes on it." He looked at me. "Can you look at it for me? No rush. Just when you're settled."

"Ok," I said, my thoughts tangled, feeling a bit like a wrung, wet towel. I was running out of emotion.

The others said their goodbyes. Odval reluctantly left Orry in Joseph's arms. Addy and Cal remained. Joseph hovered over Cal. "Is there anything else?" he said impatiently. I could tell Cal was starting to really irritate him.

"Um. No. Although…"

"Yes?" Joseph was leaning over him now.

Cal turned to me. "Rosa, I have some things that need fixing too. Can I bring them to you tomorrow? I'll bring food in return."

I thought about it. It seemed like a bad idea to encourage him but if this is how we were to feed ourselves, I couldn't really afford to say no, not yet anyway. I avoided eye contact but accepted. "Yes. Give me a few days and then drop them off."

Joseph grunted at this and walked away from us.

Cal just stood there staring for a while until Addy gave him a sharp look and snapped, "Goodbye, young man," not so gently shoving him out the door.

As if startled from a dream, he staggered backwards and left.

"How did you know this was the house I would choose? I mean, the tools, the capsule. You knew I would end up here," I said.

Addy waved me off. "Ha. You're not the big mystery you think you are, girl."

I smiled and stood with my arm around Joseph's waist.

Addy turned to us, her lips curling. "Look at you two."

"What?" I asked suspiciously.

"It's just lovely to see a young family again."

I couldn't help but cringe a little. This was harder for me than I liked to admit, this instant family made in a tube, planted out of nowhere,

The Wall

now expected to grow straight, tall, and normal. But how did you grow a normal life from that, when everything was so backwards? I tried to put it out of my mind for now and take in our home.

Our home. The words were heavy in my head. Instead of happiness, I felt guilt. Why me?

Sometimes, I felt like I was tethered to the ghosts of my past like a bunch of balloons tied to my wrist. They were always pulling at me, trying to move on, but I couldn't let them go and they couldn't let me go. It made me want to keep moving, keep running.

I tried to say something to Addy but I couldn't find the right words. I think she sensed it, touching my shoulder gently and saying, "Don't worry, girl. You'll get used to it. I'll be round to check on you from time to time." She tapped me once and said, "You know you're safe here."

I swear, when people said things like that, it made me feel less safe. It sounds like they're trying to convince me of something they're not sure of themselves.

Addy tottered out, her dark brown skirt swishing like grass shifting in the wind as she shut the door without turning around.

Bang! The timber door rattled in its frame and we were alone.

I took in Joseph's face. He had shaved when we were in quarantine but stubble was already growing back, kissing his chin and softening his strong jaw. His golden hair was weaving itself across his forehead. Such a delicate balance of hair linked together. He gazed down at Orry and then had to flick his head to keep the hair out of his eyes. So much had changed since I met him, swinging his legs atop a concrete pillar, grinning down at me like he didn't have a care in the world. We were older now—I think we were stronger too. And we had a baby.

I snorted. Thinking of how stupid it was that we had a baby. The most we'd done was kissed and we had a baby.

He looked at me, confused by my laughter. "What's so funny?"

He walked over and put his hand in my hair, gently tucking it behind my ear. I shivered and forgot what I was laughing about. He leaned down and kissed the corner of my mouth. "We're home." I felt him breathe it in, his chest expanding at the words.

Could I stay here? Could I cut the ties and let the ghosts wind their way up to the sky? I wasn't sure. But I knew I wanted to be here with him.

Orry started to cry and I settled into the old cane chair lined with furs and a ratty quilt to feed him.

24

MORE

As I fed Orry, Joseph busied himself around the house. I heard him shaking out sheets and making the bed. The snap of the cloth sent shivers down my spine. The air felt charged, nervousness and anticipation drumming out a rhythm in front of my eyes. In my mind, I was imagining doing things I had never done before and it both scared and charmed me with its possibilities.

The truth was, I wasn't sure what I wanted to do and I probably should have decided that first, instead of waiting to see how I felt as things progressed.

I heard the fridge door open and shut behind me. "They've made us some food," I heard him mumble uncomfortably.

Pots clanged, drawers were opened and closed. I wondered whether he had really cooked before. It seemed like a lot of noise for reheating food. For all his strength and confidence, I could tell his nervousness was making him clumsy. This was beyond weird, for both of us. This was the first time we had truly been alone, without a baby between us, the threat of someone waking around the fire, or a doctor or nurse barging in on us.

I wrapped Orry up and put him in the capsule, resolving to make him a cot first thing tomorrow.

This peaceful calm of domestic life was really only an idea; it was an abstract thought that had no place in reality. But I let it fool me. I let myself think about being with Joseph, sleeping with him, and everything that went with it. But it was not that simple. I wish I'd known that.

After a dinner where eyes were shooting spears of desire across the table, I excused myself to take a shower. I could hear him clattering about, cleaning up. The water was heated by the woodstove so it was lukewarm at best. I undressed and jumped in and out as quickly as possible. Homemade soap that smelled like grass and lanolin made no lather but at least I smelled somewhat clean.

I stared at my face in the mirror. It was a conflicted image. I looked like a child. A mother. I'm not sure woman was a good description for me yet.

Woman. Is that what I would be after? It seemed a little too easy for things to click into place just because of that. I shook my hair out and tried to make it look less clumpy. They'd left towels, toothbrushes, soap, but no hairbrush. Running my hands through it, I thought of my mother. The same thick mane of dark brown hair touched silver with age. The seams started to bulge a little around my chest. I missed her. I didn't want to but I did. She'd skipped into my thoughts more and more lately without permission.

I changed into the pajamas I'd found on the bed and opened the door.

Joseph was standing there, leaning against a kitchen chair. Head down like he was counting while someone went to hide. He looked up at me and bit his bottom lip, his eyes bright, and kind of dazzling.

"Are you tired?" he stuttered.

"I guess." I wasn't. At all.

He walked over to me and took my hand, leading me to the bedroom, the bed he'd carefully made. But something was dragging me back. Those ghost balloons, those puffs of air, suddenly had so much weight to them I was struggling to keep my feet. I was dragging lead bricks behind me, scratching across the floor. *Wait*, they whispered. I ignored them.

The Wall

We sat on the bed. The wood frame creaked gently. The candlelight pooled around both of us, pulling the warmth from the timber out to dance in our eyes. We were bathed in glowing light. He pulled my face towards his own and stared into my eyes. Could he see the terrified girl inside? He turned his head at an angle and smiled sweetly.

"Are you ok?" he whispered.

I nodded gingerly. I put my hands in his hair and dipped his head down. *Just kiss him*, I thought. *The feelings will go away. Maybe you can forget about things for a while. Your grief doesn't have to guide everything you do.*

I pressed my lips to his and we were gone. Kisses were long and then small bursts of short pecks followed. He kissed my neck; I followed his jawline and worked my way to his ear. His strong arms lifted me up and I swung my leg over and sat in his lap.

Back arched, I leaned down and hastily unbuttoned his shirt. It was all very fast. Rushed. Yes, it was rushed. He slid his hands under my shirt and pulled it over my head. It floated to the ground. Then he stopped. He took my body in. The way he looked at me... I didn't feel shy or exposed. His face was calm, although his breathing was fast. I could barely look at his chest; it was a little too much, too beautiful. How could someone look that good? I just watched his eyes roaming over my body, the gaze touching me with warmth.

He put his hands on my shoulders and let them glide slowly down my arms.

"I love you," he said, face flushed pink, his eyes golden, shining brighter than before.

I realized something, or at least I was starting to. "I love you too," I whispered and then I paused. "Damn it! I really love you."

I covered myself with my arms and jumped off his lap. I wasn't enough for him just yet. There were some things missing that I had to find before I would be ready for this.

He looked so confused and completely dashed. His brows pulled back. He swiped his forehead with his hand and tried to catch my eyes. "You love me, damn it?" he said. "What does that mean?"

I didn't really know what to say. I knew I was hurting him. That he probably felt rejected. I grabbed my shirt and shrugged into it, feeling awful. Like I had slapped him, even if I knew, somehow it was best for both of us.

"I'm sorry," I said, insufficiently. "I'm not sure what to say. Can we talk about it tomorrow?"

I kissed him, wholly, intensely, feeling the fire of molten gold washing over us both. I wrapped that feeling up, let it cool, and hung it like a chain around my neck. The feeling was not gone, just postponed.

I could feel his restlessness; I knew he wanted to press me for answers. But he knew me. He knew he would have to wait.

We curled up under the covers. He reached out his hand and placed it on my hip, then lifted it tentatively. "Can I?"

"Of course."

I flipped over and snuggled into the crook of his arm, laying my head across his bare chest, exhaling slowly. It would be easier if I could just let it all go, but I couldn't. And I knew the truth of the matter was—if I loved him, there was no rush. It deserved more than we were giving it.

As I let sleep grab me with its wispy, white fingers, my mind wandered to my friends, friends I sorely missed. Rash would have been able to make light of this. And as I pictured him, his dark eyebrows raised, absolute mischief in his eyes, I knew he wasn't a ghost, and maybe that's why I couldn't let him go. I didn't know what happened to him.

Clara. Clara was gone. And I carried her memory around with me, holding it close to my chest, stitching it in there. She would have offered some consolation, some wisdom, to make me see the sense of my decision.

I cursed their absence. Then I cursed my selfishness, my undeserving

The Wall

luck at being the one who survived, who got away.

I turned my head and started to weep. A pathetic, self-pitying noise that I was ashamed emanated from my lips.

Joseph's hand cupped the tip of my shoulder. "Rosa," he whispered tentatively, "was it something I did?" His words were so sincere, so full of worry. Was I always to be a source of worry for him? How could I tell him, in this moment, that I missed Rash?

I couldn't.

He pulled my body back towards his chest. It curled away from him, curled around a feeling I couldn't quite name, but that was tied up with missing, aching, unfinished business and somewhere in there, anger.

The last thing I remember thinking before sleep finally engulfed me was, *Mother, I curse you.*

You didn't prepare me for anything. I am lost and you probably don't even care if I'm alive or dead. You taught me nothing about what it would be like, how it would feel to give yourself to a man. To trust him entirely. How could you teach me anything about love? You chose so poorly and I have been paying for that choice my whole life.

I wish you had chosen me.

25

REMINDER

I forgot where we were. I let the cozy, timber home envelope me and make me feel safe. I let the people in. Let them help me. They made me believe in something that wasn't real. I forgot that with the green, the plushness, and shiny plant life that pushed up and surrounded us, with the nourishment it provided came—the fur, the claws, the teeth.

This was not our place. We were borrowers. No longer were we the dominant species. Our time had passed.

We were small in number and frame.

We were supposed to run.

Climb.

Cower

I forgot.

Joseph and I danced around each other the next couple of days. Neither of us willing to bring it up, until it went too long without being addressed and we started to just ignore it. We looked after Orry, explored the surrounding forests, cooked, and cleaned.

I began constructing a cot for Orry, which calmed me down immeasurably. I walked up to the patch of woods that sprung up just past the final row of houses. I shook down the bendy saplings, chipping my numb fingertips with tiny icicles. These trees had bad timing, much like myself. They'd seeded in the wrong season. They'd popped up just before snow had started to fall and would never survive winter. Their bendy trunks made the perfect frame for the rocking cot I wanted to make.

I cut them down and hauled them back to the house, dragging up filthy ice as I went. Quite often a neighbor would see me and offer assistance. Everyone was so friendly it made me feel a bit ill. I tried to be nice, said thank you, offered them help in return. But it all felt like pressure. I just hoped I would get there eventually.

Joseph seemed unused to idleness and after a few days, he was aching to do something. He took a spinner down to Deshi and a few hours later he came back with a job offer. He was going to work in the hospital, study under Matthew and become a real doctor.

"You sure you can handle all that blood and guts?" I teased.

"I handle you on a daily basis. Can't be worse than that!" he said. Quickly pulling it back and saying, "Sorry. I mean, I was just joking."

I rolled my eyes. Things were too polite between us.

I was gathering clients of my own. After I'd finished my cot, curious eyes poked through windows. Then hands rapped on my door. Once they saw what I could do, I was asked to build things, fix things, and come up with designs. This I could do.

Careen even came and swapped game for company. She ate with us sometimes. She seemed to have very little cooking skills despite her affinity for carving meat. I taught her the basics. It was nice feeling... like I had something to give, to offer.

One night after we had shared dinner, we decided to stoke the fire and sit up for a while. I'd started to trust Careen a little more with Orry and she held him close, touching the tip of his nose and showing him her big teeth. He reached up and clasped her pledge necklace, twisting it in his fingers. We still hadn't been asked about that and I wasn't going to volunteer.

Joseph's eyelids were fluttering; I could tell he was close to sleep. He had been at the hospital a lot. He was avoiding me.

Careen watched me, her eyes twitching a bit.

"What's the matter with you? You having a stroke?" I whispered

She blushed, her usual confident demeanor awkward.

"No," she said. "It's just, I wanted to say something. You don't make it very easy."

"What?" I was worried she was going to profess her love for Joseph.

"I met someone," she whispered. It was her treasured secret. I had the cruel thought that maybe she had invented it in her head, but held my tongue.

"That's... nice. Who?"

"Oh, he's a hunter. He's a bit older but then everyone is. He's great! I'll bring him up to meet you both." I bobbed my head along as she chattered on about him. I was happy for her. Maybe he was deaf! My ears were filling with suds and water noises as I started to feel myself drifting off too.

Then we heard it.

It was a sudden and terrifying roar, a hollowing sound that seemed to be louder and wider than any one creature could make. But it wasn't the worst noise to hear; I could have heard that noise a million times over the noise that followed.

It was the scream of the worst suffering known. Like someone had reached inside this man, pulled out his spine, and was rattling it for fun. And for all I know, that's precisely what was happening.

Careen stood up and handed me Orry, gracefully running to the rifle she had left against the wall.

"Tigers," she muttered to herself.

"What? You can't go out there," I said, shocked at how readily she jumped at the chance to put herself in danger. She'd certainly changed

The Wall

from the girl who'd left Joseph for dead.

Joseph snapped out of light sleep and strode to the door. I caught his arm and felt him stiffen.

"What are you doing?" I screeched.

"Someone's hurt; I have to try to help."

"What?" I didn't know exactly what a tiger was but by the roar and the scream that followed, I knew it must be dangerous. Careen was gripping her rifle hard, turning her knuckles white. I looked at them both, pleading with my eyes. "Please. You can't go out there, neither of you can."

Joseph glanced at me briefly. He relaxed his tense shoulders, bringing them down in a jerky movement like he was trying to convince himself not to be angry. If he was going to explain, or try to make me feel better, he decided against it.

"Barricade the door," he yelled as he stormed out, following Careen. A pair of perfect-looking, perfect idiots. I was furious, my thoughts harried and weakening. *What was he trying to prove?* I dragged a chair over and jammed it under the door. I then started my nervous pacing around the room, every now and then peeking out the window.

I couldn't see anything and apart from the initial scream, there was no sound. I tapped the glass nervously with my newly grown back nails.

Click, click, click.

Grabbing the torch, I scanned the backyard, then went to the front yard and did the same. The thin stream of light barely managed to harass the darkness out of the way so I could see one snippet of a scene. I did this for about half an hour, gripping Orry close and trying to breathe. As I walked, I got angrier and angrier, feeling flames wrapping around me and heating my temper. If he wasn't dead, I was going to kill him.

On my rounds of poking the torch out the window, something flagged in the corner of the small shaft of light. A paw. It stopped dead in the torchlight like it was a solid barrier. The creature was a still as stone but in the cold I could see mist floating away from its muzzle. I moved the torch inch by inch over its body as slowly as I could, the light shaking and dancing with the trembling of my hands.

It was the strangest creature I had seen yet. Its flame-orange fur pooled in its chest and then fanned out in a diluted white and orange spray. Along its back, black stripes ran like jagged scratches, hugging its ribcage. The black and orange markings spread all the way down to a fluffy, long tail that was only slightly shifting under the light. It was enormous.

It had been facing forward up until now, its long body pointing towards the other homes, its face focused on something further away. I flicked the torch light behind it, discovering several other paws, under several other tall, muscular creatures. There were five of them. When I came back to the leader, it turned and seemed to be looking directly at me. My heart stopped. I swear its ears reacted to the change in my heartbeat. It knew there was blood flowing through my veins. I could feel it pumping hard and inviting this terrible creature closer.

It opened its mouth wide and I could see the damaging fangs. It didn't roar—it yawned. Had it had its fill? The idea made me feel sick. *That man, that poor man.*

A shot cracked open the silence and the animal started running. I held my breath as they turned and ran through the gap between our house and our neighbors. They went file like foot soldiers in ineffectual camouflage. My gaze connected with the man that lived next door, his eyes unblinking and wide with fear in the window across from ours.

They padded through noiselessly, a whisk of orange and white blur, and they were gone.

The entire house shuddered in relief. But I couldn't un-see that scene. Now I knew they were out there.

The door rattled and I jumped. Fervent knocking startled me to action. No animal was going to politely knock at the door. I let out a

The Wall

hysterical laugh at the thought of it. 'Excuse me, would you mind terribly if I came in and ate you?'

"Rosa, open up." Joseph's voice was ragged. I knew he had to be alive. Somehow, I thought I would have to feel something if he were really in trouble.

I opened the door and several men pushed past me, dragging what I assume used to be a person under what was left of his arms. I gagged involuntarily.

They laid him down. He stared at the ceiling, a barely audible whimper coming from his bluish lips. How he was alive, I'll never know. I wondered whether will took over at that point. His body was devastated. There were parts of him that didn't look human, straggly streams of torn flesh attached to his body, or protruded out of his shredded pant leg. Anyone could tell he was a dead man. He must have been hanging on to life by sheer force of will.

Let go, I thought.

The men stood around him in a broken semi-circle, bewildered looks on their faces, gripping their guns like they were teddy bears.

I watched Joseph calmly and methodically move around his patient, wrapping up his wounds, compressing bleeders. All the while, talking to the man in reassuring whispers. It gave me insight into what he was capable of, his talent and his strength. If it was possible, it made me love him more.

He looked up, his eyes piercing and focused. "Has anyone called the hospital?"

One of the men stepped forward. "He won't survive."

Joseph's broad back shivered. The acceptance was in his face but when he looked at the man, he spoke comforting words.

Joseph put his hand to his forehead like he was trying to read something in his head. He rolled up a jacket and placed it under the man's head. Reaching into his small medical bag, he pulled out a syringe, loading it with clear fluid.

"For the pain," he said.

The man took his one good arm and crawled it to his chest with his fingertips, finding the pledge charm and gripping it tightly. His dark face was going grey as the blood drained from his body.

I kneeled down at his head, trying not to look at the rest of him, just his face. His eyes rolled around but when he found mine, they locked onto them. "Marina? Marina," he gurgled, blood pooling in his mouth.

I nodded. I would be Marina. I stroked his hair

He stared at me and I could see a smile crossing his lips as he breathed out once and never breathed back in.

It took the men, Careen, and I a couple of hours to clean up the blood. I made them cups of tea and tried to keep them in the house but they were anxious to get back out there. They wanted to make sure everyone was safe and then report to the town leaders.

Joseph was in shock. After his efforts, he'd collapsed in a chair and hadn't moved since. His face was pale, with his shirt rolled up to his elbows and crusted with blood. His eyes stared vacantly off into space.

After everyone left and Orry was settled, I turned my attention to Joseph. He was shaking a little, a dark look on his face. I tugged his sleeves down over his wrists, running my finger along the old, scooped-out scar on his forearm. I gently pulled the blood-soaked shirt over his head and tried to put a new one on.

He grabbed both my wrists tightly and shook me once. He stared at me intensely, his green eyes swirling and slightly wild.

"Just leave it," he whispered almost angrily and pulled me into his arms roughly. I balled the shirt into my fist and threw it on the floor.

I curled up in his lap and pressed my ear to his chest, listening to

The Wall

his heart beating so fast I thought it would wear out. I slowly moved my hand in circles across his skin until his breathing slowed. We fell asleep in the chair. Both reminded that we were not protected and that even though we were in a house, this was the wilderness. We were prey.

26

MEETING

The day after our encounter with the tigers, we were summoned to a meeting at the movie theater. Although to me, it seemed more like we had walked into the middle of an argument. I wondered if this was how they ran things? It almost made me miss the rigid order of the Superiors. At least they just got on with things. These people were talking in circles.

Five people sat on the stage behind a low desk covered by a frayed tablecloth. A podium was set up facing them, where people were taking turns addressing the leaders. It was a mess of yelling, swearing, and heated emotions. What I could gather was people were upset about the tigers and they were thinking of moving the 'plan' date forward. It felt like I'd flipped open to the middle of a book. I could read the words, get a sense of the action, but had no idea why they were doing what they were doing. As they talked though, things started to clear.

"We're not safe here," a man with ash-blond hair shouted, brandishing his fist in the air.

"Calm down, everyone. I'll admit that what happened was a horrible tragedy, but we all know not to go out at night. Feliks knew that too."

A woman piped up, "Maybe we should go ahead with the plans, you know, the ones we've been talking about for years. Maybe this is the motivation we need." She glanced sideways at me. I shrunk away. What did they want with me?

The Wall

"Let's think about this logically. We have few weapons and no choppers. Our numbers are small. It's not the right time," a man on the stage said calmly.

"What about the Spiders?" a woman yelled. I noticed it was Gwen. Her eyes fierce, she seemed ready to storm the concrete walls of the Woodlands right then and there.

I was lost. I turned to Cal to ask but then felt an arm link with mine. My first reaction was to shake it off. It was too familiar, that was Clara's place. The arm felt like crinkled paper and I knew it was Addy.

People obviously knew what Gwen was talking about because the emotions in the room raised higher, voices and heated breath pushing the roof off the place.

"What's a Spider?" I whispered to Addy.

She closed her eyes and took a deep breath. I felt like saying, *Get on with it, old woman*. Every time she spoke it was an ordeal, like it took too much energy to open her mouth at all. "Spiders are our people on the inside. They live in the Rings and feed us information about what's going on in there."

The name dawned on me... like the spider that had nearly killed Joseph. These people would have to be invisible, part of the rings, unnoticeable. Clever.

One of the leaders spoke again, trying to regain some order. "Look! The Spiders have reported unease amongst the people. They have now announced that no children will be born after a certain date. They have provided contraception and have already started their usual pattern of selecting out examples to punish. The Superiors do seem to be plotting something. They are pulling more children into the Classes and training most of them as soldiers. Of course, this doesn't sound good. But they seem to have a timeframe in mind. They are waiting for winter to end before they move. As far as we know, they are still unaware of our location. We have time. We need to keep gathering intel and find out what else the Superiors know."

The room swayed and swirled with hundreds of voices. Some angry, some scared. Most just trying to understand what she had just said—me especially.

A man on the panel coughed and said finitely, "We'll step up patrols of the wall border but no more talk of takeovers. We're not ready."

Takeovers? The idea filled me with equal measures of hope and fear. They couldn't possibly, could they? If they could free the people… my mind started wandering. I could see my mother, Rash, Henri. But what if the people didn't want to be freed? My thoughts turned to Paulo. Someone I hadn't really allowed into my head since I'd left. Freedom was a hot coal in his hands; he'd sooner fling it back over the wall. I couldn't imagine the people in Pau staging an uprising. They were too beaten down, too scared. I had an idea where the Survivors could start, though, to get those numbers they needed—Clara's hometown, Palma.

The idea of a Woodlands without the dark shadow of the Superiors hovering over it was an attractive idea, dangerous, but deliciously enticing. I knew if they wanted to do it, I wanted to be part of it. I needed to be.

Someone yelled out, "Has no one thought about the nursery? All those innocent children, those teenage mothers. We have to help them." At this statement, I nearly fell over. So it was nurseries they had decided upon. When Alexei had first brought it up, when I escaped the Woodlands, he'd said they hadn't decided whether they would raise the babies in big nurseries or billet them out to childless couples. My stomach turned. That could have been Orry and Hessa.

"We will help them. These things take time and planning. Let's vote and then get on to what we are really here for," a man with dark hair pulled into a plait at the nape of his neck said as he found us in the crowd and smiled. I started. Was this an ambush?

"All in favor of holding off on the plans for the Woodlands, raise your hand."

The crowd shuffled then two thirds of them raised their hands. Did I get a vote?

Joseph raised his hand with the majority. The same man with the plait looked down at us and said, "Not yet, young man. You are not pledged."

I knew very quickly, and so certainly, that I was surprised at myself. I was ready to take the pledge. I wanted a say. I wanted to be part of this community, to protect it and perhaps help it spread to my old home.

"So it is decided. Now, will the young couple who so bravely and kindly helped Feliks in his final hours please step onto the stage."

I found myself leading Joseph, eagerly wanting that charm around my neck.

It wasn't really a ceremony. It was too casual for that but it had weight to it. I felt the sense of history I was being welcomed into. This would be our home, our people, and I was pleased with that.

The man placed the necklaces in each of our palms.

"Do you know the pledge?"

We nodded.

We spoke separately. I went first. I let the words roll around in my mouth, making sure I really believed them. Realizing, of course, I did.

I am a survivor. I live beyond the wall. I give shelter to those that need it. I am not chosen but I choose to live.

It was done. And as I scanned the crowd, I saw Deshi, Apella, and Alexei smiling at us from the back of the crowd, their new necklaces shining under the warm theater lights. I needed to talk to them, find out what they thought about this idea of storming the Woodlands. Without a very thorough plan, it would be suicide.

27

WARNING

The weeks had rolled by like the rolling hills I saw when I looked out my window. The white was less than the green, the scales tipping. Winter was receding and I could see the changes, in the land and in the people. My people. I never thought I would belong anywhere. In fact, I was sure of it. But now I belonged to a place, a person, and a family.

The sense I got from these people was that they were independent but chose to be around each other. No one was forced. They were encouraged. I probably needed more encouragement than most. Trust was hard for me. It always would be.

Now that we had made our choices and our pledge, we were left to our own devices. Our home was taking shape slowly as I started receiving payment for my work. A small pile of salvaged toys had accumulated in the corner. Toys were another fairly foreign thing to us. Joseph said I should make a box to put them in until Orry was old enough to play with them.

They had tracked the pack of tigers past the city and set up surveillance at the known entry points to make sure we were never caught unawares again. Things had settled and I felt safe and comfortable. There was still talk about approaching the Woodlands but until winter was over, it wasn't practical.

Alexei said it was fascinating that the tigers now hunted in groups.

The Wall

Prior to the Woodlands, they were a solitary, shy species. Prior to the Woodlands, when people had consumed most of the planet, they were nearly extinct. I guess our near extinction had been a blessing to the wildlife.

"It's a fast forward in evolution," he said excitedly. He had decided to do what he was best at, categorizing and organizing the Survivors' history and what they'd found in the city. Apella had been asked several times to assist in helping them with their reproduction problems but she couldn't. She said she didn't trust that she would get it right this time and it brought back too many bad memories. She was content to return to doctoring.

I liked visiting them but found it easier on my own. With Joseph there, it felt like we were all keeping a secret from him. Apella was still so adamant that he never learned why she lost her baby.

I found out that Gus had approached Joseph to join him in their little surveillance group but he declined. I was relieved; the idea of him and Cal working together conjured up small horrors. He enjoyed studying under Matthew in the hospital. He took Orry with him half the time; there were always people willing to watch him. It was quite far from where we lived but transport was not a problem. Everyone used the spinners.

As I was accepted into the community and accepted it myself, I learned more and more about the way things worked. The technology was baffling. Instead of using all their energy to control people, they had developed far beyond the capabilities of the Woodlands in a lot of ways. Their biggest problem seemed to be infertility. There were no kids. I mean, *no* kids. Cal was the youngest person in the whole town. Although, now, I guess Orry was, followed closely by Hessa.

I looked over at my pile of work, eager to get started. Bataar had asked me to modify his sled, streamline it but also camouflage it better. The woman down the road had asked me to fix her dining chairs. I didn't do it for money. Money was inconsequential here. Bataar said he would give me furs and the woman down the road would cook me four dinners. It worked. Most of my business came from one person though. Cal.

We had an uneasy friendship or not even that really—we were dependent on him for food so I had to be nice to him. But I felt like he was watching me all the time, the eyes I once thought were warm and bright, now looked more solid and sticky. I usually tried to prioritize his work so I could get him out of the house quicker. But he always came back with more. At the moment, I was fixing a bunch of drawers he said wouldn't open and shut properly. Joseph said I should tell him to get lost. It wasn't that easy though. At least this way there was a definitive amount of time he would spend here. I had no doubt he would come up with other excuses to visit anyway. I felt sorry for him. He seemed lonely.

Cal was a good resource for information too. I asked him questions about the town while I worked.

"So how does the government work here? I mean, it seemed a little disorganized to me. The way people were yelling and arguing," I asked as I planed down the edge of the drawer, noticing it looked like someone had kicked the base in with their foot.

"What do you mean?" Cal said, staring at my dark hands as I smoothed the edge of the drawer, getting covered in sawdust.

"Is there one ruler, you know, like the Superiors? The man with the plait looked like he had the final say in things."

"No, not really. People nominate themselves and they get chosen by a lottery draw. There are five leaders at any one time and they rotate them every six months." It couldn't have been more different from the Woodlands.

I dusted my hands off and went to pull myself up. Cal extended his

The Wall

hand but I declined. He looked angry, for a second, and then he forced a smile to his face. "Thanks for the work, Cal. I'll let you know when I'm done," I said, trying to get rid of him.

"Are you trying to get rid of me?" he asked, his face twisted, his hand gripping the back of the chair too hard. His emotions swayed in and out of control like this. One minute he was fine, the next he seemed like he would explode with anger.

I waved my hand dismissively, "No, no. I just have a lot to do. It won't be very interesting for you." *Please let that work.*

He jumped up and down, his voice sounding childlike, "Oh I do find it interesting. I don't mind."

I wiped my forehead. "Please don't be offended, Cal, but I find it quite hard to work with people staring at me. I don't even like Joseph hovering over me when I'm working."

He looked hurt but he hung on to the last thing I said. "So you don't let *him* watch you work but you let me, at least for a little while?" He said it like he was winning. He never said Joseph's name, it was always *him* or *that guy*.

"I guess…"

This seemed to satisfy him. He got up, touching the end of my plait on the way out. I shuddered. I hadn't told Joseph about Cal's inappropriate behavior. He already disliked him without adding to it. We needed the food he brought in return for my work. For now, I had to put up with it.

Orry was with Joseph at the hospital today so it was quiet. Only wood creaking and the sounds of my tools punctuated the silence. I loved it. I emptied my mind and focused on the details before me, the simplicity of the grain, the rough give of the timber, as I turned it from something boring to something useful.

I jerked my head to the window when I thought I heard someone walking by the side of the house. I got up, rubbing the back of my neck, and peered out the window but no one was there. People were close here. It wasn't unusual to see someone poke their head in your window to ask for something. In Pau, I never even knew our neighbors' names.

I abandoned Cal's drawers and pulled out something I had been working on for myself. Under our bed was a toy train. I had carved the main engine roughly. I was basing it on the picture on the brochure we had followed so many months ago. It seemed fitting. I was turning it over in my hands, trying to work out what to do next, when I saw a reflection in the mirror facing opposite the bedroom window. It was fast but I swear I saw dark brown curls. I laid the train down carefully on the bed and went into the icy yard to investigate. I ran quickly. The cold was biting as I hadn't put a jacket on. I walked up one side of the little shack and then doubled back to the front. Cal was skulking down the front path.

"Cal!" I yelled sharply.

Maybe I should have ignored him, let him go, but I was furious. I didn't like being watched. And I wondered if this was the first time. He hunched his shoulders and turned around. Face pink, he looked at me guiltily. "Were you spying on me?" I could feel my face getting hot.

"I... I'm sorry. I forgot something," he stammered, lying.

I thought about it for a millisecond then I walked right up to him, probably closer than was necessary, and said through gritted teeth, "Yes, I think you did. Come get your drawers. I'm not working for you anymore."

The apology ran from his face like melting candlewax, revealing pure anger. Anger and humiliation. He stormed into the house, picking up the drawers, dropping them several times as he went, and stormed out again. I should have left it there, but I didn't. I held open the door and as he passed me, I muttered, "I know you broke them on purpose."

He turned to face me, his body shaking. He shrugged. It was exaggerated, like he would dislocate his shoulders with the abrupt force of it. He sighed and stared at me, his eyes blinking away tears. He looked like he wanted to say something but he couldn't get the words out. Then he clattered away, throwing the drawers under a tree, and hopping on a passing spinner.

I was relieved. I could have handled it better but I also could have handled it worse. Hopefully, he would get over it and move on. Whatever his fixation on me was, it was over.

I returned inside and put the kettle on the hearth, warming my hands around it as the water boiled. There was always comfort in these everyday things. The kettle whistled and I made some tea. The people here had technologies, but chose to live simply, hence the wood stove, the candlelight. I loved the contradiction of it, the choice of it.

I watched the steam wind its way up to the ceiling, feeling a pull in my chest. I tried not to look back but occasionally, without meaning to, my brain tunneled that way against my will. Sometimes I felt myself standing under the trees, sparks of fire twirling into the night sky. Clara could always see things I couldn't see. I wondered what she would make of this. I think she would have told me to be a bit kinder to Cal.

The sky was darkening. I closed the shutters and went outside to grab some wood. Joseph would be home soon with Orry. Mrs. 'what's her face' would be coming over with dinner. I couldn't remember her name, Mrs. Squishy something, or maybe I just thought that because her face was all puffy. I laughed.

I worked until Joseph returned. My hands were rough and dusty.

28

NOT YET

We ate our dinner, watching each other over the flicker of the candlelight. Avoiding the subject. The one that never came to any end because I couldn't decide what I wanted to do.

Orry was fast asleep in the cot I'd made, snoring and rumbling in the corner of the modest living room.

I knew I was being unfair. And part of me didn't even know why I was behaving this way. But I still felt that backwards feeling.

We went to bed early. It was still light, although darkening fast. Lying next to him, I was scared to open my mouth but also scared not to. After what had happened that first night, something needed to be said.

He spoke before I could. "I'm sorry about that night." Ever since we'd almost slept together, things had been awkward between us. We had avoided the subject for way too long.

"No, I'm sorry," I said.

Ugh! This was impossible. This was not us. It was too uncomfortable, too polite.

We both laughed. His hand grazed my bare leg and I shivered. "You cold?" I nodded, even though I wasn't. He pulled me closer to his body, so warm, almost too warm. I sighed. It shouldn't be this hard. He put his lips to my bare shoulder, slipping my shirt down and kissing my collarbone. My head was in a gold mist. I blew it away.

Concentrate.

The Wall

"Do you ever get the feeling that some of this is a bit wrong?" I asked. Staring into his beautiful eyes, wanting to dive into them and forget sense.

He raised his eyebrows, that recognizable combination of amusement and worry. "What do you mean?"

"Well, we live together, we have a child, it's like we're married, but we've never even, well, you know…" I was making a mess of this. "It's a bit back to front."

He smiled, his eyes wandering over my face towards my neck. "Well, that's easily fixed," he said with a chuckle, pulling me on top of him and kissing me passionately. *Don't get lost*, I told myself.

I extricated myself and rolled off his chest to lie facing him again. "No, I don't think it's that simple. I want to go back. Back to the start. Slow it down."

He looked shattered by the idea but he nodded. "Well, what do you want to do? Am I supposed to court you?" When he said it like that, it sounded stupid.

"Um, no. Well, sort of. Oh, I don't know. Just forget it." I leaned in to kiss him but he pulled back before my lips connected.

Amused, he said, "No, if you want this, it's fine with me, but I think there should be some ground rules." Oh great!

I thought about courting in Pau. It was about as romantic as cold porridge. Usually, the man announced his intentions to the woman. She said yes or no and they were married in a few weeks to months. I'd never seen anyone holding hands or kissing. Every time Paulo went near my mother in a romantic way, one, I nearly threw up and two, she usually jumped out of her skin like his touch gave her an electric shock, but not the pleasant kind.

In Pau, I think there was love around but it was a thin kind of love. Guarded. Everything that goes with love, marriage, and children was so very tainted. How could you give your whole if you knew it was going to be taken away from you? I couldn't imagine Joseph and me 'courting' in the traditional sense.

He was distractedly swirling his fingers in loose strands of my hair when I said, "Ok, what kind of rules?" as I eyed him suspiciously. His face lit up with mischief, dark shadows grazing his face in the dying light behind us. It irritated me. He wasn't taking me very seriously.

"You tell me if some of these things are acceptable." I nodded. "Can I do this?" He leaned in and kissed me lightly on the mouth.

"Yes."

"What about this?" He traced the curve of my neck with his fingertips out to my shoulders.

I shivered and bit my lip. "Yes." Then he brought his fingers across my chest and started towards my breasts. I shook my head. He stopped.

"Maybe I should write this down." He grinned.

"It's not a game," I said, trying to sound serious but even I couldn't suppress a smirk.

"All right, all right. We'll start slow, and no 'you know' until you say you're ready," he said, the matter of fact 'doctorness' coming out in his speech. His eyes lifted under his brow, unsure. "But you will be ready, one day, right?"

My body was ready, ready right then, but I was trying to listen to my head this time. "Right," I said. "Just not yet."

He pulled me into a tight embrace. "This ok?" he said. I giggled.

"Stop it. Now you're just being annoying!"

I fell asleep in his arms. I think we had it sorted. Maybe.

2.9

MENACE

I always thought strength came from within you, that it started there and ended there. It was of your own making.

I was wrong.

Strength is a gift placed inside you, built up by the people who love you. Fortified by the people who hate or threaten you. These are the things I will teach my son.

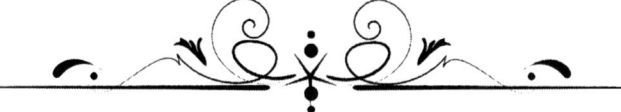

Joseph left late that morning. We couldn't bear to get out of bed, the cold chipping away at our toes, the quilt a refuge. He was enjoying stretching the terms of our new arrangement, finding different places on my body to touch, just to get a reaction. Strong fingers left a blush of warmth wherever they wandered. He finally peeled himself away and said he would be home late but that I should dress nice, whatever that meant. He was going to take me out somewhere. I couldn't imagine where. There wasn't much to choose from.

"What about Orry?" I said

"I'll arrange everything. Just be ready by eight."

"Ok," I said sulkily. I really didn't like surprises.

He kissed me lightly on the cheek, which left me wanting, and left. I watched him walk away, his thumping strides almost rocking the earth. He walked like a giant. I was still not quite used to the fact that he would be home. Home was alien. Home created flourishes of color, popping up through the cracks in the floorboards and the neat stone path, like sprouting spring flowers. He waved behind him without turning around, his scarred arm covered by a thick coat. I felt a pang of guilt for not telling him about Cal. I would do it tonight. One serious conversation at a time was probably best.

I had a lot of work to do that day; it had piled up from my procrastinating yesterday. Chair legs and sled parts taunted me from the corner. A pile of sawdust I should have swept up and taken out was migrating back to where it had started, like a tiny sandstorm moving tiny dunes. It was also my turn to look after Orry.

The day went by uneventfully. I worked hard trying to finish everything so the evening would be free. Orry was fussing. When he was like this, it was a pointless guessing game to work out was wrong. Teething, hungry, tired, sick? So I just tried to distract him. I laid him down on the floor like I used to with Hessa. He stared at me with his weird eyes, my eyes, and I explained what I was doing, holding up tools and describing their various uses. Looking at his chubby pale arms and swash of blond curls, I wondered if he would be smart like Joseph. Tracking his darting eyes and hearing his frustrated grizzle, I knew he would be more like me—crazy and likely to get in trouble.

At about six o'clock, I cleaned up and started getting ready. I swept up the sawdust again and left it in the corner. I changed into clothes they'd given me when we first arrived here. I tried on a skirt and tights but quickly wriggled out of them, selecting black pants and a long-sleeved shirt. I did my hair, remembering that day when Clara had done it and the way Joseph reacted. I blushed. He wasn't even here and I blushed. I pulled two small sections of my hair back and left the rest down.

It hurt less to think of her but I'm not sure the ache would ever go

The Wall

away. It lingered atop the pile of things I missed—my mother, the woods, Rash, and the boys. My grief wrapped around me like an ever-tightening bandage, holding my insides in but also stopping things from escaping.

I gazed down at the palette of makeup sitting squarely in my palm with great trepidation. I tried to apply it via the directions on the back of the plastic case. When I finished, I had to admit I looked awful. My eyes were over-emphasized and my cheeks too pink. I scrubbed it off. I looked… well, I looked nervous.

I started to get irritated at Joseph, wondering why he had to make a big deal out of this. I could imagine him laughing to himself at the idea of me running around trying to get ready. I wrapped Orry, who had been watching me wide-eyed on my bed while I got ready. He kicked his legs and cooed. I know I should have found these noises cute but to me they sounded like a cat getting sucked down a drain hole. These were the things I always kept to myself.

I fed him, realizing I should have done that before I got dressed as I had to unbutton my shirt. He wasn't very hungry, nuzzling into my breast and falling asleep quickly. So I dragged the cot into our room one handed, the still-greenish legs screeching and scratching across the floor. It would have left scratch marks, if the floor wasn't already so scuffed and worn. I liked it that way; it gave the place a sense of history, other families, other lives had been lived here. I put Orry down, closing the door after me. I barely had time to sit on a chair to start stressing about the night when I heard a knock at the door.

I was flustered. Was Joseph early? I opened the door wide with my shirt open just as widely. When I saw who it was, I quickly pulled it closed. "Cal!" I exclaimed with an unexpected mix of relief and anxiety.

He looked happy, relaxed, his eyes looking me up and down like I was a stick of candy. He didn't lick his lips but he might as well have.

"Can I come in?" he said with confidence, like asking was merely a formality.

I wasn't sure—a network of interlacing wire grew up in front of my face like a barrier, warning me. "Um, I'm just about to go out," I lied, as I fumbled with my buttons, doing them up wrong and having to start again.

"This won't take long. Please." He pushed his way through the door before I could answer. He was forceful and the door slammed against the wall with a bang.

A slinking, dark shadow followed him.

He walked to the middle of the room and turned towards me with purpose. "I just wanted to say, I understand now." He seemed so earnest, his face bright and hopeful.

I'm sure my face was a mess of confusion. "Understand what?" I asked, my hands balled in fists, squeezing and relaxing. Instinctively, I walked towards my bedroom door, closing it softly but fully. The latch clicked into place.

"Why you said you couldn't work for me anymore. It's your feelings for me. I wanted to say that of course I feel the same way. Now we can be together and you don't have to worry."

I laughed hard like I was expelling a wad of cotton wedged in my throat. Realizing my tactlessness, I quickly covered my mouth. But it was too late. He saw it. He heard it. He took a step towards me and I mirrored his movements, taking a step back, standing between him and the bedroom door.

"Are you crazy?" I said, barely able to control my surprise. "You're delusional. I'm with Joseph."

He shook his head violently, his expression tightening. Putting his head to the side, he crooned, "I know you don't want to hurt him but I heard you last night. You're trying to back away from him. I know you feel obligated because of Orlando. But you love me. I'm sure he will understand."

The word Orlando crept up and bit into me. No one called him that.

The Wall

That name was left back in the mounds, under dirt, rocks, and kisses that never should have happened. He was crazy.

The air in the room suddenly felt oppressive, like an electric storm was brewing above my head. I couldn't believe what I was hearing. My stomach turned in on itself as I realized he'd been watching us last night and who knows how many other nights. Why had no one warned us he was unstable?

I looked back and forth, my eyes running along the length of the lounge-room wall. I couldn't move any further away from him. I was pinned against the door. I couldn't run, not without Orry. I would have to talk my way out of this. I closed my eyes and took a deep breath. "Look I don't know why you think these things. I don't love you. I love Joseph. And I think you should leave." Honesty was all I had.

Cal's eyes darkened. He tucked his hair behind his ears, a normal behavior, once comforting, now filled me with dread. Sweat was clear on his brow, despite the cold. The sheen reminded me of slime and my disgust at him deepened. I hoped it didn't show on my face. I don't know what my face looked like to him. It felt contorted, pressed in at the wrong places. And his face was flicking back and forth between wild and calm. I didn't need to worry. He wasn't reading my face. He didn't seem to be aware of himself, let alone my expressions. *Be careful*, I told myself.

"I'm not leaving until you admit the truth," he said determinedly, thumping his fist into his thigh, edging closer. Each movement dragging with it a clawing, dark shadow.

"That is the truth. You've invented the rest in your head," I said softly. Trying to ease my way out of this like I would lever a nail out of timber I didn't want to damage. Gently.

He stopped and hit his forehead hard with the heel of his hand. An angry red mark appeared between his eyes. "Oh yeah, I'm the crazy one!" My eyes widened, the tempo of my heartbeats quickening as I felt the danger, the menace of him, swelling in front of me.

I considered how long it would take for him to reach me. It was only a couple of meters. How quickly I could grab Orry and run? How fast was he? I didn't know. I knew he would be stronger than me. He wasn't much taller but he was broad, and wiry, his arms bulging at his shirtsleeves. But I had to try.

I put one hand over the doorknob, the metal comfortingly cold against my burning skin. I turned it slowly, millimeter by millimeter, while watching him. His head was down as he talked to himself. "If he's the one in the way, maybe we should do something about that." My ears pricked and a boost of adrenaline surged at the mention of harm to Joseph.

I turned away from him while he was distracted, inching myself forward. I would do it swiftly. Open, grab, run. I counted… on one, two, three as sweat dripped down my neck and under my shirt.

Crack! His arm chopped down on my wrist, the bone splitting pain shooting up my arm. Broken. I screamed long and loud.

He clamped his hand over my mouth; it was sweaty and mixed disgustingly with the smell of handmade soap.

"Sh!" he spat "I don't want to hurt you. Just admit the truth and we can work this out."

He put his spare arm over my chest, his forearm tight, the veins popping over the skin like it could barely contain his energy, and dragged me away from the door. My legs kicked frantically, trying to push off something. Orry started crying. Cal's mouth was close to my ear, his breathing fast and uneven, and his lips wet. I strained away from it, saliva touching my earlobe. What could I say? If I lied and said I loved him, he wouldn't leave. I had tried the truth. He didn't believe me.

I struggled but his grip was too tight. He slammed me down on the floor on my back, knocking the wind out of my lungs, and straddled me. His knees pushed into my elbow joints, the bone-on-bone contact made me cry out in pain. Blood was not moving, oxygen had stopped. "Please.

The Wall

Let me go. You're hurting me." Begging. Begging could work.

He laughed hysterically, his voice strained, his eyes like hard, amber rocks, gleaming. "Look what you made me do," he said, his teeth clattering, gesturing at the mess around us. The blood. Then he wrapped his hands around some of my hair, leaned down, and held it against his cheek. I tried not to cringe; I tried not to look at where this might be leading. My fear encompassed so much.

Begging wasn't going to work.

In all of this, my thoughts were heading off in a strange direction. As I looked at his eyes, which started to swirl in front of me like pinwheels, I thought of my mother. I thought, *This is what it must be like for her*. Every day. Paulo would never lay a hand on her but the threat was always hovering. And in some ways that was worse. This was what it was like to feel powerless... to be less than a person. It angered me. It threatened me. In that moment, I knew exactly how she felt and it was horrifying.

Cal relaxed for a second, the fury slumping out of him, his eyes hungry. He leaned into my face like he was going to kiss me and the force he was applying to my elbows lapsed. It was all I needed. I brought my knees up and pushed backwards. I could hardly breathe, my chest constricted, forcing air in and out like bellows. Panic was setting in. But I kept telling myself, *Don't let him do it; don't let him do it*.

He lurched backwards and I flipped onto my stomach, scrambling to get away, heading to the corner where all my tools lay, my fingers pressing into the sawdust, sending clouds of it into my eyes.

He jumped to his feet agilely and was walking towards me slowly, his footsteps sounding heavy, pulsing through my chest and supplementing my heartbeat. My own body felt light, like I might blow through the crack under the door.

What was left of me?

"Don't run, darling." His voice was a menace, a dark-tinted scratch in the air.

I couldn't tell where he was, the floor stretched out for miles in front of me, a looming threat behind. This was not the time for things to move in slow motion. I urged time to speed up. I was nearly there, a foot of space between me and a possible weapon. I felt rough hands clamp around my ankle and yank me backwards sharply. My chin grazed the rough floorboards as he brought my head level with his boot. In a final violent action, he brought his boot down on me like he was squashing a cockroach. It made a crunching sound like a cockroach would too. Could my head burst like a berry? No, it was more like an acorn.

My vision darkened, shadowy spots appearing and dancing before my eyes like puffs of smoke. Orry. Oh God. I had to protect him. I *had* to hold on long enough to protect him. Tears were stinging like acid. I sniffed, and the familiar taste of blood ran down the back of my throat. The blow had brought it gushing from my nose and somewhere else I couldn't pinpoint. Was I broken apart? Bits of me were not responding. Some parts moving fast, some slow, some not at all.

Cal walked away from me again but he left the shadow, it lay across me like a lead weight and I couldn't move. Tearing at his hair, he yelled, "I'd rather you disappear than see you with him. I could be a good father, a better father than that guy."

Help me.

My cheek pressed to the ground; I tapped my fingers on the warm, wooden floor lightly, each finger taking an immense amount of energy to lift, the drumming giving me something to focus on. I couldn't feel any pain, or maybe my whole body was pain, there was no distinction.

White canvas shoes spattered with blood were coming at me from a weird angle, tilted like the world had sunk sideways. I blinked.

Imaginary arms linked with mine.

Help yourself.

I can't.

HELP YOURSELF.

The Wall

I'm not disappearing.

I ignored my fear, quickly folding it up for later. My eyes focused on the glinting metal a few feet away from me. *Don't count. Just go.* I dug in my heels and darted at the only weapon close to hand, my body soaring at it like a low-flying paper plane. I was as thin as paper, sharp as its edges. Could this really be happening? A hammer.

I hugged it to my chest violently, the metal reassuring my heart with a thump. Every footstep he made pounded in my brain like it was attached to an amplifier. Orry's crying broke through.

I stood. I don't know how I stood but I did, legs wobbling, one arm hanging like a dead weight.

"Get out!" I screamed, waving the hammer wildly in front of me. I couldn't see anything but blur and red. I felt the end connect with something and snag. I pulled hard and heard him cry out.

"GET OUT!" I sounded like a shrieking bird, my wings flapping, beating the air and creating a powerful wind. My voice was not my own. It was Clara's, Apella's, Mother's. Their strength in me. Like gravity, the words were solid, thrown at him with force. He took steps backwards, staring at his hands like they were not his own. Then I heard the door slam.

My broken body collapsed to the floor. I heaved myself towards the bedroom door, using my very last bit of strength. I got there and relaxed. I was cold. Curling myself around the hammer, I embraced it, convulsing once, wrapping around it like an old guard dog.

My body was slipping away, slipping into the floor.

My home. Not in my home.

I'd make myself small. Turn my body into a knot in the floorboards. Hard. Impenetrable. Strong.

The clock swirled before my eyes, the ticking unnaturally loud.

7:55.

30. WISHFUL.

In my dream, Joseph came home at 7:45 PM.

I run to the door and he tells me to cover myself up with a wink. It's violating our agreement.

In my dream, I'm not trying, unsuccessfully, to lift my head off the floorboards or even open my eyes.

In my dream, my eyes are bright and my hair is pulled back the way he likes it. It's not matted and soaked with blood, my head feeling like a hardboiled egg that's been stepped on.

In my dream, I am safe. Until I wake, I can pretend I am safe.

Because the truth is, I'm never safe.

I never was.

30

FROM HIS EYES
Joseph

As I approached the house, I could hear Orry screaming. But I didn't think much of it. He was probably fussing. I imagined Rosa running around the house, worrying about what we were going to do tonight. I knew she hated surprises but I wanted to show her I knew her. I wanted to show her I listened to her and understood what she needed.

Deshi walked next to me. It was cool and he rubbed his hands together to warm them. He'd left Hessa in town with Apella and had agreed to babysit for me. I think things were easier for him now. He had his own place, a family. But I always felt bad for him. I understood more than most how it felt to love someone and not be able to do anything about it. I hoped he would find someone here, but if he didn't, there was Hessa. Now it felt more like it did in the beginning, when we were great friends, the best.

"So what's the big plan?" he asked. Although, I was pretty sure he didn't really want to know. He didn't hate Rosa, in fact, I think he respected her, maybe even liked her, but he didn't understand the two of us together. In my mind, there was nothing to get. Whatever we had—it just *was*. It worked and would always work. There actually couldn't be anyone else.

I shrugged at his question, downplaying it. I didn't want to flaunt our romantic escapades in his face. "Just dinner and a campfire."

Deshi rolled his eyes. "Sounds boring."

I shoved him gently. "It won't be to her."

I kind of wished I could talk to him about it but I couldn't, not yet anyway. I wanted to explain how she made me feel. She was this force of nature. At any one time, she was a storm, a sun-filled day, a tornado, and I was willingly caught up in her weather. When she laughed, the air around her moved and changed. When she was angry, lightning threatened the sky. She was unpredictable but I liked to think my presence was calming to her. I felt like I provided her with balance.

We walked up the steps. The door was unlocked and creaked open eerily. I had warned her to keep it locked.

Pushing it open, Orry's screaming hit me like a warning.

I didn't see her at first—the pulled-over furniture and streaks of blood drawing my focus. But following the tracks of blood to the origin of my son screams, there she was.

I froze.

"Oh my God," Deshi gasped, as he ran towards the tiny, curled-up mass of dark hair and blood. He approached her slowly, kneeling down, blood soaking into his khaki pants.

I threatened myself to move, but when I saw her lying there, curled around that hammer, she wasn't moving. I thought she was dead. She looked impossibly small, her hair fanned out around her like someone had creepily arranged it that way. The floor beneath me seemed to rock and shift and my body started to shake. I told myself to move. My head moved from side to side in slow motion. Where was Orry—was he hurt too?

Thank God for Deshi. Deshi... the guy who got squeamish at the sight of blood, and stood back when I was attacked by that lynx. He saved us both.

He ran to me and shook my shoulders. My body was rigid and didn't react to his light attempts. "Joe. Snap out of it. She's alive. Come here."

The Wall

She was alive. I waited for the feeling of relief but it didn't come. Deshi went in to Orry, returning with a tightly wrapped, upset but unharmed, baby. "Is he...?" I asked.

"He's fine," Deshi answered but his eyes were dark as tragedy as he looked at my girl. My son was safe. Thank God for that. I knelt down next to her, cupping her shoulder as gently as I could. She looked broken and folded, like the tiniest disruption would make her body collapse. But I knew this wasn't possible. I had to get on the other side of my panic. "Rosa?" I whispered, my voice sounding breathless. The air in the room felt thin, like we were on top of a mountain.

She managed a moan but she didn't open her eyes. I turned her over and tried to stretch her out, which was no mean feat. She was clinging to that hammer like it was part of her and I couldn't pry it out of her hands. I gently shook her tiny wing of a shoulder. "Rosa, it's Joseph, can you hear me?"

She mumbled something. It sounded like, "Not in my home."

My heart sank like a lead weight. Whatever happened here, it could have been stopped. I should have been here to stop it. Anger rattled me but I pushed it down. Right now, I needed to help her.

I scooped her up as gently as I could, noticing that one arm was hanging limply at a strange angle. It was definitely broken. She was also bleeding from her scalp and had several cuts and bruises starting to form over her face.

Rosa, what happened to you?

We walked as quickly as we could towards a slowing spinner and jumped on. The bump made her moan again. She was so small, so minute in my arms. I was trying so hard not to let my anger take over but it was pressing into my back like hard hands shoving me forward. I kept thinking, *Whoever did this, I don't care what the reason, I will kill them. I will kill them.*

Deshi touched my shoulder and I flinched, every muscle tensed. It jerked me back to reality. He leaned back like he was afraid of me.

"Joe, breathe. If you keep holding your breath like that, you're going to pass out. I can't carry the three of you on my own." He smiled weakly but his eyes had no humor in them.

I lifted her unbroken arm. Her fingers were bleeding; tiny splinters were jammed under her nails like she'd been gripping into the wood for dear life. Her chin was grazed with splinters too. She squeaked and I realized I was holding her too tightly.

How did this happen? The thoughts running through my head made me feel sick. I relaxed my grip and she slumped back in my arms. I watched her chest rise and fall, too fast, noticing that her shirt buttons were done up all wrong.

"It's all right," Deshi said, trying to calm me down. "I think she's going to be ok… most of this looks superficial."

I stared at him, scared to utter the words I was thinking, "But what if they…" I stared at her torn clothes, grief drying up my words. I couldn't even say it. Even if she was going to be fine physically, how would she be emotionally?

"Don't say it, Joe, don't even go there. We don't know what happened. We won't know until she wakes up and tells us. And she will wake up. She *will* be ok."

We rode the rest of the way in silence. I just watched her breathe. I watched the air pass quietly through her beautiful, parted lips and tried to ignore the red splotches of skin that were fast turning purple all over her tiny body.

Deshi rocked Orry and reached out to stroke Rosa's hair every now and then. I was wrong about him, his feelings for her ran deeper than I realized.

The Wall

Is this what it felt like for you? When you watched me collapse in front of you, did it feel like everything was being stripped away, dreams turning to dust, nothing but grey ash covering the earth? Were you angry? Did you blame me?

You're so much stronger than you know.

She'd been under sedation for a day now. Matthew showed me her scans. Her arm was indeed broken near the wrist but it was a clean break. They set it easily. She had a pretty bad concussion and a hairline fracture in her skull that would heal on its own. The scan also showed a previous break in her jaw that had been repaired with a great deal of skill. Matthew told me it was at least a year old and asked how it happened. When I told him I didn't know, he looked perplexed and I felt inadequate.

When they rolled her onto her side, her gown slipped away, revealing one big bruise spreading over her perfect skin like someone had spilled ink on her. It was like someone had picked her up and dropped her from a height. The insides of her elbows were a blackish purple too. He couldn't tell me if she had been assaulted in any other way. He was not going to do an exam without her permission, and for that she had to wake up.

Whoever did this was a monster.

I wasn't sure how I was going to deal with it when she did wake. I wanted to hold her, cover her in kisses but Matthew warned me that if she had been assaulted, she might not want to be close to anyone for a while. That terrified me. And then I felt guilty that I was worried about something so stupid.

What I felt was powerless. I had all this anger, all this pain, and I didn't really know where to put it.

Watching her now, people would say she is so small. Frail even. Not to me. To me, she was a storm brewing and I knew as soon as she opened her beautiful eyes, she would be a thunderous force.

I just worried and wondered where the lightning strike would be aimed.

31

RESOLVED

My head felt crackly, sounds were sharp and then descended into buzzing. I kept my eyes closed and tried to focus on one thing at a time. Lifting my arm. It felt heavy and clumsy, not my own. Turning my head. That proved more difficult. I could do it but the pain was intense, like there was something jammed in my skull and when I moved it, the object wiggled and grazed my brain.

Then the reason why I felt this way came back to me in a giant and solid assault on my memory. Cal. That bastard. Anger filled me from my toes to the top of my aching head, like hot oil boiling in my blood; it sizzled and popped its way up my body until I could no longer keep my eyes shut.

They pinged open, harsh, white light trying to force them ajar, and the first thing I said was, "I'm going back to get my mother."

Joseph's head was dipped and he had his hands folded across his knees like he had been or was about to be sick. And when I spoke, his eyes lifted. They took my face in, and then my words, so his expression went from relief to surprise and then confusion, all in one shutter speeding display. As his face returned to a more calm façade, I could see myself reflected in his eyes. They said more than he could. I looked awful.

I blinked uncomfortably and ran my hands over my lips. Everything felt dry and alive.

Joseph took my good arm carefully, the one that wasn't encased in plaster, and held it between his own. "It is all right. You were attacked. You're in the hospital now. You're safe. Orry's safe."

"I know where I am," I snapped, although the effect was muted, my voice felt like it hadn't been used in months. "Water, please," I said more kindly. This couldn't be easy for him. And I tried hard to remember that but things kept slipping as the knock-knocking in my head started to drown out my thoughts.

I took a sip, slowly, the water sliding down my throat like paint. Trying not to turn my head, I noted the bag attached to my arm, the circle of empty chairs. I took in the normal, easy-to-process things in an attempt to calm my nerves but it didn't help. I dragged my elbows up to sit but I was dizzy, weak. Anger was all I could feel because to me, it was like I had been on the floor one minute and was now awake and looking for the culprit.

I started ranting. Not really making sense to start with.

"Damn boy, thought he was harmless. I was wrong, Joseph, and then I was waiting for you and I saw him peeking in the window, no that happened before, anyway, I caught him and he got mad. I'm sorry. I tried to talk my way out of it but he was so angry. He was too strong and all I thought about was Orry. I had to protect him. I tried to run but he was too fast…"

Joseph nodded his head along, grabbing at the words and trying to follow, but he was confused. So was I. I slumped further into my pillow, panting. He smoothed my hair back from my face, careful to avoid the gash in my left temple. "Sh. It's all right. Who? Who did this to you?" He was trying to sound calm, but I could hear the wound-up fury behind it.

"Cal," I said as an admission. Like it was my fault and somehow I should have been able to stop it from happening.

Everything in him tensed at once. And for a moment, I feared him. Joseph stood suddenly, pushing his chair back and sending it screeching across the linoleum floor. The metal back clanged as it fell to the floor,

The Wall

echoing in the emptiness of the room. He stomped out without looking back, both hands pushing the double doors open with a massive thud.

I wanted to get up but I couldn't. I tugged helplessly at my drips and wires but my energy was entirely sapped. I screamed but my voice wouldn't carry. *Where was he going? Did he blame me?*

I could hear yelling. Just Joseph, because whoever he was shouting at was responding quietly.

"Did you know? Where is he? WHERE IS HE?"

Oh no.

Feet shuffled across the floor and I saw my family. They were carrying steaming cups in their hands, looking at me, and then lifting their eyes to the noise behind the doors. They all had different shades of relief and death on their faces.

"Deshi, stop him. He's gone after Cal," I said hoarsely, coughing on the back of my hand.

Deshi understood but he seemed reluctant to interfere, his dark eyes running over me. I found myself curling up. "If he's the one that did this to you, then maybe I should let Joseph tear him apart."

I searched their eyes. They were all similarly resolved. What did I look like to them? A tiny girl, beaten, unable to fight for herself. That was not me.

"Addy, Addy. Please. You know this won't help anything." She nodded but she didn't move either.

I tried to pull myself up again, pulling at my IV. If no one would listen, I would go after him myself. But everything felt wrong. My body wouldn't respond the way I needed it to. Deshi put his hand over the needle I was trying to scratch out of my elbow joint, looking away when blood welled at the entry point.

"All right, I'll go. You're so stubborn," he said. But he said it with love. He jogged through the doors and stopped to talk to a nurse, who pointed him down the hall. I prayed he would catch up with Joseph before he found Cal.

Addy toddled over and pulled a hand-knitted blanket over my legs. I would have kicked it off but I felt so unreasonably cold. She did it lovingly, patting my calf. "You need to rest, dear. Stop getting so worked up."

"I'm fine," I said, lying. I held out my good arm. "Can I have my son please?"

Apella, who looked like she was a second away from bursting into tears, handed him to me. He cried and threw his head around, looking for food. One handedly, I tried to loosen my gown so I could feed him. Apella put her hand up to stop me.

"You can't, Rosa. I'm sorry. The drugs they gave you for the pain means you can't feed him."

My hand fell from my gown like a dead branch, brittle and useless. Something burst inside me. "What?" I whispered. This was unexpected. I thought I would be happy to stop feeding him, but this felt like it was too soon, like I'd been robbed of a bond with him. Or at least robbed of the choice of whether I wanted to stop or not. Apella held up a bottle and it nearly broke my heart. Things had been battle for us from the start. Feeding him had been the first thing that brought us together. Now that was gone. I shook my head sadly. "I can't," I whispered. Addy scooped Orry out from beneath my weak arm and Apella passed her the bottle. My heart took a sudden punch as I watched him eagerly take the teat and drink.

I couldn't even cry. I flopped down on the bed and regretted the sudden motion. I turned my head and Apella was quick enough to get the bowl under me before I vomited nothing. My stomach was empty. My head was empty too but for the pain and the one sentence that floated around and banged against the inside of my skull. "I want to go back and get my mother," I said again.

Apella looked surprised but she covered it with a concerned look.

The Wall

Her hair was pulled back and I noticed her ears were tiny, tiny white shells, perfect and delicate. I focused on that as I watched her small mouth deliver words I would ignore. "Sometimes when someone has a head injury, they can get stuck on one idea. I think you'll change your mind about going back."

I touched my own head, my ears were normal, but dark and and… my hair, where was half my hair? I patted down my head, awkwardly clunking myself with my cast.

"They shaved it so they could stitch your wound up neatly," Alexei said, wincing. Sure enough, as I danced my finger lightly over my head, a seam of neat stitches formed a crescent just behind my ear. I let my lips quiver.

"Oh no," I said, full of self-pity. "I look like a baseball."

Addy mouth twitched. "More like Frankenstein's monster, dear." I didn't know who that was but I could tell the comment was not complimentary. My mouth was already pulled down so I left it there.

Matthew walked in, a fresh bruise appearing under his right eye. His shirt was un-tucked and some of the buttons were missing. He looked guilty as anything.

"Where's Joseph?" I asked

"He's calming down in another room. Deshi is with him."

"Did he…?" I'm not sure if I wanted to hear that Joseph had beaten Cal to a bloody pulp or not. Matthew shook his head.

"Rosa, can I talk to you alone, please?" His eyes were creased from sleep; he looked disheveled, like he'd napped sitting in one of those metal chairs. Even if he had slept, it hadn't helped him. He was a ragdoll version of himself.

I considered his request. After all the lies I'd been told, the secrets that had been kept from me, I didn't feel like doing it anymore.

"No. If you want to tell me something, or ask me something, just do it." I watched Orry sitting in Addy's lap. He faced me and smiled that toothless, gummy smile that was more recognition than happiness. Like my face alone was enough for him. I was so glad he didn't know what was going on right now. He happily played with Addy's dried-up fingers, turned her rings around, and tried to suck on her pinky.

"Ok, well, the first thing I need to ask you is what exactly happened? Did Cal... force himself on you?"

I felt my face going red. But I had asked for this to be a public event. "If you mean did he... rape me? Then no. But the rest of this handiwork," I drew an imaginary circle around myself in the air, "was Cal."

Everyone seemed to collectively sigh with relief. I didn't say anything else. Because I knew, without a doubt, that if I hadn't stopped him, he would have. I also knew like someone knows eerily when they are about to fall or drop something that he would have killed me and maybe Orry too. I let my lids fall, closing out the concerned faces, the way they looked at me, waiting to hear the things I couldn't say. In the darkness, all I could see was his murderous eyes swirling in front of me. I shivered and Addy instinctively pulled the blanket up further over my shaking body. I clenched my teeth, my mouth closed. I told myself to pull it together. Matthew was looking at me with sad eyes, a nervous tremor running through his fingers as he checked my wounds. I heard Apella gasp as he got me to turn around so he could look at the bruises on my back and was thankful I couldn't see them. When he'd finished, Matthew sat down in the chair and clasped both hands together like he was praying, or trying to muster up some courage to tell us what was on his mind. I kind of wish he hadn't said a word.

It would have been easier to hate Cal if I didn't know the truth. If I didn't know that he was dying, had lasted longer than he should have, that he wasn't really himself. All of that. It was information that made me

The Wall

feel something for him and I didn't want to feel anything. As for Matthew, the way I saw him would be forever changed. Yes, I would much rather not have known.

This obsession with babies, with perpetuating the human race, it's stupid. Maybe we should have forsaken it. Lived out our lives and let it end there. We would end there. I'm pretty sure the world would have been better off. But then I think of Orry and I can't breathe. The conflict I feel teases at the seams that hold me together until I am slowly tearing apart, each stitch popping and breaking. Because if we let it end there, he would be alone. We would all be dead and he would be alone.

Maybe that's why it never ends.

Matthew had been silent for about five minutes, which was about all I could stand.

"What is it?" I asked, watching his hands that were gently clasped to start with, wringing each other out like he was trying to dislocate his fingers.

"I am so sorry, Rosa. This is all my fault." He looked up at me and the agony on his face showed that he truly believed it. I didn't.

"How can it possibly be your fault? Unless you forced him to do it, it can't be." Matthew was a good man. He couldn't have done this.

"I didn't but I may as well have."

"What?" I didn't understand, and looking around the room, the rest of them were as clueless as I was.

Matthew looked at the ground and stared at his canvas shoes, lifting his toes up in them, rocking his feet back and forth. "Have you ever noticed that Gus and Cal look very similar?"

I didn't see what this had to do with anything. "Yes, Cal is Gus's son; they're bound to look similar." Picturing Cal, his features, the ears poking out, the hard, sticky glare, made me cold. Remembering the way his eyes razed the room and darkened the air stunned my body and I twitched, my shoulders shaking violently.

"No," Matthew said, shaking his head. "Cal is Gus."

I searched people's eyes. They looked surprised but less so than myself. Having the science background helped them come to the answer a lot quicker than me. I went through ridiculous possibilities like Gus dressed as Cal, or Cal with a fake beard masquerading as Gus. But I had seen them together. Was there two of them, twins? How was that possible when one was much older than the other? Cal called Gus Dad. I already had a headache but this made it so much worse. I had double vision and was picturing two Cal's coming at me, laughing hysterically and calling me darling.

Matthew explained it as simply as he could: The Survivor's had come at their infertility problem from a different angle than the Woodlands. During one of their scavenging hunts, they found a clinic in one of the main cities in China. It was a research lab, filled with partial notes and equipment. It seemed like they were attempting something—some sort of mass-produced army. Matthew thought their work was complete. It was a stupid assumption. Really, they had no idea where in the cloning process they were before the bombing, or how safe it was. But the Survivors decided to risk it. Take the technology and try to make some babies. Ten families volunteered. They made a clone of the mother and the father.

"If that's true, where are all these kids? There should be twenty young people here—why is there only Cal?" It didn't make any sense and the words were starting to swish around in my brain like old dishwater. My hands searched out for something that wasn't there and then grasped a knot of sheet and squeezed it tight in my splintered fingers. Where was Joseph? I needed him here with me.

Matthew's face was pained. Deshi put a hand on his shoulder. "Let him finish, Rosa."

Matthew continued talking, "Everything went well, in the beginning…" he said in that hopeless kind of voice, the one where you wish things were different. "But there were holes in the instructions, in

The Wall

their research." It switched to pleading. "I thought I could do it, come up with the necessary growth hormones on my own, but I was arrogant. Truth is, I was stupid and desperate. I wanted a child of my own and I let that desire lead me." Now, justification… and this is where he lost me for a while. The scientific terms were whacking me on the head like the lashes I used to receive at school.

"The children grew normally at first and we thought it had been a success," Matthew continued, his voice high. Everyone was looking at their feet. "I was thrilled… the parents were happy. There were children in the community for the first time in years."

"I'm guessing it didn't last," I said darkly.

"Rosa!" Deshi snapped.

"No, no she's right. Those hormones, what I created, caused the growth of other things. Tumors." His hands were so tightly clasped, they were white. "I tried to fight the cancers but they were aggressive. They all died," Matthew said, his voice cracking at the end. "Cal was my one success. I don't know what happened. He was tumor free at his last check six months ago."

I cut him off, "So Cal's sick. I don't see what that has to do with my attack. Are you trying to make me feel sorry for him?" The whole story was wearing me down.

"Cal has a tumor in his brain, in his frontal lobe. The frontal lobes have been found to play a part in impulse control, judgment, sexual behavior, socialization, and spontaneity," Matthew said, like he was quoting a textbook. A disconnect he needed.

"What are you saying?" I asked. "Are you saying he couldn't help it, that it wasn't his fault?"

"No, not exactly, but even though he knew what he was doing was wrong, he couldn't stop himself. He feels terrible, Rosa, just terrible." I didn't want to hear that he felt bad. My head felt like it was going to explode.

"Oh my God, stop talking, just stop. I don't want to know anymore." I put my hands to my ears. "Please, get out." I felt like I was slamming my head against a wall, over and over. *Someone listen to me. Look at me. Stop lying to me. Please.*

Matthew slumped out of his chair and turned to walk away, his face so downcast he was nearly doubled over. "Wait," I said.

"Yes," he barely whispered. There was no hope in his voice at all.

That thought, it wouldn't let me go. "I want to go back and get my mother."

Every time I said it, my resolve grew stronger. The words were a march I was already part of. I would never let it go.

Matthew nodded and walked away as Joseph passed him without acknowledging his presence. His fierce green eyes were on me.

When Matthew was out of sight, I turned my attention to Addy. "Did you know about this?" I asked accusingly. The others stared around the room, trying not to get caught in the searing waves of heat that were coming from my eyes. I didn't care if she was old.

She nodded.

I glared at her, hoping her loose face would join her body and melt into a puddle.

She reacted immediately, not shying away from my glare—she met it. "It is not your right to know anything and everything about everyone. You are new here so I'll cut you some slack." She stared me down, daring me to respond. I found I couldn't. "This was not my pain to share. These were families that lost children." She huffed and her face softened. "We are on your side. But we all have our own tragedies to deal with. You need to try and understand that."

I blinked slowly, unused to being talked to like that. I wasn't sure if she was right but I felt bad for upsetting her so I left it alone. I was suddenly so weary. The tumult of information had run right over me like an avalanche and now I lay bruised and battered under meters of snow.

The Wall

But I was still doggedly and exhaustedly trying to tunnel my way out to make some sense of what just happened.

I put my hands to my hair and moaned. My head felt like it was splitting open.

Apella stood protectively between Addy and me and told everyone to leave in a sliced-back tone I didn't recognize. I needed to rest. The last thing I saw was a needle being pushed into my IV and Joseph's sad, sad face sliding together with my son's smiling one.

32.

FRAGILE

I sat in the hospital bed for three days, going crazy. People were around me all the time and I hated it. I hated the look in their eyes, the way they recoiled when they saw my bruises, the way they rushed to my side every time I swayed. I hated it. But more than anything else, I hated what it had done to Joseph. He just didn't know what to do with himself. He would reach out to touch me, and then his hands would wither away before they got to me like a leaf under a blowtorch. He blamed himself. He wanted to fix it but he couldn't. You couldn't fix something like this.

Careen was the only one who didn't treat me like I was made of glass. She told me plainly that my face looked horrible, that my hair would grow back, and that if I wanted, she would step on my attacker's neck and crush his windpipe. But I wouldn't tell her who did it. We kept it quiet. The revelations that Cal was dying complicated our feelings and no one felt the need for outright retribution.

And all the while, that thought never went away. *I want to go back and get my mother.*

I said it so many times, I think they thought it's all I could say. But no one listened. No one took me seriously. They thought I'd let it go.

"Can this come out now?" I asked, holding up my hand, which was

The Wall

still punctured with an IV needle connected to a bag. I wriggled it and pulled at the bag, knowing full well I wasn't supposed to. I wasn't a very good patient.

Joseph nodded and stood to leave. "I'll go get the nurse."

"No, you do it," I said, holding it under his nose, feeling like I wanted to jam it in his face just to force him to touch me. His behavior had been frustrating and confusing. It seemed like he was always arguing with himself about what he should do and then he sat on his hands and did nothing.

"Um, I don't know, Rosa," he said reluctantly.

"Joseph, will you look at me?" I tried to catch his eyes. He looked up and it knocked me down. So sad, so loving, so much.

"I'm fine," I said finitely. "I'm the same person and you need to get that in your head."

"But, but he could have... I should have been there." He sighed deeply. How could I make him understand?

I held his gaze, feeling the warm blush only he could create. "I have changed." He eyes were full of sorrow. "Becoming a mother changed me. Fall... falling in love changed me. But this? This will not change me. Ok?"

His shoulders relaxed a little but I knew he only half-believed me. "Ok."

I smiled. "I'm serious! Stop treating me like I'm going to dissolve into tears and screaming. I need you to believe it."

My wrist was shaking from holding it up for so long and he clasped it between his palms. I exhaled, letting out days of pain and fear. This is where I was supposed to be. "Please. Kiss me?" I whispered, not meaning to plead.

He raised an eyebrow and let out a small chuckle. Leaning in, he moved so damn slow I nearly collided with his face in my own haste. Our lips touched and everything did melt away. If there were people in the room, they were flung from the floor and out the window. They were shadows cast from golden light. Everything stretched and bent around us. This was home. Wherever we were, we could take this with us.

Again, like some aggravated prisoner in a cage, my brain rattled inside my head. I put my hand to my forehead. "Ah."

"Are you ok?" Joseph asked before the sigh had left my lips.

"I'm fine. It's just…"

"I know, I know. You want to go back and get your mother, right?"

"How did you know I was going to say that?" I asked, irritated by his assumption… even if it was right. My head pulsed and throbbed, nodding vigorously inside and out of time with the rest of me.

His eyes crinkled and he rubbed his forehead. "You even say it in your sleep. You scrunch up your face like that and you say it, over and over. Rosa, you can't, you know? You're not well enough and it's too dangerous."

I started to argue but bit down on my lip before I said something stupid. Besides, I knew I was talking to the wrong person. It wasn't up to Joseph. I knew whom I needed to talk to.

I frowned and wiggled my languid, skinny arm in front of him, "Just take this out, please."

Silently, he unwrapped the plastic bandages from my wrist and pulled the needle out slowly. It was like removing a splinter. The achy, itchy pain disappeared immediately once the foreign object was removed.

"Thank you. Now, can you get Matthew?"

Joseph looked at me like he was going to ask, 'Are you sure you want to talk to that guy?' But he left it. He smoothed my hair down and skimmed the shaved part gently.

"You look like one of the dolls in Orry's toy box," he laughed.

Orry had collected some nightmarish plastic dolls, all smooth breasts, tiny waists, and half-shaved heads. I really should have thrown them out but I was unsure of whether this was the normal thing for children to be playing with in the world of the Survivors.

"Thanks a lot," I said, secretly reveling in the return to our normal way of interacting.

No, this would *not* change me.

"I'll be back soon. I have something to show you," he said, grinning. He leaned down to kiss me again, still reluctant. He was too gentle, hovering over my face like he thought it would shatter. I resisted the urge to grab him by the collar and shake him.

I sighed. It would take time. I hoped not too long. I didn't feel like coaxing him out of this state. I had other things to worry about.

Matthew walked towards me like he was scared I would erupt. And in a way, he was right to be nervous. If I could, I would have scalded him with burning lava. But not for the reason he thought. I wasn't angry about the cloning thing, the eagerness that had led to him rushing the process. I was simply angry that he didn't tell us. People think they can hide these things. But it always comes out, usually at the worst and wrong time.

I wasn't proud of what I was going to do next but I had to use his guilt to my advantage if I was going to get what I wanted.

I tried to keep a delicate balance of looking hurt but not incapacitated, which gave me the awkward appearance of wincing with my face but sitting up stiffly like I had a plank glued to my back.

"You wanted to see me?" he said, his eyes searching for something else to look at other than my determined face. He settled on the horrid, clashing colors of the rug at my feet.

"Yes. I was wondering if you would set up a visit with Gus for me?" I said evenly, even though my insides were shuddering and pulling away from me at the thought of it.

He looked so surprised he had to sit down. He smoothed down his crinkled, check shirt that he hadn't changed in days. "What? Why?"

I stared at him, rolling over the right words in my head. "You do have some responsibility in this but so does he. I figure you both owe me a favor."

Recognition sparked in his eyes, "If this is about your mother, I can't see how…"

I cut him off, "Just set it up. Let me worry about the rest."

"All right, Rosa," he said, resigned. I was fast becoming used to him saying my name like a sigh.

As he walked away, I shouted after him. "And go home and have a shower… you look awful."

He didn't turn around but I thought I saw the corner of his face lift a little. But then I added more quietly but so he could definitely hear me, "And don't tell Joseph about any of this," and it fell just as quickly.

I stared down at The Line. Simple white chalk scratched into the pavement. And I watched myself willingly, and almost eagerly, step right on over it.

33

FACING

I dozed off after Matthew left, the mix of painkillers and my terrible headache pulling me under. I awoke to the sound of clanking saucepans and men laughing. And for a moment, I had the wonderful feeling that I was outside. That I was walking through the forest, my hands grazing the low branches of the juvenile pines, my fingers sticky with sap.

As the noise got closer, I remembered where I was and I reluctantly opened my eyes to face the cold, white walls and shiny, metal bedframes. The hospital was empty save a few nurses and one coughing old man they had bedded in the far corner.

Deshi was striding in with Orry in his arms, the child's wide eyes drawn to the light that bounced off shiny surfaces. Joseph was loping towards me with a pack slung over his shoulder, a big grin plastered on his face.

"Surprise," Joseph exclaimed, flipping his foot out and looking like the cowboy on the can of corn from so long ago.

I rolled my eyes. What now?

Deshi stepped back and ran his eyes over my whole body, rolling back on his heels. "Well, you look a little better." He smiled darkly. His eyebrows rising at my sorry state.

"I've been beat up—what's your excuse?" I said, instantly wanting to pull the comment back into my mouth. Deshi reacted ever so subtly, giving me a short, disapproving glance before turning his attention to Orry, holding him up under his arms and swinging him over to me. I held out my hands eagerly and grabbed my son with greedy fingers.

I kissed Orry's forehead and sat him up in the crook of my arm. He felt so warm, so secure in my arms. I shook my head a little, regretting what I was planning to do. Regretting it but not changing my mind.

"What's going on?" I asked suspiciously to the two beaming boys.

Joseph's demeanor was so different to that of before but then Deshi had that effect on him. "We're going to have our date." A nurse walked past, her eyes on him swinging that pack around. He was whirling around, pots and pan clanging against each other. I looked up at him and smiled, a rare, all-my-teeth kind of smile. He stepped back and collided with a trolley full of medical supplies. "Whoops, sorry," he muttered sheepishly to the nurse, who clucked her tongue as she knelt down to help him clean up the mess.

I stood up and tried to smooth down my hair, reminded of my lovely bald patch. "Did you get me a hat?" I asked, keeping my hand over the prickly, shaved part.

Deshi tossed me a knitted, wool cap, which I pulled down over my head as quickly as I could.

"Why don't you guys go? I'll take care of this," Deshi said. I watched him move elegantly around the mess, unlike Joseph, whose big body sometimes moved out of sync with the rest of him. He knelt down and started sweeping cotton buds into his palm.

He was such a good friend, to both of us. I wondered if his heart was healing. Since my attack, his attitude towards me had shifted. His voice no longer had that bitter edge to it. He seemed at peace with how things had turned out. I hoped it wasn't wishful thinking.

"Umm, just a minute. I need to speak to Matthew to make sure he's ok with me leaving." They both looked at me like I'd gone crazy.

"Since when do you ever ask for permission to…?" Deshi started,

The Wall

but I was already walking slowly towards the double doors, feeling weightless and floaty from my mix of drugs. I hoped they would wear off soon.

Joseph stood to accompany me but I waved him off. "I'll meet you out front," I said.

I pushed open the door and slipped through, feeling a chill from within I couldn't explain. Looking left and then right, I could see Matthew at the far end of the corridor walking away from me. I shouted out, but my voice was swallowed up by the long hallway. Its steep ceiling carried my crackly voice up into the rafters. It seemed wherever the Survivors lived, noise was absorbed. I wondered whether quietness was a valued quality in the people who used to live here before us. I snorted at the thought of my loud and unruly presence in such a society. Giving up on shouting, I padded after Matthew, my body dipping and swaying a little as I skidded along the shiny floor in my socks.

I was just about to call his name again when he stopped abruptly and entered a room. And for some reason, at that moment, I didn't want him to see me. I stopped and hid behind a pillar until I heard the door swing shut.

Some things you just know. I hated to believe it but somehow being attacked linked me to him and if I were a spitting person, I would have spat on the floor at the thought of it. But as soon as Matthew stopped, I knew he was entering Cal's room. And even though every inch of me wanted to scurry away from there like a cowardly mouse, I found myself being pulled to the door, my shadow dragging behind me kicking and screaming.

I peered in the window and there he was. Small, weak. The wire lattice set in the glass made him look, pleasingly, like he was imprisoned. He was hooked up to so many machines he looked like an octopus. He was facing Matthew, talking. The good doctor checked his pulse, adjusted the dripping bag above his bed, and started walking towards me. I tried to duck down quickly but my responses were so slow I found myself looking right in his baffled face.

Thankfully, he remained composed until he was out of the room.

"Rosa, what are you doing?" he asked, bewildered.

My face was loose; I felt like if I spoke, something would fall off. "I just wanted to see if you had organized the meeting?" I said meekly.

Matthew dipped his head and rubbed the crinkle between his eyebrows. The one I'm pretty sure he didn't have until he found me. "Yes, I spoke to Gus. He has agreed to see you tomorrow, at your house at twelve o'clock."

"Good," I said. "What's happening with…?" *Don't ask*, I told myself. *You don't care.* I stopped talking.

Matthew looked at his hands and then at me. I noticed he still wore his wedding ring. "He's asking for you. You know he doesn't really understand what happened, but he knows he hurt you. He wants to apologize."

I considered it. Could I be that person? Could I be strong enough to face him, forgive him? If I was going to go in there, I would have to do it now. Joseph would be looking for me soon and he would definitely object. I sighed until all the air left my lungs, trying to expel the fear and the sense that this was a mistake. I pushed open the doors and stepped through.

"You came!" Cal's face was alight with pleasure. He spoke like a child who had received a gift. His broad grin and pushed-up cheeks were too cheery to look at. They burned me with their brightness. He really was sick.

I stood in the doorway, leaning away, leaning back like there was a solid bubble surrounding him that I dare not penetrate. *What was I*

The Wall

doing?

I thought I could do it but the minute I saw his face, the violence of my thoughts frightened me. I wanted to smash the happy expression from his lips. Pull his head back by his disgusting, greasy curls and slam it against the metal bed frame until there was nothing left to hold onto.

I stayed frozen in the doorway, my hands shaking with their need to hurt him.

Cal looked at me with innocent eyes, all the menace gone, sucked out through a tumor whirlpool. But I didn't care. I couldn't. My sympathy was lost to him the moment he stepped into my home that night. Some things can never be undone.

I was shaking so hard I had to hold out my hand and steady myself on the doorframe. I felt like the whole building was shaking under my will, leering and shuddering, bits of the wall peeling off and littering the ground.

"I'm sorry. I... I can't," I managed to stammer. This was such a bad idea.

I thought I'd been handling it well up until then. That I could magically say 'I'm fine,' and it would be so. That focusing on something else would make me ok. No. I had to make a painfully conscious decision to be ok. That I would not let it change me. And I had to know that maybe it would change me anyway. For that reason, I could never lay eyes on Cal again.

I walked backwards out of the door and stumbled down the hallway, uncoordinatedly. Matthew caught up with me and grabbed my shoulders to slow me down before I fell over. I turned to face him, ready to yell at him, say something clever and sarcastic, but all that came out of my mouth was a tortured slip of a cry. I slumped down on the ground and hugged my knees. I let Matthew hold me and I poured out every last tear I had. I watched them fall and splash onto the rubber toes of his sneakers as I buried my head in his chest and soaked his shirt. And whether it was possible to make such a decision, I was determined right then that those were the last tears I would shed over this situation.

"I hate you," I said, my lips squashed against one of his shirt buttons.

"That's ok," he replied. "Addy told me to let you hate me."

I thought, *If that's true, then stop making it so hard to do so.*

34

FIRE

When I returned to my room, Joseph had come looking for me. He was sitting in one of the metal chairs, all his bravado and cheek succumbing to nervousness. I'd taken my time getting ready, splashing water over my face and dressing slowly, selecting jeans, a low-cut shirt, and a jacket. All they had were sneakers and that was fine with me. If there were a Survivor uniform, it was those canvas sneakers. I ran my finger across my chest, pressing my charm between my thumb and forefinger, feeling a strange reassurance in the dull metal.

I still felt wobbly, and I wasn't sure I was up to whatever Joseph had planned, but I desperately wanted to get out of here. Hospitals, hospital beds, the foreign beeping and dripping that never seemed to die out, were beating down my brain. I needed fresh air.

Joseph stood clumsily when I entered. The chair came with him, clinging to his extra wideness with a pack on. When it clattered to the floor, he blushed uncharacteristically and the nurse rolled her eyes at both of us.

I'd tried my best to cover my hair and dress nicely. I'd tried my best not to think about the night I'd dressed for our date the first time. The date that never happened.

"Wow!" he said.

I carefully checked my hat. Was it not covering the bald patch well enough?

"You look beautiful," Joseph said.

"I bet," I said, "next you'll say being half-bald suits me."

He chuckled. "There isn't much that doesn't suit you, darling."

Darling. Black scratches hung in the air like a claw had torn through time. I hunched my shoulders, feeling the memories trying to push their way into my head.

"What's wrong?" he asked, his tone belying his surety.

"I'm fine," I said, changing the subject. "Where are we going?"

"It's a surprise. Now close your eyes. Deshi's waiting outside so you can say goodbye to Orry."

"No way!"

"Please?"

I closed my eyes, frowning with my arms folded across my chest. "How am I supposed to walk like this? I'll walk into a wall."

His strong arms scooped me up and pulled me close to his chest. "Never expected you to walk," he said.

I relaxed. Even if this was all there was, it was plenty.

Joseph kicked open the doors and stepped quickly outside before they shut on him. The temperature dropped as soon as we were outside. The air was cool but the sun was out and it warmed my skin. I had lost track of time in the soundless, temperature-controlled hospital room. Was it afternoon? I could hear people moving and talking around us, footsteps on the asphalt, the metallic hum of the spinners as they coasted down the street. Deshi lifted Orry's face to mine and I kissed him. He slobbered on my nose.

"I'll just take him back to your house and wait for you there," Deshi said.

Joseph thanked him and we continued on. I felt ridiculous but he made me promise to keep my eyes closed.

It was a curious feeling, heightening my other senses. I could eavesdrop on other conversations around me. I heard someone talking about mobilization of Woodland forces but then we moved out of earshot. I tried to follow the words but all I caught was '... weeks... late snow'.

Joseph started talking and I got lost in the vibration of his voice in his chest and his warm breath, which smelled like fresh bread and toothpaste, on my face.

He talked about plans, how spring was coming. He asked me what I was going to do with the garden. It was an odd conversation, too normal. I wasn't sure we got to have normal. Vegetable gardens and furniture-making seemed further away from me now. It was something I had craved but now I focused on the present. Anything else was not manageable.

I sensed we were heading downhill.

He stopped suddenly and I thought we were at our destination but then he changed direction and kept walking.

It started to cool slightly, and the light against my eyelids was softer. Joseph's footfalls were softer too, hitting dirt now instead of asphalt. I could smell damp, sodden earth and pine. And fire. I smiled, the plan coming together in my mind.

"We're here. You can open your eyes," Joseph said. He wasn't out of breath in the slightest. His tone even, his breath steady. How did he manage it? I marveled at his strength.

I opened my eyes to a circle of pine trees.

Joseph leaned down and pressed his forehead to mine. "I hope this is all right. I wanted to bring you back, show you..." His voice was a rumble; it shook my chest, my heart, delightfully, like the words were in me.

I cut him off, "It's perfect, thank you." The light was filtering through the pine needles, creating sharp, crisscross shadows on the forest floor. The woods looked more like I remembered. The snow had indeed receded. There were a few icy patches but spring was slowly announcing itself.

Joseph lowered me to my feet gently but never took his hand off me. And unfortunately, I needed steadying. My head was still sore and my arm made everything awkward. I knelt down and held my palms to the small fire. It radiated warmth that seemed to reach out and engulf us both. I was glowing.

We sat together and I nudged him with my shoulder. Memories flooded through me and around me, some flying like open-mouthed ghosts swirling in a circle and some living in me, breathing with my every breath. He put his arm around my shoulders and pulled me even closer. I looked up and watched the fire dance in his beautiful eyes. The trees leaned in to hear us, to hide us from the outside. We were part of this landscape.

"Rosa, I love you." His earnest expression broke my heart but in a good way.

I nodded. My eyes wet. Love. The words were easy. What I felt was beyond that, and I didn't know how to say so.

"Do you think we'll make it?" I said casually.

"What do you mean?" he asked, his eyes wide. "I think we have some challenges ahead of us. The Woodland soldiers are coming, but I think the Survivors have a plan. I don't think we will be caught out like we were at the mounds."

That's not what I meant, but his words were heavy. I'd been so caught up in my own problems, I'd forgotten about the threats looming over the whole community. There were big issues we needed to face. The Woodland threat was like an infiltrative disease. It was creeping its deadly shadow slowly across the landscape and soon it would reach us. I imagined dark, pointed fingers impaling the fleeing people. *Did they really understand what they were up against?*

I took Joseph's hand and traced over his knuckles one by one. I heard him sigh.

"What's the matter?" I asked.

"Nothing. Nothing's the matter. I'm just so glad this hasn't changed.

The Wall

I was so scared that things would be different between us, after... but they're not."

I kissed his hand and stared into the fire. It was simple in there, in the flames. All or nothing. Consume or be consumed. Was I changed? Not in that way at least. I loved him the same. No, I loved him more. Always more. The rest? I didn't know what it had done to me yet.

"Tell me more about what's happening in the Woodlands," I said.

Joseph rested his head on the top of mine and paused. Then he pulled the backpack towards him. From it, he produced some food and spread it out on a blanket. He filled a pan with water and set it on the coals. "You should eat," he said in his doctorly tone.

I took some bread and smeared jam on it. Finding his eyes, I urged him to tell me more but he seemed hesitant.

"What is it?"

"Don't jump at this," he said carefully, "but they're going to the Woodlands in a couple of weeks."

"What, why?" I said, barely able to keep the desperate tone from my voice.

"They're retrieving the Spiders," he said.

We ate in silence for a while. I knew he was watching me, trying to peer into my brain and see what I was thinking. And what was I thinking? Exactly what he feared... If they were going back, then this was my chance. My toes were tapping in agitation.

But before I could form a plan in my head, Joseph swept it away. He didn't ask me what I was planning to do. He didn't make me promise not to go. He just put his hands on both my shoulders and squared them so I was facing him directly. He stood and I stood with him, his arms directing me like a wooden puppet. His mouth was flat but his eyes were dancing, the green flourishing, the gold flecks sparkling like fireworks and drawing me in. He moved me gently but deliberately so that my back was against a tree and then he sunk his mouth into my neck and crept his lips up to my ear.

I found myself fighting him, because he was making it take too long. I wanted his mouth, the taste of it on my own. He finally found me and I was awash in him, in the golden bands that bound us and held us to each other. Wherever my train of thought was heading, I missed it. It was gone and, in that moment, I couldn't have cared less.

We stayed by the fire until it became too dark too see the forest around us, enveloped in each other's arms and company. This was exactly right and I didn't want to leave, even if it was a false feeling. But, reminded of the great, striped creatures that stalked the night, we poured our cups of tea onto the fire and headed back to the hospital.

Matthew wasn't there but the nurse told us he said I could go home.

She handed me a bottle of pills and a bag containing the clothes I'd worn that night. She told me I would have to come back to have the cast removed in two weeks.

I nodded and Joseph and I walked home hand in hand.

Home. I craved it and dreaded it at the same time. But when we got there, it looked the same as always. Its cracked and weathered shingles creaked in the cold. Its open shutters blinked at me and welcomed me in. It was just a building, and the violence and chaos it had housed were gone. I treaded lightly over the stone path and took the steps two at a time. Standing at the doorway, I watched the house sigh and expel the menace. It whirred out the opening and soared into the sky. Gone.

Orry cried out. The warmth of the woodstove poured over me like a wave. I heard Deshi creaking over the floorboards and calming Orry with his smooth voice. And I knew it was still home. My home.

35

AGREEMENT

I slipped comfortably back into my home like a familiar, worn shoe. Deshi showed me how to make up a bottle for Orry, a process that was clumsy and time consuming. But I had to shake off the things I couldn't control. Like dry leaves clinging to a coat, they floated to the ground and I stepped on them with a satisfying crunch.

I caught up with Deshi at the door while Joseph was changing Orry's nappy.

I grabbed his arm and, for once, he didn't shrink away. "Deshi, thank you. You've been a better friend than I deserve. I… I hope this hasn't been too hard on you." I knew my words were a bit incomplete but what could I say? *I'm sorry if Joseph and I playing house is difficult for you?*

He put his hand on my shoulder and patted it. "You know what? If you had died, that would have been hard. Watching what happened to him when he saw you lying there in front of the door… Rosa, I'll never forget that face. I know things haven't been easy between us but I am glad you're ok. I want him to be happy." Deshi eyes moved to Joseph struggling with Orry's kicking legs as he tried to fasten the gurgling baby's nappy.

It was rather inadequate but I said, "I really want you to be happy too."

Surprisingly, he smiled at me, leaned down, and kissed my cheek. "I am."

And with that, I released him. He waved through the door. "See you tomorrow, Joe."

Joseph grabbed Orry's legs with one hand to still them and managed a muffled "See ya" through his gritted teeth, a nappy pin hanging out the side of his mouth.

We settled Orry and placed him in his crib. I stroked his head and watched his eyes flutter and close. I felt safe here. What was I thinking giving this up to chase down a mother who probably didn't even want me? But I felt like I had no choice—I *had* to go. Mother was beaten down, and even if I only knew that feeling for one night, it was enough, enough to know no one deserves to feel that way.

When I finally fell asleep, I dreamed a swirl of images that didn't fit. I was dancing around my living room with Orry to the music Gwen had given me, laughing and throwing my head back, singing out of tune. Then I was running through the forest, a wolf's snapping jaws at my heels. Then I was lying in bed with Joseph but thrashing around like the sheets were trying to strangle me. I fought my way free of them and landed with a thud on the floor but instead of the ground, I found myself pressed up against a Ring gate.

Staring through the bars, I could see Paulo pushing a pram with a crying baby in it, rocking it back and forth violently. I yelled out at him to stop, he was frightening the child, and when he turned to face me, I was staring into the face of a man I could barely remember, except for those eyes, my eyes.

I woke up tied in a knot of sheets, Joseph nursing a welt across his eye.

"What happened?" I asked, though I knew.

"You had another nightmare." Another? He looked at me through half-open eyes, his hair sticking up on one side from being squished into the pillow. I stared at his impossible face for a moment before pain shot through me.

The Wall

"Ugh! My head." I fumbled around on the nightstand, searching for the painkillers. As I swallowed them, I thought of my dream and shuddered.

Joseph collapsed back into bed and mumbled, "C'mere," opening his strong arms and folding me into them. He was soon asleep but my eyes were wide open. How was I going to get through this?

Joseph didn't want to leave but I pushed him out of the bed.

"Go. I'll be fine," I said as convincingly as I could. "I want things to go back to normal. You go to the hospital and I will look after Orry at home."

He left grudgingly but promised to come home early. I made sure I knew exactly what time.

I'd barely slept last night. I pulled Orry close, sleep wrapping its warm arms around me. It was dreamless. The lull of Orry's snoring brought to me an uneasy peace, until I heard an impatient rapping at the door. The sharps taps felt like they were rattling inside my head. Would my brain ever return to normal and not feel like everything was inside out?

Unwelcome noises intruded on my space. Glancing at the clock, it was nearly midday. I slid out of bed carefully and placed pillows on either side of Orry so he wouldn't roll off the bed.

The rapping continued.

"Coming," I yelled to the closed door.

As I slipped on my jeans and buttoned my shirt, I could hear more than one voice on the other side, two men complaining to each other. I ran to the door and put my hand on the doorknob. Gripping it tightly, I took a deep breath and threatened myself to relax.

Gus stood right up against the screen door, his small gut pushing through the wires, with Careen and a young man I didn't recognize flanking him. But they faded into nothing as I looked at Gus and he frowned back at me.

I'd always remarked they were similar but now I could really see it. I could see the truth of what Matthew had told me standing, disgruntled and awkward, at my front door. They were the same person, separated only by age. They had the same hair, although Gus's was cropped close and he had a short, greying beard. It was the eyes that had my feet pushing me to turn and run. They had the same amber hue, the same long, black lashes framing such cruelty in Cal's case. I kept telling myself over and over, *He's not Cal. He's not Cal.* But my body was shuddering and trying to hold me in. And keep him out.

Gus tried to pull the screen open but I was gripping it tightly and it sprang back to the frame.

Careen stepped forward and smiled. "Are you going to let us in?"

I nodded and stood back from the door, feeling like I was edging away from a wild animal.

They marched in and the younger man gave me a sideways glance, a mixture of surprise and disdain in his eyes.

Gus's face had been worried down to a weary point. He looked tired and impatient. His sat in my chair with a thump without asking and looked up at me, plumes of dust motes swirling in the afternoon sun. A sharp pain ran through me again and I found myself strategically moving behind the armchair, putting a physical barrier between the two of us.

It was silent. The words that no one wanted to say hung in the air like small balls of lightning, sizzling and spitting little twirls of electric tendrils to the floor. I decided to strike first.

I opened my mouth to speak, but sound petered out into vapor and Gus cut me off.

"Matthew informed me of your request and it is out of the question. I am very sorry for what my son has done but you are not trained for this kind of mission. I won't allow it," Gus said bluntly.

The Wall

I was flattened, but anger pulled at my restraint, lifting the pancaked edges of my confidence away from the floor. All my carefully selected arguments flew out my head. He wasn't going to listen to them anyway. *Who was he to tell me what I could and couldn't do?*

I razed my eyes across the room. Careen was smiling absently. The other man was watching, interested, like a spectator. "You're sorry?" I moved around the armchair and placed myself directly in front of him. "I'm sorry too. You will take me. Or I will bring this matter to the leaders. If you want me trained, I'll train. I have a couple of weeks. You owe me this." I looked up at the sky, as if pleading to the heavens. "At least this. I'm going. You saying 'no' means absolutely nothing to me."

I turned my back to him and waited. *One, two, three. Don't punch him. Let him think.*

I heard a resigned sigh and the creaking of an old man easing himself out of the chair, all cracks and grunts.

"Fine. You have your wish. You will start training today," Gus conceded, rubbing his bearded chin distractedly.

I thought of Cal tucking his hair behind his ears and tried to stop my eyes from widening and my breath quickening.

"Are you serious?" The young man argued, snapping his head back and forth between Gus and me. "She's a child. She'll only get in the way."

Gus eyed the protestor. "Pietre, you've just volunteered to be her instructor." His face held a self-satisfied look that at least he could punish someone for this inconvenience.

"I'll help!" Careen was jumping up and down like she was being asked to hand out candy to children.

"Oh, and she will need to be healed before you start." Gus threw the words over his disappearing shoulder.

He left us standing there.

A triangle of very different people, eyeing each other with varying levels of suspicion and excitement.

36

HEALING

I woke Orry and put him inside the capsule. Lifting it with his weight proved difficult, as I was still weak and my broken arm made everything awkward. After a few attempts, Pietre's patience ran short. He snatched the child from me and slung the capsule over his shoulder.

"Um, thanks," I said.

"Don't thank me yet. You have no idea what you're in for," he sneered.

I spoke over his shoulder to Orry's plump, little face, "Guess what, bub? I'm getting healed today; you'll get to see what happened to your father when he was fixed."

Pietre shook his head. "Oh no. We're not adding another child to the situation; find somewhere to drop it on the way to the labs."

I snarled at him. "My child is not an 'it'."

"Whatever," he said with an infuriating shrug.

After leaving Orry begrudgingly with Odval, I was escorted to the science labs like a criminal. Pietre and Careen walked next to me shoulder to shoulder. I wanted to clip them both. Well, actually I wanted to elbow him in the groin and throw a stick for Careen to fetch. She was so much like a bounding puppy. I swear I heard her panting with her tongue hanging out. I wouldn't have been the least bit surprised if she had barked. But I kept my cool. I needed their help. So I breathed deeply and imagined I did those things, which gave me some level of comfort. Eyes front, we traipsed towards the town, hopped on a spinner, and rode

The Wall

in silence until we reached the labs.

The science labs were connected to the hospital by a rickety, covered walkway, encapsulated with bent pieces of corrugated tin shaped into a crude arch. We had to walk through the hospital and up some stairs to get to it because the original entrance to the labs themselves was sealed from an old explosion. The door was folded in on itself and rubble reached the ceiling. It looked as if someone had thrown a bomb directly at the entrance.

Looking around anxiously, I worried I would bump in to Joseph, but thankfully he was not near the entrance at that time. As we walked through the doors to the hospital, I looked down the long corridor and wondered if Cal lay there still. I trembled and shut my mind to it, following my minders up the stairs.

As we climbed, Careen separated from me and jumped up the stairs, turning to look at us while she talked. Her excitement was not at all infectious—it was unfitting.

"Rosa, this is Pietre. I told you about him before," she said, none too subtly. I was surprised she didn't wink. He didn't even flinch at the mention of is name.

"Uh huh," I managed to mutter.

Pietre observed her bounding, his eyes stalking her breasts bouncing up and down, tracking her long legs with a sly gaze. I felt sick to my stomach.

When we got to the walkway, we took it one at a time. It couldn't take much weight, though Pietre commented that I could probably jump up and down on it and it wouldn't make any difference. I ignored him but he was trying my patience.

I stepped on; it creaked and swayed like a spring breeze would send it flying out into the atmosphere. The Survivors were a strange people. Why not fix it? They seemed to have the attitude of waste not, want not. If it was broken, they would fix it but they were unlikely to tear it down and build a new one. It brought my thoughts to my mother and her similar attitude, a shiver of nervousness shooting up my spine.

We descended a dark stairwell lined with small squares of light. Pushing open the doors at the bottom, we found ourselves in a shiny, silver room. There were bits of machinery laying on every available work surface. Robots whirred and lasers shone in blues and purples. Everything was new and foreign. Except for a dark face focused intently on a computer screen. Deshi.

I snuck up quietly behind him and shouted, "Hi Desh!" He jumped in his chair. When he recovered, he glared at me and chastised me like a child.

"You know, you really are so immature sometimes. I'm working on something very important," he said.

"I bet you are," I said sincerely. "What exactly?"

"I'm working on a computer bug that will open all the Ring gates simultaneously and then latch them again."

"Ooh!" I said mockingly.

He looked at me with tired impatience. A look I was so familiar with, I barely noticed it anymore.

"What are you doing here anyway?" he asked, raising his dark brows.

"I'm getting fixed up," I said, overly chirpy, swinging my elbows.

Deshi looked unimpressed. If he was interested or curious, he didn't show it. He waved us around his table without looking up from his screen. "Healing room is in there," he said, pointing to a worn, wooden door in the far corner of the room.

The Wall

When I was nine, my mother broke her wrist. She said she tripped, braced herself awkwardly, and fell on it. I never believed her. She had a ringed bruise around it, which looked far too much like someone had grasped her strongly and wouldn't let go. Someone like my stepfather Paulo. Mother had always been steady on her feet. She walked with purpose but never hurried. I'd always suspected there may have been a physical side to her abuse but if she didn't report it herself, there wasn't much I could do.

Luckily, because she was a seamstress, her hands were considered her livelihood and the Superiors granted her treatment. We were sent to the hospital for an x-ray. I sat on a chair inside the room but behind a low screen and glass window while they did it. The noises were loud and cracked like lightning. I pulled her handbag up to my chin and peeked over the edge, scared she was going to be electrocuted. It was one of the only times I ever heard her use an annoyed tone. The man stretched her arm out over a table and she snapped at him for being too rough.

This room was very similar.

There was a metal table in the center and plastic chairs lined one wall behind a glass screening window that rose to the ceiling. Hovering above the table was a glass cabinet with at least twenty pipes coming out of it in different positions. Surrounding the table were six long-armed metal contraptions connected to the pipes.

I was too scared to ask.

A woman with short, blonde hair came in behind us. Her glasses were attached to a chain around her neck. She held a clipboard and was studying it intently. Without looking up, she said, "Pietre, what are you doing here? You've used your quota for the month."

For the first time, he seemed ruffled. He ran a hand through his light brown hair and spoke to his feet. "Er... umm, sorry, Doctor Yashin. It's not for me, it's for her." He pointed in my direction with a surly look on his face. Suddenly he seemed younger, closer to our age than he pretended to be. The woman peered up from her clipboard and assessed me critically. She held up my arm in the cast and asked me to remove my hat, making ahs and hms as she wrote things down in a sharp, break-the-pencil kind of way.

"Very well," she said curtly. "On whose directive?"

"Vereshchagin."

Vereshi… what? I smothered a giggle at Gus's mouthful of a last name, receiving a nasty look from Pietre.

"Right, I'll confirm. Get her undressed and on the table for me for when I return."

I gave them both an incredulous look. There was no way I was undressing in front of either of them. As if reading my mind, Pietre smiled darkly and said, "I have no interest in seeing you naked but if you want to train, we have to do this first."

"No," I said plainly.

"Well, you'll need help getting into position on the table. You don't know which hoses go where or which way to lie. And with the cast…"

I thought about it. Careen would stand there and point out all my imperfections. Pietre seeing me was a horror I couldn't envisage.

"Get Deshi. Does he know what to do?"

They both paused and exchanged glances. Pietre nodded and left the room, returning with a disgruntled Deshi dangling off his flexed arm. And when it was explained what he needed to do, his dark face went a funny shade of green.

"No. No way. Get Careen to do it," he said, shaking his head.

"I'm not that disgusting. Please Desh. This is embarrassing enough as it is."

Deshi's shoulders slumped and I knew I'd gotten my way. "Man, Joseph will kill me if he finds out about this."

Careen smiled at me innocently and flicked my shoulder. "We'll leave you two alone."

God, she was clueless. I think she actually thought I wanted Deshi in there for a romantic reason. I snorted at the idea.

Deshi helped me undress and kindly wrapped me in a sheet, saying he would remove it when the doctor returned. He showed me how to put my arms into the metal cradles on either side of the table and my feet in similar ones at the base of the table. Lying on the icy metal with a glass coffin hanging over me, I was completely exposed. I stared up at it wondering what was going to happen, when Deshi's face appeared above me.

"Are you going to tell me what this is all about or is it better I don't know?" I gave him a look. "Right, better I don't know," he said sullenly.

The door clanged and a gust of air threatened to blow the sheet off my bony body. Deshi looked at me one last time. "It will hurt," he whispered as he shuffled behind the low wall and sat down on a plastic chair, his legs crossed elegantly.

The doctor shouted out, "Right, Rosa. Try and relax, I'm going to restrain you properly now." I heard a long beep and then the metal cradles clamped shut with a loud snap, around my wrists and ankles. I tried not to struggle but I could feel my heart thumping loudly in my chest and my breathing increasing as I started to panic. Deshi called out, "It's all right, Rosa, try to breathe normally."

I tried to think of something else, "So, what's with the glass coffin?" I asked. "Is an enchanted poison apple part of the treatment?" It reminded me of one of the 'fairy tales' I had read, Snow White. I grimaced at the thought of Deshi as Prince Charming, leaning to kiss me awake.

Deshi grunted and muttered, "Truly woeful, Rosa." I felt a pang of missing for Rash, my friend from the Classes whose bad humor and constant pranking made him the male version of myself. He would understand the need to make light of this frightening situation.

Dr. Yashin answered in a measured tone but I sensed she was amused by my attempt at humor. "We don't know exactly why they use the glass box, only that when we tried without it, two staff members were badly burned and the recipient died."

"Oh," I sighed. Humor evaporated and fear returned.

I sucked in a long breath but it hurt. Distraction was inadequate when a glass box was descending on you. I didn't want to do this. Out. I wanted to get out. My eyes were dancing crazily in my head, darting around the room, looking for the door. I felt a cool hand on arm.

Her eyes were calm, a green-hazel color. "I'm going to attach you to the machine. Just remember, we are doing this to help you. It will speed up your healing. You will feel much better when we're done." *Stop trying to convince me*, I thought, *it only makes it harder to believe you.*

She paused and looked at me with those mixed eyes, "Have you eaten breakfast?"

I didn't speak, just nodded. I knew if I opened my mouth the words 'let me go' would fly out and I would be back to square one. She pursed her lips at my response and then continued.

Painfully and methodically, Doctor Yashin reached up and drew down two of the hoses that were attached to the glass coffin. She pulled them through the glass and attached them to a catheter needle. She pushed one needle into my arm, which was not too bad. But the other one, she inserted under my scalp and it hurt like hell. I scrunched up my eyes and dug my fingernails into my palms until she was done. I felt like a pincushion science experiment, a potato battery.

"Ok. I'm going to step back now and the box will be lowered. Don't worry. In your case, it should only take five minutes. I warn you, it will hurt a great deal." She moved my chin so I was facing the ceiling. "Keep your head straight." She patted my arm gently, and pulled away the sheet, disappearing from view.

I thought the being naked part would be awful but I was completely distracted by the fact that a giant glass box was being lowered over my body. It dangled and swayed until the mechanical arms took over and

The Wall

straightened it into place. I heard the sound of air sucking and knew I was sealed in. I was a spider under a drinking glass, my mind scuttling and straining to find purchase on the straight edges. *Breathe*, I kept telling myself. But I was holding it and then gasping for short bursts.

"Relax!" I heard the doctor shout again. "It will start in ten seconds."

I thought, *Is she joking? How could anyone relax in here?*

I counted.

One, I watched all but four hoses retract from the box and the mechanical arms seal the holes with rubber stoppers.

Two, a cycling, whirring noise began, like someone was spinning an enormous, metal wheel.

Three, something clicked into place.

Four, the whirring stopped and a humming began.

Five, the whirring started again and sounded faster.

Six, I couldn't breathe. I needed to get out.

Seven, I could see blue liquid tracking down the tubes, entering my glass sarcophagus, and a blue gas filling the box.

Eight, I held my breath, not wanting to inhale the gas.

Nine, it felt cool when the blue liquid hit my skin and I could feel it spreading through my body.

Ten, I had to breathe, my body convulsed, and I drew in the gas, which dried my throat instantly and burrowed into my insides like a thousand needles.

Now I understood why they restrained me. *Oh my God, please. Please, someone kill me. Kill me now.*

Five minutes of this was four minutes and fifty-nine seconds too long. I screamed and strained. I lifted my hips off the table as my body fought against the pain. My eyeballs felt like they were trying to jump out my head. I was aware of every drop of that liquid as it moved through my veins, burning the vessels as it went. I prayed for death—I prayed for anything to end it. I begged for them to stop but my strangled screams were met with silence.

"Rosa, it will end in 3... 2... 1. Try to stay awake."

I blinked away tears, sure my eyeballs were bleeding, sure my whole body was burnt to a crisp. But after a few seconds, the pain released its grasp on my body and I felt fine. No, better than fine. The glass coffin rose above my head, wobbling, and the doctor appeared in my view again. Carefully removing the needles, she felt my head. The clamps released and I put my hand to my head, surprised to find a few centimeters of hair had grown to cover my bald spot. I was then suddenly reminded of my nakedness and swung up to grab the sheet on the floor. The dizziness I'd been feeling from my concussion was gone. The dull ache in my wrist was gone too. I felt like I could run for miles and never tire.

I gave Deshi a look, which he returned with concern. "I have to get back to work, Rosa. I hope you are feeling better." He strolled quickly out of the room, anxious not to get caught up in my plans. Careen and Pietre came in right after him.

"Cool, huh?" Careen bubbled excitedly and I couldn't help but grin back. Yes, it was pretty impressive.

Pietre just stared down at his dirty fingernails and muttered unsympathetically, "We could hear you screaming from the other end of the labs."

The doctor cut my cast off and I dressed quickly under my sheet, telling them to turn their backs as I buttoned my shirt. I didn't miss the scoff from the boy soldier. Finished, I jumped up quickly, like lightning.

"Thanks, Doctor," I said casually.

"You're welcome," she replied in amusement. "Just try and take it easy. You will feel strong but you will also have a reduced sensitivity to pain. I don't want to see you back here again." I nodded. She pulled me

The Wall

to her side and whispered in my ear. "I was truly sorry to hear about what happened to you."

I blushed. I didn't know everyone knew about it. And it made very uncomfortable to think people pitied me.

"Um, thanks." I didn't really know how to respond. She nodded and left, pressing something into Pietre's hand as she glided out the door. He muttered to her with a scary smile on his face.

He turned to me, still hanging in the door like he didn't want to step into the room. "Here, take these," he said flippantly.

Two pills flew in an arc towards me. I caught one fuzzy-edged pill in my palm but the other rolled under a trolley.

"Why? What for?" I stammered as Pietre let the door slowly close between us.

"Because if you don't, you'll die," he said sharply, the words slicing through the closing gap like an arrow.

I jumped off the table like a spring and scrambled to find the second pill. Pushing the trolley aside, it clanged into the wall and bounced back towards me. My fingers grasped the powder-white disc and I carefully held it, worried my new strength would turn it to dust. I shoved them both in my mouth, feeling them grazing my throat as I swallowed them without water. I was about to yell a tirade of abuse at Pietre when a ripple of nausea rolled through me like a tidal wave. I turned to the bucket placed neatly at the foot of my bed and vomited pure blue.

Careen's perfect face appeared in the doorway. She cracked a pristine smile as I raised my head from my bucket. I wiped the tears from my eyes, my hands streaked blue. Puzzled, I looked to her for explanation.

"Oh yeah," she said, flipping her hair behind her ear. "Don't wear any white for a while." She tapped her chin thoughtfully with a slender, white finger. "Actually you're safer to just wear blue for a few days. You're gonna pee, sweat, and cry blue."

"Fascinating," I said sarcastically as I turned back to my bucket to continue emptying the contents of my stomach. Now I understood why the doctor seemed displeased that I had eaten.

I heard a tapping. I followed Careen's foot to her face. "What?" I asked, irritated.

She looked uncomfortable. "Um, we'll just wait outside until you're finished, ok?"

I was about to say, 'fine', when the rumble of nausea overtook me again.

The door pressed shut.

As we left, after the vomiting fireworks, I asked Dr. Yashin what the pills were for.

"The liquid can't stay in your system for more than fifteen minutes, or your body starts to shut down," she said matter-of-factly.

I gulped. "What do you mean?"

"Just imagine how you felt in the procedure times a hundred, then suddenly, everything just ends," she said, playing with her glasses chain.

"I don't remember Joseph crying blue tears," I muttered.

Pietre whistled low and said, "Maybe he's not as big a baby as you." I couldn't even be bothered glaring at him.

Dr. Yashin shook her head disapprovingly. "Yes, I heard about his operation. They took his heart out, injected the blue solution, and then injected the antidote minutes later. This was done before they placed it inside his body."

"Oh," I said, because I couldn't come up with anything intelligent to say. I felt out of my league. Overwhelmed. There was so much about these people I didn't understand—or couldn't understand.

I turned to the soldiers, Careen and Pietre. "So, what about this training?"

37

TRAINING

When training started, I split myself in two. One half walked towards Joseph, lay in his arms, kissed him, and let his warmth grant her safety. The other half walked away, walked into the woods.

COMBAT

The morning after my procedure, my body jerked in the bed like I'd been electrocuted. A hard shiver. It felt like some of the blue stuff was still swirling around my insides, poking at what was left and looking for any remaining damage. Joseph lay next to me, warm and beautiful. I gave him a gentle kick with my heel and he groaned and rolled towards me. Reaching out, he pulled me into his arms. I folded like a V, unable to fight him in his sleep. Unable and unwilling. He moved his hands up under my shirt, unaware of what he was doing. I blew my hair out of my face and rolled my eyes. If he was going to do this, I'd rather he was awake. I turned in his arms and kissed his nose. "Joseph, wake up." He blinked at me cross-eyed for a second and then chuckled. Opening his arms, he stretched out and yawned, folding them behind his head.

"What time is it?" he asked, mid-yawn.

"Nearly eight, you need to go."

His eyes shone in the morning sun and told me he wasn't going anywhere. Still drowsy from sleep, he rolled over and pinned me under his big arms, coasting just above my body. I smiled up at him but something twisted in his face and he paused. "Sorry, is this...?"

"I'm all better now. See..." I flipped over and I rolled up the back of my shirt, "no more bruises. I feel great."

Joseph finally shook off his drowsiness and frowned. "Obviously, I'm glad they did it but I still don't understand why. Your injuries were pretty superficial. I didn't think they used the machine unless it was a life-threatening injury."

I pulled myself up onto my elbows and met his questions with a kiss. Quickly following it up with, "Yes, of course, Dr. Sulle, but you have to go. You'll be late." I needed to leave for training really soon.

"Oh, right," he said, his mind distracted momentarily. He jumped out of bed and made his way to the shower, pulling off his shirt as he walked. I had to sigh. The sight of his now-tanned, naked back, little freckles dotting the skin around his neckline, was too much. I considered joining him in the shower. I could imagine the hot water running over our bodies, my hands... but I let my shyness talk me out of it.

Training, I reminded myself.

Joseph left with Orry in one arm and a medical bag in the other. Five minutes later, Careen and Pietre were knocking on my door.

"Geez!" I said in surprise. "Were you hiding in the bushes?"

"Something like that," Pietre snapped as he pushed his way into the house without invitation. He looked me up and down with an unwelcome stare. "You can't wear that. You need to put on something more... flexible."

I regarded my clothing. I was wearing jeans and a button-up shirt. I appealed to Careen questioningly.

"Just put on leggings and a t-shirt," she said happily. "Blue," she called after me.

I changed and they led me down our house steps. At least they weren't shoulder to shoulder like yesterday, but I still got the sense I was being babysat. They turned right and we headed towards the thick patch of forest that edged the top line of houses. We were close to the Wall and its silhouette hung over the roofs of the small timber cottages. Dark, spindly shadows dripped down the trunks and darkened the foliage of the forest we were about to enter.

They disappeared into the brush and it closed around them like a heavy curtain. I followed.

I watched the two of them. They were unlike Joseph and me in so many ways. Pietre moved through the woods like the trees presence offended him and should jump out of his way and salute. Careen followed behind him, mirroring his footsteps. She never touched him unless he initiated it. And when he did, it was like he claimed her.

He was rough and cursed a lot, which reminded me of my Construction boys. A feeling that rocked and ached my heart. But apart from the cursing, he was nothing like them. He seemed hardened and certainly unused to not getting his own way.

When there were no more branches to slap and abuse, the forest gave way to smaller shrubs. The woods had now sprung green and yellow. It had changed as if overnight. From bleak and cold, life just managed to press itself against the icy panes of winter, to buzzing and bursting with pollen dust. Life was defrosting, long, green stems beckoned and bent in the breeze. Little crackles of noise, leaves shifting, gave evidence of small, scurrying creatures that had poked their wet noses out of hibernation. I inhaled deeply, the smell of layers of rotting foliage, the shed skin of trees, wafted up from where we trampled. It was thick and sweet, damp and moldy, but wonderful. I doubted Pietre noticed.

Every movement was so deliberate and violent with this man. He stomped into the center of the clearing and spun around to face me, anchoring his feet in the dirt like his toes were talons.

"Your training will be separated into three parts." He held up his fingers and counted them off, folding them down like he was snapping his bones. "Fitness, Combat, and Survival Skills." He appraised my tiny frame. "I think we'll start with Combat since I think we all know that's what you will need the most help with."

Careen giggled and I shot her a glare.

He put his hands on his hips and told me to try to take him down. I laughed, my body shaking with the preposterousness of it. It felt good to laugh. Was he serious? He growled, his teeth bared like a wolf, and assured me that he was.

I shook my head, "No." I wasn't going fight anyone on my mission. This was stupid. I turned to Careen, who leaned back gracefully and lunged at him. Her feline qualities were exaggerated as she glided through the air and grabbed his throat. They scrambled, grunted, and wrestled until Pietre had her arm twisted behind her back. Immobilized. They were enjoying this and I felt like I was getting a gross insight into their love lives.

I held my stomach. "Can you guys save it for the bedroom, please?"

Pietre gave me a sickening smile and Careen looked clueless.

"Fine, let's try shooting the stunner," he said, jumping up and wiping the dirt from his hair, attempting, unsuccessfully, to smooth it down.

He placed the gun in my hand, knocking my lower limbs out to a wider stance with his forearm, like I was an uncooperative table leg. Then he pressed his cheek against mine, the rough sandpapery stubble grazing my skin. I blushed and my heartbeat picked up, unused to the contact from a stranger. "Now aim for that tree." He pointed to a narrow birch about two meters away from me, still skinned stark, its peppered trunk scarred from winter and starving deer stripping its bark away. It was only ten centimeters in diameter.

I wrapped my fingers around the gun loosely. I wanted to drop it. I hated the feel of the cold metal in my hands, the power it held to harm. I had no intention of taking this with me to my mothers. I closed both

The Wall

eyes and took a literal shot in the dark. I heard the click and then a winding up, whizzing noise as the charge built. Then the wires spat out and frittered to the ground. I'd lowered my arms as it discharged and it landed in the dirt at my feet.

Pietre was in a rage. "You can't close your eyes when you shoot. You could have shot yourself in the foot!" He retrieved the wires and straightened my shoulders forcefully, like he was squaring a peg. "Try again. This time with your eyes open!"

We tried shooting the stunner over and over until the sun was high in the sky and my arms felt like listless willow branches, shaking and bowing from holding them out in front of me for so long. I think by the time we were done, I could at least open one eye when I pulled the trigger.

At the end of the first day, I walked in the door and the other half of me took over. The lies began. Joseph wasn't home yet so I rushed around, making an obvious mess so he would think I'd been working all day. I ran my hands along the rough edge of a cabinet carcass and sprinkled sawdust on my forehead. I began making dinner, which was reheating one of the many casseroles, which had been deposited in our fridge after my attack, mostly from Addy, but some from Gwen and Odval too. I smiled at their kindness, overwhelmed and undeserving. As I lifted them up, inspecting what each container had in them, something fell to the floor. It was a little music device and stuck to it was a note with Gwen's scrawl running across it. It read: *Angry Music*.

I shrugged and clipped it to my waistband. Placing the earphones in, I switched it on. It blasted and my head jerked back from the volume. Once I had adjusted it, the words bashed me over the head again and again with fear, anguish, and pain, but I couldn't stop listening. As Joseph opened the door, the words crept out and sailed towards him.

I told you to be patient
and I told you to be kind
…now all your love is wasted
…who will love you?
Who will love you?

The blood drained from my face and I pulled the earphones out violently, managing a thin-lipped smile. I glanced down at the tiny screen and noted the name of the musician. This Bon Iver guy was inside my head, his anguish matching my own.

He dropped his bag on the floor and watched me carefully. But then Orry cried and Joseph had to respond. He went to the kitchen to make Orry's milk at the sink. I kept my back to him but acknowledged his presence with a slight nod. I felt like a criminal, so I slammed bars between the two people I was fast becoming. This was 'at home' Rosa. *Believe it*, I told myself, cursing Gwen under my breath even though part of me wanted to hear the rest of the song. Did he get what he wanted? Did he shame her into being better?

Orry settled and Joseph laid him on his tummy on one of Addy's rugs.

I clucked my tongue. "You know he'll vomit on that. He's just had a bottle." Although, you probably wouldn't even notice on one of Addy's creations since they all looked a little like a rainbow had vomited on them as it was.

Joseph chuckled and walked towards me. I relaxed, slipping into the comfortable and desirous atmosphere he created. "You know you sound like Addy when you talk like that."

I put my hands on my hips and did my best imitation of Addy, rattling and bobbing my head as I spoke, "Babies need to be independent." I raised my index finger, waggling it in his face. "You've got to let them work things out for themselves. A face full of vomit and he'll soon work

The Wall

out not to do it again."

Joseph threw his head back and laughed. It filled me with certainty, like a limp sail suddenly pressed open by a surge of wind. He placed his hands on my waist and pulled me towards him so our hips were touching. "That's very good. You've been practicing." He ran his fingers across my brow, brushing of the sawdust. "Working hard?"

I felt my heart beating faster and the blood rush to my cheeks. I took a step backwards. "Yes, it's good to get back into it. It gives me something to focus on," I lied, as I slapped imaginary dust off my pants. He looked at me doubtfully for a second but shook it free.

"Yes, I suppose that's true. I like getting back into working at the hospital... even if it is with Matt." It was unlike Joseph to be so unforgiving but he hadn't let go of what Matthew had failed to tell us. Also, as far as I knew, Cal was still under Matthew's care in the hospital, which had to be hard.

After we put Orry to bed, I took the opportunity to turn the focus onto him and let him talk my ears off about his day until we dozed off on our couch, carelessly intertwined like the gnarled roots of a Banyan tree.

I woke up the next morning in our bed and realized Joseph must have carried me. The first day of training had been exhausting and I was sure it would only get worse. Pietre didn't strike me as someone who would go easy on a beginner, especially not me.

This is how it started.

Every morning, I would see Joseph off at the door. He would take Orry every other day and I would drop the baby with Odval on my days.

If Joseph suspected anything, he never said so. He was so preoccupied with his medical training. It had stepped up recently because they were preparing for the mission. People were getting checked out and checked off a list and preparations were being made for the incoming Spiders. Some of them had been injured during interrogations and there were also likely to be injuries during the rescues. Gus asked Joseph to go along as the medic but he said he felt like he didn't have enough experience yet to be solely responsible for the groups' health.

I did a good job of separating the two things I was doing. When I was with Joseph, I stuffed the training Rosa in a box and locked it. I immersed myself in him and Orry. I intended to tell him… I just wanted to wait until I was stronger, trained better, so I would have more back up when he tried to convince me not to go. Well, that's what I told myself.

I became friends with my lies. They wrapped around me like curls of white smoke, whispering the necessary answers in my ears. When Joseph noticed a scratch on my arm, I told him I got it rushing through my work. When I appeared tired, I said it was the nightmares. When he questioned the pile of work that had accumulated in the corner, I said people were giving me more time to finish because of what had happened but they were still bringing things over. The lies came quickly and easily and it scared me. Inside, I felt like a coward. He knew what I'd wanted to do and I should have just told him the truth straight away. Instead, I slunk into a corner, made excuses, and let one half of me lie and the other half wrap my arms around him like nothing had ever happened.

FITNESS

As expected, Pietre was a hard taskmaster. He had me running laps, climbing trees, and doing sit-ups and push-ups. But I didn't mind it. I liked the way my body responded to the exercise. My stomach flattened and my arms became ropey and toned. I was never going to look like

The Wall

Careen, the terrible and formidable threat of a woman, but I had my own kind of fitness.

Tree climbing was my favorite thing. Being light and agile, I could clamber up even thin-boughed trees quickly and quietly. I selected a tall Poplar tree. Its slim branches were low to the ground and stuck straight out at a 45-degree angle. The whole tree looked like it had been pulled through a water pipe and the branches hadn't uncoiled. As I sat on a bendy branch to catch my breath, a vein of guilt ran through me. I'd strayed far from that busting, pregnant girl. I sighed. I grieved. I was so different to what I used to be. That girl slipped over a cliff when I wasn't looking, a clatter of loose dirt spilling over rocks, the only evidence she ever existed.

Sitting here now, with the rough bark scratching my backside, the spiky buds pressing into my head and arms, I couldn't imagine how I had once been comfortable up here. But then I was with Joseph. He softened everything.

"What are you thinking about?" a breathless Pietre asked. He was looking up at me between the branches, his eyes curious.

"Nothing."

"You know, if this is too hard for you, you don't have to go. You could give up," he suggested.

"You'd like that, wouldn't you?" I snapped, wriggling around and trying to sway the tree. Maybe I could eject him from it.

"I would."

I glared down at him and jumped to my feet, sending scratchy bits of bark and poplar buds towards his annoying face.

"Why do you hate me so much?" I asked.

He wiped his face and squinted up at me. Pursing his lips, he considered my question.

"I don't hate you. But my mother was one of the Survivors that didn't make it out of the mounds. So for that… I feel a little bit of payback is necessary." Leaves dotted his hair and he tried to shake them off without falling from his perch.

I shifted my feet to disperse my weight better. I was shocked at this revelation but tried not to show it. My voice felt small, "So you blame me?"

"No."

"Then what?"

"She died so you could live. I guess I wanted to make sure you made it count."

I was confused. I didn't understand where that left us. All I knew was I was trying as hard as I could. Grudging respect maybe? At least that's how I felt. My lips curled a little as I realized I seemed to have a knack for having serious conversations in trees. I wondered if my life could get any more ludicrous. Of course it could.

I swung myself up to the next branch and muttered, "I'll make it count."

And I'm pretty sure I heard him respond with, 'you better' as he made his way down towards the sodden earth.

I climbed to the top of the tree. No one could reach me up there. I gripped the trunk and moved like a monkey, never staying put for too long until I reached the uppermost branches. I stayed there longer than I should have, letting myself sway in the breeze, willing my body to become nothing so I could float over the Wall. The pressure was weighing on me and I considered the fact that I might fail, that I wouldn't make it count. I was overflowing and just wanted to be empty—if only for a second.

Running my hands over the straggly bark, I thought about Addy. Why hadn't she come to visit me? I was sure Matthew probably told her what I was doing. Maybe she disagreed with my choice. It didn't make any difference, I suppose, but I wanted her to support my decision. She of all people understood the importance of family.

Careen's voice pierced the silence. "Rosa, what are you doing up there? Don't you need to pick up Orry?"

I scrambled down the trunk, skinning both my knees in my haste. Odval would be waiting for me.

When I got home on day eleven, Apella was in my chair. I would say sitting but that's not what she was doing, everything about her was set on edge. She was like a porcelain figure, her legs folded neatly, her composure perfect, her whole existence looking out of place perched atop a pile of Addy's crocheted rugs. She looked down at her hands, which were clasped lightly in her lap, and then up at me through a curtain of blonde hair. I tried to smile at her but it came out all wrong on my face. How could I lie so easily to Joseph and not to her?

"Rosa, I'm concerned about you. You haven't visited in a while. Is everything all right?" I could tell the words pained her. She was never one for sentiment and this was difficult for her.

I waved her off, "I'm fine."

She rose delicately and wafted over to me, gently placing her cool hand on my cheek. "Please come see me before you leave," she said sadly. I didn't know what to say so I nodded.

SURVIVAL SKILLS

Finally I had something I could teach Careen and Pietre. Wandering through the forest, I picked out the various edible plants and showed them. The sun was sifting through the leaves and actually warming the earth slightly. Pockets of yellow pinecones moved like little, bearded faces poking out of the pine needles. The azaleas I'd pointed out to Orry had started to flower. It was beautiful but it was also a warning. If the weather was clearing, the Woodland soldiers may be ready to start their trek. They would begin their search for us.

Careen listened with interest as I tried to educate them, Pietre quietly fumed.

"See these?" I said, bending a branch towards their faces. "They're sweet. A bit chewy but a good source of calories."

Pietre eyed it with disgust. I let it snap back into place, hoping it would whip him as it returned.

"Why would I eat a pinecone if I can shoot a rabbit?" he asked, crossing his arms like a child.

Careen touched him affectionately and he flinched. A devilish look spread across his face. "I think it's time we showed you how to hunt."

I shriveled away from his stare. I didn't want to hunt. Killing things was not in me. I knew that. I stood my ground. "I don't need to learn to hunt; I survived out there for months, pregnant, eating only nuts and berries."

He sneered at me. "You want me to sign off on your mission? Then you'll hunt."

Careen protested, "Look, I think she's shown that she can handle herself out here. I don't think…"

"Think?" he snapped. "Who asked you?"

She closed her mouth. I was so surprised at her. She could more than handle him. If she wanted, she could snap him over her thigh and toss him in the dirt. I didn't understand why she would let him tell her what to do. Observing their relationship over the last week and a half reminded me of Paulo and Mother. It made me wonder if this was normal. If so, it made me feel like I was the undeserving winner of the boyfriend lottery. Joseph would never speak to me that way. Although, what I'd done lately would warrant it.

The Wall

"I'll do more combat skills if you want but I'm not hunting," I said. I was sure if I killed an animal in front of him, I would burst into tears and there was no way I was going to let that happen.

"Fine," Pietre said, his eyes burning.

38

FINAL DAY

I'd said I would try harder with my combat skills but I couldn't help but argue with some of the more specialized moves Pietre wanted me to learn. I couldn't see myself cartwheeling across the front lawn of my parents place and leaping onto the roof. Pietre had mixed training up in the last few days and we jumped from skill to skill like a test. It reminded me harrowingly of *the* Test at the Classes.

"I don't see why I need to know how to disarm a man. Paulo doesn't own a gun, none of the citizens do," I said, crossing my arms and squatting over the fire I'd just made from nothing but a rock and some dried grass. "Look," I gestured. "I can do this."

Pietre sneered at me. Standing back, I could almost see the waves of anger rolling off him. "Yes, but lighting a fire won't help you in the Rings. You need to be able to defend yourself if someone comes at you." He stormed towards me and flung his forearm to my neck. Forcing me up with his other arm, pinching my underarm skin, he pinned me against a tree and lifted me off the ground. My legs kicked uselessly as my windpipe slowly closed. "You have to *believe* I won't hurt you. That in fact, I can't," he said, staring at me intently, cocking his head to the side as he searched my eyes.

I was much smaller than him, weaker, and a not nearly as skilled as a fighter. Of course he could hurt me! This wasn't about some attitude adjustment I needed to make.

"Let me go," I managed to gasp, although my breath was running out fast. I could see Careen standing behind me, blurred by my wet eyes, as I felt the fight leaving my body. She shifted nervously, clamping her hands together like she was trying to stop herself from interfering.

He watched my eyes roll up. I was about to pass out. His eyebrows drew together as he studied me with morbid curiosity, like when I watched my neighbor kill a chicken. It was a spectacle to watch it run around with its head missing, even if it was disgusting. His face relaxed and he let me fall, throwing his hands up in exasperation, relenting.

I fell to my knees, clutching my throat and coughing. Glancing at one of the knives at my feet, I let anger overtake reason. I wrapped my hands around it tightly and stood. I hated being tested. It eroded my skin and cornered my judgment, until all I could see was my need for retribution.

"She's impossible," he yelled at Careen. "I can't see how this is going work." He turned his back to me, digging his feet into the dirt like a bull about to charge.

I'd hoped I would hit the tree to his right—just graze his ear or something clever like that. I wanted prove to him I had learned something, that I wasn't useless. I pulled my arm back and threw. The knife cartwheeled through the air. I stood there, hands at my sides, mouth agape, as it circled its way towards the middle of his back. I sighed with relief when it landed, handle first, between his shoulder blades with a satisfying thud and bounced to the forest floor.

I couldn't help myself; I let out a triumphant, "Bah!" and fell to the ground laughing. Careen covered her mouth to muffle her giggles.

Pietre twirled around and I thought he was going to punch me in the face. Instead, a mean smile curled his lips. "Better," he said as he picked up the knife and wiped it on his trousers. He placed it in my hand and pulled me up straight. He wrapped his fingers around my own and my breath caught unpleasantly. "Hold it like this and keep both eyes open when you aim." He stood behind me, whispering into my ear, and I tried to focus on the knife and not the warmth of his hard body pressed into my back. "Ok, retract your arm and make sure you release it here," he held my hand level with my face, "and not here." He brought our hands down to my waist. "Good, now throw."

I threw the knife and it landed just left of the center of the trunk of the tree. I let myself smile a little. Realizing he still had his hand wrapped around my own, I wiggled out of his grasp and turned to face him. "Thanks."

He shrugged. "Just get on with it. We don't have time for this." He looked to Careen, who was beaming like a proud parent. "We don't have time for you either but we're stuck with you," he said, pointing a knife at me accusingly.

He beckoned Careen over, nuzzling into her neck and turning my stomach. Was that what Joseph and I looked like to others? I hoped not. "Why don't you show her how it's done, honey," he said into her hair. *Ick!*

Careen gathered up five short-handled knives and threw them in succession. When I looked at the tree, she had made a circle pattern. "Show off," I muttered. Her ears pricked but she ignored me, strolling elegantly to the tree and plucking out the knives with ease. This was never going to be my thing. I felt sorry for the tree.

After I'd proved to Pietre that I could at least throw the knife so it landed blade first into a target, he let me move on to something else.

He fished around in his small duffle bag and I was worried he was going to pull out another weapon for me to master. Instead, he withdrew a handful of dark grey material and threw me a wad. On closer inspection, I could see they were gloves and little booties. "Put those on. This is mission specific and you must be able to do this if you want to come

The Wall

with us."

I rolled my eyes. Who did he think he was, Genghis Khan? I put on the equipment, wondering what possible use they could have.

As Pietre shoved and cursed his way through the slapping branches, I watched his back ripple and tense with fascination. He was wound up tighter than a spring and I knew I was the one that wound him even tighter. He wore a dusty blue t-shirt and dark jeans, the standard canvas shoes wrapped around his ankles. He was not as tall as Joseph and not as broad. He looked like a Survivor, strong, lean, and ready to jump to action at any second. His hair was the part that amused me the most. He seemed to always need to be in control but his hair didn't cooperate. Light brown in color, it was spiky and stuck up at all angles, like he had just rolled out of bed. He was forever trying to smooth it down. I wished he would leave it. It was the only part of him that seemed accessible and less hard. Careen followed him, her feet barely touching the ground as she walked. She was like a cat, lithe, beautiful, and slightly feral.

I, on the other hand, moved quietly but carefully, around the trees, under the branches. I inhaled and reveled in the smells of the woods. I treated them as I would my home, with respect.

I followed them until we found ourselves at the Great Wall.

Pietre spun around to face us, running his hand through his hair for the hundredth time. I clambered my way through the brush, always lagging behind, and stood before them. Pietre's body lurched as if stunned and he strode towards me with an angry look on his face. I suppressed the feeling that I should run. He grabbed my arm and jerked it to his face, inspecting it.

"What?" I shook him free, looking to Careen for help. He pulled a cloth from his back pocket and clamped it to my wrist. His stare was intense and I didn't like it.

"You're bleeding," he stated, wrapping a large gash on my arm quickly and tightly.

"Huh," I remarked, fascinated with the fact I hadn't felt a thing. I peeled back the cloth and the cut bubbled blood like a backed-up plughole. It was quite deep but I had no recollection of how I did it.

"You need to be careful; you're not paying attention to your surroundings," he snapped, irritated. "Remember, you have a low sensitivity to pain at the moment."

"Are you concerned about me, Pietre?" I teased.

His eyes flicked to me disparagingly as he kicked off his shoes. He wasn't concerned, just annoyed. I was a bothersome bug he wanted to squash.

"Just help yourself, so I don't have to."

Help yourself. The words crushed me as I remembered the last time I'd heard them or thought them. I tightened the bandage over my bleeding wound, and wrapped a mental bandage around the oozing wound Cal had left in my head.

"Fine," I said shortly. "What are we doing now?" I gazed up at the wall. It was in full shadow, with the sun hovering just past the turrets. It felt cold and oppressive. I didn't like being this close. It still gave me the chill associated with being closed in. I'd managed to find some history books, books with real facts in them, during my stay in the hospital. The Wall had been built to protect the Chinese Empire from various threatening groups but also to control trade. The books also revealed there were bodies sandwiched between the great stones that made up the beastly structure. It was a towering graveyard.

Careen narrowed her eyes at me as she handed me the booties. "Put these on your feet and follow us." I wondered what her chilly stare was about but I had no time to ask.

I watched as Careen and Pietre approached the wall and jumped suddenly, landing on the surface like two lizards. They scrambled up the wall, keeping their bodies pressed as flat as they could to the sandy, grey stone. I followed, slipping a little, but managing to keep my grippy hands and feet flush with the wall. They were both sitting between the turrets, legs swinging over the edge, when I got to the top, somewhat breathless, but my heart drumming in a fulfilling rhythm. That was much more fun than throwing knives.

They held hands. Careen made a point of leaning her head on his shoulder and glaring at me suspiciously. Her mood had changed since our altercation in the woods and I had the sense she was jealous at Pietre's concern for my arm. I scoffed at the thought. Pietre was not interested in me, and I certainly wasn't in him. We were just stuck with each other, as he'd said.

"Well, at least we know you'll survive getting over the wall," Pietre said, grimacing. I think he'd hoped I would fail at this also. "Now, let's discuss the rest of our mission."

We talked and planned until the sun dipped below the wall and bits of fluffy, pink clouds wafted towards the sky. I'd lost track of time. I was going to get home late, after Joseph.

I lowered myself over the turret and scrambled down the Wall, skidding and scraping my arms as I went. I felt less in control, like I was sliding down ice. I tried to put my shoes on as I walked, hopping on one leg whilst trying to jam a shoe on my foot, but I tripped over. "What's the rush?" Careen said as she caught my arm.

I explained to Careen I hadn't told Joseph about the training and he would be angry. She nodded through my huffed explanations and waited until I finished to speak. She blinked at me with her perfectly symmetrical blue eyes. "You have to tell him, Rosa. He'll understand." Her faith in him was not reassuring. She flipped her hair and shrugged off her seriousness. "That was fun wasn't it, the climbing?"

I looked at her, confused by the sudden change in her mood and conversation, I should have been used it by now but she was so strange sometimes. "I guess…" I said, raising my eyebrows. We slowed down to a walk as we approached the edge of the trees.

Careen said goodbye and I watched her gracefully pluck her way between the plants at the tree line. She made sure she stayed just out of sight, practicing her camouflaging skills.

Pietre stayed with me. He was acting shifty and it made me uncomfortable. I stepped out of the cover of the trees, peering back and forth to check for people. I could see our house from here. I wondered if I had time to run to Odval's and collect Orry before Joseph returned but decided against it, too much too explain. I took two steps towards home and Pietre called me back. I turned around and he approached me. He took both my shoulders and sort of shuffled me into position so my back was completely facing my home. He held up my arm and ran his fingers along the blood-soaked cloth. "Take care of this properly," he said and then he leaned in slowly and whispered into my ear. "There. All done—now he knows."

I turned and felt the sound clipped from the air, my heart stopped beating and the ground wobbled under my feet. Joseph was standing at the top of the road, having just stepped off a spinner. He regarded the two of us for a moment, then his eyes fell to the ground and he walked calmly into the house. Panic rose. I don't know what he thought he saw. All I knew was—Pietre was a bastard.

I shoved Pietre's chest hard but he was unaffected, giving me an unfeeling stare. Unsympathetic. "Why did you do that?" I asked.

"I was doing you a favor." *The hell he was.*

I thought about the way he'd purposefully moved me and leaned in so close, his lips brushing my ear. "But he could have thought that you and I were…"

At this, he laughed wholeheartedly and cruelly. "You and me? You know, that's why I like Careen. She's simple; she knows what I need and she gives it to me," he sneered. "This," he motioned between the two of us, "would so not be worth it."

"You're disgusting," I spat.

I turned towards my house and ran with desperate, stumbling footfalls. Although, I wasn't sure what I was running towards.

39

LIES

As I ran towards the house, I pulled out the handheld communicator I'd been given and called Odval. My fingers were shaking so hard I missed the buttons several times.

"Can you hold onto Orry for a while longer?" I asked, trying not to sound as frantic as I felt, my feet trying to pick their way between the cobblestones and only managing to trip up on every loose one.

She paused. I could hear Orry babbling in the background. "That's fine. Is everything ok?"

I forced myself to smile while I spoke, "Yes, yes, everything's fine. Um… Joseph and I just wanted some time to ourselves, if that's all right? Just a couple of hours…"

"You know I love having him here. How about I keep him overnight and you pick him up in the morning? I need you to have a look at my bed; I think some of the springs need…"

I cut her off. "Yep! That'd be great. I'll come by early in the morning." I was at the door. I cursed myself. We were leaving tomorrow. How had I let it get this far without telling him?

I'd ruined everything.

I steeled myself, taking a deep breath and pushed the door ajar, listening to it creak and screech with anticipation. Or maybe that was just the noise in my head.

The Wall

I stood in the doorway, panting, watching him move around the house, changing out of his work clothes, putting dirty clothes in the hamper. Doing normal things when there was nothing normal about what he'd just seen. I stood on the edge, an observer. I was gripping the sill with my toes but I didn't want to step in. Stepping in meant owning up. I just kept my eyes on Joseph, noticing him, noticing the changes I'd failed to see before now.

Before he used to have to fill every gap, every break in conversation with chatter. Now there was a stillness to him, a contemplative age that smoothed his face and dwarfed my own maturity. Was it his purpose, his need to help people? I envied it so much. I couldn't quiet my thoughts for even a second. I was a whirlwind, a hurricane that swept in and destroyed everything in my path.

His control was unbearable. I'd expected him to come at me. Shout and scream. But he ignored me.

I pulled a bandage from the first aid kit and wrapped my wrist tightly, while he moved to the kitchen and tried to wash the dishes. The dull collision of ceramic against steel the only sound the house could abide. I stepped forward and the floorboards creaked under my feet. I was sneaking up on him like a thief in my own home. He stopped washing, letting a cup fall into the sudsy water, gripping the sides of the sink with his head bowed. Every muscle in his arms was tensed, like he was silently trying to rip the sink from the bench. It warned me not to come any closer.

"It's not what you think," I squeaked, my throat closing over slowly like the petals of a night bloom. "Pietre and I, he… we…" Damn it!

He turned to face me, suddenly looking huge, a powerful man looming over me, daring me to come up with something to explain my behavior. "What do *you* think I think?" His face was tight but I could see the hurt in his eyes.

"That there's something going on between Pietre and me...?" As I said it, it seemed the most unlikely conclusion to come to.

He laughed at me and I shrank smaller still. It was a bitter sound. "You and him? That's ridiculous. I know exactly what you're doing. Damn it, Rosa, you're training. You're... leaving me." He started muttering to himself, saying something like he should have guessed but he didn't want to see it. The words sprinkling out like salt onto the weathered floor.

I took a step closer and he took a step back. "No," I whispered. "I'm not leaving you. I'll be back." I was pumping my hands now, trying to calm him. It didn't work.

His whole body shook and he put his hand up as if to say, *Stop! Don't come any closer.*

"Where's Orry?" he asked, his eyes flitting around the room, avoiding my own.

"He's with Odval. He's safe." I felt pitiful. *How could I explain this to him?*

He turned his back to me again, turning on the tap and leaning down to take a drink. Every breath in his body was exaggerated, the anger building, his chest and shoulders seeming to swell with it.

He spun to face me; I felt my own resolve hardening. This was not the best way to tell him but I still felt this was the right thing to do. I straightened myself and faced him front on, nose pointed upwards in defiance.

"When do you leave?" he asked, the words squashing their way out of his hard-set lips.

"Tomorrow," I said quietly.

He sighed deeply. "Then I'll go with you," he said determinedly.

Watching the heat and anger swirl around the both of us, I wondered, *How do you break someone? Do you have to be callous and unfeeling?*

The Wall

Or did you think your bond was strong enough to take it? And it wasn't, you were wrong.

"No. You can't." I watched his face crumple, his eyes looking right through me. "Someone needs to stay with Orry. Besides, you're too loud," I said with a weak smile. "You couldn't sneak up on Addy, and she's deaf!"

He wasn't amused.

He stood two meters from me, his arms folded calmly across his chest. I watched them rise and fall with his breath, watched him try to control his anger.

"Well, I guess you've thought of everything, haven't you?" he said resentfully. Then his eyes sparked. "Except for one thing."

I didn't want to ask but I had the feeling he would say it anyway. "What's that?"

His eyes were fuming, the green boiling over, his temper rising. Gold could be an angry color.

"I won't let you go."

I took a deep breath. "Joseph, you know you can't stop me. I'm going."

He was losing it, throwing any argument at me he could to stop me from going. He was pitching his arms in the air, pacing back and forth, "Don't you think I would like to rescue my parents? Why do you get to and I don't?"

The answer to that question was easy. "It's different, you know that. Your parents are safe. They are happy. They... love each other. I'm thinking of my baby brother or sister too. Orry's blood."

Silence followed for what seemed like forever as he glared at me. I hadn't moved and my legs started to ache. I shifted my weight back and forth. *How could I make this make sense to him? Could I?* I leaned on the back of an armchair and waited for him to speak.

When he opened his mouth, the force was still strong but some of the anger had drained away. "Why is this so important?" He knew why. "Aren't you happy with Orry and me?" His tone was bewildered, strained.

It broke my heart to hurt him like this. But then, it was already kind of broken. I considered his question. Didn't he realize that's why I needed to do this?

I slid towards him slowly, gliding across the floor in my socks like an ice skater, talking as I moved. "Of course I am." I grasped his hands but he shook me free like I was trying to cuff him. Surely, we had to be stronger than this. "That's why."

"I don't understand." He laid his head in his hands like the words were giving him a headache.

"Don't you think everyone deserves this, what we have?" I pleaded.

Recognition flickered in his eyes.

"Rosa." He jolted back suddenly, wringing his hands. He pulled his hair back from his eyes. My heart skipped and all I could see was him. Like one of Orry's pop-up books, he stood clear, the rest of the world turned blurry—boring two-dimensional representations of the real thing. "I'm so angry with you," he stuttered. "How could you… I mean, what am I supposed to do if… damn it." He clasped his hands together and looked at the floor. He was never lost for words. The gravity of our situation had pulled them away.

I could have walked away. Maybe I should have. Let him cool off or tried harder to convince him I was right. Instead, I took two steps towards him and connected with his lips before he could speak again.

40

BEGINNING & ENDING

His arms were slack at his sides for a moment, like I'd shocked him into submission. But I pressed hard against his chest. I literally threw my body at the problem, holding the two crushing walls, the opposing opinions, at bay with my twig-like arms. I felt heat taking over, lips colliding and kissing deeper than they had before. I thought, *He may set me back, put me in my place, be the sensible one as always and tell me to stop.* But after a few seconds, his arms gripped me tightly. They dragged up my back and under my shirt with such pressure I could barely breathe.

He pulled my shirt over my head and threw it on the ground. Lifting me up, he moved towards the bedroom door, bracing my back against the doorframe as he kissed my neck and slipped my bra strap off my shoulder to kiss my collarbone. I shivered, goose bumps growing all over my skin. He ran one hand over the lace of my bra and wound it behind my back to release the clasp. When he did it so swiftly, I resisted the urge to ask him if he'd done it before. Then words would never have hoped to find me as he brushed his lips across my chest and I thought I would die.

Joseph lowered me onto the bed, keeping his hand in the small of my back, my body arcing over his strong forearm. He paused and looked at me for what seemed like forever. The curtains were closed, sunlight creating a golden frame around the fabric. It felt like the room might burst into flames, the light sparking and curling upwards. I sat up and pulled his shirt over his head. Pressing my palms to his chest, I marveled at his body. Strips of yellow light danced across his sun-kissed skin. Undeserving didn't really cover it.

This was the point of no return. But we were already too far gone. There was no going back from here. He tugged back the covers and folded me into them, sliding in next to me. I wiggled out of my pants, kicking them to the side. The world was melting around us. Breath was quick, taken between lips meeting each other, to skin, to be lost in layers of fresh-smelling hair. Hearts were beating strangely. We didn't know what we were doing but we knew exactly what to do. He rolled over until he was hovering above me, just like he had done a hundred times before, but now there was nothing between us. All I could think was, *I want to be closer. I want every bit of my skin to be touching every bit of his.* I pulled him down, feeling the warmth enveloping me. The soft pressure of his lips on mine, drawing me in, tasting dewy and sweet.

He pulled back, coasting above me, too much space between our bodies. His arms flexed under his weight. His beautiful, green eyes were glistening like faceted emeralds, roaming all over my tiny frame, waves of heat touching every inch of my skin.

Shyness disappeared. I felt desperation, an aching need, and I tried to pull him into me. But he hesitated.

"I love you," he said.

I thought, *Don't speak. Don't stop. Show me.*

And then the whole room was humming gold as we discovered more about each other than we'd ever imagined. We were undone and pulled back together. Even the dust in the corner was sparkling like dying stars.

Nothing prepared me for it, the moment. I was moving on a river, my body ebbing and moving with the current and then, suddenly, I was pulled out and cracked open, a fissure of gold light pressing out of my chest and skimming forth over the room.

I was nothing before this.

The Wall

This was forgetting.

This was living.

Somewhere, I lost my thoughts. I was weightless, tied to a hundred birds in flight, soaring through empty space. Thoroughly warm and entirely safe.

This was everything.

41

GOODBYE

Now I know you. I know me. And I know how much you will hate me when you find out I am gone.

It was still dark. I shuffled out of bed, carefully lifting Joseph's heavy arm from my waist without waking him. A lamplight shone from the lounge room, casting heavy shadows across the door and softly illuminating his sleeping face. I stared at him for one terrible minute, watching him breathe, the pulse in his neck beating slowly, calmly, my own heart stretching through my shirt and reaching out to lie back in his arms. *Could I leave him?* All of my doubts sprung up between the floorboards and wrapped around my ankles like vines, threatening to tie me to this spot, hovering over him forever.

My mind shifted back through the night and the notion I might not be able to do what we did again weakened every joint in my body. I wanted to fold up like a wooden puppet and give in. It would be easy to lose myself to this, to the shrug of love, let it wrap me up and ignore all the horrible things going on around me. I sighed deeply, feeling it catch in my throat. Maybe someday that's what I would do, but not today.

I padded out of the room as quietly as I could, feeling less and less sure. I couldn't say goodbye. He would only try to stop me or follow me. This was best. Oh God! I hoped he would forgive me.

As an afterthought, I grabbed Orry's carved train, clutching it reassuringly to my chest. I touched it to my chin, feeling the roughness, the unfinishedness of it. I'd broken so many promises.

I changed into my camouflaged clothing in the lounge room, grabbed my backpack, and placed the train at the bottom. Without a flourish, without an admittance or noise, I slipped out the door. I didn't look back but my whole body was straining against my will to climb back into bed with Joseph. I walked down the street, feeling as if I was tied to my home and, with every step, the ropes were stretching and snapping. This was so much harder than I thought it would be. But I couldn't regret what we did. Never.

What was I going to do for two hours? We were leaving at dawn. I felt restless and wasted. Tears started to come and I found myself kicking into a run and tearing down the dark streets towards the one place I thought I might find some consolation.

I rapped on the worn, wooden door frantically, my chest feeling hollow, a painful lump rising in my throat as I became more and more hysterical. No one responded so I started knocking more loudly, the skin on my knuckles busting and white. A light clicked on and I heard her creaking across the floorboards, surprised her weight even made a noise. A shadow passed in front of the curtain.

"Addy, let me in. Please," I pleaded, pressing my forehead to the door, the 'please' sounding more desperate than I meant it to.

The door opened a crack and the old woman peered out into the darkness hesitantly. When she recognized me, she relaxed. "Rosa, what are you doing here? It's four AM. Goodness child, come inside before you freeze to death."

"I'm sorry to wake you. I'm sorry, I… oh, damn it." Addy raised her eyebrows at my cursing but she softened when I succumbed to crying.

Nothing I tried to say came out right. Nothing made sense.

Addy led me to the living room and sat in an armchair. I laid my head across her lap and soaked her dressing gown with salt water. She shushed me and stroked my hair until I calmed down long enough for me to tell her what was going on.

I lifted my head and stared into her grey eyes. "He's going to hate me. He thinks I'm leaving him. I don't know, maybe he's right. Maybe I am, but not forever. Oh Addy, do you think I'm doing the right thing?"

She took both my hands and squeezed them hard, looking deep into my defective eyes, looking past them and into me.

She said, "I was told once, we can't choose when we are born. We can't choose when we die either. The important thing is what we do with the time we have."

I stared at her blankly. "What do you mean? Do you think I am doing the right thing or not?" I was shaking her arms. It was like shaking a handful of barley.

"Think about it, Rosa," she said, winking one crinkled eyelid at me.

I scrunched up my blotchy face. I wasn't in the mood for riddles. I stared around her cluttered dwelling. Handmade dolls and little porcelain ornaments covered every available space. Crocheted rugs and scarves dripped off the ends of coffee tables and chairs. There was a lifetime of possessions here, a lifetimes worth of making, sharing, living.

Right then, I got it. This wisdom, this unearthly knowing that the crumpled-up woman had inside her, was more valuable than most things I could think of. That's why they separated us. We can never be full, never have that understanding, when we are forbidden to seek counsel from our elders. It was very clever. Clever and evil.

Without it, we were like a packet of shiny pins, all looking for a hold, always ending up clattering to the dirt, half-buried or finding someone else's sharpness. I felt gratitude and guilt for the privilege of being able to pin part of myself to her. The other thing I knew was, like she said, I had to make my time count for something. I had to try to save my mother and her child. Whether it was right or wrong, I was going to try and Joseph might never forgive me. The realization filled me with renewed hope and a plummet of dread.

Addy insisted on making me tea and feeding me. I knew better than to argue with her. But as the sun rose, I said my teary goodbye, hugging her and kissing her forehead, which felt like dry hessian and smelled like dried lavender.

As I walked towards the hospital, pictures of Orry floated around in my head. Orry smiling at me, blinking his odd eyes, and gurgling. The pain I felt for leaving him was so strong I could barely breathe. I should have said goodbye to him but I was too much of a coward. I knew if I saw him, saw the adoration in his eyes when he looked at me, I would never go. I felt bad I was leaving Odval out of the loop but Orry was safe with her and she knew where to find Joseph.

Goodbye, my loves. Please wait for me.

I climbed the stairs wearily. Soon, Joseph would wake and notice my absence. I should have left a note but I had no idea where to start or how to explain. Nothing I could write or say would make this hurt any less. I touched my neck and ran my finger along the edge of my pledge charm, thinking of when I was wearing nothing but that necklace and letting my breath hum out of me for a second of recollection.

Apella's door was ajar and the soft glow of candlelight shone through the gap.

"I think you should tell her. She's much stronger than you realize," I heard her calm, cool voice say.

"Yes, but will it really help her to know? Won't it just hurt her more?" I recognized Matthew's low tones, the protective strain behind the words.

"Matt, I have come to love Rosa as a daughter and I would do anything to protect her. But she must know. She will find out eventually. So it should be sooner rather than later and in a way we can control." Alexei's voice was shaky but strong in its meaning.

I leaned closer to the door. My heart warmed but in an uneasy way at the word, 'daughter'. I had no idea he felt that way about me. Did I see him as a father? Perhaps. I certainly found him embarrassing. I had affection for him but little patience. From what Joseph explained to me, that was precisely how one should feel about their father. Family was wrapping itself around me in defense. *Don't go.*

I knocked lightly on the door with my knuckles. It creaked forward slightly. The room went silent. I wondered if I should pretend I didn't hear anything. Probably.

I walked in and Apella was sitting at her kitchen table, hands warming around a steaming mug. Matthew was standing facing Alexei, who was wearing pajamas, what was left of his hair sticking straight up, with his glasses sitting too loosely on the end of his nose. What a ridiculously awkward man he was.

I kept my eyes on Matthew. "Just tell me. I don't want to be lied to anymore. Whatever it is, just say it." So much for pretending I didn't overhear.

Matthew stood over me. His blue eyes shone in the candlelight but were barely able to draw attention away from the dark circles that hung under them. He put his hand on my shoulder. "Cal passed away earlier tonight."

I stepped backwards like he had punched me in the stomach. Dead. Dead?

It was harsh to say it but I muttered under my breath, "Well, I guess it's all worked out quite neatly for you, hasn't it?"

Apella walked over to me and helped me into a chair. Well, she arranged my frozen limbs and forced them to cooperate into a sitting position. "Rosa, you're being unfair."

"I know," I said woodenly. "Why didn't you use the healing machine on him?"

"It doesn't work on cancer. It can only repair normal cells. Even if we had used it, he would have continued to get sick."

"Right," I said, blinking unevenly. I didn't know what to say. Was I supposed to be relieved? I didn't feel much of anything. I didn't really know Cal, not the real Cal. I should have been sad for him and his family but all I felt was a bottomless nothing. "Thanks for being straight with me," I said.

"Are you all right?" Alexei asked, crouching down to look into my eyes. I managed a half-smile balanced with confusion.

"I think so?" It came out like a question.

"I have to go," Matthew said quietly. "We leave at dawn."

I pulled my head out of my soft, squishy cloud long enough to register that Matthew was coming with us. I hoped he was going to one of the other towns. I couldn't look into his penitent face anymore.

Apella and Alexei hovered over me, waiting for me to do something. Erupt into tears... melt into a puddle of self-loathing, I don't know. I was blank. My mind turned white as snow and I was nowhere in it. Apella shook my shoulder and I heard her whisper, "She's in shock. Get her a glass of water." Alexei's hand slipped off my leg. I hadn't even noticed it was there. I could feel my eyes blinking slowly, snapping scenes like a camera. Table. Cup. Fireplace. Strange picture of person screaming.

What was I doing before this?

My two unlikely parents kneeled before me. Alexei held the glass to my lips and I sipped slowly. Apella tucked my hair behind my ear so she could see my eyes. "Rosa, you have to get going. You'll miss the train." Her words were far away, an echo.

Alexei's rough hands grabbed my face and held my eyes to his. It occurred to me that I'd assumed his hands would be soft like a baby's, like he'd never worked a day in his life, but I was wrong. I'd been wrong about so many things. "We are both so proud of you, for what you are about to do. You're very brave, Rosa. Do you know that?"

Things clicked over. Wheels started turning. Brave? I was brave? I could be. I will be. I slid the door down on the past with a bang. Nothing could be gained from dwelling on this news. I will be brave.

I stood and they stood with me. "Thank you both so much." I hugged them and strode to the door. Newfound strength welled from their faith in me. I turned and gave them a smile. "You're good parents. Though I don't know where you find the strength, with a daughter like me." I heard a sigh from both of them and the sound of Alexei laughing quietly.

It was a gift. I wasn't sure if I felt they were my parents but they were as close as I had at that moment.

I ran down the stairs, telling myself over and over, *You can do this. You can do this.* I tripped my way towards the station on the other side of the Wall, trying hard not to think about Joseph's hand searching for the warmth of my body beside him and finding nothing but cold, empty sheets.

42.

LEAVING HOME

The plan was to ride the spinners as far as we could. In some cases, that was within a few kilometers of the target town. In others, it was a few days' walk to the outer ring of the town. We couldn't use the dogs. They were too noisy and we couldn't hide them or feed them once we reached the wall of the outer ring we had to climb. Deshi had invented a small device to be placed over the latch of the gate of Ring seven. It would open every gate simultaneously for four hours. We were to slip in and out as quickly as possible. Some Spiders had been detained in other towns. With those, the Survivors would incapacitate the guards and grab them. No killing allowed.

Each Spider had a homing device embedded in their upper arm, so at the time of rescue, we would all know exactly where to find them using our handheld trackers. The Spiders knew we were coming and would be ready. We didn't know their names and they didn't know ours—it was safer that way.

None of this really applied to me but Careen and Pietre went over and over the details as our spinner traveled out from dawn to a bright scarlet-and-pink sunrise. I just stared out the window, dreaming about my night with Joseph, blushing at the thought of our skin touching, his lips brushing over new places. I missed him like a pulsing hole in my heart. Careen snapped her fingers in front of my face.

"Rosa, this is important." Her head was a flaming hue with the sunrise penetrating through the curtain of her strawberry hair. It matched her temper.

Pietre had a handheld and he was showing us where the spinner would stop and how far we had to walk. It looked like we got the worst town. Pau Brasil was at least sixty kilometers from the train line.

My mind receded like the tide, pulling on the facts like sand, grabbing the information for a second, only to have it wash out of my grasp with the next wave. I pictured Joseph waking and realizing I was gone. Orry would already be awake and searching for the comfort of warm milk in his belly. Odval would be wondering why I was taking so long. I ran my fingers along the cool, plastic table, swirling circles and imagining the weight of my child in my arms.

"We will walk at night and hide by day. There's no snow, at least, but it means there may be Woodland police patrolling the borders. Is there anything useful you can tell us about Pau Brasil?"

My ears pricked and my senses returned as I remembered how much I hated Pietre. "Not really, they're all the same," I mumbled without looking at him.

"Figures," he said snidely.

My head snapped up, regarding his snarling expression with distaste. Did he ever really smile? My anger reached out like a straggly hand looking for something to hold onto. It found Pietre's hateful face and dug in with pointed fingernails.

"Don't speak to me," I said, my face brimming with hot-blood anger. "I haven't forgotten what you did. You're an intolerable man. Well, not even a man—a boy. And I wish you would drop off the end of the earth!"

Joseph would be storming around the house, banging into things and clumsily getting dressed. He would be so sad; I will have made him so sad. He will hope I've changed my mind. I could see his face looking to the door, hoping I was coming back. My heart heaved at the pressure I put there. *What was I doing?*

The Wall

As I expected, Pietre enjoyed my outburst and a sickening smile crossed his lips. He put his arm around Careen, who looked up at him confused, and pulled her closer. I directed my voice at Careen's blinking face. "I know the plan and I would like to get some rest before we charge off into the wilderness again, all right?"

She nodded. Poor girl, she had no idea what was going on between Pietre and me.

I returned to staring out the window. I tried to force my face to relax but I felt like I was trying to unroll a tightly wound map. Every time I took the band off and tried to flatten it out, it would curl back up again. I sighed deeply. We would travel for a week like this, close to each other, invading each other's space. Already it felt like the sides of the spinner were pressing down on me. I didn't know how I would stand it. Pau Brasil was the last stop on the line.

Along the way, we would stop and drop off the others close to their assigned towns. Each group had a designated time they had to return by if they were to catch the train back. This was entirely dependent on our little group. We would have to bring the spinners back from the end of the line and pick everyone up. "Timing is extremely important," Pietre drummed into to me, pressing his finger into the table until it turned white and beating me about the head with the information. I rolled my eyes and nodded, arguing with him was pointless and a waste of my moping energy.

The landscape was peeled back. It whirred past us and held no interest to me anymore. Bleak and brown. Greenery mottled the background like camouflage clothing but I was blind to the beauty. The leaves rustled like the trees were shaky fingers scared to touch us. They reflected my anxiety. I still couldn't decide if I'd done the right thing. I hoped maybe when my feet hit the grass and I was trekking towards my mother, I would feel differently. But my purpose escaped me. It was like trying to find my key; I knew it was on me somewhere.

The spinners stopped every six hours for toilet breaks and leg stretches. It was unnerving going from the cool, pristine environment of the spinners, to the dank, mossy richness of the woods. Usually, I would have loved the difference. It would have motivated me. The others were certainly energized. They could see change around the corner. Normally, the atmosphere would have been infectious. I could see the anticipation rolling around them like a velvety blanket, comforting and reassuring them they would be ok. But I could only catch the corner of it and it seemed frayed and easily torn. All I could see was naivety. I worried they didn't realize how dangerous this would be. They seemed too confident that nothing could go wrong.

I spent the first break, and every one after that, quickly peeing and squatting on a rock. I sullenly dug in the dirt with a stick to see how big a piece of dirt I could excavate without it breaking into smaller pieces. The others practiced their moves and went over their plans. Gwen approached me on the first day. She put her hand on my shoulder, an unfamiliar move for her, and it felt more like a slap. Her face scrunched, showing those odd dimples on her cheeks. "Is it Cal?" Her voice wavered. Did she grieve him or was she just nervous?

I shook my head, but I wasn't sure. It could be. My brain refused to deal with his death the same way it had refused to back down from coming out here in the first place. It threw ineffectual but heavy covers over the things that might stop me. I sucked on my lip and let my eyes brush over to her for a second. I couldn't speak, if I did, I would cry.

She patted me again. "Look, if it is, you shouldn't blame yourself, no one does. He was sick long before you arrived. You should put it behind you."

I nodded and watched her feet as they shuffled away from me, kicking a rock in frustration. I think that was the problem or at least part of it. I had put it behind me, but not dealt with it, so it just sat there. An angry ball of anger and sadness that kept a steady distance behind me, but always followed. And I always knew it was there.

I dragged at myself, my own company as irritating as being with people. I knew this wasn't helping but I did nothing other than feel sorry for myself. I wished I'd done things differently but it was too late. I could feel Joseph moving through the town, his heavy footsteps heavier still with the weight of my desertion on his mind.

I saw Matthew through the shifting trees, his face as dark as the bar-like shadows cast across his face. He was as miserable as I was. We never spoke. I wondered if we would ever speak again or if he was done with me. It would be fair enough if he was.

By the time we got to the last stop before Pau Brasil, everyone stopped bothering to talk to me and left me to my self-pitying behavior.

Doing my usual scratching in the dirt, I etched a pattern of concentric circles when my arm was wrenched up violently. "I've had it with you," Pietre snapped. "I thought you wanted to be here. If we're going to get through this mission, you need to get yourself together." He was shaking me like a ragdoll and I let him.

"I'm s-sorry," I said between shakes. But he was sewn-up furious and couldn't be undone with an apology. The world was wobbling in my vision, trees were wriggling like snakes, the world was heaving. "Stop, please! I-I said I'm s-sorry, Pietre." My voice quavered with the world as his fingers pressed hard into my arm. I felt a pang of pain as the joint in my shoulder started to strain from him twisting it.

In my reverberating vision, I saw red hair alight in front of brown, scratchy trees.

Without a word, she punched him hard in the jaw. I heard the crunch of knuckles connecting with bone. I saw his eyes roll delightfully into the back of his head as he stumbled backwards and hit the ground, letting out a small, "Ugh". He sat in a daze for a second and then he scraped himself off the ground, storming lopsidedly away from us, clutching his face. I stared at Careen, mouth agape.

"What? He was taking it too far. He needed to be taught a lesson." Smiling with her perfect white teeth, she held out her hand and I took it. She looked into my eyes seriously. "He's right though. You need to snap out of it and focus. You have a job to do."

She was right.

We walked away, with him cursing her in the distance. "Shouldn't you go apologize or something?"

Careen raised one eyebrow in a perfect arc and smiled wickedly, "He'll get over it. It's not like it hasn't happened before." She grabbed my arm somewhat urgently and we skittered across rocks and dirt towards our spinner.

We climbed in the carriage. Careen closed the door and pressed the lock button down. "I've had enough of him today, haven't you?" she said. I smiled. I'd had enough of Pietre from the moment I met him. I was glad Careen was starting to agree with me.

A bit of light poked through the trees now and settled in our hair. I could do this. Despite Pietre's stupid way of demonstrating it, he was right. I was here and I had to stand by my decision. One more night and we would set off for Pau, for my mother and my baby brother or sister. I needed all the strength I could muster for this. The rest of my woeful feelings would simply have to wait.

43

LATE SNOW

The weather had been mild right up until the last stop, the sun lightly warming and only the slightest breeze to rustle our hair. But the temperature started to drop as soon as we pulled up to the Pau Brasil stop. We shrugged on our packs, and the door hissed open. The cold wind hit our face like a block of ice had formed around the outside of the spinner. Quickly, we pulled out our winter coats and gloves. Pietre held the map in front of his face, constantly wiping the sleety rain from the screen and pointed northwest, directly towards a dark grey, craggy collection of rocks. It couldn't be called a hill more than a hostile, sharp and uninviting tumble that looked like it would cut you just for looking at it. So this was the outside of my old home. It seemed fitting. I closed my eyes and prayed we would not be climbing over it.

It was barely light. Just enough to see the black mass of rock and the dark, thickly wooded forest sprawled beneath it, the trees leaning towards it as if in worship. Everything else could be shadow or form. It was too hard to tell. I imagined eyes watching us as we traipsed headlong into the howling wind, each drop of rain pelting our faces like sharp bits of gravel.

Pietre yelled, his voice barely cutting through the wind, trying to convince himself as much as Careen and me, "Bad weather is a good thing. It will keep the predators away." I thought, *After a night of walking through this, I might want a wolf to end my misery.*

We walked all night. Freezing cold and soaking wet, there was nothing to do but keep putting one foot in front of the other. I was sandwiched between an angry and determined Pietre in the lead, and an unrepentant Careen in the back. I couldn't think, couldn't talk, could only walk. We couldn't hear each other anyway. The way the wind swirled around us and slammed against the grey rocks that seemed to continue to rise higher and higher out of the ground to our left, it was like some deranged woman was screeching in our ears, her hands cupped to her jagged mouth, warning us to turn back. It went on for hours, endless hours.

As the sun rose, the wind eased and we could at least hear each other speak. We were so cold our lips were blue—every extremity felt like it was splintering and migrating away from the rest of my body. I honestly don't know how we managed to keep walking, but we did. We found a cave not too far off course and made camp. We couldn't make a fire; it would be too easy to spot, especially during the day. So we huddled together in our sleeping bags and tried to sleep, pressing ourselves into the shadows of the scooped-out cave that felt and smelled like the inside of a rotted carcass.

I thought I would have trouble sleeping, but after a night of walking, my body collapsed in dreamless exhaustion. I only awoke when someone was again shaking the life out of me.

"Rosa, wake up. We have to get moving again," Careen whispered.

Pietre snored loudly, sleeping sitting up awkwardly, with his back pressed against the bare rock. I kicked him with my boot and his eyes snapped open, the sheen of purple still evident along his jaw where Careen had punched him. He rubbed his chin absentmindedly and winced when his hands brushed over the bruise. Smiling, he held his

The Wall

arms out to Careen and grappled her into an embrace. She fought him at first but then relaxed against his chest. My eyes started to sting for how much I missed Joseph and Orry. When I watched the two of them in their bizarre, dysfunctional relationship, I was jealous.

"I'm not sorry," Careen whispered.

"I know, me either," Pietre said.

When they'd finished snuggling, which I took to mean he'd forgiven her for hitting him, we started out for another night of walking. I took a deep breath and closed my eyes, hoping when I opened them the entrance to the cave would not still be streaming water. I prayed for the rain to end.

I wish I hadn't.

Our packs were heavy and we were so fatigued, but we kept moving, doggedly putting one foot in front of the other, stumbling every so often in the dark and following the red arrow on Pietre's handheld.

It was still impossible to talk, not that I had much to say. Thoughts were rubbed clean from the constant outward assault on my senses. All our concentration went into not falling over, not losing each other or losing our way.

The world was black and slimy, the pale light of the handheld illuminating only the closest branches, slick with rain and slippery with moss. It showed us what direction to take but it didn't account for tree roots and jagged rocks. The number of times we fell over in the mud or walked directly into a huge rock, seemingly placed there just to annoy us, I couldn't count. I started to despise that red arrow, blinking tauntingly and not seeming to bring us any closer to our destination.

At the end of the second night, the rain eased and we all sighed in relief. Pietre even clapped me on the back happily. Pulling off his hat and running his hand through his hair, he gave me a genuine smile. I pulled back in surprise.

"What?" he said, looking boyish and self-conscious all of a sudden.

"Nothing, you just look different when you smile," I commented shyly, instantly regretting it.

"I smile plenty," he snarled, returning to his abrasive self. "Just not when you're around."

I shrugged. I'd expected that.

We'd been walking to the right of the jagged rock formation and dragged our sorry bodies up into another cave. This one was shallower and smaller, but at least it wasn't wet and pelted with horizontal rain.

We ate quickly and shrank into our sleeping bags, lying touching each other. Normally, I would have objected but I was actually quite grateful for the warmth. Even though the rain had cleared, the air was so much colder.

My eyes didn't want to open. My poor body clock was so back to front. Waking at dusk and going to sleep at dawn was killing me. My body ached from sleeping on the rock floor and I felt like I was frozen to it. I wiggled around and heard cracking and something sliding across my bag with a nylony 'zip'. Careen had turned towards Pietre and her warmth deserted me.

I looked out the cave opening. It was still light. I blinked, unbelieving, and prayed for the rain to return.

A late snow.

The woods had been transformed to winter again. The entrance to the cave frowned to the outside, white iced around its mouth. Jagged icicle teeth grinned at us and swallowed us whole.

I shook Careen's shoulder and she batted me away with the flat of

The Wall

her pale hand, smacking me the face. I punched her shoulder hard and she sat up with an irritated look on her face. But when she saw the snow, her face changed to utter dismay. *What the hell were we going to do?* It had been hard enough to walk in the rain in the dark. With icy rocks and roots to slip on, it was going to be disastrous.

Careen rattled Pietre. He sat up violently. "Crap!" he said and then he proceeded to curse for a good couple of minutes while we watched. His shoulders and head hunched, he kicked things around our tiny cave.

Finally, I'd had enough. "Will you shut up? There's no point in getting angry—we have to keep moving." Jolted out of his rampage, he took a deep breath and shrugged.

"You're right, we…" The sound of metal slicing the air silenced us both. We turned our heads to the cave opening and saw a blade flying towards a young deer that had, surprisingly, not been scared off by Pietre's cursing.

Pietre's eyes opened wide in horror and his mouth fell open as the blade hit the creature in the throat, blood spurting out onto the fresh snow. The poor deer stumbled around uselessly, trying to shake the blade from its neck, and collapsed awkwardly against a tree. Sweet black eyes frozen like its surroundings, unblinking.

Pietre was furious. Angry whispers progressed to shoving as he manhandled Careen to her feet and shook her. "Have you got a brain between those pretty ears?" he spat.

"What?" Careen said bewildered, between shakes. We were genuinely baffled at his anger. I thought what she'd just done was awful but I didn't understand why *he* was so upset? I thought he enjoyed this kind of thing.

"Do you think we can eat a whole deer, or even carry the carcass somewhere safe? You've just alerted every wolf in the area there's a fresh kill waiting for them." Pietre put his hands down and flexed his fists while he talked. "And once they're done with the deer, who do you think they will come after next?"

Careen eyes became pools of alarm as she realized her stupidity. "I'm sorry," she stuttered. Pietre turned his back to her and started shoving his things into his pack.

He swung around and jumped out of the cave, burying his legs up to the knees in snow. Bashing his way to the deer's body, he grabbed it by the back legs and threw it into a branch. It was grotesque and as good a warning as any to get as far away from it as possible.

The sun had set. The blood was dripping down the tree trunk and pooling in the snow like a red ink blot. Pietre turned his head up to us, his eyes showing a hint of panic, and said bleakly, "We have to run."

We ran in the darkest dark, bashing our way through trees and slapping branches. The snow had stopped falling but it was icy, cold, and slippery. Every time I put my foot down, I would think it was safe, only to find my heel digging into a sharp rock or a buried branch catching my foot and sending me flying face first into the snow. Every now and then Pietre would stop abruptly and listen, his ears pricked for the sound of a wolf following us. But we heard nothing, save footsteps crunching through the powdery snow and our own breathless panting.

After hours of running, I stopped. I couldn't breathe. My heart and lungs a connected bulge of stabbing pain. I had to rest for a second. I reached out in the dark and found Pietre's sleeve. I tugged it and he halted. "I… have… to stop… for a… second," I said between puffs.

"No. We have to keep moving."

"Please?" I begged, releasing his shirt and bracing myself over my knees, desperately trying to drag in another breath.

He hadn't ignored me. I couldn't hear his footfalls moving away. He raised the screen to his face and tried to ascertain how far we'd traveled by tracing his finger along the path we'd followed.

"One more hour. Then we'll stop and find shelter," he said, gripping my wrist and squeezing it uncharacteristically gently.

I couldn't do one more hour. Careen was puffing and panting behind me but she didn't back me up. She was probably feeling too guilty for forcing us to set this ridiculous pace.

He didn't wait for me to answer but I saw the handheld floating further away from me. Then I felt the drag of someone pulling me along like a donkey. I had no choice. I put my head down and thought of my mother.

The blinking arrow brought us closer to the rock formations and sometimes when I stuck out my hand, it grazed the natural wall. The rock was sharp and cold, but reassuring. If wolves were chasing us, we could scramble up there quickly if we had to.

I was desperately trying to keep up but I was so much smaller than the two of them. One of their steps was two of mine. My legs pulled up out of the three-foot deep ditches of snow and slammed down hard against the earth, begging me to slow. Trying to keep myself motivated, I imagined the wolves were right on our heels and the adrenaline caused by my fear spurred me on. All I could hear was our breathless pants and our chorus of crunching boots. We sounded like twenty men, not three.

A wolf howled.

I heard a shuffle of fabric as something caught and nylon ripped open with a neat shriek.

Then, a sickening snap.

I reacted quickly, stumbling over to the glowing screen of the handheld. I kneeled down and found his face. I clamped my hand over his mouth but not before he let out one hollow scream.

He pulled himself to sitting, my hand still over his mouth, his hot breath on my palm. In the half-light, I caught him nod and I released my hand. I risked the torch in my pack and turned it on, shining it on his face and down his body.

His expression was painful, his jaw tight, but to his credit he didn't scream again. His face was greenish white and beads of sweat were forming on his brow, despite the cold.

Several wolves howling broke my concentration. They'd heard him. They were coming.

Careen was standing over us, her hand covering her mouth in shock, her body trembling slightly.

I tried to think. *What should I do? What would Joseph do?*

Pietre spoke before I could make any decisions. "My leg is broken. You'll have to leave me." He clenched his jaw and tried to find a more comfortable position but found none.

I was stunned. "What? No." No way was I leaving him there to be eaten.

"It's ok; at least I'll slow them down. Give me the stunners and a torch," he said calmly, holding out his hand.

Careen fumbled around in her bag and handed him two stunners. He dragged himself towards a tree and leaned his back against it. I couldn't believe what I was hearing. These Survivors. This self-sacrifice stuff was so over the top. "I'm not leaving you here. Get up. We'll help you walk." I tried to get him to put his arm around my shoulder but he sank into his position like an immovable rock.

"No, you won't. The mission is too important. Besides, they'll catch up to us and then we'll all die. Just stay out of it, Rosa. This is *my* decision."

I stood there, exasperated. This wasn't going to happen. I wouldn't let it. There had to be another way. *Think. Think.*

I took a few steps towards him and smacked the side of his head with my torch. His eyes went blank and he slumped forward. The stunners tumbled out of his hands, coming to rest at his feet, stark black against the white.

44

FEAT

"Rosa, what the hell did you do that for?" Careen whispered angrily. I ignored her and set to cutting down a straight branch with my knife. I lined it up, cut it down to size, and used the set of bandages we had to splint Pietre's broken leg. I unrolled a sleeping bag, unzipped it, and tried to roll him inside. He was so heavy, a dead weight.

"Careen, help me." The clueless redhead squatted down with me and we rolled him into the bag, zipping it up. I shone the torch up at the rock formation, searching for a cave entrance, a hole, anything. My heart fell when the only opening I could see was three meters off the ground.

One mournful, long note sounded off, not far away.

"We have to get him up there," I said, pointing with my torch, tracking the seam of rock where snow had settled. It zigzagged upwards to the entrance, showing us a way up. It was only a foot and a half wide but it would have to do. Careen nodded and we started to drag him towards the base of the cliff.

Pietre wasn't a huge man but unconscious, and not giving us any help at all, it was like he weighed three-hundred kilos. We pushed, pulled, and heaved until we'd dragged him halfway up the cliff. Resting on the ledge for a second, I thought my arms might actually twist and fall off if I tugged on them hard enough. My lungs burned from the cold, my legs strained as we tried to roll him up and over the next ledge, his whole dead weight crushing us both.

He woke up and started cursing and wriggling, his unaware antics sending him sliding down the ledge and on top of us. My heart buckled at the idea we would have to start all over again. Without thinking, I grabbed his broken leg to stop him from slipping all the way back down. I clamped down on it hard, wrapping both my arms around him while pinning my front to the rocks' surface. My muscles pulsed, ticking involuntarily. He shrieked and then, silence. *Thank God.* He passed out from the pain, but then we were back to dead weight.

I don't know how we did it. It was a blur of pain and pressure. The wolves were approaching—the air was stripping my lungs. But we got him up there. We pushed him up over the ledge and into the cave like a sack of potatoes. We watched as he rolled over a few times, deep into the cave like a loose one, and came to a stop, nestled awkwardly around a boulder. I stood at the edge, shining my torch down over the side of the rock, shaking my head in disbelief. What we just did was impossible. The rocks petered down towards the ground with barely a foot of outcropping to cling to. I'll never understand how we did it.

Careen rolled and then arranged Pietre at the back of the cave. She laid out some food, one stunner, and filled his water bottle with fresh snow. We piled both our sleeping bags on top of him and stood to look out of the entrance. She put her arm around me and pulled me close. I turned to face her and hugged her fiercely. Her body initially stiffened but gradually relaxed.

"If we can do that, we can do anything," I cried. Tears streamed down my face. It was so hard, more physically testing than anything I'd ever done. And the worst was yet to come. *How would we survive this? Especially without Pietre.*

"That's good," she said into my hair, her hand resting on my shoulder, "because now we have to outrun wolves."

45

RUN

The new plan. Well, the only plan, was to leave Pietre in the cave and run all the way to the edge of the town. We'd left our sleeping bags with Pietre and removed anything inessential so we weren't weighed down. We didn't even take water bottles—we would rely on snow. Careen was going to run east a kilometer or so and kill something, hopefully something big, to distract the wolves. Then she would run back to the cave and we would set out together.

We would have to travel in daylight, which was risky, but we weren't going to be able to camp, which meant we weren't going to be able to sleep. Panic deserted me at this time. It should have strangled me, but I don't know, the fact we were facing death, just pulled everything into sharp focus. We had to do it. We had no choice. We would run and we would take our chances.

Squatting in the cave waiting for Careen was agonizing. I felt ready to spring—to run. I ate what little my stomach could handle and drank some water. I stretched my legs and checked back on Pietre every now and then. When he woke up, he would be in terrible pain and I was thankful I wouldn't be around to see his scowling face when he did open his eyes. Looking at him now, he seemed peaceful except for the bulging bruise on his temple.

I heard a rustling in the trees and snapped my head back around to its origin. Pale hands pulled through the branches, covered with snow-iced leaves. Careen.

She climbed up to the cave entrance. She explained that she'd managed to kill an elk and carve it up crudely so she could deposit bits of it around in the trees. I shuddered and then I laughed. Careen looked at me like she thought I was going crazy.

"You all right?" she asked in a tone indicating she clearly didn't think I was.

I laughed again. "A butcher and a carpenter running for their lives in the woods... It sounds like the start of a really bad joke."

She gave me another wondering look, like, *What is going on inside that head of yours?* But she didn't say anything.

It would take the wolves some time to get all the pieces down. Careen had also marked trees heading in the opposite direction to our cave with blood. It would lead them away from Pietre's sleeping body. I composed myself at the chilling visual. Always blood. Hopefully, this elk's sacrifice would save us.

Careen had a little water and ate something. She leaned down and ruffled Pietre's hair. Kissing him lightly on the cheek, she whispered something to him and then strode purposefully towards me. She may have wanted to be a butcher but everything about her screamed warrior. This was it. We had no one to rely on except each other. The sun rose, peeking through the branches, spilling blood-tinged light over the black rocks and bouncing off the snow.

I could feel them in my chest, pounding paws digging in and pushing off in unison.

"Let's go."

We hit the ground and broke into a frantically paced run. We had no idea what kind of head start we had or whether our diversions would work. We only knew what direction to run and that's what we did. We put our heads down and sped across the snow as fast as we could. Careen ran behind me, knives clutched in both hands. I clasped the handheld in front of me, turning and veering, keeping the red arrow straight. It said we had fifteen kilometers to go. I wish I hadn't known that.

Running. Running. Running.

The edges of my vision darkened like I was passing through a shadowy tunnel. Exhaustion approached me, clamping its ragged fingers around my shoulders and trying to pull me backwards. But I kept my head down and kept pushing forward.

On and on, one foot in front of the other, ignoring the buzzing in my ears and the thickness of the surrounding air. I was moving through bitter honey.

I pictured Joseph's face in front of me. I heard Orry's laugh and saw it dancing in the trees. I held out my hands for them but they disappeared into a wisp of smoke.

"We have to stop," I managed to expel.

"We can't," Careen replied halfheartedly.

"One minute." I put my finger up.

I quickly took a drink, leaned myself against a tree, and sunk into it. I imagined it wrapped its branches around me and lifted me to the sky. I'd be out of air but out of reach. I closed my eyes. I would just close my eyes for one minute, just rest for two seconds. My mouth cooled and my breath steadied. I would just sleep for five minutes. Greyness. Pinprick edges and haze.

Careen slapped me back into consciousness. I awoke with a start, putting my hand to my face, feeling light, scratchy icicles running off my cheeks from her snow-covered glove.

"Wake up. We are not giving up now. We're nearly there. Look," she said, holding the handheld that was frozen to my palm in front of my face. It read two kilometers. It was barely midday and we were almost there. I guess fear makes you fast.

Hope got a hold of me and rattled me awake. We might make it. We could find a tree to sleep in. We could still get this done in time.

The sound and the sight of three wolves approaching grabbed at the hope and tore into tiny pieces right in front of me. We were dead.

Their muzzles were bloodied. Their eyes focused on the two, white-clad puffs, two Woodland girls who didn't belong out here in the Wilderness. Careen grabbed my shoulder and squeezed. Our eyes connected and I inherited her wildness. I thought of nothing other than survival. We turned and ran.

They were so close. Their low growls rumbled in my ears and then a quick bark followed as they pursued us through the undergrowth. Branches whipped at my face as I scrambled up and over rocks. The unnatural, cool steel of wind-turbine posts suddenly creating an extra obstacle course we had to weave around. They churned the air and confused sound. I peeked back at the wolves; they shook their heads, their ears flapping against their heads. The whirring confused them too and slowed them down a fraction. Careen stayed at my back. I knew she could run faster than me and I didn't understand why she hadn't overtaken me yet.

I twisted my head back to look at her and realized she had stopped. She was standing legs parted, knives up, ready to throw.

I watched in slow-motion terror as she threw them both. One connected with a black wolf's chest. The great dog skidded in the snow, smashing face first into the ground with a single yelp, and then went silent. The other knife landed in the front leg of another, but it only seemed to make it angrier and it didn't slow its pursuit. Careen spun around, weaving her hand into mine, and ran next to me. I'm not sure

The Wall

who was leading. We dragged each other along.

We didn't care how much noise we made. We were intensely focused on getting close to the wall and up a tree as fast as we could.

The handheld flashed. Two-hundred meters.

Oh my God. We might actually make it. I looked up and noticed the trees were spreading out, becoming sparser and sparser as we approached the wall. There would be nothing to climb.

My concentration lapsed for a fragment of a second and that was all it took. I put my foot down between two rocks, my boot wedged, and I fell forward, my face planted in the snow. All I could see was white. All I could hear was growling. They were right on top of us now.

A hand grabbed the back of my jacket, yanked me up, and threw me forward. A jaw snapped closed, connecting with nothing but air, teeth on teeth, just missing my calf. The wall was right there. I could see it. Grey concrete topped with white snow like a molding cake. But it was too late. We'd run out of time.

I don't know what I was hoping for, but I sprinted at the wall for all I was worth. Maybe I thought someone might see us, rescue us, pluck us from the ground and place us back inside the walls. I didn't want to die.

We slammed against the wall at the same time. I pounded it with my fist weakly but my mouth wouldn't open. I realized quickly and depressingly that I would rather die than be captured and put back in there.

We planted our backs to the concrete, waiting for the wolves to spring at our throats and tear us to shreds. This would not be a quick death.

Careen took my hand and squeezed.

The two remaining wolves had slowed to a walk. They had us cornered and they knew it. They moved slowly, their tongues hanging out, the injured one limping slightly. Their eyes were wild, the bloodstains around their mouths making them look monstrous and invented. They

lowered their bodies to a ready crouch. I blinked slowly.
Joseph, I'm sorry.

46

REFUGE

I concentrated on the mouth of the black wolf. Its crusty lips lifted, gums baring polished, white fangs. Pink-tinged saliva dripped from its growling jaw. My heartbeat slowed to match the viscous trickle. It slowly bulged with the extra weight of more liquid joining it and then plopped onto the fresh, powdery snow, spreading like a stain and disappearing as it melted through the ice.

The wolves pushed off and flew through the air. Their fur stood on end, sharp as needles, as their bodies created an elegant arc, paws outstretched and pointed like they were part of a dance. They were awe-inspiringly beautiful even as they were terrible.

Something cracked like lightning, and the scene transformed. Mid-flight, their fur singed black and they fell like clumps of snow from over-weighted branches to the ground, three feet in front of us. Their chests heaved in pain. The foul smell of burning flesh crept up my nostrils.

We stood like statues, afraid to move, our eyes passing over the lumps of futile fur. Careen stepped forward and swept her foot over the snow under one of the wolf's limp legs. "Scorch spot," she whispered breathlessly as her dusting revealed a metal curve about three-inches wide, buried in the snow. I turned to her with a withering look. She tapped it with her foot and leaned down to press her ear to it with her hands behind her back. I did the same, hearing a faint, ominous humming.

"They're called Scorch Spots. Be careful! Don't put your hands and feet on the ground at the same time and don't come too close," she warned, in between panicked breaths. I got up awkwardly, my legs starting to spasm under my weight. "Anything with four legs gets zapped as they cross the threshold. I remember them from my Guardian training. They protected us from animals on outside patrols."

The wolves looked at us through piercing, yellow eyes. So un-human but so human was their need. *Help,* they pleaded. And despite the fact they tried to kill me, they were wild animals and deserved a better death than this. Careen obliged, slitting their throats neatly as her hands shook from exhaustion and sheer nervous energy. The wolves bled out in seconds.

I put my shoulder to one, trying to heave it over, but it was immense and what little strength I had was sapped.

"We can't move them," I said in a high, stepped-on voice. This would draw attention if it hadn't already. Careen scooped up some snow and threw it on the black wolf's back. It contrasted so strongly. The pure, cold white against the rough, dark fur and warm, flowing blood. I shuddered at its barbarity and its necessity. We heaped snow and broken branches on their bodies as fast as we could. When we were done, we ran around the wall until we'd put a good distance between us and them, hugging the smooth concrete.

Careen's eyes were slightly crazed when they snapped to me. My first clarified thought was Pietre. I hoped he was ok. "We have to find somewhere to hide," she whispered, although it sounded more like a soft shriek. Even Careen could panic.

I surveyed our surroundings. The black rocks had petered out and stood only a few feet from the ground. There were straggly pines about two-hundred meters back into the forest but they didn't look very strong. Wind turbines shot up everywhere. The bases of the posts were big and set in each one was a small maintenance door. I pointed one out to

The Wall

Careen.

"What about in there? Could we kick it in?" My voice was still breathless, the high edge of terror still dominating. Careen just nodded and we lugged our exhausted bodies to the nearest one.

The door was flimsy and easy enough to jimmy. Careen, not so carefully, jammed the edge of a knife in and wrenched it until the door came loose. We crept inside the small space and pulled it closed.

Inside, the darkness was impenetrable. I could see nothing and only hear Careen's ragged breathing and shuffling legs. Exhaustion hit me like a falling rock, splitting me open and riddling me with holes. I could move no longer, my brain emptied. We lay against the curve of the hollow post, listening to the whipping of the air above and the creaking and turning of the mechanisms within.

We slept wound around each other, breathing low and shallow, fearful but unable to stay alert. And as I drifted into unconsciousness, I couldn't for the life of me care what happened next.

How could I care about anything when I was this tired?

BEFORE THE STORM

I awoke in pain. My back crunched up against cold steel, Careen's heavy legs resting over my calves. I couldn't feel my feet. I wiggled out from under her and pins and needles surged up my legs. Dragging my leaden body around, I felt for the door, suddenly scared we'd locked ourselves in. I didn't want to come this far and have it end here. I moved around the wall with my hands and couldn't find the opening, starting to panic. We'd be trapped.

I pressed harder with my fingertips, feeling for any point of difference. Finally finding the edge of something, I pushed. The cold hit me hard but at least it wasn't snowing anymore. It was night, a sprinkling of stars and a crescent moon lighting up the darkness. The silhouettes of the wind turbines looked like giant claws stretching to the sky to pull the stars down. I fumbled around, trying to find the handheld, and checked the time. It was close to midnight. We didn't have long.

I rattled Careen. "We need to change."

Changing brought me close to hysterics—as two girls tried to dress in a narrow space that only got narrower as we stood. There were arms and legs everywhere, bumping heads and hands put in places they shouldn't have. By the end, we were both laughing so hard we were crying.

"Ha! The last time I was naked with someone it was a bit different than this," Careen laughed.

"Me too!" slipped out before I could stop myself.

The Wall

She stopped moving and grabbed for my arm in the dark.

"So you and Joseph finally...?"

My face felt hot and I was glad she couldn't see me, "How did you know we hadn't already?" I snapped in an unwarranted outburst.

There was a pause and I pictured Careen searching around in her head for an answer.

"It was the way you moved around each other, like there was a current running between you." She giggled. "Also it was the way he looked at you like if he stared hard enough, your clothes would just fall off!"

I snorted, barely able to contain my amusement. Careen was so bubble-headed, but sometimes she cut right through all the excess rubbish, the politeness. She pushed past the issues pressing at the sides and put her finger right on the heart of the matter.

Being more experienced than me, I had to ask, "Does that change? I mean, after you've slept with each other that first time?"

She slapped out at me in the dark, grazing my side with her fingertips. "No, silly! It's just that, now, you can actually do something about it!"

"So it didn't change things between you and Pietre?" More silence.

"Pietre and I haven't done that yet," she said quietly.

"Oh," was all I could say. I was glad she couldn't see my face, my eyes wide and unblinking with surprise. Pietre had lied to me. Good for Careen. She had more control in that relationship than I realized. It made me think I didn't know her that well and the more I found out about her, the more I liked. I mean, she certainly was an acquired taste, but then, so was I.

I thought about Joseph and Orry, waiting for me at home. At least I hoped they were waiting for me. A jagged lump rose in my throat, bringing water to my eyes. I would never find someone who loved me as much as Joseph did. I missed my family so much I felt like I would be sick. It was a physical pain that twisted and turned in my stomach.

I wiped the tears from my eyes, found Careen's arm, and squeezed.

"You ready?"

There was no response. "Careen, did you hear me? Are you ready?" I whispered through gritted teeth.

"I nodded," she said irritably.

I rolled my eyes. "In case you haven't noticed, we're in the dark. I can't see you."

"Oh yeah, whoops," she said in her light and light-headed tone. "Yes, I'm ready. Let's go." And like that, she was back to the same old Careen.

We stepped outside and were surprised to find the snow had disappeared almost as quickly as it had arrived. The ground was muddy and the air mild. I fished out the handheld and handed it to Careen. She swished and swiped the screen until the homing beacon signal appeared on the screen—a little red dot that seemed to be moving within a very confined space, back and forth. The Spider lived in Ring Five. She shoved it in her pocket. A slight glow emanated from her right side where it sat.

Inside our packs was an additional set of camouflaged clothing, as well as gloves and booties for climbing the wall. Careen had the device that would open the gates. We were to get in and out quickly, making as little noise as possible.

We crouched down low and padded swiftly towards the wall, leaving our conical refuge behind. My heart was beating so fast I was sure Careen could hear it. Here we were, back at the place it all started. I swallowed hard when were close enough to the wall for its shadow to chill my bones. I severely understood the gravity, the danger, of what I was about to do.

What if I failed?
What if they caught me?
What if I never got back home?

48

RESCUE

Stealing up to the edge, it was so hard not to turn around and run in the other direction. It loomed over us, just tipped by the light of the crescent moon, a towering wall of concrete that seemed to reach past the trees and into the sky.

Careen turned to me. "Are you sure you want to do this? You could come with me."

"No. I'm not sure," I said, but I had to. I had to try. "Give me a leg up."

She hesitated. I put my leg on her knee and she pushed me up the wall. The gloves and shoes stuck to the concrete like glue. It was still a strange feeling, fun. I clambered up the wall like a gecko. I didn't look back. I didn't look inward either—I would see Joseph and Orry's faces and I would change my mind.

Deshi said we had four hours once we disabled the gates. I reached the top and stopped to take a breath. Pau from this angle looked like a maze. It reminded me of one of the many toys Orry had accumulated, a circular piece of plastic with a metal ball inside. You had to tip the game back and forth to work the ball through to the end of the maze. The sense of being rattled around like that ball was strong. I fought the dizziness off, took one last look, and made my way down the other side.

Careen was right behind me. She landed soundlessly on the dirt inside and glanced my way. "Good luck," she whispered, her breath making clouds. "I'll meet you on the outside at four." And then she sprinted off towards the first gate. I watched as she took a small, black disc and placed it over the locking mechanism of the gate. The camera followed her and locked onto her moving body as she pushed in and twisted it counter clockwise. A light flashed red. *Red, red, red...* It needed to turn green. I held my breath and we both stared at it. Red, red, red... *green*! Relief flooded over me. Careen nodded and slipped through the gate silently, giving me one last look of concern before she disappeared.

I should have followed but I stalled. In that moment, I felt it. Looking up at the wall that now contained me, everything felt wrong. My home was wood and stone. This place was unnatural in every way and I couldn't shake the feeling I shouldn't have come. Again, I had to swallow the bad feelings. I needed to get to Ring Two, and to do that, I needed to run. I tucked my gloves and booties in my pocket and got moving.

As I crept in and around the shadows, I let my eyes wander. So this was Ring Eight. Being sixteen when I left, I never got to see it. It was narrow, barely any space between this wall and the wall for Ring Seven. The houses were squashed together. They were tiny and even more basic than my old home. They couldn't have been any bigger than our old lounge room.

I couldn't help myself. Most of the lights were off but one or two homes still had a candle burning. I stepped lightly up the path. Being naturally stompy, it took every bit of my concentration to be stealthy. My toes cramped in my shoes, my legs bandied minutely. The Pau Brasil tree was holding its breath for me as I snuck up to the dirt-crusted window. I sighed softly. My heart ached for the trees. At home, there were no Pau Brasil trees, because it was not native. It belonged somewhere else, in another country, another world that gave up on its people long ago. I sympathized with the tree right then, feeling as out of place as it did.

Through the window an old man sat, smoking on an old dining chair like he was part of it. He was thin, thin to the point of looking close to death. He was an unwashed bag of bones, his pants held up by a piece of string. I thought of Addy, the way everyone looked to her for advice, her importance in the community. This man was a waste of space and the Superiors would not waste their time or resources on him.

There was nothing else in the room, save a pile of papers on the floor and an old stove. The old man coughed, the thin cigarette dropping from his lips, and startled himself to a more aware state. He didn't look my way, or if he did, he didn't notice me. His eyes were vacant and chilling in their despair. Joseph was right. It was beyond sad... a bunch of old people, waiting to die. My hate for the Superiors dug deeper. A ravine, carved out by a river of blood. I crept back along the path and kept moving. Silently, stealthily.

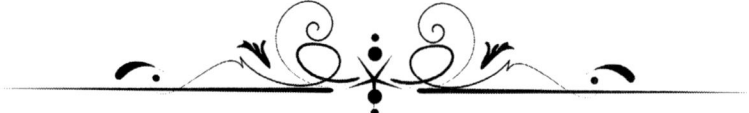

Footfalls light. Cool air pressing down on my lungs. Run. Run. Slip through the gates. Quietly. No creaks. Everything controlled, muscles tense. Don't trip, and for God's sake, don't make any noise. This was a mistake. No. Just keep moving. It was too late to change my mind now.

I arrived at Ring Two and scanned the streets for a marker. I walked through one row of houses and couldn't find anything familiar. When I moved to the next set of houses, I covered my mouth to stop from laughing. The house was the same as our old house, the same color, the same garden. And there they were, mother's hideous purple-and-yellow curtains hanging in the lounge-room window.

A wave of hopelessness hit me hard. *What was I going to do?* I had practiced the speech in my head but now it sounded stupid. There was too much to say and not enough time. What details could I provide to her that would make her come with me without question? Fear compressed me. *What was I thinking, coming here?*

I turned around, ready to abandon my mission. But then I heard it. The soft cry of a baby. I instinctually moved towards the familiar sound. A light turned on at the side of the house. Like a moth, I was drawn to it. And at the same time, I almost didn't want to look. This was where it had all started—this was the baby that sent me away, sent my life down an unimaginable path. I owed it everything and blamed it for everything.

I took off my bag, peeled myself from the wall of the house like old tape, and willed myself to look. Inside, my mother was holding the baby, patting its back gently, and humming. From all the pink, I figured it was a girl. I had a little sister. A crown of shiny, black hair capped the baby's head. Mother lulled it to sleep, stroking its hair and smiling as she lay the child down in her crib. I felt a pang of jealousy, like a hand had reached out and slapped me. Mother looked content. She was happy. Without me.

This was a mistake, I knew now. I don't know what I was expecting. If she'd treated the baby with the same mollified disinterest she did me—that would not be any better than this. Maybe this was for the best. At least now I knew she was safe and the baby was safe. I should have just turned around and left, but this little ball of anger was spinning inside me, chipping away at the sensible side, leaving a girl, raw, stripped of what she thought she knew. She wasn't incapable of caring for a child; she just couldn't take care of me.

I tapped lightly on the window with the back of my finger, trying hard not to smash it through. She looked up and registered immediately. Her eyes horrified. Her mouth wide open in shock. Thankfully, she didn't scream. She shut her eyes for what seemed like forever. Trying to calm herself or maybe hoping she'd imagined me. When she opened them again and I was still there, she motioned for me to go to the back door with a sharp flick of her hand. Then she backed quietly out of the baby's room.

I was excited and fearful as I tiptoed quickly to the back and hid in the shadows of the corner of the house, waiting for her to come out. Hope still clawed at my ankles.

Paulo must have been inside sleeping. I certainly didn't want to see him.

I heard the latch, and saw one foot step out onto the mat, bare, thin, and pointed just like my own. The anger melted and I felt the overwhelming urge to run to her. To hug her. I wanted to tell her about all the horrible things that had happened to me and all the wonderful things I'd seen. I wanted to sit in her lap and have her comfort me like that night so long ago, when Paulo's brother and wife had been captured. I wanted the mother I'd never had.

She stuck her head out carefully, looking from side to side like she was testing the air to see if it was breathable. I moved into the light slightly and motioned for her to come to me. She moved like a mouse, timid and scurrily.

"Rosa, what are you doing here?" she whispered in a tone that could only be explained as absolute horror. Her head bobbed around, looking back and forth nervously. She reached out and put her hands on my elbows, pinching them, the barest of contact. She was cold. Shaky.

"I have a sister," I blurted out, shell-shocked. "Look, Mother, there's no time to explain everything but I've come from the outside, from beyond the Woodlands. I want you to come with me. You and the baby. It's better there. It's so much better than living in Pau with him." I angled my head towards the house.

She faced me silently. Her eyes looked off to the distance, tracking an invisible object just over my shoulder. She put her hand to my face, tucked a strand of loose hair behind my ear, and cupped my cheek. Even now, after all that had happened, she still couldn't look me in the eye.

We stood at even height; it was like gazing in an ageing mirror. I waited for her to say something but she just took a step back and shook her head. *No.* My heart started to tear open and blood poured around it, drowning me. Straightening her nightdress and looking at her feet, she put distance between us. There was always distance between us.

"I can't," was all she said, and then she turned around and went back inside, locking the door behind her.

The rejection sounded and felt like fabric ripping, tearing at me, jagged and messy, the ripping sound deafening only in my ears. I was such an idiot. I stood there for a long time slack and drained, the moon highlighting the lack of color in my face. I was stripped down. Bare. She didn't want me. I stood there, hands at my side, willing myself not to cry.

I stood there for too long.

Strong hands clamped down on my shoulders and jolted me back to awareness. Memories of blood-stained lips, hearts cut out, slick, black hair, and cruelty pummeled my already beaten-up brain.

"Rosa." His voice was laced with that familiar, controlled anger. "You should not have come here."

I turned around slowly. Smiling defiantly. "Nice to see you too, Paulo."

4.9

RESCUE ME

Paulo swung me around so his arm was about my neck. He had me in a headlock and dragged me inside. I struggled, but in a muted way because I didn't want to make any noise. If Paulo or a neighbor called the police, that would be it. I would be dead.

He threw me into a chair, the old, wooden legs teetering until all four were back on the ground. "Don't move," he hissed, his voice aching to yell at me.

I could have run, but fear the authorities would be right behind me had me trapped. His eyes bore down on me—they were furious, hateful, and perhaps—could it be?—frightened. He rubbed his chin and went to the sink, spitting. Mother walked in. Her face fell and she burst into tears.

The kitchen looked identical to our old one, everything scrubbed clean. The only difference was a stack of sterilized bottles leaning against each other on the dish rack.

"What are you doing here?" Paulo asked and then he paused, swiping the air angrily like he could knock my presence out of the air. "No, don't tell me. I don't want to know. Whatever idiocy you are caught up in, I will not be party to it."

I thought about it. The less I said, the better. Even though it was tempting to drag him into it, Paulo would report everything, and I had to think about Careen and Pietre.

Falling back into bad habits, I laughed and said innocently, batting my eyes, "Why? Aren't you pleased to see me?"

He slammed his fist down on the table and I jumped. *Take this seriously*, I told myself. *You have to get out.*

"I thought I was finally free of you. Pleased? No, I am *not* pleased." Every word was tainted black, lashing around his face like the lick of a whip.

"Well, I'll leave then. I can see I'm not welcome." I started to stand, but he was too quick. Before I could move, he had his hands on my shoulders, holding me down. I squirmed under his touch, his fingers pressing hard into my collarbones.

"Paulo, no," my mother pleaded quietly. "We should let her go. She's done no harm."

He considered it for a second, his head cocked to the side, counseling himself. There was a tiny ray of hope. But then his eyes changed, they hardened. Hope was squashed like a bug.

"No, we need to call the police. She shouldn't be here."

Releasing me, he walked straight to the phone hanging on the wall over the kitchen counter, picking up the handset. It was an old phone, ceramic and heavy, with a reel dial. He put his finger in the first hole and pulled the number. I watched as it revolved its way back into place.

He forgot. I was not afraid of him.

I sprung from my chair and wrenched the handset from his fingers, pulling it as hard as I could. It stretched and strained and then the phone flung from the wall, taking plaster and paint with it. It took him a second to respond, his face suspended in disbelief, but when he did, it was like all our fights were wound up into this one action. He pulled his arm back and slammed me hard with the back of his hand. I flew through the air like a scrap, clipping my temple on the corner of the kitchen table and crumpling to the floor. But I pulled myself back up, bracing myself. The world was spinning, but I wasn't going to go down so easy.

My mother was wringing her hands, standing by, watching him hurt

The Wall

me. *Help me*, I thought. *For once! Don't be afraid of him. Help ME!*

Paulo gripped the phone. The numbers spun in front of my eyes even though they were still. All the control, all the stifling stiffness, was gone. He shrugged it off like a shroud, revealing the cruel twist of a man beneath. He was going to kill me. I could see it in his eyes—they were a swirl of empty black, ominous, terrifying.

He kicked me in the stomach hard and I fell backwards to the floor again, my head half-hidden under the chair. He clapped the chair out of the way. Telephone raised, ready to strike. He had me pinned.

I had the ridiculous thought that this was a very bizarre way to go, beaten to death with a telephone. My mind conjured up the vision of my death plaque. *Here lies Rosa Bianca. Killed by a telephone. If only they hadn't put her on hold for so long...* A laughed slipped out between my lips. Of all the stupid things to do. His eyes were dancing. He licked the corner of his mouth. He would relish this. The humor was instantly eroded and all I could feel was a numb, stepped-on panic.

I couldn't scream—they would hear me. And I would never let him see me cry. I closed my eyes, flashes of Joseph circling me with his big, strong arms, our son laughing and watching light dance against the timber walls, green hills and trees. Trees everywhere. *I'm so sorry.*

The dull bang of metal hitting flesh, and mostly bone, disturbed us both. We looked up to see my mother's small, brown face, her eyes tired but defiant. Just there in the corner of those eyes, I could see me. I gasped as a small trickle of blood worked its way from her eyebrow down her cheek.

She raised the kitchen pan in her hand and struck herself in the face, hard. It would be comical if it weren't so frightening. She looked at Paulo, her eyes stony. Then she ran for the front door, unlocking it shakily, her hands struggling to grip the key.

She turned to me, and said, "Run, Rosa," and then she walked out the door screaming, "Help! Help! He's beaten me. He's going to hurt my baby!"

Lights were going on. People were stirring. Soon there would be sirens.

Paulo let go like my skin was on fire. The situation was turning on him and he cowered away from me, eyebrows knotted. A chunk of slick, black hair snaked down his forehead. I saw him for what he was, a small, petty man who had no heart and therefore should have no place in mine. I felt a small amount of pity for him. Very small. His life was over.

"You know, it didn't have to be this way, Paulo," I said as I stood unsteadily. I carefully took two steps backwards, holding his gaze, and then I bolted out the back door. The flimsy screen slammed several times. *Creak, bang, creak, bang.*

I heard him mutter, low and desperate, "I know."

I ran down the side, picked up my bag without breaking stride, and turned away from my old life for good. *Goodbye, Mother.*

Why do we go around in circles? Wasn't I just here? Nothing changes. Nothing ever changes.

I ran. Tears streamed down my face. I failed. I couldn't save either of them. I hadn't even asked my sister's name. I ran through the list of things I'd wanted to say. *You're a grandmother. I'm safe. I'm working hard. I love you. I miss you. I need you.* All of it sitting in my stomach, scrawled on a crumpled-up piece of paper, the ink seeping into my veins.

Could I let it go? She didn't want me. So maybe I could stop worrying about her now. I shook my head, answering my own question. No. It wouldn't be that easy.

The night air was piercing, like it was part acid cloud. My puffy eyes made it hard to focus, hard to see the dark shapes I needed to follow. I tightened my hair and wiped my nose with my sleeve, a streak of snot pulling across my face and hardening there. I was at the gate to Ring Three now. I crept up to it and carefully wrapped my fingers around the iron, remembering rust stains on my school jacket, a life that didn't

The Wall

belong to me now, and probably never really did. I breathed a sigh of relief when it opened easily.

Following the curved line of the concrete wall for a while, I then made my way into the street and snuck past several houses. I kept my eye out for my old house but I couldn't find it without the purple-and-yellow curtains. They all looked exactly the same.

I stole down a street, hugging the unsheltered curb, feeling more and more like I shouldn't be here and how I couldn't wait to be home. A mechanical creaking stopped me in my tracks. It sounded like a giant door pulling open, then glass shattering and muffled voices. I froze. There were very few places to hide. I padded into the front lawn of one of the houses and tried to mold into the shape of the Pau Brasil tree, noticing the lined-up bins on the curb in front of every house. What day was it? Wednesday. Bin collection.

"Damn it," I muttered under my breath.

It was getting closer, inching its way towards me. I watched as a giant, mechanical arm lifted bins to the opening and shook. A man followed the truck, picking up the different recyclables and emptying them into compartments in the base of the truck, below the mouth meant for garbage. I'd never seen it done before. It was so early, 3AM. What an awful, bottom-of-the-rung job.

A man sidled up to the boxes, picked them up awkwardly, and bouncily walked to the truck, whistling as he went. The driver stuck his head out the window and yelled at the man intermittently, or maybe it was a boy. He was short and thin. He moved like he wasn't collecting garbage. This boy was taking a stroll through a flowered field, sweeping his hands across the blooms, and looking up at the sky. It was clear he wasn't taking what he was doing very seriously. The man in the truck yelled at him over and over, his hairy arm gesticulating and banging the door. But the boy seemed unperturbed, walking out of sight, snapping his hand together like a talking mouth, wobbling his head and imitating the driver. I tried not to laugh, covering my mouth with my hand. The tears were drying up now.

The truck was one house away and I prayed the headlights would not cast their light on me. My feet were quite obviously sticking out from the thin trunk. I cursed the ineptitude of the tree for being such a poor shelter. My feet were in sneakers; they would know I wasn't from here. My eyes, my clothes, they would know straight away.

The truck lurched forward, squeaking to a stop at the house I was standing in front of. The headlights illuminated the front door. I knew they would see me. I held my breath and stood on the tips of my toes, trying to press myself further into the bushy foliage and pathetically thin trunk. I should have run. I'd had time. But the boy loading garbage had distracted me and now it was too late.

Metal clashed, glass clinked against glass, and the truck moved. The headlights weren't shining on me anymore. But the boy was still there, picking up some loose bottles that had spilled out of an overloaded box.

"Make sure you get everything, boy," the driver growled impatiently as he rolled to the next house.

"Yeah, yeah," the boy replied, shaking his head.

I looked down at my feet to see a green glass bottle had rolled under my tree.

The boy picked his way up the path, collecting bottles and sticking them under his arm. I moved around the tree, trying to stay out of sight. Thinking, *This is it... I'll be caught and it will be for nothing.*

He got to the front door and turned around. I held my breath. A few more steps and I would be safe. *Keep moving*, I willed. *Don't look under the tree.*

He was just off the path when he stopped suddenly, like a thought had occurred to him. He turned around and marched straight towards my hiding place. He leaned down and scooped up the bottle at my feet. He stopped way too long, staring at the dirt. No, he was staring at my

The Wall

shoes. My lungs burned for air.

I relaxed. Gave up. I inhaled deeply. There was no way I could escape this. The boy would call the man in the truck, who would alert the neighbors. I would be up on the center podium tomorrow and my mother would have to watch as they cut my heart out, slit my throat, or did whatever horrible punishment traitors received.

I let out a sigh and closed my eyes, fists clenched, thinking maybe I could punch him, do some damage before I was dragged off.

My thoughts went to Joseph. I was so selfish for wanting to come here. My heart clenched and jolted. I would never see him again. I would never see my son again.

"Soar?" I opened my eyes. "What the hell are you doing here?" A sharp whisper emitted from a dark shadow of a face. I knew that voice.

I peered into it, trying to pick out the features, dark brows, dark eyes, my height. Then he smiled.

"Rash."

The word escaped my lips like a soft wind.

50

GHOST

I gripped both his hands with my own, hard, feeling his skin, his pulse, making sure he was real. They were the same as always, rough, cool. My mouth moved quicker than my brain and the words tipped out of me like a barrowful of dirt.

"Yes, it's me. Look, we don't have much time but I've come from the outside. There's a settlement. If you want to come with me, I'll take you. It's so much better there. You can be free, safe," I blurted out in one breath.

Rash watched me, absorbing my words, absorbing me. He looked the same but there was a new sadness behind his twinkling eyes. I wondered how he had ended up here, collecting garbage.

He smiled broadly and that smidge of sadness disappeared like a mirage. He squeezed my hands back fully, the complete action of a friend, a brother who had never let me go. I felt a stitch being sewn, my heart pulling itself back together. "I can't go. I have a promising career sorting through other people's garbage for the rest of my life," he said with a wink. He pulled my ear close to his mouth and whispered, "Let's get outta here."

I shivered from the warmth of his breath and smiled.

The driver of the truck was now really worked up, thumping the side of the truck in a temper. "You hopeless good for nothing idiot. Get over here before I chuck you in the compactor."

"With charming coworkers like that guy, why would I even think of leaving this dream job?" he whispered, and my heart swelled. "Coming!" he shouted to the driver.

He tried to move but I jerked him back. I couldn't let him go. I couldn't believe he was standing in front of me.

"I'll need those back," he said warmly, his eyes resting on our joined hands.

I nodded and released him, feeling instant pain at the separation. I whispered, "Meet me at the gate for Ring Eight at 3:45 AM. Can you get away?" I asked.

"Hey, for the ghost of Construction Class, anything!" Rash said and he sidled away casually, without looking back.

He may have been useless as a laborer but he could act. He slipped naturally back into his garbage-collector role like nothing had happened. And like that, an old ache eased. It lifted and left a tiny, white scar behind as a reminder, but one of my ghosts was freed.

I stood there, waiting for the lights of the truck to recede into the distance. Filled with new energy, I weaved through the shadows like I was air and light. Rash, I found Rash. How he was here, I couldn't fathom but I'd found him—he was coming with me. I would let this good news cradle me against the grief that was threatening to destroy me, the grief of losing my mother, twice.

I stole my way through the gates without incident, noticing for the first time how empty the streets were. Even on a quiet night there were usually a few police patrols strutting down the pavement, talking loudly and being generally obnoxious. Where was everybody? My feelings of joy at finding my friend were coated in a sap of suspicion. Dust swirled up my nose as a vague breeze swept across the ground. The air never moved very far in here.

I hoped the Spider Careen retrieved would have some answers for us. I prayed her rescue had gone smoother than my own.

Ring Eight—the end of the line in so many ways. It was the end of Pau Brasil; it was the end of life for its inhabitants. For me, it was the end of Woodlands. I would never come back here.

I waited in the shadow of an empty bin on the curb. I would have to wait for at least an hour so I hunkered down on my knees and rested my back against the side of the bin. It was empty but the stench of past garbage was almost too much. I took my breath in small bursts through my mouth, wondering what they did with all the rubbish.

I lifted my hand to my face gingerly, feeling the bulge where Paulo had struck me throb under my fingertips. Paulo. I smiled darkly. By now, the police would have him in custody. Maybe that's why there was no one in the streets. They were all attending the disturbance I'd made in Ring Two. It seemed unlikely. There should be more, I was sure of it.

I watched as two men in police uniforms set themselves up in a little shed that rested against the outer ring. They must have been on watch and had just changed shifts. They began to play cards on a flimsy table the man had carried in under his arm, talking loudly. There was an older, heavy-looking man with big, muscled arms and stringy hair that fell in a flap over his balding head. The other had a small snip of a face and when he spoke, his voice matched it perfectly, whiny and full of pinched resentment.

"Didn't you want to go?" the older man snorted.

"They said I couldn't go, bad legs," the snip said, slapping his thigh. "There's a lot of walking, y'know."

"Sure, sure," the older one said, punching the whiny one's arm. "You're just worried the scary Survivors will getchya with their magical powers." He wiggled his fingers at the young one like he was casting a spell.

The Wall

"Shut up! You're not going either—what's your excuse?"

"Too old," he said and went quiet for a while. I shifted on my haunches. "Ha! I win. Another round?"

"Why not? Nothing going on around here," the younger one shrugged.

I tried to put this together, not that it was hard. This puzzle had flat edges and only two pieces to match up. If the police were not here, they had begun their search for the settlement. Only I didn't know how long ago they'd left and whether they'd found anything.

After about an hour of watching and listening to this back-and-forth conversation, which mostly consisted of the big one teasing the whiny one and the whiny one, well, whining, I started to wish they had caught me or that the bigger one would slap some sense into the snippy man. He complained and carried on about every single thing. How hot it was during the day, how cold it was at night, how his leg ached in varying temperatures. It seemed to me it ached in every temperature. I was about to stand up and offer to amputate it for him when I saw Rash leaning against the gate, looking for me.

It didn't take him long to see me crouching behind the bin, rolling my eyes. He walked towards me and my heart started to pound. He would expose us both. But he walked straight past me without casting me a shadow of a glance and made his way up to the policemen. They had a hushed conversation and he shook hands with the older one. They walked away from their post.

Charm can get you quite far it seemed.

The dark mischief walked towards me with his beautiful grin. I felt my own mouth lifting. He was here. He was real.

"How did you do that?" I asked in wonderment as I took his hand and let him pull me up.

"Oh, I just told them I saw an old man had carked it in the house around the corner and he had some nice stuff."

I was disgusted but relieved at their greed.

I took both Rash's hands and shook off the grotesqueness this place was steeped in with a shudder. I stared at my friend. My ghost. He returned my stare and then cupped his hand to my face; it felt like he might pass right through me like smoke. When I saw his eyes, the disbelief and happiness reflected there, I realized I was a ghost to him too.

"Wow, Soar." He traced my jaw with his finger. "No scar."

I took his hand between both of mine. "Not on the outside anyway."

"I guess you have a pretty interesting story to tell me," he said, flashing his white teeth and winking.

I laughed quietly, touching my stomach. "I certainly do, but not now." I pulled out the spare gloves and booties from my pack, my fingers brushing the toy train I had shoved in there the morning I'd left my son. My heart squeezed uncomfortably. "Put these on," I said, bounding towards the wall, feeling light as a feather and as heavy as a block of lead sinking to the bottom of a lake.

I'd lost my mother and gained my friend. But loss is loss. It wouldn't be so easy to exchange one for the other. My grief would follow me.

But for now, I had to show Rash how to climb the wall like a lizard.

Rash took to climbing fairly easily, swearing under his breath at how unfit he was when he slipped. But he didn't slip much. We got to the top and looked back at Pau. I was about to say something meaningful. To say farewell this place I'd called home for sixteen years when Rash gripped my wrist and held up my hand, making it wave jerkily. "So long, suckers!" he said, way too loudly, and swung himself down the other side, shimmying down the wall impressively quick.

I smothered a giggle, rolled my eyes, and followed. Finding the wall

The Wall

a bit slippery with morning dew, I slid down the last part of the wall and landed on my butt in the mud.

"Graceful as always," Rash said, extending his hand. I slapped it away and was about to make a snide comment about his lack of gentlemanliness when I heard footsteps coming towards us. Careen's face appeared, floating in the half-light, illuminated by her handheld. A dark figure walked beside her. Tall and lean. They were muttering to each other. Even at their hushed tone, I could hear a melody in his voice. It was familiar but in a removed kind of way, like an overheard conversation. The voice grated. It grazed the edges of my memory and tried to pull something reluctantly to the surface.

I ran at Careen and jumped, knocking her to the ground in a fierce embrace. She was shocked to say the least. "What's wrong with you?" she exclaimed, but her voice was relieved and she responded to my affection with a squeeze, our chests squishing together.

I shuffled backwards. "Sorry, I'm just glad you're ok," I muttered, embarrassed, realizing we were being watched by a stranger. The figure chuckled lightly, a sound that rang bells in my ears. I shook my head to clear it.

"Where's your mother and the baby? And who's this?" Careen said as she lurched towards Rash threateningly.

I scrambled to my feet and put myself between them. Rash stood there with his hands up, smirking. "Hey. Settle down there, lovely lady. I'm a friend," Rash said. He leaned over to me and whispered, "Are all the Survivors this gorgeous?"

Careen's head snapped towards me questioningly.

I rattled out the quickest response I could, blurting out too many details and not enough, laughing hysterically as I explained how Paulo had tried to kill me with a telephone. The dark figure lurked in the background, swaying from foot to foot like he was going to run at me. I squinted at him as I spoke, but I couldn't make out a face in the squandering light. "She wouldn't come," I said, starting to sob, the pressure of my failure wrenching my insides. "She didn't want me." I was pathetic.

Rash and Careen put their arms around me. "It's ok, you tried," Careen said soothingly.

"Yeah and you got a great consolation prize," Rash said.

"You're hardly a prize," I snorted.

"That's the spirit!" he said, elbowing me in the ribs playfully.

"Ouch." I was so sore from my scuffle with Paulo.

"Whoops, sorry," he said sheepishly.

Careen touched my ribs again and I winced. Her voiced sounded terribly serious when she said, "I think he broke a rib, Rosa. Can you walk?"

I was confused. I'd been walking, running for hours. I was walking right now. I took a deep breath and again felt that sharp, strangling pain I'd taken to be my heart breaking. Careen ran her hand along my jaw and up to my temple. "You probably have a concussion too." Her words seemed far away. I felt fine. I focused on the shadow man.

He was silent, too silent, and it bothered me. I took the torch from my pack and walked towards him, my legs jabbing out from under me like they weren't my own.

"And who's this?" I asked suspiciously. Something about him didn't sit right. I flicked the torch on, the stream of light blinding. His eyes were tightly shut as the brightness showered his face. I lowered it a little so he could see. So I could see him.

He opened his eyes and smiled nervously. I drew in a breath and it poisoned me. My heart refused to beat.

Finally, I held the missing piece of the puzzle. But as I placed it in its rightful spot, the picture shook and changed. Old realities shifted, confusion dominated. Suddenly, half my life made a whole lot more sense but just as surely, the other half of my reality split open spectacularly.

The Wall

He blinked and opened his mouth to speak.

Don't speak.

Shadows darkened and light penetrated. *Could you feel insane with rage and full of joy at the same time?*

One blue eye and one brown.

The world was spiraling down or I was plummeting through the earth—I couldn't tell. But as I fell to the ground, shock and exhaustion pulling me under, one thought pushed its way to the surface like an oily bubble and burst.

My life, my whole life...

My father was a Spider.

Acknowledgments

This book is for every woman who's been beaten down, has got back up and said 'this is not going to define my life'.

It's for those of you who had the strength and courage to say 'it was not ok' and I won't let it happen to anyone else.

And for those who aren't there yet, just know you *are* strong enough; you can do it, and one day if you want to and when you're ready, you will.

It takes enormous strength to endure and strength to fight back, I am in awe of each and every one of you.

About the Author

Daughter of a Malaysian nuclear physicist father and an Australian doctor mother, Lauren Nicolle Taylor was expected to follow the science career path. And she did, for a while, completing a Health Science degree with Honors in obstetrics and gynecology. But there was always a niggling need to create which led to many artistic adventures.

When Lauren hit her thirties, she started throwing herself into artistic endeavors, but was not entirely satisfied. The solution: Complete a massive renovation and sell their house so they could buy their dream block of land and build. After selling the house, buying the block and getting the plans ready, the couple discovered they had been misled and the block was undevelopable. This left her family of five homeless.

Taken in by Lauren's parents, with no home to renovate and faced with a stressful problem with no solution, Lauren found herself drawn to the computer. She sat down and poured all of her emotions and pent up creative energy into writing The Woodlands.

Family, a multicultural background and a dab of medical intrigue are all strong themes in her writing. Lauren took the advice of 'write what you know' and twisted it into a romantic, dystopian adventure! Visit Lauren at her website: www.LaurenNicolleTaylor.com.

Clean Teen Publishing

CPSIA information can be obtained at www.ICGtesting.com
Printed in the USA
LVOW08s1017050214

372450LV00001B/55/P

9 781940 534183